STUDIES IN
MAJOR LITERARY AUTHORS

edited by
William E. Cain
Wellesley College

A ROUTLEDGE SERIES

STUDIES IN MAJOR LITERARY AUTHORS

WILLIAM E. CAIN, *General Editor*

The Artist, Society & Sexuality in Virginia Woolf's Novels

PR
6045
.072
Z8669
2004
West

Ann Ronchetti

ROUTLEDGE
New York & London

Published in 2004 by
Routledge
270 Madison Avenue
New York, NY 10016
www.Routledge-ny.com

Published in Great Britain by
Routledge
2 Park Square
Milton Park, Abingdon
Oxon OX14 4RN U.K.

Routledge is an imprint of the Taylor & Francis Group.

10 9 8 7 6 5 4 3 2 1

Library of Congress Cataloging-in-Publication Data

Ronchetti, Ann.
   The artist, society, and sexuality in Virginia Woolf's novels / by
Ann Ronchetti.
      p. cm. — (Studies in major literary authors; v. 34)
   Includes bibliographical references and index.
   ISBN 0-415-97032-6 (hardcover: alk. paper)
   1. Woolf, Virginia, 1882–1941 — Criticism and interpretation.
2. Woolf, Virginia, 1882–1941 — Political and social views. 3. Woolf,
Virginia, 1882–1941 — Characters — Artists. 4. Woolf, Virginia, 1882–1941
— Aesthetics. 5. Social values in literature. 6. Artists in literature. 7. Sex
in literature. I. Title. II. Series.
   PR6045.O72Z8669 2004
   823' .912 — dc22   2003027446

For Luise Schneller Ronchetti and Peter Ronchetti,
and in memory of Barbara Schneller

Contents

Abbreviations

The following abbreviations are used in the text and notes as needed:

AROO   *A Room of One's Own*
BA   *Between the Acts*
BP   *Books and Portraits: Some Further Selections from the*
       Literary and Biographical Writings of Virginia Woolf
CE   *Collected Essays of Virginia Woolf*
D   *The Diary of Virginia Woolf*
JR   *Jacob's Room*
L   *The Letters of Virginia Woolf*
MB   *Moments of Being: Unpublished Autobiographical Writings*
MD   *Mrs. Dalloway*
ND   *Night and Day*
O   *Orlando*
P   *The Pargiters: The Novel-Essay Portion of* The Years
TG   *Three Guineas*
TL   *To the Lighthouse*
VO   *The Voyage Out*
W   *The Waves*
Y   *The Years*

Permissions

Excerpts from *Collected Essays,* Volume II, by Virginia Woolf, copyright ©
1967 by Leonard Woolf, reprinted by permission of Harcourt, Inc.

Excerpts from *Collected Essays,* Volumes III and IV, by Virginia Woolf,
copyright 1950 by Harcourt, Inc., and renewed 1967 by Leonard Woolf,
reprinted by permission of the publisher.

Excerpts from *Moments of Being* by Virginia Woolf, copyright © by Quentin
Bell and Angelica Garnett, 1976, reprinted by permission of Harcourt, Inc.

Excerpt from *The Letters of Virginia Woolf,* Volume I: 1888–1912, copyright © 1975 by Quentin Bell and Angelica Garnett, reprinted by permission of Harcourt, Inc.

Excerpts from *The Diary of Virginia Woolf,* Volume I: 1915–1919, copyright © 1977 by Quentin Bell and Angelica Garnett, reprinted by permission of Harcourt, Inc.

Excerpts from *The Diary of Virginia Woolf,* Volume II: 1920–1924, copyright © 1978 by Quentin Bell and Angelica Garnett, reprinted by permission of Harcourt, Inc.

Excerpts from *The Diary of Virginia Woolf,* Volume III: 1925–1930, copyright © 1980 by Quentin Bell and Angelica Garnett, reprinted by permission of Harcourt, Inc.

Excerpts from *The Diary of Virginia Woolf,* Volume IV: 1931–1935, copyright © 1982 by Quentin Bell and Angelica Garnett, reprinted by permission of Harcourt, Inc.

Excerpts from *The Diary of Virginia Woolf,* Volume V: 1936–1941, copyright © 1984 by Quentin Bell and Angelica Garnett, reprinted by permission of Harcourt, Inc.

Extracts from *The Voyage Out, Night and Day, Jacob's Room, Mrs. Dalloway, To the Lighthouse, Orlando, The Waves, The Years, Between the
Acts,* and the *Collected Essays of Virginia Woolf* used by permission of
the Society of Authors as the Literary Representative of the Estate of
Virginia Woolf.

Extracts from *The Pargiters* by Virginia Woolf published by Hogarth Press.
Used by permission of the executors of the Virginia Woolf Estate and
The Random House Group Limited.

Extracts from *Moments of Being* by Virginia Woolf published by Hogarth
Press. Used by permission of the executors of the Virginia Woolf Estate
and The Random House Group Limited.

Extract from *The Letters of Virginia Woolf* by Virginia Woolf published by
Hogarth Press. Used by permission of the executors of the Virginia Woolf
Estate and The Random House Group Limited.

Extracts from *The Diary of Virginia Woolf* by Virginia Woolf published by
Hogarth Press. Used by permission of the executors of the Virginia Woolf
Estate and The Random House Group Limited.

Extracts from *A Room with a View* by E. M. Forster used by permission of
the Provost and Scholars of King's College, Cambridge and the Society
of Authors as the Literary Representative of the Estate of E. M. Forster.

Acknowledgments

This study has had a long gestation. I am grateful to Dianne Hunter, who directed my earlier work on Woolf's self-reflexive artist-figures, and to Dirk Kuyk for his engaging introduction to the Symbolists and aestheticism. Howard Harper proved an invaluable guide through the stages of dissertation writing, supplying encouragement and inspiration through his comments and his own scholarship on Woolf. I am also indebted to Allan Life and the late Harold Shapiro, having benefited from their extensive knowledge of Victorian literature and culture. This book would not have been possible without the support of David Bartholomae, Rush Miller and administrators at the University of Pittsburgh, who granted leave to work on it. Thanks also to Phillip Wilkin and Fern Brody for picking up the slack, Charles Aston for his timely assistance, and Evelyn Ronchetti for her enthusiasm and ability to keep a secret.

CHAPTER ONE

Introduction

Perhaps nowhere in her essays does Virginia Woolf render her view of the writer's relationship to life as his or her subject matter as succinctly as she does in "Life and the Novelist," first published in *The New York Herald Tribune* on November 7, 1926. She begins her essay by noting what she believes is a significant difference between the novelist and other artists: "The novelist—it is his distinction and his danger—is terribly exposed to life" (CE2: 131). Unlike those artists who paint or compose in their studios, the novelist deliberately positions him- or herself among others in order to receive those impressions that become the raw material of fiction: "He fills his glass and lights his cigarette, he enjoys presumably all the pleasures of talk and table, but always with a sense that he is being stimulated and played upon by the subject-matter of his art" (CE2: 131). As Woolf is quick to point out, however, the actual crafting of the work of fiction for most writers takes place in isolation:

> They have finished the wine and paid the bill and gone off, alone, into some solitary room where, with toil and pause, in agony (like Flaubert), with struggle and rush, tumultuously (like Dostoevsky) they have mastered their perceptions, hardened them, and changed them into the fabrics of their art. (CE2: 131)

Published a year after *Mrs. Dalloway* (1925), her first critical success, Woolf's essay presents a view of the writer as a traveler between two worlds, the world of everyday life, in which he or she interacts socially with his or her fellows, observing their behavior and the surrounding scene, and the world of the study, to which the writer retreats in order to transmute his or her impressions into the work of fiction. In *Ivory Towers and Sacred Founts: The Artist as Hero in Fiction from Goethe to Joyce*, Maurice Beebe explores the geography of this terrain both for practicing writers of the nineteenth and twentieth centuries and for the often self-reflexive artist-figures in their fiction. Beebe identifies two traditions that illustrate the degree of a writer's involvement in everyday life. That of the Sacred Fount "tends to equate art with experience and assumes that the true artist is one who lives not less, but more fully and intensely than others. Within this tradition, art is essentially the re-creation of experience" (13). Alternatively, the Ivory Tower tradition, one that flourished in late nineteenth-century European literature, "equates art with religion rather than experience," and considers it above life (13). In this tradition, "the artist can make use of life only if he stands aloof" from it (13).

Tracing the origins of the *Künstlerroman* back to Goethe's *Die Leiden des jungen Werthers* (1774; final version 1787) and *Wilhelm Meisters Lehrjahre* (1795–6), Beebe describes the condition of "the typical artist-hero" as that of a

> ... Divided Self ... wavering between the Ivory Tower and the Sacred Fount, between the "holy" or esthetic demands of his mission as artist and his natural desire as a human being to participate in the life around him. (18)

In his analysis of the fiction of Balzac, James, Proust, and Joyce, Beebe argues that in the best fiction, the two traditions "are successfully reconciled" (66). For example, "The typical Jamesian artist," Beebe notes, "is polite, clean, witty; a cultivated person as much at home over tea cups as at his desk or easel" (200). And Joyce's Stephen Dedalus is granted "the right, even the need, to form at least a partial compact with life" (295). Concerning Joyce himself Beebe states, "Not only is his art based on his experience, but he was also one of the most domestic of writers" (261).[1]

Despite its seemingly simplistic nature, Beebe's argument highlights the importance of the theme of the artist's relationship to life in the work of several major late nineteenth-century and modernist authors. The fiction of Virginia Woolf also deserves scrutiny for its handling of this subject. As an experimental novelist, Woolf sought to develop a fictional method that would enable her to suggest the nature of life as experienced by the individual consciousness from moment to moment. As essays like "Modern Fiction" (1919) and her diary entries reveal, Woolf was impatient with her generation's Victorian legacy of fictional conventions in the materialist mode, "this appalling narrative business of the realist: getting on from lunch to dinner" (*D3*: 209). She longed to develop a higher form of realism that would convey the "myriad impressions—trivial, fantastic, evanescent, or engraved with the sharpness of steel" received by "an ordinary mind on an ordinary day" ("Modern Fiction," *CE2*: 106). Throughout Woolf's writing career, life remained the basis of art as far as she was concerned; in her diaries and essays, she praises the work of authors as widely disparate as Cervantes, Defoe, and Chekhov for their ability to present the truth of life as experienced by individual human beings.[2] What she longed to see was a novelistic form that would more accurately and succinctly convey the essence of our experience of the world, that would "stand further back from life," giving "the outline rather than the detail" ("The Narrow Bridge of Art," *CE2*: 224–5).

Like a number of her predecessors and contemporaries, however, Woolf was also much absorbed with questions of the artist's relationship to the world, and the degree to which social and sexual engagement enhances or hinders the extent and quality of his or her creativity. As is often the case in the earliest fiction of a writer's career, Woolf's first novels, *The Voyage Out* (1915) and *Night and Day* (1919), address these questions from a number of angles. Both books present young people who are amateurs in the arts or some intellectual endeavor, or would-be artists or writers who have reached the age where key life decisions must be made—whether to pursue the bar or academic life, as in St. John Hirst's case, or whether to continue one's career as a lawyer or move to the countryside to write, as in the case of Ralph Denham. Unlike other major authors, however, Woolf's absorption with this theme continued throughout her writing career, receiving even greater attention in *To the Lighthouse* (1927), *Orlando* (1928), *The Waves* (1931), and *Between the Acts* (1941), each of which has as a central character an aspiring or practicing artist or writer who must wrestle with his or her identity as a creative individual and as a human being, and negotiate his or her relationship to society and the world at large.

A brief survey of Woolf's background and the cultural context in which she reached maturity as a writer reveals a number of factors that may account for her unusually strong preoccupation with the nature of the artist's relationship to life. Woolf was born into a large Victorian family with a formidable artistic and intellectual heritage. Her maternal lineage included the Pattles, who had ties to the Pre-Raphaelite painters; as a young girl, Woolf's mother, Julia Jackson, had often visited Little Holland House, her aunt Sara Princep's home, and a "hothouse of aestheticism," according to Phyllis Rose in her biography of Woolf (10). Guests there included Holman Hunt, Burne-Jones, and Tennyson, among others.[3] Another visitor, sculptor Thomas Woolner, who with Rossetti and Holman Hunt had founded the Pre-Raphaelite Brotherhood, was one of Julia's suitors. Julia herself had served as a model for painters Burne-Jones and Watts, sculptor Marochetti, and photographer Julia Margaret Cameron, who was also her aunt (Panken 20).

While growing up at 22 Hyde Park Gate in Kensington, Woolf faced a constant reminder of the family's connection to Thackeray in the person of her mentally disturbed half-sister Laura, Leslie Stephen's only child by his first wife, Harriet Thackeray, a daughter of the famous novelist. Anne Thackeray Ritchie, Stephen's sister-in-law and a popular novelist in her own right, proved a lively, robust presence with her frequent visits to the Stephen household during Woolf's girlhood.

By 1882, the year of Woolf's birth, her father, Leslie Stephen, had already become a prominent literary figure in England, editing *The Cornhill Magazine* and assuming the general editorship of the *Dictionary of National Biography*, for which Stephen himself would write a number of the entries.

Woolf in effect grew up in a house with an elderly father who was also an intellectual and a man of letters in the habit of retreating to his study on the fourth floor for hours on end. Stephen provided his young daughter with ample opportunity to observe at close hand the various compromises that family life demanded of one of his scholarly temperament over the years. Her portrait of Mr. Ramsay, based largely upon her father, in *To the Lighthouse* foregrounds some of these compromises with particular poignancy.[4]

As Woolf's biographers have noted, Stephen encouraged his daughter to become a writer by giving her access to his personal library and discussing history, biography, and literature with her. According to Katherine Hill, Stephen expected Woolf to become his "literary and intellectual heir," following his lead as an essayist, reviewer and historian (351).[5] But as a number of biographers and critics has argued, Woolf's assumption of the role of writer served a crucial function in enabling her to negotiate the demands of living and establish an independent identity. Rose states that already as a young girl, Woolf was "training herself to be a writer, finding in writing a happier reality, an alternative to family life" in the tumultuous Stephen household (29). Louise DeSalvo views Woolf's early writing efforts as an attempt "to carve out an identity separate from the rest of the family" (*Virginia Woolf* 242–3). As Woolf's own comments in her diary attest, writing became essential to her well-being: "I cd. make some interesting perhaps valuable notes, on the absolute necessity for me of work" (*D5*: 44). For Woolf, writing served as a vital means of integrating reality and uniting the various facets of the self; while driving through Richmond one evening, she realized

> . . . something very profound about the synthesis of my being: how only writing composes it: how nothing makes a whole unless I am writing. . . . (*D4*: 161)

For one for whom writing served such critical functions, then, the relationship of the artist or writer to the world became a central concern. Woolf's gender brought added immediacy to the issue, as the relationship between women artists and society was particularly problematic for the women of her generation. Raised in a household that respected learning and intellectual activity, but nonetheless insisted upon adherence to traditional gender roles, Woolf, like her sisters, was also expected to marry and have children. Her ambivalence toward marriage and motherhood may be traced to her loss at age thirteen of her overworked mother, who apparently catered selflessly to the needs of her emotionally demanding husband and their extended family. The death only a few years later of Woolf's half-sister Stella during her first pregnancy most likely reinforced Woolf's fears concerning heterosexual relations (Rose 15). And as DeSalvo argues, Woolf's subjection to sexual abuse by her half-brothers George and Gerald Duckworth adversely affected the expression of her sexuality in adulthood (*Virginia Woolf* 87). As painting did for her sister Vanessa, writing would become Woolf's means of establishing an autonomous identity apart from that of wife and mother. For Woolf it seems to have become a substitute for motherhood as well. Her diaries are sprinkled with references to her books as her children, and she occasionally describes the process of writing in terms of sexual reproduction and maternity.[6]

Although Woolf was understandably fearful of heterosexual relations and claimed herself "a great amateur of the art of life" (*D5*: 346), as an upper middle-class woman with a modest independent income, an unusually supportive husband, and no children, Woolf occupied a comparatively privileged position as an aspiring woman writer. Throughout her life, however, she felt handicapped in her profession as a result of her sheltered upbringing and limited formal education. As she noted in her diary in 1928, she "should have liked a closer & thicker knowledge of life" (*D3*: 201). Woolf bitterly resented not having had the opportunity to obtain a university education, and explored at length the reasons why the "daughters of educated men" (*TG* 4) were largely denied this opportunity in her polemical work, *Three Guineas* (1938). Throughout her life, Woolf remained painfully aware of the limitations that her gender and class imposed on her as a writer, as *A Room of One's Own*, *Three Guineas*, "Professions for Women," and "The Leaning Tower" make clear. The most lamentable was her restricted exposure to life in its variety and complexity. As her biographers and friends have noted, Woolf was in the habit of asking people from other classes numerous questions about their daily lives in an effort to extend her awareness of the diversity of human experience.[7]

Given Woolf's status as a daughter who was herself struggling to establish an autonomous identity as a woman and a writer in an intellectually prominent upper middle-class family with direct ties to the world of artists and writers, it is not surprising that she was much concerned with questions of the artist's relationship to social and sexual life and the surrounding world. At least two other factors account for Woolf's deep and lifelong deliberation on these questions. The first is a legacy that Woolf shared to varying degrees with a number of other writers of her generation—that of Walter Pater and aestheticism. The origins of this late nineteenth-century literary and cultural phenomenon extend back to the earliest years of the century, ranging from such diverse sources as Keats's fascination with sensation, the Neo-Platonism of the Oxford Movement, the Pre-Raphaelite Brotherhood, Ruskin's art criticism, and Matthew Arnold's cultural criticism, as well as the Symbolist movement, which emerged in Paris in mid-century and was itself influenced by the poetry, fiction, and critical theories of Edgar Allan Poe.

That Woolf was aware of these authors and movements and had read their works (with the possible exception of some of the French Symbolists), one can safely assume, based on her frequent use of her father's wide-ranging library, which included numerous titles in literature and literary history.[8] Arnold would have been a constant ghostly presence at 22 Hyde Park

Gate, particularly in Leslie Stephen's study, as Stephen had by that time assumed Arnold's mantle as England's "leading man of letters" (Rose 5). That Woolf read and appreciated Ruskin, though not uncritically, is evidenced by the fact that she produced two known essays about him—"Ruskin," first published in the collection *The Captain's Death Bed and Other Stories* (1950), and *"Praeterita,"* originally published in *The New Republic* on December 28, 1927.[9]

Woolf's exposure to Walter Pater is thought to have begun with her reading of the first edition of Pater's *Imaginary Portraits*, published in 1887, a presentation copy of which the author had left at the Stephen home during that year. As Perry Meisel notes in *The Absent Father: Virginia Woolf and Walter Pater*, this was the only book by Pater in Leslie Stephen's library until 1898 (12). Meisel conjectures that "perhaps as early as 1902," Woolf acquired Pater's works in Macmillan's Edition de Luxe (1900–1901) for her own use (16). Of these, Woolf apparently held *Marius the Epicurean: His Sensations and Ideas* (1885) in particularly high esteem at the time. In "Old Bloomsbury," written many years later during the early 1920s and read before Bloomsbury's Memoir Club, Woolf recounts one of her half-brother George's nocturnal visits to her room while her father lay dying of cancer downstairs: "It was long past midnight that I got into bed and sat reading a page or two of *Marius the Epicurean* for which I had then a passion" (*MB* 160).[10] During her writing career Woolf never produced an essay exclusively on Pater, although two essays, "English Prose" (1920) and "The Modern Essay" (1922), praise him for his style (Meisel 81–2). In her preface to *Orlando*, she coyly acknowledges Pater's influence, among others. One should also note that in September 1898, Woolf began attending classes in Latin taught by Pater's elderly sister Clara, who, as Meisel notes, was closely associated with Oxford aestheticism and had been involved in establishing Somerville College, the second of Oxford's colleges for women (Meisel 17, 19).[11]

Meisel provides a detailed analysis of the influence of Pater and his aesthetic principles on Woolf's writing, particularly on her work as critic and reviewer. In the two authors' critical essays he notes a shared "vocabulary of judgment and analysis" (73), a search for the perfect fusion of form and matter in the work of art (59), the desire that superfluity be eliminated from the work of art (56), the requirement that the author or artist exercise self-discipline, or "ascesis" (Pater's term; 56), the criterion that the author's or artist's work express his or her personality (40), and the use of shared figures of speech (xiv), especially alchemical or metallurgical metaphors, to describe the artist in the act of receiving impressions and transforming them into a work of art. Meisel detects Pater's influence on Woolf's fiction in its concern with "the languages of sense and perception" (44), its detailed descriptions of its characters' thoughts and sensations (13), and its use of "the moment," which Meisel traces back through Conrad and Hardy to Pater, Wordsworth, and Hegel, among others (47).

Part of Meisel's thesis is that Woolf appropriated aspects of Pater's aestheticism as a young writer in an attempt to break with the patriarchal Victorian tradition that fiction should be morally edifying, one to which her father and many other prominent literary figures of his generation subscribed. As Meisel notes, Leslie Stephen denounced aestheticism in "Art and Morality," an essay published in *The Cornhill Magazine* in July, 1875, arguing that art must be morally upright and foster ethical behavior (1–3). It appears that Stephen, like so many opponents as well as proponents of Pater's aestheticism, misread his work, especially the notorious conclusion to *Studies in the History of the Renaissance* (1873), the first edition of that work, as advocating the indulgence of the senses for one's personal gratification (Beebe 152). As James Hafley argues, Pater valued art for its ability to revitalize the spirit, frequently commenting upon its moral and ethical value (101).

Perhaps the most important lessons that Woolf absorbed from Pater as far as the relationship of the artist to the surrounding world is concerned were the need for a finely honed receptivity to life, the experiences it offers, and the people and objects it places in one's way, coupled with an ability to examine and express in one's art the effect these observations and experiences have upon one subjectively. This view by no means requires that the artist lead an active life of doing among his or her fellows, but it does preclude the self-willed isolation of the artist from society as exemplified by Des Esseintes, the aesthete-hero of Huysmans's influential novel *À rebours* (1884). As is widely acknowledged, the English aesthetes and decadents of the late nineteenth century read Pater assiduously, but also took their cue from the French Symbolists, cultivating a desire "to stand apart from the common life and live only in the imagination," as Edmund Wilson notes in *Axel's Castle* (32). This devolution of Paterian aestheticism was hastened by the resurrection and transformation of the persona of the dandy as cultivated by Wilde and satirized vigorously in Gilbert and Sullivan's *Patience* (1881). Among the Bloomsbury group, E. M. Forster satirized this persona as early as 1908 in his characterization of Cecil Vyse in *A Room with a View*.[12] Woolf herself would also find fault with aestheticist affectation approaching this extreme;[13] one detects evidence of it in her portrayals of St. John Hirst in *The Voyage Out*, William Rodney in *Night and Day*, and Ashley in *The Years*.

In addition to the influence of Pater and aestheticism, Woolf's thinking about the artist's relationship to life was doubtless stimulated by her friendships with the Cambridge men and assorted artists and writers who comprised Bloomsbury. For Woolf, the influence of Cambridge began through her father, a graduate of the university, and continued through her brother Thoby and his numerous Cambridge friends and acquaintances with whom they formed the Bloomsbury group. Woolf's ambivalence towards Cambridge and its graduates is well documented. As Phyllis Rose notes in her biography, Woolf equated Cambridge with her experience of being excluded from a university education (34). To her, there was something slightly ridiculous about the strange behavior of Thoby's college friends: "They sit silent, absolutely silent, all the time; occasionally they escape to a corner and chuckle over a Latin joke. . . . Oh women are my line and not these inanimate creatures" (*L1*: 208). As Alex Zwerdling notes in *Virginia Woolf and the Real World*, Woolf differed from her Cambridge friends philosophically, putting "much less faith in the triumph of reason" than they (294). Rose observes that Woolf "seems to have defined herself against them, insisting on the value of a distinctively 'feminine' and even untutored approach to life" (39). As George Spater and Ian Parsons point out, Woolf's opportunities to debate issues and ideas with these young men nonetheless served as something of a substitute for the university education she never received (39).

Furthermore, it was through these graduates that Woolf was exposed to the thought of Cambridge philosopher G. E. Moore, whose Platonism and views on the role of art reflected Pater's to a certain extent. As Quentin Bell notes in his two-volume biography of Woolf, the Cambridge graduates tended to view Moore's *Principia Ethica* (1903) "practically as the gospel of their time" (*VW1*: 139). One cannot ascertain the degree of importance that this book had for Woolf, who read it for the first time in 1908 (Rosenbaum, *Victorian Bloomsbury* 226), well after the Bloomsbury group had coalesced, and whose written comments on it are inconclusive.[14] However, the work did serve to affirm the group's "belief in the intrinsic value of art" (Johnstone 45), in that it claimed that "the most valuable things, which we know or can imagine, are certain states of consciousness, which may be roughly described as the pleasures of human intercourse and the enjoyment of beautiful objects" (Moore 188). Among critics and historians of the phenomenon that was Bloomsbury, S. P. Rosenbaum has perhaps gone farthest in exploring the parallels between Moore's ethics and Pater's aesthetics: "both relied upon an intuitional ideal, valued aesthetic experience for its own sake, thought of that experience primarily in terms of perception, and were unconcerned with its temporal dimensions" (*Victorian Bloomsbury* 30). As Rosenbaum notes, however, for Moore as well as for Bloomsbury, relationships between individuals were "at least as important as aesthetic experience. . . . love was not subsumed under art" (30).

Overall, Bloomsbury's relationship to Pater and aestheticism was a complicated, uneasy affair, riddled with considerable ambivalence. As Rosenbaum notes, virtually everyone in the Bloomsbury group had read *Marius the Epicurean*, drawn by its concern for relating the sensations and impressions of its protagonist (*Victorian Bloomsbury* 144). Pater's style, however, was alternately admired and disliked by different members of the group (154), and Rosenbaum states that as the years passed, Bloomsbury came to value Pater's essays more than his fiction (144). As Ulysses D'Aquila notes, the aesthetic movement really had a much stronger foothold in Oxford, where Pater was educated, served as tutor, and lived much of his adult life, than it ever did in "intellectual Cambridge" (5n6). Rosenbaum makes this point even more emphatically:

> Bloomsbury's aesthetics developed out of puritan, utilitarian Cambridge rather than Anglo-/Roman Catholic Idealist Oxford. Pater's skeptical, even solipsistic, epistemology, and the Idealist implications of Wilde's theory that nature imitates art were refuted for Bloomsbury by the common-sense philosophical realism of Moore, which gave to Bloomsbury's aesthetics a solidly logical underpinning. (*Victorian Bloomsbury* 30)

In her introduction to *Art & Anger: Reading Like A Woman*, Jane Marcus submits that Wilde's works and experience were instrumental in Bloomsbury's espousal of sexual freedom (xix), but as Meisel notes, the Bloomsbury group also wanted to maintain a distance from the aesthetic movement (34), troubled by the charges of homosexual behavior leveled against Pater at Oxford and successfully brought against Wilde in the ruinous second trial of 1895. It should be noted, too, that Bloomsbury aesthetics also evolved from formal concerns posed by the work of the Post-Impressionists, with which both Clive Bell and Roger Fry as art critics and promoters of Post-Impressionism were quite familiar. As C. Ruth Miller remarks, Woolf's writing has been interpreted by some as an effort "to fulfil in her own medium the criteria developed by Clive Bell and Roger Fry for the visual arts" (45).

An eloquent apologist for Bloomsbury, J. K. Johnstone attempts to summarize its relationship to art, artists, and the world. Bloomsbury's main concern, he argues, was simply "to help the artist to create, and every one to enjoy, good works of art" (95). Johnstone assigns Fry a critical role in establishing the group's view that "art is autonomous": "He showed where art touches life and where it is separate from it" (95). Noel Annan adds that according to Bloomsbury, the only obligation an artist really had was to express him- or herself (26); certainly the group was remarkable for creating a climate in which its artists and writers would not be hampered by any moral strictures concerning the purpose of art.

Despite Bloomsbury's distinct lack of a manifesto proclaiming commonly held beliefs and values, the group continued to come under attack, sometimes being falsely accused of an overly refined aestheticism that it never espoused, and other times for being elitist and seemingly unconcerned with the larger issues affecting art and its role in society. Among the accusers were individuals as diverse as Wyndham Lewis, T. S. Eliot, Bernard Shaw, D. H. Lawrence, and F. R. Leavis,[15] the latter of whom was particularly harsh in his assessment of the Bloomsbury manner:

> Articulateness and unreality cultivated together; callowness disguised from itself in articulateness; conceit casing itself safely in a confirmed sense of high sophistication; the uncertainty as to whether one is serious or not taking itself for ironic poise; who has not at some time observed the process? (257)

Bloomsbury's pacifism during the First World War and its members' rejection of many of the privileges and opportunities accorded them by their largely upper middle-class backgrounds alienated it from the British mainstream. Bloomsbury was also viewed as "an exclusive cultural mafia" (Zwerdling 102) that had considerable influence over the literary reviews of the day and the choice of art that would be exhibited in London's galleries (Edel 245).

To assume, though, that Woolf was a member of a group of artists and writers who had little concern for the role of the artist in relation to society is unjust. Although Leonard Woolf was primarily an essayist and critic, his efforts on behalf of British socialism and the formation of the League of Nations were substantial, as was the impact of Maynard Keynes's theories upon British economic policy. Keynes also helped to establish the nation's Arts Council, for which he served as its first chair in 1945. Johnstone argues that Bloomsbury liked to view itself as a promoter of civilization and the arts; the Woolfs' Hogarth Press and Fry's Omega Workshops were meant to serve this purpose, among others (40). As Woolf's 1940 biography of him reveals, Fry was most influential in introducing British audiences to contemporary continental European painting, both through his tireless lecturing before the public and his published art criticism as well as through his staging of the first and second Post-Impressionist exhibits in London in 1910 and 1912. Although ambivalent about personal involvement on behalf of reform,[16] Woolf as a young woman taught history and literature at London's Morley College, a night school for working people, for three years (Bell, *VW*1: 105–7).

Apart from the influence that Bloomsbury's brand of aestheticism, its Cambridge perspective, and the ideas of Moore, Bell, and Fry may have had on Woolf's thinking about the artist's relationship to the surrounding world, the Bloomsbury group also served as a laboratory in which Woolf could closely observe the lives of practicing artists and writers, the consequences of their choice of domestic arrangements, and the manner in which they negotiated the temptations as well as the demands of their art, their families and lovers, society and the world at large. These lives were quite varied, ranging from the uneventful, somewhat reclusive, urban bachelorhood of Saxon Sydney-Turner, who was musically talented, but never fulfilled what Woolf wrote were his friends' expectations of greatness (Bell, *VW*1 102), to the socially active life of Molly and Desmond MacCarthy, the latter a prolific theater critic and an unusually gifted conversationalist; from Lytton Strachey's Berkshire *ménage à trois* with Dora Carrington, a troubled young artist, and Ralph Partridge, her husband, to Woolf's sister Vanessa Bell's life of rural retirement at Charleston in Sussex, where she painted with Duncan Grant, raised her three children, was frequently visited by Roger Fry, Clive Bell, and the Woolfs, and tolerated the presence of Grant's lovers.

Woolf found her sister's unusual life as devoted mother, successful artist, and custom-flouting bohemian particularly engrossing, deeply envying her maternity, but also occasionally disparaging her *métier*, painting, as "a low art" (qtd. in Bell, *VW2*: 147). In *The Sisters' Arts: The Writing and Painting of Virginia Woolf and Vanessa Bell*, Diane Gillespie provides a thorough analysis of the competitive as well as supportive relationship between the two sisters and the effect their respective lives, art forms, and creative work had on each other. As Gillespie notes, Woolf and Bell "measured themselves against each other" from youth onward (10), Woolf frequently viewing her sister as "more procreative than creative, as more the artist in life than the artist per se" (3). Nonetheless, each sister valued the other's critical opinion and would occasionally provide a subject for the other's art. The two even collaborated on the production of Woolf's books, Bell supplying illustrations for *Kew Gardens* (1919, 1927) and *Flush* (1933), and for the dust jackets of a number of others.

In evolving her view of the artist's relationship to life, then, Woolf had a number of sources to draw upon—her observations of her sister's life and the lives of her artist and writer friends and acquaintances, the philosophical and aesthetic ideas bandied about at Bloomsbury gatherings, her exposure to Pater and the aesthetic movement, her observations of her scholar-father's life, and an unusually rich heritage of family lore relating to the nineteenth-century artists, writers, and intellectuals to whom her family was connected. In *A Room of One's Own* (1929), Woolf considers the woman artist's relationship to the world, exploring the economic, social, political, and psychological factors that historically have hampered the creative woman in pursuit of her art. In such essays as "Life and the Novelist" (1926), "The Artist and Politics," and "The Leaning Tower," the last two first published in *The Moment and Other Essays* (1947), Woolf addresses particular facets of the artist's relationship to the world. Her other essays provide numerous glimpses of her thoughts on the subject in their considered comments upon the lives and works of specific writers or creative talents. However, Woolf's fiction equips her with a much broader canvas upon which to test possible theories concerning the optimal relationship between the two, and to arrive at some kind of synthesis that satisfies her intellectually as well as emotionally.

As will be seen, Woolf's early novels reveal an aesthete's preoccupation with the coexistence of two opposed worlds, one of contemplation and imagination, of the exercise of one's intellect and creativity, juxtaposed with a workaday world that is generally indifferent to such activities. For the artist-figures in her earliest fiction, establishing one's position in relationship to these worlds is of paramount importance if one hopes to create the conditions needed for successful productivity as an artist. In *The Voyage Out*, Woolf's first novel, Terence Hewet—down from Oxbridge and leading an aimless, albeit harmless, existence on 700 pounds a year—is a would-be novelist whose thoughtful, sympathetic nature readily draws him towards others. Rachel Vinrace, a sheltered young woman with significant musical talent, is initiated into a social world in which the opportunities for women, artistic and otherwise, appear severely circumscribed. Both of these fledgling artists, particularly Rachel, expend considerable energy in attempting to determine what their relationship to the everyday world should be. By the time of *Between the Acts*, Woolf's last novel, the barrier separating the two realms of being dissolves; the stuff of everyday life, past and present, becomes the basis of Miss La Trobe's dramatic art, and is ultimately transformed by it in a pageant tracing the history of England and its literature to the present day, produced with villagers on a country estate.

Both La Trobe's art and her life are shown to be rooted in the reality of daily life; far from being a brooding Ivory Tower artist at some remove from the world, she is presented as an imperfect woman who happens to be a playwright living among other imperfect men and women. This manner of rendering artist-figures in Woolf's later fiction reflects a transition in the portrayal of artist-figures in modernist and postmodern fiction that Lee Lemon identifies in his *Portraits of the Artist in Contemporary Fiction*. Lemon argues that prior to World War II, the major novelists frequently depicted their artists as "isolated rebels" (ix), exhibiting "Byronic contempt" (xii) for the quotidian in their search for truth and beauty. One can find evidence of this in the characterization of such artist-figures as Stephen Dedalus and Eugene Gant. The "Byronic artist" (xii), Lemon states, has been replaced in the postwar *Künstlerroman* by the "Wordsworthian artist," whom he describes as "primarily an ordinary human being trying to live in a world peopled with individuals as important as himself" (xiii), citing as examples artist-figures in the fiction of Durrell, Lessing, White, Fowles, and Barth. One may observe this more humble, fully human artist-figure emerging in Woolf's fiction as early as *The Voyage Out* in the portrayal of Miss Allan, a middle-aged literary historian. As will be seen, Lily Briscoe in *To the Lighthouse* embodies a number of traits of the new fictional artist-hero. One might argue that Woolf's relatively early abandonment of the Ivory Tower artist-figure as a central character in her fiction serves as additional evidence of her status as a herald of postmodernism among the modernists.

Through her fictional artist-figures, Woolf also explored an issue closely connected to that of the artist's relationship to the world—one that was of particular importance to aspiring women artists: How does the exercise of one's sexuality affect one's creativity? Specifically, is celibacy or sexual involvement advantageous or inimical to one's artistic development? Do heterosexual relations and their consequences raise insurmountable obstacles for would-be artists, especially women? As Maurice Beebe points out, this issue has occupied writers for quite some time, having accumulated its own store of written commentary. In *Walden*, for example, Thoreau states his opinion unambiguously:

> The generative energy, which, when we are loose, dissipates and makes us unclean, when we are continent invigorates and inspires us. Chastity is the flowering of man; and what are called Genius, Heroism, Holiness, and the like, are but various fruits which succeed it. (219–20)

The notion that the artist must withhold his or her "generative energy," diverting it into artistic creation only, seems to have prevailed in a number of the *Künstlerromane* of the nineteenth century. Beebe cites Flaubert's *L'éducation sentimentale* (1869), James's *Roderick Hudson* (1876), and Gissing's *New Grub Street* (1891) as examples of novels in which the male artist-figure ruins his career by succumbing to passion (18; dates mine). According to Beebe, Gissing's fiction in particular illustrates the destructive force of the *femme fatale* (98), a latter nineteenth-century manifestation of woman as vampiric seductress, wreaking havoc in the lives of her victims.[17] However, as Beebe notes, there also is a number of late nineteenth- and early twentieth-century novels in which the artist-hero "feels that he cannot function without love," among them, Hardy's *The Well-Beloved* (1897), Norris's *Vandover and the Brute* (1914), Dreiser's *The "Genius"* (1915), and Wyndham Lewis's *Tarr* (1918) (18; dates mine).

Woolf's earliest novels seem to suggest that heterosexual involvement takes a high toll on aspiring artists of both sexes. In *The Voyage Out*, Mr. Pepper comments on the foiled writing career of his old Cambridge friend Jenkinson of Peterhouse, whose creative promise is permanently suppressed by marriage and addiction. Rachel Vinrace, the novel's young heroine, senses a "terrible possibility" (176) lurking in heterosexual relationships that threatens to destroy the individuality and creativity of the persons involved. By the time of *To the Lighthouse*, however, the marital status of its central artist-figure, Lily Briscoe, a single woman who leads a marginal life with her father, no longer matters so much as the internal changes she undergoes in trying to complete a painting of Mrs. Ramsay first attempted ten years earlier. The portrait of Lily that emerges at the end of the novel is that of an individual who has reached a degree of psychosexual maturation that enables her to achieve the vision for which she has sought so long in her art. Woolf's most fanciful novel, *Orlando*, like *Between the Acts*, presents the image of the woman artist as a sexually actualized being who is also artistically productive. In *The Waves*, Bernard, whose consciousness the novel privileges over those of the five other major characters, is a storyteller and aspiring writer who is also a socially integrated, upper middle-class family man. The artist, Woolf appears to conclude at the end of her career, cannot be too involved in life, socially or sexually, regardless of the setbacks or suffering such involvement may entail.

As will be seen, however, the gradually increasing social and sexual integration of Woolf's artist figures in the course of her fiction is countered by a corresponding trend toward portraying them also as outsiders, individuals who, though equipped with friends and family and living in the midst of things, are in some way marginalized, either because of their gender, class, nationality or sexual orientation, or by choice, preferring to remain apart from mainstream social and political values and activities. Miss La Trobe, a woman of mysterious origins who appears to have had at least one lesbian relationship, is perhaps the best example of this trend in the late fiction. However, one also sees evidence of it in the characterizations of Septimus Warren Smith, Lily Briscoe, Neville and Louis in *The Waves*, and William Dodge in *Between the Acts*.

There are several possible explanations for the appearance of this trend in Woolf's portrayal of artist-figures in her fiction. It may be partly the legacy of aestheticism and its Ivory Tower artist, who constitutionally prefers not to be associated with the mundane business of society, getting and spending, cultivating socially and politically useful ties, and attending to matters of empire. More positively stated, it may reflect the need of the Paterian observer of life to stand at somewhat of a distance from his or her subject in order to experience impressions unimpeded by the pressures of involvement in the public life and issues of his or her time.

On the other hand, it seems to reflect Woolf's evolving political consciousness, intimately linked to her feminism, which increasingly values the position of the "outsider," as she refers to it in her diaries and in *Three Guineas*, for his or her ability to stand relatively free of the influence of powerful patriarchal institutions in assessing what he or she observes as an artist or writer. This more advantageous position of greater objectivity need not be assumed merely to escape the influence of the conservative Establishment; it can serve as a refuge from the pressures of emerging social or political trends from either end of the ideological spectrum.

Woolf experienced this situation particularly keenly during the 1930s, when she and the Bloomsbury group came under attack, accused of being a coterie of privileged individuals caught up in an antiquated aestheticism that ignored the pressing social and political issues currently being addressed by such young, socially engaged writers as Auden, MacNeice, Spender, and Isherwood in their poetry, drama, and fiction. In *World within World*, Spender characterized Bloomsbury along these lines:

> Living in their small country houses, their London flats, full of taste, meeting at week-ends and at small parties, discussing history, painting, literature, gossiping greatly, and producing a few very good stories, they resembled those friends who at the time of the Plague in Florence withdrew into the countryside and told the stories of Boccaccio. (144)

As has been demonstrated, this view was hardly justified, especially in reference to the author of *A Room of One's Own* and *Three Guineas*; Spender would doubtless modify it were he writing about Bloomsbury today. As a result of such criticism, Woolf eventually did come to believe that during the 1930s she had permanently lost favor as one of England's major writers, but surprisingly she felt braced and liberated by this supposed change in her status: "One thing I think proved; I shall never write to 'please' to convert; now am entirely & for ever my own mistress" (*D5*: 105). As Woolf discovered, there is a real freedom to be had by an artist or a writer in having been made, or choosing to be, marginal.

The appearance of an increasing number of outsider artist-figures in Woolf's later fiction may also reflect Woolf's growing wish for anonymity in writers. As C. Ruth Miller notes, "The need for anonymity in art and the pernicious effect of any attempt to use art as a platform are themes which recur throughout Virginia Woolf's writings" (11). In a 1920 diary entry, Woolf discusses the danger of "the damned egotistical self; which ruins Joyce & [Dorothy] Richardson to my mind" (*D2:* 14). Quite a few of Woolf's critical essays on authors praise their subjects for their ability to withhold their identities and avoid the distortion created by personal grudges in the writing of their fiction; among this particular pantheon are Austen, Turgenev, and James.[18] As Carolyn Heilbrun notes, Woolf's reviews for *The London Times* were anonymous (*Writing* 40), as was the case for other reviewers for that newspaper.

For Woolf, however, this longing for anonymity also represented an attempt to escape the limitations of selfhood, a "flight from public and private identity" (Rose 209). As James Naremore argues, the majority of Woolf's later novels "are narrated by what she has called a 'nameless spirit,' which, by its very existence, asserts a 'common element' in life—something not isolated, not separate, not perishable" (76). It is significant that among the unpublished work Woolf left behind following her death was an essay entitled "Anon," intended to serve as the first chapter of "a Common History book—to read from one end of lit. including biog; & range at will, consecutively" (*D5:* 318). As Brenda Silver notes, the intent of this essay was "to explore . . . the role of the artist in articulating the emotions embedded in the human psyche and shared, however unconsciously, by the community as a whole" (380). For Woolf, then, it would seem that outsider status serves as a valuable first step for the artist or writer on the road to attaining the kind of anonymity that enables him or her to transcend selfhood and become a medium through which collectively shared emotions and experience find their expression in the work of art.[19]

What follows is a necessarily limited analysis of selected artist-figures—practicing, amateur, and aspiring—in Woolf's novels which attempts to illustrate the general trends in the evolution of Woolf's thinking about the artist in relation to life identified in this introduction. In treating the novels chronologically, I will try to avoid succumbing to what Miller has characterized as the "developmental fallacy," the temptation to assume that "each work in a writer's canon represents a refinement of its predecessor" (x), but only where it does indeed appear to be a fallacy when applied to Woolf's novels.

CHAPTER TWO

The Voyage Out

As many critics have noted, Woolf's first novel, *The Voyage Out* (1915), combines elements of the novel of manners, the novel of ideas, the *Bildungsroman*, and the lyrical novel, for which Woolf would eventually become well known.[1] Much of the novel concerns itself with social relations among a group of English tourists vacationing in Santa Marina, a small South American resort on the Atlantic coast. During the course of the novel, the main characters debate such topical issues of Woolf's time as the suffragette movement and women's rights as well as the relative merits of a life of public service and the artist's, writer's or scholar's life. Literary and aesthetic matters, such as the value of modern literature as opposed to the classics, or of literature as opposed to music, are also discussed.[2]

The Voyage Out can be considered a female *Bildungsroman* in that it traces the social and psychological development of a naïve and ill-educated—but intelligent and musically talented—young woman who is exposed to social life and relations between men and women for the first time at the age of twenty-four. Like the protagonists of most novels in the *Bildungsroman* genre, Rachel Vinrace embarks on a psychological voyage of self-discovery,[3] here, under the tutelage of her aunt Helen Ambrose. Unlike the lives of the genre's typically male protagonists, however, Rachel's life does not evolve toward greater freedom and expanding possibilities; rather, it devolves from relative freedom to increasing restrictions in a narrowing sphere of action, ultimately ending in her premature death from an illness following her engagement to Terence Hewet.[4]

Published when Woolf was in her early thirties, *The Voyage Out* exhibits the hallmarks of a first novel in its mixture of novelistic genres, its frequent, extended descriptive passages in which Woolf practices evoking landscape and place,[5] its use of characters as mouthpieces for its author's views, and its numerous autobiographical elements. As James Naremore notes, Woolf bases much of Rachel's character on herself (7), and several critics have found correspondences between the novel's other characters and Woolf's friends and relatives, as well as between events in the novel and in Woolf's early life.[6] For Woolf, the laborious writing and rewriting of the novel, which went through at least five drafts (Gordon 97), comprised an effort to explore the possibilities for autonomous selfhood and artistic productivity available to a talented young woman of her class, limited education, and relatively sheltered upbringing. As Rachel's ultimate fate suggests, Woolf's prognosis was not to be optimistic. In her quest for freedom and self-determination, Rachel continues to be confronted by society's restrictive expectations for young women, ultimately beginning to fulfill them by becoming engaged to Hewet despite her ambivalence towards marriage and her sense of a "terrible possibility" (*VO* 176) lurking in heterosexual relationships.

Among the characters in *The Voyage Out*, there are no professional artists, fiction writers, or poets; rather, the characters include a number of amateurs and dilettantes from relatively privileged backgrounds. Among these are Mrs. Flushing the painter; Helen Ambrose, who has an eye for beauty and is working on an elaborate piece of embroidery; Hewet, the aspiring young novelist; St. John Hirst, his scholarly Cambridge friend who occasionally turns out a poem or a play; and Rachel herself, who exhibits a real gift for playing the piano. The novel does present, however, a number of characters who are professional scholars, among them, Hughling Elliot, a Cambridge don; Ridley Ambrose, Helen's husband and an editor of the classics; and Miss Allan, a middle-aged teacher who is also writing a history of English literature.

Among Woolf's central concerns in the novel is an ongoing debate as to the relative merits of the public life of action and the private life of the artist, writer or scholar devoted to creative work and the life of the imagination or research.[7] This bifurcation of living into opposed modes evokes the two contrasting spheres of existence that preoccupied Matthew Arnold in his poetry and prose.[8] It also recalls the separate realms of experience delineated by the Symbolists in their poetry and fiction, and exhibited by late nineteenth-century aesthetes in their desire to retreat from worldly life into a life of sensation and imagination.[9]

Woolf introduces the debate early in the novel during a shipboard dinner conversation among representatives and advocates of both sides. Present are Rachel, the Ambroses, Willoughby Vinrace, Rachel's father and a captain of industry who operates a thriving shipping business out of Hull, Mr. Pepper, a cantankerous old friend of Ambrose, and Clarissa and Richard Dalloway, upper-class socialite and Member of Parliament respectively who between them represent public life in service to the empire. With considerable affectation, Clarissa Dalloway nonetheless sums up the competing claims of the two worlds rather succinctly:

> 'When I'm with artists I feel so intensely the delights of shutting oneself up
> in a little world of one's own, with pictures and music and everything

beautiful, and then I go out into the streets and the first child I meet with
its poor, hungry, dirty little face makes me turn round and say, "No, I
can't shut myself up—I *won't* live in a world of my own. I should like to
stop all the painting and writing and music until this kind of thing exists
no longer." Don't you feel . . . that life's a perpetual conflict?' (45)

Later, in private conversation with Rachel, Richard Dalloway aims to
affirm his role as a servant of the empire in a self-effacing way, comparing
the state to "a complicated machine" that will be threatened if "the meanest
screw fails in its task" (66). Woolf causes Dalloway to undercut his seeming
courtesy when he later startles Rachel by forcefully embracing her. Both the
Dalloways and British imperialism are treated satirically in a private cabin
conversation between the couple in which Clarissa extols England:

'One thinks of all we've done, and our navies, and the people in India and
Africa, and how we've gone on century after century, sending out boys
from little country villages—and of men like you, Dick, and it makes one
feel as if one couldn't bear *not* to be English!' (50–1)

The debate between the relative merits of public and private life continues
throughout the novel, having particular urgency for young men such as
St. John Hirst, who must choose between continuing his life at Cambridge
as a promising scholar or entering public life by training for the bar in
London. Woolf also gives the debate physical embodiment in her placement of the novel's characters in Santa Marina. Those living in the villa on
the hillside above the town enjoy the solitary, contemplative life of artists
and scholars. Ambrose leads a sequestered existence editing the odes of
Pindar in his study. Helen Ambrose cares for him, works on her embroidery, and pursues her interests in the arts and the world of ideas. Rachel
spends most of her time reading books, playing the piano, and daydreaming in her room. The sheltered, leisurely way of life offered by the villa
enables its occupants to follow their personal inclinations and construct
private worlds that are innately authentic and free of the distorting influence of the external world. The latter is represented in the novel by the
social life of the hotel, filled with summer tourists from Europe, in which
individual identity is barraged with behavioral conventions, traditional expectations and the pressure to conform to them. Although Hewet and
Hirst have rooms there, they escape the hotel's frequently stifling social life
by visiting the Ambroses at their villa.

From their vantage points at the villa or seated in the hotel's great hall,
the novel's main characters are not so much participants in social life as
they are observers of it.[10] Keeping a psychological distance from others,
they exhibit a preoccupation with observing their fellows, demonstrating
varying degrees of sympathy for them. In his youthful arrogance, Hirst is
undoubtedly the most critical, occasionally comparing the hotel guests to
grotesque lethargic animals (177). Hewet, on the other hand, is considerably
more charitable, exhibiting a broader, more mature understanding of those

around him. Observing young Arthur Perrott in conversation with Evelyn Murgatroyd, Hewet imagines Perrott mentally calculating whether it would be right to propose to a woman, given his limited financial circumstances (137). Although sequestered for much of the novel with her husband in their villa, Helen observes her companions and acquaintances closely, combining acerbic pronouncements about some with a sympathetic, intuitive understanding of others, such as Hirst and Rachel. She and her niece are also in the habit of descending into the village in the evening in order to "'see life'" (98).

Of the four principal characters, Rachel's sheltered upbringing and unschooled intelligence make her particularly impressionable and vulnerable to the shocks given her by her observations. Rachel's experience as the heroine of a novel that can be viewed as a female version of the *Bildungsroman* recalls that of Pater's protagonist in *Marius the Epicurean: His Sensations and Ideas* (1885), which, as was noted earlier, Woolf had read with considerable ardor as a young woman. Although their backgrounds and experiences are quite different—Marius goes to Rome where he studies rhetoric and becomes an assistant to Marcus Aurelius, whereas Rachel is exposed to society in Santa Marina, where she becomes engaged, the two as young people in the process of forging their identities share a number of circumstances. Both have been reared in conditions of retirement, both have been orphaned by one or both parents, both make a "voyage out"—Marius, to Pisa and then to Rome; Rachel, across the Atlantic to South America—where they begin to seek answers to basic questions concerning how one should live, and both die of illnesses at relatively young ages.

But perhaps the most significant similarities between the two are their roles as observers of the lives of those around them, and their deep susceptibility to the impressions they make upon them. Marius's journey takes him to Pisa and Rome, where he has an opportunity to observe at close hand the lives and characters of a number of people—Flavian, an ambitious, handsome youth who is also an aesthete and a poet; the emperor Marcus Aurelius; the writer Apuleius; Cornelius, a young Christian soldier; and Cecilia, the Christian widow whom Cornelius loves. Also examined and evaluated are the schools of thought or religions associated with these individuals— Cyrenaicism, Stoicism, Platonism, and Christianity. By the end of the novel, Marius has been drawn to Christianity, at first seduced by the beauty of its ritual and then moved by the warmth and spirituality of its practitioners. Following a visit to his country home, Marius volunteers to take the place of his Christian friend Cornelius as a captive, and dies of an illness induced by exhaustion while he is being led back to Rome.

Rachel's education in life accelerates when she embarks for South America on her father's ship in the company of the Ambroses. During the course of the novel, Rachel alternately puts herself in the midst of social life and retreats from it in anger, fear, or boredom. Her forays into social life include her conversations with the Dalloways on board the *Euphrosyne*, her visits to the hotel, and her participation in the mountain expedition, the hotel dance celebrating the Warrington-Venning engagement, and the journey up the river to a native village. Some of these experiences, such as her talks with the Dalloways and the engagement dance, make a great impression upon her, sending her back to her room or outdoors to wonder at the people she has met or mull over the event (173).

Equally frequent, however, are Rachel's agitated retreats from others, usually to the shelter of her room and her music, or to the natural world and fantasy. Feeling excluded by Helen and Clarissa's discussion of their children on shipboard, Rachel leaves them abruptly: "She slammed the door of her room, and pulled out her music" (57). Patronized by Hirst at the dance, Rachel leaves the hotel ballroom in a rage, escaping into the garden where she imagines herself a Persian princess riding in the mountains with her retinue of female attendants (155). Although primarily an observer of life, Rachel, unlike Marius, lacks the sophistication to control her emotions and put her experiences in perspective. Her vacillations between the world of social life and the private world of the self are pronounced, and her death as the result of an undiagnosed illness following her engagement conveniently ends her struggle to negotiate the demands and attractions of the two spheres of existence.

As Woolf makes clear, Rachel's difficulties in coming to terms with the world of everyday life and formulating an identity are compounded by her gender and the severely circumscribed roles available to her in that sphere. Dalloway's sexual assault on shipboard and the tensions Rachel experiences during her engagement make her aware of a threatening dimension in the heterosexual relationship, a destiny she increasingly resists. Rachel's limited exposure to social life on the ship and at the hotel has already demonstrated to her how few her options as a young woman seeking to exercise her creativity and develop an autonomous identity actually are.

Woolf frequently depicts the married women whom Rachel meets on board the *Euphrosyne* and in Santa Marina as intelligent individuals with creative ability who are unable to realize their potential as autonomous beings or as artists. The only relatively contented married woman portrayed in the novel is Mrs. Thornbury, who relishes her maternity and enjoys caring for others. Nonetheless, Rachel observes that Mrs. Thornbury has lost much of her individual identity, having been reduced to archetypal motherhood through marriage (318). Mrs. Flushing, who is childless, squanders her talents and energies in various enthusiasms and impulsive actions, such as deciding to journey up the river. Her paintings, though stylistically characteristic of her exuberance, lack artistic control and appear to serve as a convenient outlet for her energies (234). Mrs. Elliott, also childless, does some amateurish sketching, and is shown to be an expert knitter. Confined to her role as a society matron, Clarissa Dalloway, impeccably groomed, meticulously transforms herself into a work of art; Rachel compares her to "an eighteenth-century masterpiece—a Reynolds or a Romney" (47).[11]

Helen Ambrose engages in creative activities such as embroidery, but appears to be more intellectually oriented as well as seriously conflicted in her role as a wife and mother. In the novel's opening scene, Helen tearfully mourns a temporary separation from her children. Several days later, however, she confides to Clarissa Dalloway, "'Nothing would induce me to take charge of children'" (43). She is frequently bored by her own sex (20), welcoming the occasional companionship of Hirst and his rigorous intellect: "He took her outside this little world of love and emotion. He had a grasp of facts" (304). At times, Helen exhibits a cynicism thought unseemly in women, upsetting her husband (309). She frequently shows impatience with social conventions and routine activities, seeking release from them. As Howard Harper notes in *Between Language and Silence: The Novels of Virginia Woolf*, Helen appears to be "a woman chafing against a destiny which will prohibit her from ever becoming anything more than 'Mrs. Ambrose'" (12). The internal tension that Helen exhibits as a married woman confined to a narrow social role serves as an omen for Rachel, who fears similar consequences for herself in marriage.

The remaining women among Rachel's acquaintances in Santa Marina are unmarried. Susan Warrington, Evelyn Murgatroyd, and Miss Allan present her with the limited range of options available to the single women of her class and time. Having reached thirty, a dangerously old age for an unmarried woman of the upper middle class, Susan eagerly accepts Arthur Venning's marriage proposal, which rescues her from the humiliating company of younger unmarried girls. Susan's changed status and new identity as a future wife give her renewed confidence, which degenerates to a degree of complacency that alienates Rachel.[12]

Unlike Susan, who gratefully follows the prescribed path for young Englishwomen, Evelyn Murgatroyd is keenly aware of the possible consequences for women of heterosexual involvement. Revealing photographs of her mother and father indicate the extent to which her mother's personal development has been stunted by her illicit relationship with Evelyn's father and the stigma of having given birth to Evelyn out of wedlock:

> Mrs. Murgatroyd looked indeed as if the life had been crushed out of her; she knelt on a chair, gazing piteously from behind the body of a Pomeranian dog which she clasped to her cheek, as if for protection.

> 'And that's my dad,' said Evelyn, for these were two photographs in one frame. The second photograph represented a handsome soldier with high regular features and a heavy black moustache; his hand rested on the hilt of his sword; there was a decided likeness between him and Evelyn. (250)

As a defensive reaction to her mother's fate, Evelyn identifies with the vitality and power of her father's image, exhibiting enthusiasm and admiration for military enterprises and heroic adventure. Her naive definition of life as "'Fighting—revolution'" (130) is both comic and pathetic. Evelyn's eager adoption of masculine values simultaneously becomes a means of garnering male admiration as well as an attempt to avoid the behavioral constraints her society deems appropriate for young women.

Despite her continued self-deception, Evelyn consciously expresses several of the reservations about marriage that Rachel harbors privately. Acknowledging her own vaguely articulated need for something more than conventional marriage (366), Evelyn casts a critical eye upon the apparent complacency of the two engaged couples, Susan and Arthur, and Rachel and Terence, suspecting that "one could get nearer to life . . . enjoy more and feel more than they would ever do" (320). Evelyn's emphasis on the importance of "doing things" (321) as opposed to merely "being" reveals the extent of her understanding of the limited sphere of action allowed women of her class. Her own eagerness to join absurdly grandiose causes, however, reflects the extent of her self-delusion and her inability to direct her energy into more realistic action.

Of all the women whom Rachel has come to know during her stay in Santa Marina, Miss Allan, a middle-aged teacher, most approximates the ideal of the capable, independent woman who lives with dignity in a patriarchal society. Despite Woolf's admiration for this gracious, intelligent person, she appears unable to resist using her characters to depict Miss Allan as a *femme manquée* whose life is lonely and difficult (115). There is the suggestion of a certain degree of masculinity in Miss Allan; she is seen by the hotel guests as "the square figure in its manly coat" (115). Her assured self-possession, her lively wit, and her logical mind reinforce this rather masculine image. She might even be viewed as an example of the ideally androgynous individual except for a curiously asexual quality that denies her full humanity.

The air of deprivation surrounding Miss Allan and her life of self-discipline and hard work serves as a subtle warning to young women like Rachel who attempt to envision an independent life within their culture. However, Miss Allan's unique literary productivity in *The Voyage Out* suggests that at this relatively early point in her life, Woolf suspected that the independent, celibate life might be the one most favorable for, and even necessary to, full artistic creativity for women. Of all of the characters in the novel who are involved in some creative activity, whether it be Hirst and his poem about God, Ambrose and his translations of Pindar, Helen and her embroidery, or Hewet's ruminations about his novels-to-be, Miss Allan is the only character who completes her undertaking, a survey of English literature, during the course of the novel (316).

Although Rachel does not profess to have any artistic ambitions as far as music is concerned, it is clear that playing music occupies a central place in her young life and in her psyche; through it, she is ultimately made aware of the danger her engagement to Hewet poses to her emerging identity as an independent being. Rachel's music serves a number of important functions for her. As was noted earlier, she turns to the piano when she feels rebuffed by others. Playing music allows her to gain control over her emotions in following the notation of the score. Furthermore, when she plays, Rachel exercises her unusual talent, reaffirming her individuality and uniqueness in the process, particularly after having been ignored or rejected by others. At the hotel dance, Rachel responds to Hirst's damaging taunt about her lack of formal education by forcefully asserting her talent as a skilled musician, claiming she plays "'better . . . than any one in this room'" (153).[13]

Music also represents a form of transcendence for Rachel, enabling her to move beyond self-consciousness as well as the external reality that surrounds her. Hewet notes with pleasure this aspect of Rachel's relationship to music: "He liked the impersonality which it produced in her" (291). As was discussed earlier, impersonality becomes an important criterion for Woolf in assessing the work of other writers. Evolving to its logical extreme in Woolf's consciousness, it eventually metamorphoses into a desire for anonymity on the part of the artist or writer, a characteristic that Miss La Trobe exhibits as the producer of the pageant in *Between the Acts*.

Playing the piano serves an additional function for Rachel that can also be of use to others. *The Voyage Out* contains numerous references to Rachel's search for a deeper reality beyond everyday appearances that evoke Marius's search for an ideal realm beyond earthly life, especially as he begins to examine Platonism and Christianity's basic tenets.[14] Not only Rachel, but a number of the other characters in the novel search for a "pattern" in their experience of earthly reality that seems to emerge, albeit fleetingly, from time to time, affirming the presence of a kind of underlying order, if largely invisible, to the inhabitants of the visible world. This search also has its counterpart in Pater's *Marius the Epicurean*.[15]

In playing the piano, Rachel reverses her usual habit of passively awaiting insights into a deeper reality by actively imbuing earthly reality with a sense of order and meaning through her music. Woolf conveys the structuring function of music in particular by describing the effect of Rachel's playing in architectural terms: "Up and up the steep spiral of a very late Beethoven sonata she climbed, like a person ascending a ruined staircase" (291). Rachel turns this ability to the benefit of the hotel guests after a particularly exhausting night of dancing when she continues to play before them as dawn breaks:

> They sat very still as if they saw a building with spaces and columns succeeding each other rising in the empty space. Then they began to see themselves and their lives, and the whole of human life advancing very nobly under the direction of the music. They felt themselves ennobled. . . . (167)

Here the conveying of a broader order is also clearly connected with the creation of collective feeling and identity in the image of "the whole of human life advancing very nobly" to the structure of the music. As will be seen, the latter becomes one of Miss La Trobe's primary goals in staging her pageant before the gentry and villagers in *Between the Acts*.

Because her identity as an accomplished musician as well as playing the piano itself are so vital to her, Rachel is particularly troubled by the prospect of Hewet's intrusion into her world through marriage. In a revealing scene toward the end of the novel, Rachel and Hewet, recently engaged, are together in her room—her formerly private sanctuary, Rachel playing the late Beethoven sonata referred to earlier while Hewet makes notes on the nature of women for his projected novel *Silence*. Thinking aloud, Hewet repeats some commonplace theories of his day concerning women while Rachel continues playing. Finishing the piece, she turns to him in playful exasperation:

> 'No, Terence, it's no good; here am I, the best musician in South America, not to speak of Europe and Asia, and I can't play a note because of you in the room interrupting me every other second.' (292)

Hewet replies that the Beethoven sonata Rachel has been playing is not conducive to his work, likening the piece to "'an unfortunate old dog going round on its hind legs in the rain'" (292).[16] A few moments later, Hewet pronounces his opinion of Rachel's reading choices: "'God, Rachel, you do read trash! . . . And you're behind the times too, my dear'" (292). Although this dialogue is presented as affectionate banter, future sources of conflict appear to be imbedded in it. As the clock strikes twelve, Hewet concludes that they have been wasting the morning, stating that he ought to be writing his book, and that Rachel should be writing replies to the congratulatory notes the two have received upon their engagement (295). Implied here is a belief that Rachel's new social role should now take precedence over her musicianship. Initially appearing to compliment her, Hewet also expresses his frustration with what he senses to be her aloofness and her independent bent:

> 'But what I like about your face is that it makes one wonder what the devil you're thinking about—it makes me want to do that—' He clenched his fist and shook it so near her that she started back, 'because now you look as if you'd blow my brains out. There are moments . . . when if we stood on a rock together, you'd throw me into the sea.' (297–8)

Toward the end of the scene, Hewet confronts Rachel about her remoteness in particular: "'There's something I can't get hold of in you. You don't want me as I want you—you're always wanting something else'" (302). Rachel concurs, sensing that "she wanted many more things than the love of one human being—the sea, the sky" (302). Fearful of the constraints that married life with Hewet may impose upon her, Rachel continues to long for something larger, less defined, and more impersonal. As in much Symbolist poetry, Rachel seeks this other reality in nature, especially in the sky and the sea, to which she is frequently drawn during the course of the novel.[17]

As has been seen, Rachel's reluctance to accommodate herself to the everyday world of men and women is strengthened by her growing awareness of the potentially stifling limitations imposed on women who agree to assume traditional social and sexual roles in her culture. In *The Voyage Out*, however, Woolf also demonstrates her broader concern for the unfavorable effect of gender roles and heterosexual relationships on the individuality and creativity of women and men alike. During the first extended dialogue of the novel, Ridley Ambrose and Mr. Pepper discuss the fate of an old Cambridge acquaintance, Jenkinson of Peterhouse, whose "'really great abilities'" as a potential writer were never realized (15). "'Drink'" and "'drugs'" appear to be largely responsible for the withering of his creative potential. However, there is also a hint that married life and domesticity are partly responsible for the failure: "'Married a young woman out of a tobacconist's, and lived in the Fens—never heard what became of him'" (15). In the second case discussed by the two men, that of Jenkinson of Cats, Mr. Pepper places the blame for creative paralysis more squarely on the mindless eccentricities bred by contemporary domestic life, such as "'sticking Norman arches on one's pigsties'" (16).[18] Woolf once again explores the consequences of conjugal domesticity for creative men in particular in her characterization of Mr. Ramsay in *To the Lighthouse*.

In the ongoing debate concerning the relative merits of public life as opposed to a life of retirement devoted to artistic productivity or scholarship, both Woolf and her principal characters exhibit considerable ambivalence regarding the two modes of living. All in all, however, *The Voyage Out* tends to privilege the sequestered life over the social life, especially for the creative individual. One indicator of this preference is the fair amount of criticism of urban life and of British civilization in particular, especially its imperialism, to be found in the novel. In its first chapter, Woolf depicts the Ambroses' London as a gloomy city swarming with masses of undifferentiated workers rushing to and fro, threatening to overwhelm the individual who insists on his or her uniqueness:

> In the streets of London where beauty goes unregarded, eccentricity must pay the penalty, and it is better not to be very tall, to wear a long blue cloak, or to beat the air with your left hand. (9)

Woolf's image of London seen on shipboard from a distance as "a crouched and cowardly figure, a sedentary miser" (18) anticipates the "little deformed man who squatted on the floor gibbering, with long nails" (77) who appears to threaten Rachel in her nightmare following Dalloway's sexual assault. Civilization, urban life, and personal violation appear to be closely related here, as well as in the later novels.[19]

Woolf also includes a number of satirical references to British imperialism, the end result of "civilized" life in England, in the novel. Clarissa Dalloway's embarrassing tribute to British might during her shipboard cabin conversation with her husband has already been noted. Helen sardonically reviews the contents of a letter from Rachel's shipping magnate father in which he describes how he successfully intimidated striking native dockworkers by shouting "English oaths at them" (196). Using Rachel as her observer, Woolf ironically relates the minister Mr. Bax's Sunday sermon about the hotel guests' "duty to the natives" of Santa Marina (230), echoing Kipling. Appropriately, the guests themselves are largely of the class that furnishes men for service to the empire; as Hewet notes, one of Mrs. Thornbury's numerous children has just been appointed governor of the Carroway Islands (294).

In addition to the negative portrayals of urban life and the empire in *The Voyage Out*, the temperaments of three of the four major characters are drawn primarily to the life of retirement devoted to artistic and scholarly activity. Helen's flinty interactions with the Dalloways and the hotel guests, her interests in the arts and ideas, and her eccentric dress mark her as an intellectual and a bohemian of sorts. Hirst's caustic observations on hotel social life and people in general mark him as an elitist who is only truly comfortable with fellow scholars in a university setting.[20] Woolf portrays him as something of a reclusive, late nineteenth-century decadent as well; following Hirst's condescending words to Rachel at the dance, Hewet tries to explain to her that she must make allowances for him as one who has spent most of his time "'in front of a looking-glass, in a beautiful panelled room, hung with Japanese prints and lovely old chairs and tables'"(156). While at the hotel's Sunday service, Hirst irreverently reads Sappho's "Ode to Aphrodite" in Greek and in Swinburne's translation while seated in the rear of the chapel (230).

As has been noted, Rachel's skittish participation in hotel social life, her frequent uneasiness in company, her retreats to her room to play Bach or Beethoven, her affinity for the natural world, especially the sea, and her search for a deeper reality or order underlying the visible world mark her as one temperamentally best suited for a fundamentally private life in which she may pursue her music and the workings of her imagination. By the end of the novel, her engagement to Hewet strikes one as an anomalous development in her life that death quickly and conveniently rectifies.

Some critics view Rachel's dissolution in illness and death as unconsciously willed, as both a means of escaping from the dismal prospect of enforced existence in an everyday world that severely limits her life as a woman, and a means of casting off the burden of selfhood, merging with the universe in death. It is probably safer to assume that these motivations would be the author's, and that Woolf was projecting her own wishes in assigning her highly autobiographical heroine such a fate; by the time *The Voyage Out* was published in March 1915, Woolf had already made two suicide attempts, the second as late as September 1913 (Bell, *VW2*: 228).[21]

Of the novel's four principal characters, Terence Hewet appears to belong more squarely in the realm of social interaction and public life. His deep interest in observing and talking with others, his actual need for companionship and social involvement (310), his knack for organizing social activities such as the expedition into the mountains, and his generally sympathetic, intuitive nature all serve as evidence of his being primarily a social creature. There is a possible hint of what might be characterized as naïve aestheticism in Hewet's plans to write a novel about silence; more positively, he shares Rachel's Paterian longing to discern an order underlying earthly reality.[22] One senses, however, that upon returning to England, he will continue to be actively involved with others, quite possibly in spheres beyond that of letters such as politics or social reform. At this stage in Woolf's writing career, Hewet represents the emergence in embryonic form of the engaged artist-figure who practices his or her art while living fully among others. Bernard of *The Waves* and Miss La Trobe of *Between the Acts* represent the maturation of this view of the artist in Woolf's fiction.

CHAPTER THREE

Night and Day

Unlike *The Voyage Out*, Woolf's second novel, *Night and Day* (1919), confines its action largely to an urban setting—London and its environs in the early years of the twentieth century. This unusually long work, widely considered Woolf's most conventional novel,[1] is written in the genre of the novel of manners and is concerned with sorting out the fates of five relatively young people whose misperceptions about each other and lack of self-knowledge result in mismatches that are eventually dissolved. New, more promising couplings emerge, resulting in two imminent marriages as the novel slowly moves towards its comedic conclusion. The novel consists largely of the principal characters' visits to each other's rooms or houses, the narrator's presentation of their thoughts and feelings, and their drawing room conversations, where dialogue rather than deeds or external events advances the action.

Despite its conventional appearance, *Night and Day* reflects Woolf's interests as an emerging experimental writer in its frequent exposition of the states of mind of its main characters. In a manner reminiscent of Henry James as well as her psychological novelist contemporaries such as Lawrence, Woolf appears to be concerned with providing an anatomy of her characters' emotions as they interact with one another, gradually discern the illusions under which they have been operating, and acknowledge the emergence of new emotions which will affect their relations with one another. In particular, the principal characters are involved in learning to recognize, understand, and master their emotions, especially that of love. The combination of the novel's restricted setting and sphere of action and Woolf's detailed analyses of states of mind tend to make it rather claustrophobic and particularly taxing for readers accustomed to the selective use of detail to suggest psychological states characteristic of the more lyrical works of Woolf's maturity such as *To the Lighthouse* and *Between the Acts*. Like its predecessor, *Night and Day* must also be considered an apprentice novel; Woolf herself admitted in a letter to Ottoline Morrell dated February 20, 1938 that she learned much from writing it (Rose 96).

It is in *Night and Day*, however, that Woolf introduces a practicing professional artist-figure for the first time in her novels. This figure, the great English poet Richard Alardyce, grandfather of Katharine Hilbery, is deceased, but nonetheless continues to exert considerable influence upon the lives of the Hilberys, particularly that of his granddaughter.[2] Both Mrs. Hilbery and Katharine are preoccupied with writing a definitive biography of the man, but Katharine bears the burden of showing literary pilgrims to their home her grandfather's personal effects—the "relics"—kept in a little alcove resembling a shrine dedicated to his memory off the drawing room (15). The dead man's grasp extends well beyond the demand for such vestal duties, though; wherever she goes, Katharine finds that new acquaintances, upon learning of her relation to Alardyce, expect her to exhibit a keen interest in poetry, and to be herself somehow poetical (20, 317). Considering the difficulties of a life lived in the shadow of a great literary ancestor, it is not surprising that Katharine shows a marked lack of interest in poetry and literature generally. Throughout the novel, she insists she knows nothing about literature and does not read books. One senses in the portrayal of Katharine's relationship to her famous grandfather Woolf's attempt to work out a number of issues associated with her anxiety as a young woman struggling to forge her own identity as a writer in the shadow of an father who was an illustrious man of letters.[3]

Among the novel's amateur artist-figures is the minor character Henry Otway, Katharine's poor country cousin, a young man who has abjured a career in trade, "and persisted, in spite of the disapproval of uncles and aunts, in practising both violin and piano, with the result that he could not perform professionally upon either" (209). Woolf expands upon this perfunctory Austenesque statement by informing the reader that Otway has only "the score of half an opera" (209) to show for his thirty-two years. He earns a modest living by teaching violin and piano to the young ladies of Lincolnshire.

William Rodney, an old family friend of the Hilberys and Katharine's fiancé, is the only amateur artist-figure among the novel's main characters. A socially timid, over-refined son of an old west country family, Rodney works as a clerk at the Bureau of Education by day, retiring to his bachelor's rooms atop an eighteenth-century house in Lincoln's Inn Fields in the evening, where he cultivates his aesthetic sensibilities, reading the classics from his collection of first editions, examining his pictures and photographs of statues, playing melodies from Mozart's operas on his piano, working on a verse play in the genre of Renaissance pastoral drama, and composing an occasional sonnet to be used in courting Katharine.

Woolf's characterization of Rodney as an aesthete is curiously mixed, but overall unsympathetic. Rodney is portrayed as a combination of an eighteenth-century antiquarian with a fondness for the Elizabethans (he delivers a paper on the Elizabethan use of metaphor to a group assembled in Mary Datchet's rooms) and a rather anxious, enervated Prufrockian aesthete whose obsession with appearances and socially correct behavior renders him ridiculous to his contemporaries.[4] Admiring Katharine's beauty, style and poise, Rodney becomes annoyingly proprietary following their engagement, treating her as a treasured object in a manner that recalls Cecil Vyse's valuation of Lucy Honeychurch in Forster's *A Room with a View*. Far less self-assured than Vyse, however, Rodney alienates Katharine with his petty complaints about her supposedly negligent behavior and his overconcern for appearances, including her own.[5] For Katharine, Rodney comes to represent another manifestation of the past and its more formal, restrictive traditions attempting to assert control over her life; her break with Rodney and subsequent engagement to Ralph Denham constitute an effort to seize the present for herself and determine her own future.[6]

In William Rodney, Woolf presents a version of the Ivory Tower aesthete whose conceitedness and social ineptitude stymie his efforts to integrate himself with the social life of his time. In Cassandra Otway, Katharine's cousin, Rodney conveniently finds a worshipful, relatively docile young woman of artistic talent and interests who enables him to assume the role of teacher and inculcator of culture (it is not surprising that Woolf chooses to make him work for the Bureau of Education). Unlike Katharine, Cassandra is far more willing as well as able to play the role of Stella to Rodney's Swift.[7]

Although not amateur poets or closet dramatists like Rodney, the novel's other major characters share Rodney's dual needs for a retreat in which to engage in some kind of creative work or independent study and a sense of connectedness to the life around them. The effort to satisfy both needs is in fact the major theme of *Night and Day*, reflected in its title. How can one order one's life so as to inhabit both the daylight world of social engagement, activities and responsibilities and the nocturnal world of the solitary dreamer, artist, scholar or thinker? How can one retain a firm grasp of facts, of external realities while simultaneously allowing for feelings and the inspiration bred by the imagination? As Katharine remarks to herself,

> Why . . . should there be this perpetual disparity between the thought and the action, between the life of solitude and the life of society, this astonishing precipice on one side of which the soul was active and in broad daylight, on the other side of which it was contemplative and dark as night? Was it not possible to step from one to the other, erect, and without essential change? (338–9)

As will be seen, this novel presents a view of family responsibilities as potentially debilitating, inhibiting the expression of one's "nocturnal" side and the formation of an independent identity. Heterosexual relationships, on the other hand, are seen to hold out the promise of liberating the self from the social constraints of the daylight world while simultaneously reconciling the need for individual autonomy with the need for a sense of connectedness to others. Katharine's evolving relationship with Ralph Denham comes to embody this positive potential in the novel.

Like William Rodney, Ralph Denham is also an economic "slave" (72), obliged to work during the daytime as a lawyer in a City firm to support his aging mother and numerous younger siblings. Denham is an energetic member of the aspiring middle class, ambitious for himself and his family despite their financial problems and their lives of shabby gentility in Highgate.[8] In the evening after supper, Denham retreats from the turbulence and cares of family life to his room atop the house, which has the disordered, impoverished appearance of an artist's or writer's garret. In this room, Denham studies the law and writes papers on legal topics, one of which has been published in a prominent review edited by Katharine's father. This refuge, however, is also the site of Denham's daydreams about the future and fantasies concerning Katharine, whose dark beauty, poise, aloofness and mystery appeal to him so powerfully. In the novel's symbolic scheme, Denham's room represents his solitary nocturnal side, where he broods upon his hopes and Katharine, looks out of his window, which provides a romantic view of the lights, rooftops and chimney pots of London at a distance, and tends to his pet rook, whose presence evokes the famous midnight visitor of Poe's "The Raven," as well as the poem's despondent solitary speaker.

A materialist reading of Denham's longing for Katharine would most likely view it as a manifestation of his desire to attain the privileged social class to which she belongs. Their earliest interaction, fraught with tension as a result of Denham's acute consciousness of their class difference, would suggest as much: "'I suppose you come of one of the most distinguished families in England'" (17). But Woolf makes it clear that Katharine appeals to elements in Denham beyond any desire for upward mobility as well. For Denham is possessed of a rebellious inner spirit that his elder sister Joan finds perplexing; she can envision him "suddenly sacrificing his entire career for some fantastic imagination" (125). To her, Denham exhibits an "odd combination of Spartan self-control and . . . romantic and childish folly" (31). The narrator informs the reader that Denham's daydreams "gave outlet to some spirit which found no work to do in real life," a spirit which he sometimes viewed as his "most valuable possession" (127). Katharine's aristocratic aloofness and mystery appeal to this romantic side of Denham, who associates her with "beauty and passion" (292), and proceeds to transform her in his fantasies (24). Denham's associations of Katharine with "the spaces of night and the open air" (192) give her the quality of a *fin-de-siècle* siren, whose attractions Denham, like a moth hovering around a flame, cannot resist. Toward the end of the novel, Denham begins to keep an evening "vigil" outside Katharine's house (396), imagining Katharine as "a shape of light, the light itself" that radiates from the three tall windows of the drawing room (395).[9]

Denham's powerful infatuation with Katharine causes him to transform her into a romantic ideal, despite his conscious efforts to appreciate her for herself.[10] As he confesses to her during one of their nocturnal walks in the city, he has made her his "'ideal'" from the beginning (298). Denham's rather rigid, uncompromising personality, his rejection of "the second-rate" and "the unworthy" (329) is such that he must of necessity idealize Katharine, and it is this obsessive behavior that creates the major obstacle to their union once Katharine has broken her engagement to Rodney.

It also reflects a Platonic element in Denham's character, however; dissatisfied with the inferior reality of the visible world, he insists on projecting a superior reality beyond it, symbolically embodying this ideal in Katharine; although she might take her leave, "his belief in what she stood for, detached from her, would remain" (385). Katharine's metaphysical significance for Denham reaches its zenith later in the novel when the couple experiences a moment of heroic transformation replete with the imagery of flames and light often found in Pater's work:

> . . . he and Katharine were alone together, aloft, splendid, and luminous with a twofold radiance. . . . They were united as the adventurous are united, though one reaches the goal and the other perishes by the way. (398)[11]

Denham's desire for union with Katharine, then, is not simply the result of social ambition or of wanting to escape the demands of an onerous family. Transforming her in his fantasies, Denham enables Katharine to nurture his underdeveloped romantic side by incarnating his personal ideal, giving him a dizzying sense of mastery in gaining her. At the same time, like one of Lawrence's lovers, he has the realization that they are in the grip of a reality larger than themselves, one that will consume them even as they are transformed by it:

> They were victors, masters of life, but at the same time absorbed in the flame, giving their life to increase its brightness, to testify to their faith. (505)[12]

Like Denham, Katharine is eager to shed the burdens and limitations of family responsibilities. Her lot is to attend to the numerous domestic matters shirked by her amiable but impractical mother and her retiring scholar father. At the Hilbery home on Chelsea's Cheyne Walk it is Katharine who must deal with intrusive, gossiping relations, preside over the tea table, and pay household bills. Living under the shadow of her deceased grandfather's fame, Katharine must also assist her easily distracted mother in preparing her grandfather's biography (a work that increasingly threatens never to materialize), and show visitors Alardyce's portrait, manuscripts and personal effects.[13] The result of this enforced preoccupation with the past is a sense that she is barely aware that "she was a separate being, with a future of her own" (114). If Rodney and Denham feel themselves slaves to their jobs, Katharine bemoans her "slavery to her family traditions" (352).

Although her material circumstances are far better than Denham's, Katharine's life in service to her family seems doubly frustrating because of the restrictions upon her freedom placed by her gender and class, and the selfless role of dutiful daughter she is expected to fulfill. Like Denham, Katharine indulges in daydreams, but ones that are clearly more escapist than his. Some are also fantasies of mastery. Katharine imagines herself taming ponies, steering a ship in a storm through treacherous waters (45), alone on a hilltop among bracken (434), or, more tellingly, riding with an unidentified "magnanimous hero" along the seashore or through a forest (107, 141, 197, 270). The latter, a recurring fantasy, seems the more remarkable in that it continues well after her engagement to Rodney, who clearly fails to satisfy her at some primal level.[14]

Despite the general perception of Katharine as a sensible, practical young woman, she nonetheless exhibits traits that give her a mysterious, otherworldly air. Woolf's description of her appearance early in the novel conveys the aura of a romantic figure from an earlier era. Wearing "old yellow-tinted lace" on a dress set off by an "ancient jewel," Katharine has "dark oval eyes" and exhibits a "spirit given to contemplation and self-control" (13). On two separate occasions she is favorably compared to Shakespeare's Rosalind (175, 306). Katharine often exhibits an air of abstraction, walking past Denham on the Strand one day without noticing him (130). Her absent-mindedness results in the loss of a basket of oysters and, on another occasion, her bag (137, 332–3). Denham is not oblivious to her remoteness, sensing in her "something distant and abstract" that simultaneously "exalted . . . and chilled him" (421).

Woolf also associates Katharine with the night. Like Pater's Marius and Rachel Vinrace in *The Voyage Out*, Katharine appears to be in search of a deeper reality beyond that of everyday appearances. In a characteristic gesture, Katharine turns away from a room full of people to gaze out the window upon a night sky:

> She heard them [voices] as if they came from people in another world, a world antecedent to her world, a world that was the prelude, the antechamber to reality; it was as if, lately dead, she heard the living talking. The dream nature of our life had never been more apparent to her . . . . (352)

The night comes to be associated with Katharine's mental expeditions beyond the quotidian to a Platonic realm where

> . . . dwelt the realities of the appearances which figure in our world; so direct, powerful, and unimpeded were her sensations there, compared with those called forth in actual life. (141)

As the novel demonstrates, Denham senses Katharine's dissatisfaction with the visible world, one that mirrors his own; their relationship promises to liberate her from the restrictions of daytime existence, permitting her to explore at greater length the mysterious realm she can only glimpse from time to time in her seriously limited daily life.

One of Katharine's major means of escaping the oppressive domestic obligations of her life on Cheyne Walk also has nocturnal associations. Late in the evening, Katharine is in the habit of retiring to her room where she furtively studies mathematics and astronomy in solitude; the narrator compares such late-night activity to that of "some nocturnal animal"(45).[15] In part, Katharine's pursuit of mathematics is clearly a reaction to her grandfather's fame as a poet and her parents' absorption in literature, which she disdains as being "'all about feelings'"(146).[16] Occupied with her parents and the exigencies of social life during the day, Katharine treasures the impersonality offered by working at mathematics at night, "'something that hasn't got to do with human beings'" (195). Estranged from Rodney, Katharine takes refuge in the sciences, in abstract concepts that paradoxically seem more real to her (284). Even more importantly, mathematics, like music for Rachel Vinrace in *The Voyage Out*, provides Katharine with an arena in which to craft an independent identity and gain a sense of mastery over something other than the family tea table; withdrawing into the subject one night, Katharine feels herself "mistress in her own kingdom" (479).

Not surprisingly, Katharine, like other young women of her class and time, consciously equates the prospect of marriage with liberation from the restrictive influence of parents and the opportunity to establish an independent existence in one's own space. As Katharine frankly admits to herself, she wants to marry Rodney partly in order to have her own house (194). However, her daydreams of personal liberation as a hoped-for result of marrying Rodney frequently take the form of pursuing mathematics and astronomy without restriction (216). Woolf even enables Katharine to suggest that a woman's personal fulfillment can enhance the conjugal satisfaction of her spouse: "'if I could calculate things, and use a telescope . . . I should be perfectly happy, and I believe I should give William all he wants'" (195). By the time Katharine becomes emotionally involved with Denham, the equation of heterosexual involvement with opportunities for personal development in her mind becomes more intuitive and spontaneous. While walking along the Embankment with Denham, who tells her at length about his family, Katharine feels extraordinarily happy as "books of algebraic symbols, pages all speckled with dots and dashes and twisted bars, came before her eyes" (300).

Katharine's choice of Denham over Rodney signifies many things. For Katharine, Rodney represents the claustrophobic world of the past inhabited by her literary parents and imposed upon her by the legacy of her famous poet grandfather. Rodney's petty complaints and preoccupation with appearances mark him as representative of her social class at its worst—irritable, formal to the point of stuffiness, restrictive. Katharine also discovers that Rodney harbors decidedly old-fashioned attitudes towards women: "' . . . who wants you to be learned?'," he remarks to her (138). Denham, on the other hand, promises a life in which Katharine will be free to develop her own interests;[17] like her, he is drawn to the sciences, especially botany, and shares a passion for facts. For Katharine, Denham represents the future and unfulfilled potential. As the narrator states, both

> . . . shared the same sense of the impending future, vast, mysterious, infinitely stored with undeveloped shapes which each would unwrap for the other to behold . . . . (493)

For Denham, union with Katharine comes to symbolize the transcendence of limitation and the attainment of an ideal. She also enables him to relinquish his desire to retreat to a country cottage to write a history of the English village, making him feel that personal fulfillment is indeed possible within the context of human relationships (379). Most importantly, however, Denham and Katharine share a mystical bent that involves both in a quest for a deeper reality. As Mary Datchet notes, the two have "this hidden impulse, this incalculable force—this thing they cared for and didn't talk about" (177). Denham tries to articulate this impulse for himself and Katharine: "'we're in some sort of agreement . . . we're after something together'" (299).

In *Night and Day*, then, the prospect of marriage to one's beloved appears to offer both the satisfaction of the need for relationship and the promise of opportunities for personal development that characters of such independent temperaments as Denham and Katharine crave. Marriage in this novel, as in comedies generally, represents an escape from old familial restrictions and responsibilities and offers the hope of independence and a new life. In the case of Denham and Katharine, their union promises to reconcile the two worlds of night and day, the need for solitude and the freedom to pursue one's interests and the need for social integration.

This seemingly rosy conclusion to Denham and Katharine's struggles is nonetheless tempered by numerous examples in the novel of threats to individual autonomy and fulfillment dormant in heterosexual relations and the marriage bond. In the novel's opening dialogue, Mrs. Hilbery and her guests consider the fate of Katharine's female cousin, who has married an engineer and as a result is forced to move to Manchester. As chauvinistic Londoners, they have a difficult time imagining what this pitiable woman might be able to find to do in the Midlands (10). On one occasion, Mrs. Seal, Mary Datchet's colleague in the office of the women's suffrage society who is self-conscious about her lack of formal education, hints that "'domestic circumstances'" have prevented her from becoming "'an intelligence'" (170).

As in *The Voyage Out*, Woolf makes it clear that marriage and domestic responsibilities place limitations upon the personal development of men as well as women. One of Katharine's aunts, Millicent Cosham, recalls that another relation, Uncle John, burdened with a wife and seven children, has had to settle for a judgeship in India, which is not quite "'the top of the tree'" (151). Cyril Alardyce, Katharine's young second cousin, has scandalized the family by maintaining a liaison with a woman who is about to bear his third child. He lectures at a workingmen's college, and appears worn with cares (120); "'they've got nothing to live upon'" (121), Mrs. Hilbery notes with concern. There are also allusions to Katharine's famous grandfather's failed marriage, including the suggestion that it led Alardyce to drink and dissipation (102).

Although *Night and Day*'s conclusion provides the comedic promise of two happy marriages, one of the novel's main characters, Mary Datchet, is left outside the charmed circle of the engaged. Mary represents Woolf's first effort in her fiction to deal at length with the independent New Woman, a late Victorian social and literary phenomenon for which Woolf reveals some ambivalence.[18] Although not an artist or a creative writer, Mary is dedicated to her work as a volunteer in the office of a women's suffrage society. She also has Woolf's prerequisite independent income and, in this case, rooms of her own, the latter a fact for which Katharine expresses her envy (272). Mary uses her evenings to plan strategies to advance the cause and continue working on a political treatise she is writing. Woolf's portrayal of Mary is generally quite sympathetic; although lacking the dark beauty and romance of Katharine, Mary reveals herself to be a sociable, sensible and sensitive individual, holding evening gatherings in her rooms, showing considerable political acumen in her work on behalf of women's suffrage, and always making herself available to friends who need an understanding ear. She also exhibits "an indefinable promise of soft maternity" (166), a potential which Denham finds particularly appealing. However, Mary remains too much a creature of daylight, of the quotidian, to spark Denham's desire. When she discovers that Denham is deeply in love with Katharine, she is shown to resign herself to a life of work dedicated to her social causes.

Woolf's difficulty in portraying Mary lies in her ambivalence about Mary's work as a reformer and her status as a woman who lives without heterosexual love. The scenes set in Mary's office have a decidedly Dickensian quality to them, as do the surnames of her colleagues. Mr. Clacton and Mrs. Seal are depicted as colorful eccentrics, Clacton assuming the role of the self-important social reformer who is also an amateur aesthete during his lunch hour (82), and Mrs. Seal exuding a frenetic enthusiasm for the cause that often renders her ridiculous.[19] Woolf's lifelong misgivings about social reformers and zealots of any stripe can be found in these scenes, as in the conversations of the Hilberys *en famille*. As Mr. Hilbery remarks,

'It's curious . . . how the sight of one's fellow-enthusiasts always chokes one off. They show up the faults of one's cause so much more plainly than one's antagonists.' (100)

It seems that in *Night and Day* Woolf cannot resist the opportunity to satirize some of the more naive-sounding reforms as well as reformers. One of Mary's new acquaintances, an earnest young man named Mr. Basnett, has devised a plan

> ... for the education of labor, for the amalgamation of the middle class and the working class, and for a joint assault of the two bodies, combined in the Society for the Education of Democracy, upon Capital. (355)

Following Mary's realization that Denham does not love her, Woolf's narrator seemingly prematurely relegates her to the ranks of the loveless, who must turn to their work for consolation. While walking along Charing Cross Road, Mary momentarily transcends her own existence, taking a broad view of the human condition, and concludes that life is "'not happiness'" (260). Committing herself to the cause (women's rights), Mary feels that her "lot" has been "cast" forever with the

> ... shadow people, flitting in and out of the ranks of the living— eccentrics, undeveloped human beings, from whose substance some essential part had been cut away. (265)[20]

The air of finality surrounding these moments seems forced; after all, Mary is a young woman in her mid-twenties who has arrived in London just six months ago. Furthermore, her sensible personality as Woolf delineates it does not strike one as being of the sort that would so readily write off hopes for future happiness, even under the pain of the present moment.

Apparently at this stage of her career, Woolf cannot countenance a professionally oriented woman's life as being successful without heterosexual involvement; Mary's dedication to her work must be made to seem compensatory. Examining a leaflet to be issued by the suffrage society, Mary thinks "she would be content to remain silent for ever if a share of personal happiness were granted her" (258). Her faith in the cause becomes "faith in an illusion" (258). Confiding in Denham later in the novel, she states that her work is "'the thing that saves one—I'm sure of that'" (391). In an effort to give Mary her due, Woolf attempts to correlate Mary's "passion" for her work with Katharine and Denham's passion for each other. While strolling about nighttime London at the end of the novel, Katharine and Denham look up at the light in Mary's windows: "'She's happy too,'" says Katharine. "'She has her work'" (505). Unfortunately, however, the numerous instances which cast doubt upon the centrality of Mary's work for her make this correlation unconvincing.[21]

Woolf's conflicted portrayal of Mary's relationship to her work in *Night and Day* nonetheless continues to illustrate her problematic view of the relationship between heterosexual love and work, creative or otherwise, for women first presented in Rachel Vinrace's experience in *The Voyage Out*. One senses that in Woolf's mind, Mary would mature into a figure not unlike Miss Allan—witty, intelligent, gracious and productive in her work, but still to be pitied for her mateless status and her hard, apparently lonely life.

One might argue that the seeming deprivation resulting from the absence of heterosexual love in the lives of such figures as Mary and Miss Allan serves to illustrate Woolf's evolving view that some form of relationship is required by those engaged in independent pursuits such as art or scholarship in order to realize their full potential both in their work and as human beings. I would argue, though, that Woolf's earliest novels exhibit an overvaluation of the significance of heterosexual relationships for women.[22] Those women who are not in such relationships seem doomed to lead lackluster lives in their chosen occupations. Those who are must risk the threat of the relationship interfering with their work as creative individuals or professionals. At this stage in Woolf's writing career, the wide circle of friends, warm family affections and engaging personality of a character as socially integrated as Mary are not enough to insure such a woman a fulfilling, productive life.

Katharine and Denham's final position at the end of the novel, however, does represent a dramatic advance over that of Rachel and Hewet in *The Voyage Out*. In Katharine and Denham's relationship, Woolf provides a positive image of heterosexual involvement as an aid to individual autonomy and personal development; a comfortable middle ground between the solitary productivity of the Ivory Tower and the social integration of the Sacred Fount appears to have been reached, at least momentarily. However, one must keep in mind that neither Denham nor Katharine is an artist or a creative writer. Furthermore, Woolf's narrator does not indicate the degree of Katharine's commitment to the study of mathematics and astronomy. Finally, the happy resolution of their difficult courtship must be seen partly as a concession to the conventions of the comic novel of manners. One would need to be able to look into Katharine and Denham's future life together to determine whether their relationship actually helps or hinders their growth and productivity as individuals involved in different intellectual enterprises.

CHAPTER FOUR

Jacob's Room

With *Jacob's Room* (1922), Woolf departed from the traditional realism of *Night and Day* in an effort to evolve an experimental novelistic style that would be uniquely hers.[1] Unlike her first two novels, *Jacob's Room* shows little concern with plot, consisting instead of chapters subdivided into episodes providing impressionistically rendered glimpses of various periods in the short life of Jacob Flanders, a young man who dies in the First World War.[2] Also included are scenes from life in such places as Scarborough, the seaside resort where Jacob grows up; Cambridge, where he attends the university; the Cornwall coast, where he vacations as a child and a college student; London, where he works in an office following graduation; and Greece and Italy, which he visits alone shortly before the war. As these glimpses provide a rudimentary history of Jacob in different milieus from early childhood to young manhood, the novel does bear a resemblance to the *Bildungsroman* genre employed earlier by Woolf in *The Voyage Out*, but differs most dramatically from it in its refusal to permit the reader access to Jacob's mind and to trace his personal growth and intellectual development.

Rather, *Jacob's Room* can be seen as an ironic, modernist version of the *Bildungsroman*, portraying its central character largely from a distance and from the perspective of a number of other characters in the novel. Certain physical and behavioral traits as well as personal interests consistently recur in the glimpses afforded of Jacob, but his inner being remains a mystery to narrator and reader alike.[3] As the novel's title suggests, *Jacob's Room* presents selected details of the context of Jacob's brief life, rather than those of his innermost self. Woolf's technique in this novel effectively illustrates its narrator's contention that it is practically impossible to know others well: "It is no use trying to sum people up" (31, 154). Those familiar with Woolf's fiction will recognize this as a recurring theme in the novels.

Part of the irony of *Jacob's Room* viewed as a *Bildungsroman* lies in the premature death in war of its subject, Jacob Flanders, an ending quite uncharacteristic of the genre. Indeed, when compared to the sense of unlimited possibilities available to Ralph Denham and Katharine Hilbery at the conclusion of *Night and Day*, Woolf's previous novel, *Jacob's Room* presents a series of images of blighted potential, not only in Jacob's tragic fate, but also in the unremarkable lives of the novel's other characters, major and minor. The novel's narrator, on occasion irritatingly obtrusive, offers a series of bittersweet observations that portray life as limiting and even imprisoning. Appearing at the end of the novel's first chapter, the image of a crab pathetically trying time and again to climb out of Jacob's beach pail serves as a controlling metaphor for a number of the lives presented, albeit briefly, in *Jacob's Room* (14).[4] As will be seen, loss, deprivation, and limitation are shown to characterize many of them. Opportunities for creative or scholarly activity or simply for personal fulfillment are circumscribed by class limitations, gender roles and expectations, and unhappy marriages. In this novel, civilization and heterosexual relations more often than not hamper the individual's efforts to attain a meaningful, satisfying life.

Unlike the main characters in Woolf's first two novels, none of those in *Jacob's Room* is a practicing or aspiring artist-figure, writer, or scholar. Among the minor characters is a number of amateur artists and scholars who are themselves portrayed as marginal figures, or whose work lacks significance. At the beginning of the novel, Charles Steele, the seascape painter who includes Mrs. Flanders's seated figure in the scene he is painting, is described as "an unknown man exhibiting obscurely" who is "much gratified if his landladies liked his pictures" (8). The novel's narrator reveals that the irreverent young artist Cruttendon who so impresses Jacob during his stay in Paris will spend his adult life in Kent, forsaken by his wife, painting orchards "savagely, in solitude" (130). The novel's only aesthete, Everard Benson, a host of tea parties, whose rooms are decorated "in the style of Whistler, with pretty books on tables," wins the disdain of both the narrator and Jacob, who considers him "a contemptible ass" (104). Among the solitary researchers to be found under the dome of the British Museum is the Dickensian Miss Marchmont, bewigged and wearing an "old plush dress," who is looking for something "to confirm her philosophy that colour is sound—or, perhaps, it has something to do with music" (105).[5] The hard-working feminist Miss Julia Hedge resents the fact that she must grapple with statistics on behalf of the cause rather than enjoy copying poetry, as does Jacob while seated in the Reading Room: "Death and gall and bitter dust were on her pen-tip" (106).

One might argue that Jacob's literary bent—he is fond of reading the Greeks, Romans and Elizabethans—marks him as an aspiring writer or scholar, but the narrator's limited portrayal of him can be seen to present him as simply one of many young, intelligent, recently graduated Oxbridge men of his era with a seemingly undemanding job in London who has yet to choose his lifework.[6] Among Jacob's wide-ranging interests are also the study of butterflies and moths—a boyhood hobby which still occasions nocturnal jaunts into the countryside—and history, political theory and government, the latter stimulated by his visits to Greece and Italy, where he envisions writing letters on the subject that "might turn to an essay upon civilization" one day (136). Jacob's post-university writings include a paper attacking a bowdlerized edition of Wycherley which he unsuccessfully tries to get published, an essay "upon the Ethics of Indecency" (78), and "long letters about art, morality, and politics to young men at college" (94). Clearly, Jacob exhibits vocational potential that could take many different forms, but as a young adult in his twenties, he has not quite reached the point of making his choice, a prospect that still irks him:

> 'One must apply oneself to something or other—God knows what. Everything is really very jolly—except getting up in the morning and wearing a tail coat.' (72)

Like so many promising young men of his generation, though, Jacob falls victim to the demands of the nation and his gender role, dying quite possibly on the very fields whose name he shares.

If Jacob's life is sacrificed as a result of the demands placed upon his sex, youth and patriotism during wartime, the lives of the novel's female characters are also severely limited by their gender. In Clara Durrant, sister of Jacob's college friend and in love with Jacob, Woolf portrays yet another dutiful daughter of her own class whose personal growth is stunted by her sheltered upbringing and who chafes under the socially imposed restrictions of her culture. Jacob's admiration for Clara is tempered by pity; he envisions her "a virgin chained to a rock . . . eternally pouring out tea for old men in white waistcoats" (123). Living in the shadow of an assertive mother who enjoys debating political issues with her nation's peers, Clara exhibits a child-like reticence which makes Bonamy, Jacob's friend, think of her as "the silent woman" whom Jacob may one day marry (152). But Bonamy also senses the repressed human potential within her, viewing Clara's as "an existence squeezed and emasculated within a white satin shoe" (152). Painfully aware that her family and her culture have already placed her on the marriage market, Clara momentarily loses patience with her role as a nubile young woman at a dance, tearing up her dance card and tossing it into the fireplace (85).

The other unmarried women in Jacob's life, Fanny Elmer, Florinda and Laurette, dominate the most unattractive end of the narrow spectrum of possibilities permitted young single women of the Edwardian era. Apparently financially independent to a certain extent, Fanny shares a room with a schoolmistress and spends her time sitting for Slade School painters such as Nick Bramham, engaging in desultory reading, and window-shopping. Desperately in love with Jacob, she resolves to "learn Latin and read Virgil" in order to make herself more interesting to him (121). She even attempts to read *Tom Jones* when she learns that Fielding is one of Jacob's favorite authors. Mulling over the "dowdy women" whom she believes are the typical female readers of such classics, Fanny thinks, "there is something . . . about books which if I had been educated I could have liked—much better than ear-rings and flowers" (122). But Fanny correctly surmises that her under-developed mind will never be able to hold Jacob's interest; he will forget her as soon as he travels to Greece.

Florinda is perhaps Woolf's most extensive, albeit quite limited, fictional portrait of the *demimondaine* who supports herself by sitting for painters and exchanging sex for the companionship, favors, and protection of indi-vidual men. Unlike Clara and Fanny, Florinda's "unanchored life" (78) appears to have originated in poverty and homelessness; she does not even have a last name, "and for parents had only the photograph of a tomb-stone beneath which, she said, her father lay buried" (77). In her face, Jacob sees something that is "horribly brainless" (80), and is naïvely taken aback when he views her at a distance upon the arm of another man. At the farthest end of the spectrum is the intelligent young prostitute Laurette, whom Jacob visits in a brothel. Unlike Florinda, she appears to have fallen mysteriously from a higher station in life (105).

In the brief glimpses of the lives of these young women provided by the narrator, Woolf exhibits something akin to the determinism commonly asso-ciated with such naturalist writers as Zola and Crane and also found to a cer-tain extent in Chekhov—one observes it again many years later in *The Years*.[7] In *Jacob's Room*, however, these rather grim young lives are not the only ones bound by fate and circumstances. The novel offers numerous examples of adult lives often frustrated or rendered miserable by marriage. The invalid daughter of a prominent Scarborough family, Ellen Barfoot is packed off in a bath chair to the town's seashore promenade every Wednes-day afternoon so that her husband, Captain Barfoot, may discreetly visit Mrs. Flanders, whom he admires. Ellen is "a prisoner—civilization's prisoner" (25), locked into a physically as well as socially visible position that renders the maintenance of appearances essential. The restless wife of a Scarborough clergyman, Mrs. Jarvis often roams the moors with a book of poetry, trying to convince herself that she would never be so desperately unhappy as to "leave her husband, and ruin a good man's career, as she sometimes threat-ened" (27). During a private conversation at a London party, Mrs. Withers murmurs to her male confidant that her husband is "cold" (110).

While in Greece, Jacob meets and falls in love with the elegant Mrs. Sandra Wentworth Williams, a beautiful woman who exudes a wistful, sensitive aura and is in the habit of seeking relief from her unbearably dull, bourgeois marriage by enlisting young men she meets in fleeting affairs of the heart. Woolf's narrator cannot resist treating her satirically:

'I am full of love for every one,' thought Mrs. Wentworth Williams, '—for the poor most of all—for the peasants coming back in the evening with their burdens.' (141)[8]

But there is also a hint of the vampiric *femme fatale* about her; noting Jacob's "severe" character, she realizes "that she could deceive him" (169). The narrator imagines her at home in England, when "she would suck back again the soul of the moment" she had spent with an admirer (161). According to the narrator, it is women like Mrs. Wentworth Williams who are the bearers of cynicism to such as Jacob, who contains within himself "something caustic . . . the seeds of extreme disillusionment, which would come to him from women in middle life" (159).

As in Woolf's first two novels, though, *Jacob's Room* also offers examples of men relinquishing their full potential in marriage or suffering the consequences of an unhappy match. Mr. Dickens, hired by Captain Barfoot to take his wife to the esplanade every week, is a man who is scorned at home by his rheumatic wife and his daughters. By way of compensation, he enjoys being "in charge of Mrs. Barfoot, a woman" during these excursions (26). A conversation at a party reveals that Mrs. Durrant's husband gave up ownership of a yacht—and the freedom it implies—upon marrying her (61). Mr. Clutterbuck, a family friend of the Durrants, escapes from his unhappy marriage by frequently retreating to the Durrants in Cornwall and London as a houseguest (88).[9] And Evan Williams, impeccably correct in his behavior, is so demoralized by his own shortcomings and his wife's dalliances that he has effectively given up hope of ever achieving anything extraordinary, thinking that at best, he might be able "to publish, with Macmillans, his monograph upon the foreign policy of Chatham" (145).

Throughout the novel, Woolf's narrator presents examples of the difficulty of civilized life in general and heterosexual relations in particular. Commenting upon the common wish to be momentarily free of the demands of social interaction, the narrator concludes, "as for men and women, let them go hang" (141). Although the information about Jacob provided in *Jacob's Room* is purposely limited, there is enough evidence to indicate that he would find the social obligations entailed by marriage quite onerous. He shows a marked impatience for social life at the hotel in Greece where the guests dressed up in the evening "and talked nonsense— what damned nonsense" (138). As far as women are concerned, Jacob is capable of a certain degree of courtesy—lifting the fearful Mrs. Norman's dressing-case off the train, for example, or holding Mrs. Durrant's ball of wool for her. But like so many of his peers who have undergone the subtle indoctrination in predominantly masculine values and mores at such male preserves as Rugby, Oxford, and Cambridge down through the decades, Jacob finds the experience of most women puzzling and quite foreign to his own. A momentary expression of vacuousness on Florinda's face triggers in him "a violent reversion towards male society, cloistered rooms, and the works of the classics" and anger toward the power that has so arranged the realities of life (82). The presence of wives of dons at the Sunday service in King's College Chapel annoys him, as does that of touring Frenchwomen on the Acropolis: "'Damn these women—damn these women!'" (151).[10]

The narrator wryly comments that the "violent disillusionment" they engender in him

> . . . is generally to be expected in young men in the prime of life, sound of wind and limb, who will soon become fathers of families and directors of banks. (151)

Such disillusionment quite possibly finds a home in seriously depressed men like Evan Williams in middle age as well.

As *Jacob's Room* strongly suggests, the masculine mores and values that Jacob absorbs at Rugby and Cambridge are those that alienate the sexes from each other and drive British civilization, including education, commerce, and the war machine that ultimately consumes Jacob's life. Toward the end of the novel, the narrator provides a chilling description of the abstraction of war and the seeming mindlessness with which young men allow themselves to be caught in its grip and destroyed:

> The battleships ray out over the North Sea, keeping their stations accurately apart. At a given signal all the guns are trained on a target which (the master gunner counts the seconds, watch in hand—at the sixth he looks up) flames into splinters. With equal nonchalance a dozen young men in the prime of life descend with composed faces into the depths of the sea; and there impassively (though with perfect mastery of machinery) suffocate uncomplainingly together. Like blocks of tin soldiers the army covers the cornfield, moves up the hillside, stops, reels slightly this way and that, and falls flat, save that, through field-glasses, it can be seen that one or two pieces still agitate up and down like fragments of broken match-stick. (155–6)

As Woolf's narrator ironically concludes, such activities "are the strokes which oar the world forward . . . . dealt by men as smoothly sculptured as the impassive policeman at Ludgate Circus" (156). It is "this unseizable force" (156) that drives Jacob and countless young men like him to their seemingly inevitable deaths.

Throughout the numerous glimpses of blighted lives found in *Jacob's Room* runs a bittersweet air of fatality that gives the novel its poignancy. The narrator's lyrical descriptions of the physical world and natural phenomena convey a sense of the vastness and timelessness of the visible world and the insignificance of most individual lives in comparison. Seated among the ruins of a Roman fortress atop Scarborough's Dods Hill, Mrs. Flanders occupies only a moment in eternity, as does Jacob on the Acropolis above Athens. Walking in Hyde Park in the spring, Miss Eliot experiences "a curious sadness, as if time and eternity showed through skirts and waistcoats, and she saw people passing tragically to destruction" (168). In a philosophical mood, the narrator offers a Platonic view of human life as "but a procession of shadows" (72).[11]

On occasion, the natural world adumbrates the demise of the individual existence, as in the case of the narrator's description of a tree falling in the woods that foreshadows Jacob's death: "A terrifying volley of pistol-shots rings out—cracks sharply. . . . a tree has fallen, a sort of death in the forest" (32).[12] Most of the time, however, the visible world serves as the context for the repetitive actions of generations of faceless individuals who are born, live their brief lives, and die. Like countless women before and after them, Mrs. Flanders and Rebecca tend to the children, "plotting the eternal conspiracy of hush and clean bottles while the wind raged" around the house (13). Commenting upon the sad beauty of the Cornish landscape, the novel's narrator acknowledges the unavoidable limitations of the individual life lived so fleetingly against the backdrop of eternity: "We start transparent, and then the cloud thickens. All history backs our pane of glass. To escape is vain" (49).[13]

Unlike most of the characters briefly depicted in *Jacob's Room*, Jacob Flanders is released quite early from the prison-house of life. Woolf's deliberately limited portrayal of Jacob as well as his laconic personality and inscrutable inner self have the effect of making him a youthful Everyman upon whom his friends and acquaintances as well as the reader can project the characteristics they find most attractive in human beings: "' . . . so distinguished-looking'," thinks Mrs. Durrant of the young man who might have become her son-in-law (61); "' . . . so unworldly. He gives himself no airs'," records Clara, who might have become his wife, in her diary (71). "'You're such a *good* man'," Florinda blurts out while seated across from him in a restaurant (80); " ' . . . the greatest man he had ever known," concludes a somewhat inebriated Dick Graves, who can no longer contain his admiration (111). For Fanny and the reader alike, Jacob himself, like the war which claims him, turns into an abstraction, "more statuesque, noble, and eyeless than ever" (170), by the end of the novel. Like the Greek busts to which he is often compared, Jacob becomes the embodiment of a Platonic ideal—the eternal promise of youth, a youth frozen in time like that of the lovers on Keats's Grecian urn, spared the inevitable compromises, limitations, and sorrows of adult life in an indifferent world.

CHAPTER FIVE

Mrs. Dalloway

Three years after the appearance of *Jacob's Room*, Woolf published *Mrs. Dalloway* (1925), the book that established her reputation as an important contemporary novelist. Like Joyce's *Ulysses*, first published in book form three years earlier in Paris, *Mrs. Dalloway* appropriates the unities of time and place, presenting the thoughts and experiences of three main characters—Clarissa Dalloway, Peter Walsh, and Septimus Warren Smith—during the course of a single day in London in June of 1923. The action of *Ulysses*, which also takes place on a June day, but in Dublin in 1904, includes a burial, a birth, a visit to a brothel, and—the day's most significant event—the late-night meeting of Leopold Bloom and Stephen Dedalus, the novel's protagonists. The day experienced by the main characters in *Mrs. Dalloway*, however, has equal if not greater significance for them; after an absence of five years, Peter Walsh returns from his life as a colonial civil servant in India and renews his painful friendship with Clarissa, who had refused his proposal many years ago to marry Richard Dalloway instead. During the same day, Septimus Warren Smith, a mentally disturbed young war veteran under the care of the physician Sir William Bradshaw, takes his life by throwing himself from a window; Bradshaw reports the event to Clarissa's husband later that evening at the Dalloways' party, which Peter attends, bringing together the disparate experiences of the three main characters at the end of the novel.

Woolf's first three novels concern themselves with the development of young people who are on the threshold of adult life and face having to make critical choices as to how and with whom they shall live. *Mrs. Dalloway*, however, is essentially a novel about middle-aged characters taking stock of their lives. With the exception of Septimus Warren Smith, whose young life, like that of Jacob Flanders, is blighted and destroyed by the war,[1] the major characters in the novel—Clarissa Dalloway and Peter Walsh—are involved in reacting to the day's sights and events, recalling the past, assessing their lives thus far, and considering the effects of their relationships upon their current existence. These characters and the novel's narrator also examine the lives of a number of other middle-aged characters—Richard Dalloway, a Member of Parliament and Clarissa's husband; Hugh Whitbread, a retainer of the Court; Sally Seton, an old friend of Clarissa and Peter; the physician Sir William Bradshaw and his wife, Lady Bradshaw; and Miss Kilman, tutor to Elizabeth Dalloway. In abandoning elements of the *Bildungsroman*, or novel of development, employed in her early novels, Woolf, along with other contemporaries such as Joyce and Proust, evolves a genre that might be termed the *Erfahrungsroman*, or novel of experience, in which adults assess their lives, the choices they have made, and the impact of events that have befallen them.

As in Woolf's earlier novels, most of the artists, musicians, poets, writers, and researchers in *Mrs. Dalloway* are amateurs. Of the practicing artist-figures and scholars in the novel, all appear only at the end of the novel at the Dalloways' party, where each is satirized. Clarissa's old friend Sir Harry is a professional painter of questionable distinction (266). Apparently an heir of the school of Constable, he specializes in paintings of "cattle standing absorbing moisture in sunset pools" (266). Also present at the party is "little Jim Hutton," whom Clarissa characterizes as a "very bad poet" and who appears in red socks (268). Earlier in the novel, Miss Kilman has mentally condemned Clarissa for being a daughter of "the rich, with a smattering of culture" (186). Indeed, the Dalloway household is very far from being a center of artistic activity and patronage in the traditional sense. Rather, Clarissa invites such figures as Sir Harry and Jim Hutton to her parties for their social value—Sir Harry is something of a *bon vivant* and Hutton plays the piano beautifully—knowing full well that their work as painter and poet is insignificant.[2] The presence at the party of Professor Brierly, the Milton scholar, whom Clarissa views as "a very queer fish" (267), provides another opportunity for Woolf to continue her satirical treatment of academics.

Among the minor female characters, a number practices a particular art or craft as an avocation, one that offers a creative outlet for the pressures and frustrations of their limited lives. Having lost her teaching position because of her German ancestry and her failure to condemn Germany during the war, the physically repellent Miss Kilman leads a marginal existence tutoring Elizabeth Dalloway in history, attending religious services and lectures, and, despite her tin ear, attempting to play the violin as a source of consolation (188). As an exuberant, comically defiant young woman, Clarissa's old friend Sally Seton seemed destined for a bohemian existence in the arts: "she would paint, she would write" (276). To both Clarissa's and Peter's surprise, however, Sally has married an owner of cotton mills in Manchester. In mid-life, Sally demonstrates pride in her five sons and her extensive beds of rare hibiscus. Her garden, however, also serves as a welcome retreat, where she finds a degree of "peace" that she fails to receive from others (293–4). Characterized by Clarissa as "the typical successful man's wife," Lady Bradshaw has had to accommodate herself to her husband's formidable will: "Sweet was her smile, swift her submission" (152).[3] As a dutiful wife, Lady Bradshaw accompanies her physician husband on his rounds, patiently waiting in his elegant gray car, or taking professional-grade photographs of old churches nearby (143).

Among the remaining female characters, two of an even older generation have been more successful in channeling their creative energy into unusually productive activities. Clarissa's maiden aunt, old Miss Parry, was in her younger years the picture of energetic Victorian spinsterhood, having traveled widely (and dangerously) in Burma, collecting orchid specimens and documenting them in her watercolors. At Clarissa's party, she cannot resist telling Peter that her book on Burmese orchids was praised by none other than Charles Darwin himself and was issued in three editions before 1870 (272).[4] Likewise privileged by wealth and social standing, the elderly Lady Bruton, proud of her descent from military and civic leaders, "men of action, who had done their duty" (167) and possessed of a "pent egotism" that "must eject upon some object" (164–5), uses her social position aggressively to advance political and social causes, asking Richard Dalloway and Hugh Whitbread to lunch to help her draft a letter to the *Times* promoting emigration to Canada.

Lady Bradshaw, Sally Seton, Miss Parry, Lady Bruton and Clarissa all inhabit a world of privilege, nurtured by a highly organized patriarchal social system. The men in their lives in turn serve the empire and its needs, whether as physicians, Members of Parliament, court retainers, or captains of industry. As women, however, they constantly confront the limitations imposed upon them by their rigidly defined roles as wives, mothers, and daughters of their class. As in the cases of Sally Seton and Lady Bradshaw, creative activity becomes marginalized as a result of these restrictive roles, which largely determine their lives—roles particularly difficult for women whose temperaments do not naturally gravitate toward the social and the domestic.

Clarissa Dalloway, however, embraces her role, accepting the realities of her social position as an MP's wife and turning them to her advantage in practicing her art as a hostess and society matron. In fact, one could argue that Clarissa has actively sought this role in her deliberate choice of Dalloway over Peter Walsh as her spouse. As Peter observes to himself, Clarissa had always been socially ambitious: "she was worldly; cared too much for rank and society and getting on in the world" (115). But contrary to his and Sally Seton's shared opinion, it is not snobbery that has motivated her so much as wanting to be in a position to exercise her artistry as a hostess. This embracing of the actualities of her life reflects a willingness to compromise—to accept the personal limitations of her role in order to have access to a medium in which she may ply her art. As a social artist, Clarissa Dalloway operates at the center of Beebe's Sacred Fount, where life—human relations in all their diversity and complexity—assumes the form of art.[5]

If one compares Clarissa's experience with that of Peter Walsh and Septimus Warren Smith, the two other main characters, one detects an increasing inability to make use of one's experiences to foster one's creativity. Clarissa thrives as a hostess—a social artist—as a result of her choice of a husband and a particular way of life. As one who was expected to become a writer and occasionally entertains the idea of researching topics of interest in the Bodleian in his retirement, Peter Walsh has not been able to master the events of his life and turn them to his fullest creative advantage. An aspiring poet from the working class, Septimus Warren Smith is overwhelmed by the events of his young life, which dissipate his creative focus and ultimately destroy him.

As will be seen, despite quite pronounced differences—in gender experience and in class origin—the three main characters share similarities of temperament. All at one time wrote or hoped to write; all demonstrate a refined sensibility and an unusual receptivity to beauty, especially as manifested in the physical world; all experience great pleasure simply in being alive. Each of the three is also a tenacious individualist, despite the common roles or activities in which he or she is or has been involved. Finally, each also exhibits a perspective that is critical of others and, in Peter's and Septimus's cases, of the prevailing order as well. As participants in, and observers of, their times, Clarissa, Peter, and Septimus, albeit to widely varying degrees, are also outsiders, maintaining a distanced stance from the life around them. In the case of Septimus, the alienation from social life bred by his combat experience degenerates into madness—perhaps the ultimate manifestation of one's apartness from others save for death itself, which he also reaches before the end of the novel.[6]

Unlike Septimus and Peter, Clarissa's upper-class background has given her a distinct advantage in life. Recalling with pride that her eighteenth-century ancestors were courtiers (6), Clarissa frequently reverts to scenes from her girlhood at Bourton, her family's country estate. As a girl, Clarissa appears to have exhibited a literary bent; Sally Seton recalls how she produced "reams of poetry," and remembers begging Peter to rescue Clarissa from men like Dalloway and Whitbread "who would 'stifle her soul' . . . make a mere hostess of her, encourage her worldliness" (114). Under Sally's influence, Clarissa would read Plato, Shelley, and William Morris, and the two would sit for hours in Clarissa's bedroom, planning social activities with lofty, naïve reformist goals, such as establishing "a society to abolish private property" (49).

Although Clarissa's social ambition easily overrides such youthful idealism, she retains something of it in her party-making, which involves bringing disparate people together and "making a world of her own" (114):

> Here was So-and-so in South Kensington; some one up in Bayswater; and somebody else, say, in Mayfair. And she felt quite continuously a sense of their existence; and she felt what a waste; and she felt what a pity; and she felt if only they could be brought together; so she did it. And it was an offering; to combine, to create . . . . (184–5)

Looking at her image in her bedroom mirror, Clarissa thinks of herself as one who provides a time and a place in which the bored and the isolated among her acquaintances can meet to experience moments of warmth and connection (55).

Ultimately, however, Clarissa comes to regard her party-making talent as simply "her gift," believing she has no other skills, artistic or otherwise (185). One wonders, of course, how accurate this self-effacing assessment is, and how much her failure to nurture other, dormant talents may be the result of her social conditioning as a daughter of the upper class or her willful repression of them. Certainly she senses an artificial element in her role as a hostess; at such times, she is "something not herself" (259). As Peter recalls, however, Clarissa has always exhibited a strong "social instinct," even as a girl, when she introduced him in a particularly mannered way to an acquaintance, and he chaffed her for being the "'perfect hostess'" (93). Despite Peter's criticism of her fondness for socializing and her husband's concern for her health—she has a weak heart—Clarissa in her maturity is compelled to continue giving parties because she feels it is what she does best.

To a large extent, Clarissa's need to entertain also reflects her abundant zest for living. As Peter reminds himself, her capacity for enjoyment is seemingly boundless (118). Her trip to a florist's, where she savors the colors and scents of fresh cut flowers, as well as her walk in her Westminster neighborhood remind her of her intense pleasure in the moment:

> In people's eyes, in the swing, tramp, and trudge; in the bellow and the uproar; the carriages, motor cars, omnibuses, vans, sandwich men shuffling and swinging; brass bands; barrel organs; in the triumph and the jingle and the strange high singing of some aeroplane overhead was what she loved; life; London; this moment of June. (5)

Because Clarissa harbors no illusions about a guaranteed afterlife, she ascribes great significance to the life that has been given her, a fact that occasionally evokes "terror" in her (281).

For this reason, the prospects of aging and death loom large in Clarissa's mind, as they do in Peter's.[7] Returning from her morning walk and discovering that she has not been invited to accompany her husband to luncheon at Lady Bruton's, Clarissa suddenly feels "shrivelled, aged, breastless" (45). Inspecting her image in her mirror, she rallies quickly, however, reminding herself that she is still not "old," having just turned fifty-one (54). As a defense against the finality of death, Clarissa harbors a pandemic notion of her identity, sensing herself to be "everywhere" (231). She entertains the possibility that after death,

> ... somehow in the streets of London, on the ebb and flow of things, here, there, she survived, Peter survived, lived in each other, she being part, she was positive, of the trees at home; of the house there, ugly, rambling all to bits and pieces as it was; part of people she had never met;

> being laid out like a mist between the people she knew best, who lifted her
> on their branches as she had seen the trees lift the mist, but it spread ever
> so far, her life, herself. (12)

Clarissa's main ways of celebrating life and alleviating the prospect of
death are to live for others, to do kindnesses, and to bring people together.
Recalling Clarissa's religious skepticism, Peter satirically characterizes her
attitude toward life while also admiring her feisty defiance of fate:

> As we are a doomed race, chained to a sinking ship (her favourite reading as
> a girl was Huxley and Tyndall, and they were fond of these nautical
> metaphors), as the whole thing is a bad joke, let us, at any rate, do our part;
> mitigate the sufferings of our fellow-prisoners (Huxley again); decorate the
> dungeon with flowers and air-cushions; be as decent as we possibly can.
> Those ruffians, the Gods, shan't have it all their own way . . . . (117)

Despite her spirited resistance of the forces of chaos and death in her
doing for others and bringing them together, there remains in Clarissa
something solitary and impersonal that coexists with her social self and
finds its objective correlative in her attic bedroom, where she retreats at the
end of each day to read memoirs and sleep alone in a narrow bed. As an
ambitious hostess, Clarissa is gratified to have her house full of guests
(261), but here is "an emptiness about the heart of life; an attic room"
(45), where she can retreat, nun-like, to her innermost self, which prefers
to forego intimacy with another and retains "a virginity preserved through
childbirth which clung to her like a sheet" (46).[8]

The suggestion of approaching death in the imagery of Clarissa's narrow bed, her candle "half burnt down" (46), and the winding sheet of her
psychic virginity evokes a sense of physical stasis, a condition akin to
Eliot's "still point of the turning world" ("Burnt Norton," 62) in which the
soul is finally free of external realities and capable of listening to its own
rhythms. For Clarissa's virginity of soul needs privacy and autonomy, as do
the individuals in a marriage:

> . . . there is a dignity in people; a solitude; even between husband and wife
> a gulf; and that one must respect . . . for one would not part with it
> oneself, or take it, against his will, from one's husband, without losing one's
> independence, one's self-respect—something, after all, priceless. (181)

As Peter is fully aware, Clarissa's seeming coldness is not simply a matter
of what he considers to be insufficient feminine warmth and sensuality in
heterosexual relations, but a condition of her mind. One of the major reasons why Clarissa has chosen Richard over Peter as her spouse has to do
with her determination to protect her spiritual independence, which
Richard freely grants. With Peter, however, "everything had to be shared;
everything gone into" (10). Clarissa's apparent deficiency of passion for
Richard has protected her from the intensity of love, which, like institu-
tionalized religion, she feels, destroys "the privacy of the soul" (192).[9]

This independence of mind is also a valuable trait of the artist, who, even as he or she culls material from the life surrounding him or her, must eventually be able to view it with a certain degree of objectivity, take its measure, and fashion it into art. As Clarissa's medium is human relations, she exhibits an uncanny ability to size up a situation swiftly and accurately: "She sliced like a knife through everything" (11). As a hostess, she has the invaluable ability to assess personalities instinctively (11). Although Clarissa tries to convince herself that she is no longer judgmental (11), she is, as Sally Seton rightly observes, "hard on people" (291), having decided not to invite her rather colorless cousin Ellie Henderson to her gathering (178). This criticalness, unappealing though it occasionally is, serves her well as she plans events that will bring others together successfully. Above all, Clarissa is favored with a willful vitality which Peter characterizes as having a degree of "toughness" he has not seen anywhere else (236).

Unlike Clarissa's, Peter Walsh's life has not proved nearly so successful or satisfying. As Sally Seton recalls at the Dalloways' party, his friends had expected him to become a writer (285). As a young intellectual with socialist views, Peter would visit Clarissa at Bourton, where they would debate issues as well as share their interest in poetry: "(she was a Radical then)" (234). Clarissa chose to marry Dalloway, however, and Peter was sent down from Oxford, eventually enlisting in the civil service in India.

Broad though Peter's interests have remained, his writing has been limited to letters, which Clarissa characterizes as "dry sticks" (9). He considers researching and writing about topics of personal interest in his retirement, but at the moment is in London trying to expedite the divorce of Daisy, the much younger woman he hopes to marry. Much to his humiliation, he knows that he will need to ask Richard Dalloway to help him find another government job soon. At lunch together, Lady Bruton, Hugh Whitbread, and Richard, fond as they are of Peter, share the same view of his life as a failure, remembering how he had been refused by Clarissa and "gone to India; come a cropper; made a mess of things" (161). Peter is keenly aware of their assessment; while examining both Clarissa's and his own life, he recalls the idealism of their youth and compares it to their present lives: "it was this; it was middle age; it was mediocrity" (236).[10] If Clarissa's life appears mediocre to Peter, she certainly does not view it as such, and jealousy of her comparative success appears to be motivating him at least partially in making such an assessment. Unlike Clarissa, Peter has been unable to make positive use of the materials of his life. His creativity has surfaced from time to time—he has invented a plough for use in the Indian district where he served, for example—but for the most part, his best energies have been subsumed in years of lackluster colonial service.

Peter's emotional life has been unsatisfying as well. If one can isolate a single cause for his unremarkable middle age, it would appear to be his unusual sensitivity, which he feels has handicapped him. Like Clarissa, he experiences intense moments of heightened awareness. Observing an ambulance streaking by from his vantage point opposite the British Museum, he is overwhelmed by the thoughts of life and death it evokes (230). Peter is also highly receptive to beauty, as his appreciation for the effects of the "yellow-blue evening light" over London makes clear (246). The intense emotions that such experiences stir in him have, he feels, worked against him, particularly while a member of India's colonial elite: "It had been his undoing . . . this susceptibility" (230).

It is because of Peter's emotional vulnerability that Clarissa's refusal of his proposal has had such an enormous impact upon his life. The reader is led to believe that Peter decided to enter colonial service in India partly as a result of her rejection of him, even though members of his family had served in India for three generations. As if to assuage the blow of Clarissa's refusal, Peter married a woman he met on the boat to India, a development that disturbed Clarissa greatly. Twice during the course of the novel, Peter claims that his involvement with Clarissa has seriously injured him emotionally. To himself he acknowledges that she "had sapped something in him permanently" (241); to Sally Seton he confesses that his relationship with Clarissa "had spoilt his life" (292). A brief, interrupted visit to Clarissa at midday leaves him in tears and embarrassed by what she has "reduced him to—a whimpering, snivelling old ass" (121).

Throughout the day, Peter spends much of his time in denial, trying to convince himself that he is no longer in love with Clarissa, but rather with Daisy, a twenty-four-year-old married woman with two small children whose pathetic effusiveness reassures him of his desirability (238). Peter also attempts to minimize his need for others: "one doesn't want people after fifty" (120). In addition, he expends considerable mental energy trying to assure himself that his life has not been a failure: "his life was not over, not by any means" (64).[11]

This effort also involves coming to terms with his years of colonial service on behalf of the empire, about which he is quite ambivalent. Looking at his reflection in a plate-glass window, Peter sees a man of substance who, he likes to think, had wielded considerable influence as a colonial administrator (72). Returning to London after a five-year absence, he cannot resist admiring the achievements of English civilization, including "butlers; chow dogs; girls in their security," despite his dislike of "India, and empire, and army" (82). While observing a squad of young recruits single-mindedly marching up Whitehall, he thinks, "one might laugh; but one had to respect it" (77).

Peter's critique of the empire is also implicit in the distaste he continues to exhibit for Clarissa's social role as an MP's wife; she throws parties for Richard's political benefit, but Peter thinks Richard would be "happier farming in Norfolk" (116). Peter's most intense feelings of dislike for the prevailing order find their focus in the figure of Hugh Whitbread, Clarissa's old friend and a wealthy, servile court retainer. Throughout the day, Peter cannot avoid thinking of him with contempt, reducing him to "a first-rate valet" (111). Indeed, Hugh's last name evokes rather appropriately the blandness and conventionality of his personality. That Peter's sentiments regarding Hugh are not entirely unjustified is also evidenced by similar assessments of him made independently during the day by Sally Seton and Richard Dalloway, who note that Hugh is becoming "an intolerable ass" (173).

Despite Peter's dislike of the social hierarchy and all it represents, he is still quite willing to be exposed to it and to Clarissa's annoyingly effusive social manner—"'It is angelic—it is delicious of you to have come!'," she gushes to Lord Gayton (270)—in deciding to go to the Dalloways' party. Although refusing to acknowledge fully his need for others, he justifies his decision to attend by admitting his need to interact with them (244). But what draws him most powerfully to the party is the presence of the woman with whom—try as he may to deny it—he is still in love: "What is this terror? what is this ecstasy? . . . . It is Clarissa, he said" (296).[12]

Ultimately Peter must be viewed as something of an outsider—one whose unusual sensitivity, broad intellectual interests, and critical mind have set him apart from many of his colleagues in service to the empire. Despite his great charm and his self-acknowledged dependency upon women, he remains a rather pathetic figure—as Sally Seton observes, "an oddity, a sort of sprite" (289). He is also made to appear rootless, having "no home, nowhere to go to" (289). Clarissa's house in Westminster remains the geographical center of his emotional life, but the welcome he can expect to receive there must always be measured at best.

In Septimus Warren Smith, Woolf depicts the ultimate form of alienation—madness, in this case brought on by service to the empire in the trenches of France. In a sense, Septimus represents what Jacob Flanders might have become had he returned to England after combat duty. Pronounced differences in temperament, however, may well have predisposed Septimus to suffer an extreme reaction to the horrors of war that Jacob would have been able to resist, had he lived. The narrator presents Septimus as one of any number of young, unsophisticated idealists from the provinces cherishing the age-old dream of moving to a big city and becoming a great poet or writer (127). Somewhat condescendingly, the narrator describes Septimus as "one of those half-educated, self-educated men" who has acquired his learning after work from library books chosen "on the advice of well-known authors consulted by letter" (127).

Prior to the war, Septimus worked as a promising young clerk at an estate agent's office; in the evening, he attended Miss Isabel Pole's lectures on Shakespeare in Waterloo Road.[13] Perhaps flattered by his adulation, Miss Pole fueled his sense of being destined for greatness by lending him books and sending him notes: "Was he not like Keats? she asked" (128). As a result of her encouragement, Septimus became enamored of both Miss Pole and the world of ideas; as the narrator satirically notes, one might have found him on any night "finishing a masterpiece at three o'clock in the morning and running out to pace the streets" (129).

Septimus's naïve idealism was such that he was among the first to enlist when his country entered the war, hoping

> . . . to save an England which consisted almost entirely of Shakespeare's plays and Miss Isabel Pole in a green dress walking in a square. (130)

His laudable conduct won him the admiration and love of Evans, his officer, and the two became inseparable.[14] Not until Septimus became engaged to Lucrezia, a young Milanese hat-maker, did he realize that something was awry. His initial pride in having felt so little upon Evans's death prior to the Armistice (130) turned into horror as he realized that he could no longer feel; this becomes the "appalling crime" for which he believes he is "condemned to death by human nature" (145) in the form of Dr. Holmes and Sir William Bradshaw, his physicians.

Although Septimus is completely at the mercy of his mental illness,[15] the forms his madness takes and the brief moments of sanity he occasionally experiences reveal a highly developed sensibility and a critical mind that might have been well suited to creative activity had his experience been other than it was. Septimus's euphoric moods are frequently stimulated by the beauty he perceives in the world around him. Resting in a chair in Regent's Park, he is both soothed and elated by what he sees around him:

> . . . wherever he looked at the houses, at the railings, at the antelopes stretching over the palings, beauty sprang instantly. To watch a leaf quivering in the rush of air was an exquisite joy. Up in the sky swallows swooping, swerving, flinging themselves in and out, round and round, yet always with perfect control as if elastics held them; and the flies rising and falling; and the sun spotting now this leaf, now that, in mockery, dazzling it with soft gold in pure good temper; and now and again some chime (it might be a motor horn) tinkling divinely on the grass stalks—all of this, calm and reasonable as it was, made out of ordinary things as it was, was the truth now; beauty, that was the truth now. Beauty was everywhere. (104–5)

Septimus retains this Keatsian capacity to enjoy the physical world—indeed, sheer existence itself—up to the last minutes of his life. Sitting on the sill of the window from which he throws himself, he pauses:

> He did not want to die. Life was good. The sun hot. Only human beings—what did *they* want? (226)[16]

Even in his madness, Septimus shows his creative bent. While seated in Regent's Park, he sings "an immortal ode to Time," with Evans's voice answering his antiphonally from behind a tree (105). In the boardinghouse room Septimus shares with his young wife is a table drawer containing sheets of paper bearing his thoughts, ideas, and curious drawings (223). During a rare moment of lucidity, Septimus aids his wife in designing a hat, showing "a wonderful eye" in selecting and arranging colored material (217).

Septimus's critical abilities extend beyond the visual, however. During his first consultation with Sir William Bradshaw, who has taken over his case, mention of the war evokes in his mind the image of a "little shindy of schoolboys with gunpowder" (145). When Bradshaw announces that Septimus will be sent to a home for the disturbed in the countryside, Septimus cannot resist remarking with caustic wit, "'One of Holmes's homes?' "(147). Mad though he is, Septimus never fails to understand what is most repulsive about such overbearing individuals as Holmes and Bradshaw, and the damage they are capable of inflicting upon the lives of others. To Septimus, they represent predatory humanity at its worst, manifestations of Tennyson's "Nature, red in tooth and claw" in human form:

> Human nature . . . was on him—the repulsive brute, with the blood-red nostrils. Holmes was on him. (139)

Clarissa Dalloway articulates more clearly what Septimus rightly detects in her own reaction to Bradshaw while thinking about Septimus's suicide later in the evening, acknowledging the physician's professional stature, but also sensing him to be "obscurely evil . . . capable of some indescribable outrage—forcing your soul, that was it" (281).[17] As she reasons further, if Septimus has been exposed to Bradshaw's power as a patient, he might well have concluded, "Life is made intolerable" (281).

Indeed, this is precisely Septimus's fate. His quarrel has never been with existence itself or with the physical world, which he greatly enjoys and appreciates. Rather, his great sensitivity and emotional vulnerability have rendered him unfit for the rigors of twentieth-century life. Initially victimized by his service on behalf of the empire in France, he faces further victimization by Sir William Bradshaw, also in service to the empire, who threatens to separate him from his wife—his last link to human society and fellowship. His suicide is rendered not as submission to a longing for death but as a final act of the will, an assertion of his independence: "Holmes was at the door. 'I'll give it you!'," he shouts before he throws himself from the window (226).

Clarissa understands this full well, sensing her kinship with Septimus: "She felt glad that he had done it; thrown it away" (283). For a willful woman in questionable health who frequently considers her own mortality and relentlessly celebrates life, the thought of Septimus's act sparks a momentary sense of relief and liberation—a reprieve in the constant struggle to create meaning and order: "He made her feel the beauty; made her feel the fun" (284).[18] As for Septimus, in choosing to take his own life, he defies the prevailing order and asserts his autonomy, reclaiming control over his life in the act of ending it, something that his culture has prevented him from doing for quite some time.

CHAPTER SIX

To the Lighthouse

Published two years after *Mrs. Dalloway* in 1927, *To the Lighthouse* supplies not only an in-depth view of the lives of one upper middle-class British family while on holiday prior to the First World War, but also Woolf's fullest exposition of the creative process as experienced by a single artist in her fiction. Setting the novel's action on a remote island off the coast of Scotland during September of a year before the war and then, following the war, during the same month ten years later, Woolf provides something akin to a laboratory view of the complex relations that make up the lives of Mr. Ramsay, a scholar of philosophy, his wife, and their large family of eight children. Also presented are the relationships between members of the family and their summer guests, who include William Bankes, a widowed botanist, and Augustus Carmichael, a poet, both of whom are old friends of Ramsay; Charles Tansley, an ambitious young doctoral student; and Lily Briscoe, an unmarried woman and friend of the family who paints.[1]

The opening, prewar section of the novel traces the activities of the family members and their guests during the course of a day at the Ramsays' island summerhouse largely from the perspectives of Mrs. Ramsay, Ramsay, Bankes, and Lily. Among these are Lily's efforts to paint a portrait of Mrs. Ramsay seated knitting indoors framed by a window with her youngest child, James; Mr. Ramsay's solitary meditations and conversations with Tansley or Bankes while pacing up and down the terrace; a ramble along the cliffs and seashore taken by Nancy and Andrew, two of the Ramsay children, in the company of the young couple Paul Rayley and Minta Doyle, also guests of the Ramsays, who become engaged by the end of the afternoon; and a dinner featuring *boeuf en daube*, a special recipe of Mrs. Ramsay's grandmother, that brings family members and guests together at the end of the day.

The second part of the novel consists of a comparatively short, lyrical section that suggests the effects of the war years upon human consciousness as well as the world of the Ramsays—Andrew dies in the trenches of France; Prue, a young bride, dies of an illness associated with her first childbirth; and Mrs. Ramsay herself dies quite suddenly of an undisclosed illness. The section simultaneously traces the gradual decay of the uninhabited summer house, which two local cleaning women, Mrs. McNab and Mrs. Bast, rescue from near-oblivion following ten years of disuse and restore in preparation for the family's return.

In the novel's final section, Woolf interweaves the morning's two central activities—Lily's attempt to recreate and finish from memory the painting of Mrs. Ramsay and James begun ten years earlier, and Mr. Ramsay's expedition to the lighthouse with his teenaged children James and Cam—by alternating sections containing Lily's thoughts while painting with sections revealing those of the Ramsay children while sailing towards the lighthouse with their father. During the morning, Lily occasionally moves to the edge of the terrace to follow the progress of their boat, imaginatively if not visually; the two activities are formally linked when the Ramsays land on the lighthouse rocks and Lily, sensing they have reached their destination, completes her painting with a final brushstroke.

If one compares Parts I and III of the novel, Part I is largely about the life of the Ramsay family as experienced by the Ramsays themselves and as observed by William Bankes and Lily Briscoe, who are not only outside the family circle, but may be considered marginal individuals beyond their relationship to the Ramsays as well. A keen observer of the complex dynamics of the Ramsay marriage and the relationships between family members, Lily also assumes the role of the artist as observer in her attempt to paint a picture of Mrs. Ramsay and James, using formal principles to help distance herself from her subjects and work out the relationships between the abstract shapes that will comprise the picture. In Part III, Lily is able to transcend the barrier separating the experience of life and the production of art found in Part I in her renewed effort to complete the picture begun ten years ago, drawing upon her memories of Mrs. Ramsay and allowing her own conflicting emotions regarding her to emerge and guide her work as a painter. As will be seen, during this process, Lily also comes to terms with her ambivalent feelings toward Ramsay, achieving a silent conciliation with him that represents a benchmark in her own development as a woman.

By focusing largely upon Lily Briscoe and Mrs. Ramsay in *To the Lighthouse*, Woolf enables herself to investigate two of the forms of creativity available to women—that of painting, practiced casually by many women and men of her own class, but quite seriously by her sister Vanessa, and that of women in their traditional domestic roles as wives, mothers, and social managers, of which her own mother, Julia Duckworth Stephen, was apparently a prime example.(2) As has been noted, Clarissa Dalloway represents Woolf's earliest extended portrayal of the married woman as social artist in her fiction. But in *To the Lighthouse*, so vitally concerned with the specific conditions that affect women and their creativity, Woolf continues to pursue the larger question of the artist's relationship to life generally and to domesticity and sexuality in particular, regardless of gender.

As if to challenge any notion concerning the ideal conditions for creativity among men, Woolf presents three adult male characters in *To the Lighthouse* who display varying degrees of ability as poets, scientists, or scholars in quite different social and sexual circumstances. Perhaps the character who surprises readers the most in this regard is Augustus Carmichael, a rather inscrutable, retiring presence at the Ramsays' summer house who ends up producing a successful volume of poetry during the war. An endless source of frustration and personal doubt for Mrs. Ramsay, Carmichael will have none of her solicitousness, seeming perfectly content to while away the hours dozing, meditating, composing an occasional poem or reading French novels in his lawn chair at some remove from the others. Shuffling past Mrs. Ramsay in his yellow slippers or settling into his chair to pursue an opium-induced reverie, Carmichael appears an example of the burned out *fin-de-siècle* aesthete, preferring his own imaginative company to that of others.[2] However, he is not the superannuated Ivory Tower artist he initially appears to be. As Mrs. Ramsay's ruminations about him reveal, his life, which has included "an early marriage; poverty; going to India," has not been a particularly comfortable, sheltered one (20). Mrs. Ramsay blames Carmichael's distrust of her upon his wife, having herself watched "that odious woman" drive him from his home (63). Although Carmichael seems content to limit his interactions with the Ramsays and their guests, he is not without feeling for others; he shows a surprising devotion to Andrew, and, according to an acquaintance of Lily, "'lost all interest in life'" upon learning of his death in the war (289).

Carmichael's appearance is deceiving; far from being oblivious of his environment, he observes it intently, if silently and intermittently. As Mrs. Ramsay notes, both she and Carmichael share an artist's appreciation for Rose's arrangement of fruit on the dinner table (146). As Lily realizes in Part III, Carmichael has silently shared her thoughts concerning the Ramsays and the expedition to the lighthouse during the morning (309). Carmichael's seemingly decayed, aloof demeanor conceals a keen intelligence that has been buffeted by life; he produces a volume of poetry that has much resonance for a generation of readers recently shaken by the horrors of war.

If Carmichael's personality is undemonstrative but feeling, William Bankes's is sociable but emotionally repressed. Equally repressed emotionally herself, Lily values Bankes for his disinterestedness, his mild temperament, and his measured, reasonable response to life, unlike the self-dramatizing Ramsay. Like Mrs. Ramsay, however, she is also aware of Bankes's fussiness, his obsession with propriety and order in the smallest details (39–40). As a childless widower, Bankes, too, has suffered, but rarely expresses his pain directly. Sensing that he has "dried and shrunk" (35) in comparison to Ramsay the emotionally enriched family man,

Bankes is obviously hurt that Cam has refused to give him a flower, as her nursemaid directed (36), and occasionally admits to himself that he "would have liked" to have a daughter (83).

Although Bankes's work as a botanist is thought by Ramsay to be first-rate, one senses that his creativity as a scientist has been curbed by his overriding need for control—of his thoughts as well as his emotions and the circumstances of his life. In the first part of the novel, Bankes recalls another significant loss in his life—his once vibrant friendship with Ramsay—that he characteristically tries to contain in his own mind despite the pain it brings him. After Ramsay's marriage, the friendship lost its "pulp," resulting in "repetition" whenever they met (35). Bankes likens his former friendship with Ramsay to "the body of a young man laid up in peat" for many years (35).

In mourning this loss, Bankes in middle age also wrestles with feelings of social and professional inadequacy, trying to convince himself that "he never let himself get into a groove" and that he still has many friends (133). While conversing with Lily about art, he tellingly claims, "We can't all be Titians . . . Darwins," that one could not have men of their stature without "humble people like ourselves" (110). Like many other men of his generation, Bankes subscribes to Carlyle's theory of great men changing the course of civilization, and secretly regrets that he apparently is not destined to be one of them.[4] He tries to mitigate his irritation at Charles Tansley's raw assertiveness by considering that Tansley may well be the next great man:

> But perhaps . . . here is the man. One was always waiting for the man. . . .
> At any moment the leader might arise; the man of genius, in politics as in anything else. (142)

Ramsay privately shares Bankes's engagement with the "great men" theory, but also questions it, whereas Bankes is content simply to accept it. While pacing up and down the terrace, Ramsay asks himself whether great men are indeed responsible for "the progress of civilisation" (67). As the reader learns, this question is particularly critical for Ramsay, as he has desperately hoped that he might be one of them. If anything, one senses in him such an overriding preoccupation with the question of his own genius and fame that it may well have impeded the actual work he supposedly does as a scholar-philosopher. Ramsay alternately disclaims his hoped-for genius, believing he has none (55), and longs for its affirmation, silently demanding reassurance from Mrs. Ramsay shortly afterward:

> Mr. Ramsay repeated, never taking his eyes from her face, that he was a failure. She blew the words back at him. 'Charles Tansley . . . ' she said. But he must have more than that. It was sympathy he wanted, to be assured of his genius, first of all . . . . (59)

Unlike Carmichael and Lily Briscoe, Ramsay has difficulty attaining the disinterested, unself-conscious state needed for the emergence of creative inspiration, an ability that Woolf increasingly valorizes in her fictional artist-figures. It is only after Ramsay has been reassured by the presence of his wife and his renewed faith in the quality of Sir Walter Scott's fiction at the end of the day that he can momentarily relinquish his obsession with the question of his genius, which he frames in terms of reaching the philosophical equivalent of the letter Z: "if not he, then another" (179).

In addition to his potentially crippling self-consciousness, Woolf suggests that domesticity itself may have inhibited Ramsay's creative ability as a philosopher. Bankes believes that Ramsay's family has augmented, but also diminished him, noting his "habits . . . . eccentricities, weaknesses" as possible evidence (37). Mrs. Ramsay gathers from Bankes that her husband's latest book is not his "best" (62); Charles Tansley, on the other hand, exhibiting the characteristic brashness of a promising young academic, thinks that "Ramsay had dished himself" in marrying and fathering a large family (136). While strolling on the terrace with Ramsay, Mrs. Ramsay is aware that her husband also believes that his marriage may have hindered his work, preventing him from having produced "better books" (106).

To a certain extent, Ramsay does indeed appear to ascribe his limited professional achievements to the onerous responsibilities involved in being a *paterfamilias*. Looking out over the sand dunes and recalling his habit of taking solitary day-long walks in the countryside before his marriage, he thinks that if he could only regain that solitude, the great work might be written, but then quickly tells himself that as the father of so many children, he has "no right" to such a choice (106). One does not know, though, to what degree Ramsay may be using the argument of domestic burdens and family responsibilities simply to rationalize the fact that he has not accomplished what he had hoped (70). Mrs. Ramsay, at any rate, seems to sense a genuine correlation between the demands of family life and Ramsay's difficulty in fulfilling his promise, doing her utmost to spare her husband involvement in petty domestic matters such as the need to have the greenhouse roof repaired.

As critics have noted, much of Mrs. Ramsay's energy is devoted to easing the difficulties in the lives of her husband and children, and nurturing her husband's pathetically insecure ego. With Mrs. Ramsay, Woolf expands her portrait of the traditional wife and mother as social artist and engineer of relationships as well as creator of enduring moments of community and order in the face of life's arbitrariness and nature's indifference to humankind. When compared to Clarissa Dalloway, Woolf's first extended portrayal of this type of woman as artist, Mrs. Ramsay is presented as a richer, more complex figure, first, because she is more deeply enmeshed in her spousal and maternal roles than Clarissa, and second, because Woolf depicts her not only by revealing her own thoughts, which comprise a large part of the novel's first part, but also by presenting her through the eyes of several characters—Lily, of course, but also Bankes, Ramsay, Tansley, and her children. The isolation of the family and its guests in a summer house also enables Woolf to present Mrs. Ramsay's role within the family more fully; she is never alone for several hours at a time, as is Clarissa, during the course of her day. Rather, one obtains both glimpses and in-depth views of the various forms Mrs. Ramsay's artistry takes hour by hour throughout the first part of the novel.

These are the external reasons why one senses Mrs. Ramsay's greater complexity as an example of the wife and mother as social artist. In characterizing her, however, Woolf also constructs a multifaceted personality that extends to greater opposing extremes than Clarissa Dalloway's does. As an earth-mother figure in service to a patriarchal culture, Mrs. Ramsay privileges the men in her family over her daughters, feeling that women had "something" which men lacked (129), and were therefore capable of caring for themselves:

> . . . she had the whole of the other sex under her protection; for reasons she could not explain, for their chivalry and valour, for the fact that they negotiated treaties, ruled India, controlled finance; finally for an attitude towards herself which no woman could fail to feel or to find agreeable, something trustful, childlike, reverential . . . . (13)

From a Marxist perspective, one might argue that Mrs. Ramsay worships the power of men as rulers of her world, identifying—at least as much as a woman of her time can—with such men in her role as the controlling force in her much more limited domestic sphere. From a purely psychological perspective, she is flattered by the attention and respect this powerful sex accords her, which augments her sense of her own worth as a human being. Mrs. Ramsay's "mania" for marriage and matchmaking (261), her seeming anti-intellectualism, her tendency toward self-effacement and her worship of her husband's mind all reflect her apparent devotion to her traditional role as a nurturer of men and advocate of their well-being.

At the same time, however, there is a genuinely subversive element in Mrs. Ramsay's relationship to men that emerges in her self-confessed preference for "boobies" like Paul Rayley, as opposed to "clever men who wrote dissertations" (85), and in her late-night visits to Lily's room, where she freely mocks the male guests she has so diligently humored by day:

> Arriving late at night, with a light tap on one's bedroom door, wrapped in an old fur coat . . . she would enact again whatever it might be—Charles Tansley losing his umbrella; Mr. Carmichael snuffling and sniffing; Mr. Bankes saying, 'The vegetable salts are lost.' (76)

One has the impression of a critical intelligence submerged in the gender role she so unremittingly enacts throughout the day.

Unlike Clarissa Dalloway, Mrs. Ramsay appears to have genuine interests beyond her role as wife and mother that in another era might have become her lifework instead. In the habit of visiting the sick, both on the island and in London, Mrs. Ramsay has developed a real concern for matters of public health, deploring the condition of the milk distributed in London and the absence of a hospital on the island (89). When she is moved to express her views on these subjects during dinner, her earnestness is met with derision by her family:

> ... she described the iniquity of the English dairy system ... and was about to prove her charges ... when all round the table, ... like a fire leaping from tuft to tuft of furze, her children laughed; her husband laughed; she was laughed at, fire-encircled, and forced to veil her crest. ... (155–6)

As far as her family is concerned, Mrs. Ramsay's credibility extends only as far as the boundaries of the traditional gender role she has so fervently embraced; aspiring to investigate the state of the nation's dairies or "elucidating the social problem" (18) is obviously beyond them.[5]

Such conflicting traits within Mrs. Ramsay give her a depth and complexity that Clarissa Dalloway, who is simultaneously more cerebral than Mrs. Ramsay and more limited in her interests and understanding, does not have. As social artists, the two women also have quite different relationships to "life," the medium in which they both work. If Clarissa practices her art at the center of the Sacred Fount, Mrs. Ramsay plumbs its depths in practicing hers. Unlike Clarissa's, Mrs. Ramsay's exposure to life in its various forms is much broader and deeper. As the wife of an emotionally demanding husband and mother of eight children, her skills as a nurturer and mediator are constantly being enlisted in ways that Clarissa's are not. Mrs. Ramsay's interests in her community and in social welfare generally take her well beyond the boundaries of her class as she visits the sick and the dying, who provide her with an unusual opportunity to see life from the perspective of the poor in moments of crisis.

Perhaps because of the amount of poverty and suffering she has observed in her own lifetime, Mrs. Ramsay views "life" not so much as the obverse of death, to be celebrated relentlessly, as Clarissa does through her parties, but as an enemy capable of inflicting much pain, being "terrible, hostile. . . quick to pounce on you if you gave it a chance," and requiring firm management in order to curb its destructive potential (92). Worrying about the fate of Paul, Minta, Nancy, and Andrew, who have not returned from their beach walk, Mrs. Ramsay senses herself once more confronted by "her old antagonist, life" (120). At times she feels guilty about having brought eight individuals into the world to be victimized by this adversary, but then, figuratively "brandishing her sword," she attempts to convince herself that they will be "perfectly happy" (92).

Mrs. Ramsay's social artistry is as much an attempt to keep dissolution and chaos at bay as it is a celebration of community. Following the lighting of candles at dinner, the assembled family and friends are momentarily aware of their isolation together on the island, and sense "their common cause against that fluidity out there" (147). Unlike Clarissa Dalloway's,

Mrs. Ramsay's experience of life is such that it leaves her with a deep-seated pessimism that she cannot always conceal from her husband, who senses "the sternness" in her, which "saddened him" (98). Married to an emotionally volatile man who is frequently anguished, Mrs. Ramsay ironically notes that her husband is "happier, more hopeful" overall than she (91).

Despite her adversarial relationship with life and her determined efforts to fortify her family and friends against its ravages, Mrs. Ramsay, like Clarissa Dalloway, is also an appreciator of beauty and a creator of meaningful moments that endure in the memories of those who experience them. Her visual pleasure in Rose's arrangement of fruit has already been noted. Mrs. Ramsay's appreciation for physical beauty in men and women alike is so strong that it keeps her from firing her gardener, Kennedy (100–1). Perhaps the most famous example of Mrs. Ramsay's transformative powers is her ability to enable Cam to imagine a frightening animal skull mounted in her room, when wrapped in Mrs. Ramsay's shawl, as "a bird's nest . . . a beautiful mountain" (172). At times, Mrs. Ramsay finds the creation of memorable occasions of unity, meaning, and pleasure daunting, as at the beginning of the dinner, when she realizes that the burden of "merging and flowing and creating" is hers (126). That these sometimes arduously created moments endure is evidenced by Lily's memory ten years later of a morning on the beach with Mrs. Ramsay and Charles Tansley that was particularly remarkable for the unusual cordiality which Mrs. Ramsey mysteriously enabled Lily and Tansley to show each other (239).

This scene also illustrates an additional feature of Mrs. Ramsay's artistry—her ability to affect individuals favorably simply by her presence:

> That woman sitting there writing under the rock resolved everything into simplicity; made these angers, irritations fall off like old rags; she brought together this and that and then this, and so made of that miserable silliness and spite . . . something—this scene on the beach for example, this moment of friendship and liking—which survived, after all these years complete . . . there it stayed in the mind affecting one almost like a work of art. (239–40)

There is something in Mrs. Ramsay's temperament which, when combined with her personal beauty, draws others to her and seems to bring out qualities in themselves that they do not normally exhibit. Despite his characteristic misogyny, Charles Tansley cannot resist Mrs. Ramsay's allure during the course of their errand in the village, feeling "extraordinary pride" in accompanying her. She unconsciously enables him to see her inner and outer beauty, despite her graying, middle-aged womanhood—to feel "the wind and the cyclamen and the violets" as they walk together (25).

In a sense, Mrs. Ramsay herself becomes a living work of art, attracting others to her, causing them to want to gaze upon her and get closer to her. With James, she becomes the icon of the Madonna and Child framed by the window that Lily tries to incorporate into her painting; alone, she becomes an object of desire, for Lily and the others as well as for her husband. Although a botanist, Bankes cannot help thinking of Mrs. Ramsay in terms of classical and Renaissance art; she could easily be an older incarnation of Botticelli's *Primavera*, "very clearly Greek, straight, blue-eyed.... The Graces assembling seemed to have joined hands in meadows of asphodel to compose that face" (47). Mrs. Ramsay knows how fond Rose is of selecting jewelry for her mother every evening (122), recalling her own deep feeling for her mother as a girl (123). Following the dinner, Prue silently acknowledges her pride in her mother, whom she views as unique, "the thing itself" (174).

As will be seen, Lily's relationship to Mrs. Ramsay is quite complex, compounded as it is of admiration, longing, annoyance, criticalness, and endless fascination. In the first part of *To the Lighthouse*, Lily observes the dynamics of Mrs. Ramsay's relationship to her friends and family, particularly her husband, while trying to paint a portrait of her seated with James behind the window. In the novel's final section, Lily attempts to paint Mrs. Ramsay again, calling up memories of her that help her unleash her creativity and complete the painting while simultaneously resolving her psychological conflict with Ramsay, whom she has been unable to accept in his role as Mrs. Ramsay's emotionally demanding spouse. This convergence of Lily's material artistry with memories of Mrs. Ramsay's social artistry results in Lily's attainment of a new stage in her development as a woman. Art in the form of painting and life in the form of Mrs. Ramsay's psychological legacy to Lily cooperate to stimulate her personal growth as well as her artistic creativity.

As Lily discovers, the allure of Mrs. Ramsay brings to the fore her psychological conflict between the need to maintain her emotional autonomy and the common human need for intimacy. Unlike Rachel Vinrace in *The Voyage Out*, Lily appears to be quite conscious of the existence of these two seemingly opposed needs within herself, having chosen to protect the sanctity of her emotional independence, which appears to be the stronger of the two, by physically and psychologically stationing herself at the periphery of social life. Like Augustus Carmichael, who occupies a somewhat similar position in relationship to the Ramsay family as well as the world, Lily values the advantages and protection this position offers, suspended as it is between the solitary inner world of the self and the imagination and the outer world of social activity and interpersonal relationships, where unruly emotions may threaten one's integrity as an individual. The promise of a stable and ordered existence in this intermediate realm provides Lily with the sense of control over her emotional life that she feels she must have.

To protect her autonomy, Lily cultivates objectivity and her skills as an observer.[6] Unlike Rachel Vinrace or Katharine Hilbery, she demonstrates a finely honed awareness of her own motivations as well as those of the people surrounding her. While quite critical of Mrs. Ramsay's pity for men, which seems to stem from an undefined inner need (128), Lily is also capable of acknowledging what she believes to be "her own poverty of spirit" (152) in comparison. Lily's impersonal, objective stance as an observer reveals its defensive nature by setting limits to the number and quality of her relationships with others. Her interaction with Charles Tansley at dinner constitutes an "experiment" in which she withholds or offers words calculated to have a distinct effect upon his behavior (139). Lily appears to be most at her ease when in the company of Bankes, whose own impersonality—his "disinterested intelligence" (262–3)—and asexual behavior pose no threat to her emotional well-being.

In the novel's first part, Lily's painting provides another means of maintaining her emotional autonomy. Her medium requires of her the physical distancing and observer's skills that she also uses in relating to others in everyday life. It is significant that Lily pitches her easel at the edge of the lawn, midway between the sea and the house where her artistic subjects, Mrs. Ramsay and James, are seated. One cannot be too close to Mrs. Ramsay if one wishes to appraise her objectively. As Lily later notes to herself, one needed "fifty pairs of eyes" to take her measure (294). Acknowledging the distorting effect of Mrs. Ramsay's appearance, Lily adds that one pair must be "stone blind" to her beauty (294).

For Lily, the process of painting requires the shedding of one's personal traits, ego needs, sexuality, and social role until one has reached the state of impersonality necessary for an aesthetic vision to emerge and direct one's creative efforts:

> She took up once more her old painting position with the dim eyes and the absent-minded manner, subduing all her impressions as a woman to something much more general. (82)

By draining herself of her identity, Lily attains the state of mind needed for the emergence of inspirational material from the unconscious. She shares this ability with Mrs. Ramsay, who finds an occasional moment in which to shrink to a "wedge-shaped core of darkness" (95) that promises her "limitless" freedom to explore the realm of the imagination. As in Mrs. Ramsay's case, the intrusion of others with their personal needs and demands inhibits the free play of Lily's imagination and her creativity as an artist. In the third part of the novel, Ramsay's silent demand for sympathy blocks Lily's efforts to resume painting (224). As in *The Voyage Out*, Woolf appears to imply that for women, emotional intimacy with men impedes one's aesthetic creativity.[7]

The conditions for painting, then, utilize and reinforce defenses that Lily has already developed in determining her relationship to everyday life. Eliminating external sources of disturbing emotions in the process of isolating and depersonalizing oneself in preparation for painting is not enough, however. Some means must be found to manage powerful emotions thrown up by the unconscious in response to the subject of one's art. For this purpose, Lily the formalist makes use of the abstract principles of design emphasized by the Post-Impressionists in order to assert control over her response to Mrs. Ramsay's maternal power. Mother and son are depicted as a triangular purple mass, so lacking in representational detail as to cause Bankes to suspect that Lily may have treated her subjects irreverently (262).[8]

Too often, though, formal considerations prevent Lily from being receptive to unconscious impulses and recapturing her aesthetic vision. The course of her painting in the first part of the novel is dominated by the conscious consideration of design principles—connecting masses of color, for example—that prevents her from translating her vision into art (82–3). It is only in the novel's final part that Lily is able to relinquish formal concerns momentarily, allowing unconscious emotions to flow from her and express themselves in her painting (235).

Like Rachel Vinrace's music, Lily's art frequently serves as a retreat from emotionally disturbing experiences in the external world, supplying her with the reassurance provided by a familiar activity and reaffirming her identity as an individual. During the dinner in the first part of the novel, Lily's irritation at Mrs. Ramsay's pity for Bankes is quickly dispelled by thoughts of her painting; she decides that she will move the tree closer to its center (128). Lily again takes refuge in thoughts of her work after experiencing emotional rebuffs from Tansley (130) and Paul Rayley (154). Unlike life among the Ramsays, replete with "unrelated passions" (221), Lily's art provides an important source of order and stability in her life. Her brush becomes "the one dependable thing" in a contentious, disorderly world (224).

For Lily, painting is also a means of asserting her identity and maintaining her integrity as an individual. Her resistance to her longing for intimacy is weakest when her doubts about her artistic ability and her individuality are strongest. At times like these, Lily reveals just how dependent her identity is upon her image of herself as an artist. At such times, she is also sorely tempted to relinquish her struggle as an artist and succumb to her longing for Mrs. Ramsay and the fertile milieu she creates around herself:

> Such she often felt herself—struggling against terrific odds to maintain her courage; to say: 'But this is what I see, this is what I see,' and so to clasp some miserable remnant of her vision to her breast, which a thousand forces did their best to pluck from her. And it was then too, in that chill and windy way, as she began to paint, that there forced themselves upon her other things, her own inadequacy, her insignificance, keeping house for her father off the Brompton Road, and had much ado to control her impulse to fling herself (thank Heaven she had always resisted so far) at Mrs. Ramsay's knee and say to her—but what could one say to her? 'I'm in love with you?' No, that was not true. 'I'm in love with this all,' waving her hand at the hedge, at the house, at the children. (32)

Usually keenly aware of her own motivations, Lily ironically is unable to acknowledge the central role her painting has played in forming her sense of self. During a conversation with Bankes, she remarks that she would continue to paint "because it interested her" (110).[9]

Like two children excluded from a party given by their parents, Lily and Bankes stand at the periphery of the charmed circle of the Ramsay family, observing the interactions of its members with envy as well as perplexity and dismay. Bankes indirectly reveals his longing for intimacy and a sense of connectedness by wistfully expressing his desire for a little daughter and trying to mitigate the sense of loss occasioned by the decay of his friendship with Ramsay, as noted above. Lily infrequently acknowledges her longing for intimacy to herself, and rarely reveals it, even in an indirect way, to others.

Unlike Rachel Vinrace, Lily's rejection of heterosexual relations appears to be based primarily upon her observation of their effects upon women, not upon intuitive knowledge. Mrs. Ramsay's relationship to her husband and his male friends serves as a primer of the accommodations to men's needs made by women in traditional heterosexual relationships. Lily is extremely critical of Ramsay's egotism, the enormous emotional demands he makes upon his wife (40, 72), and his unwillingness to give her support in return (223). Conversely, she is deeply disturbed by Mrs. Ramsay's deliberate insincerities and lies, her "irresistible" social manner (152), her willful "highhandedness" in manipulating others (75), and her willingness to nurture her husband at considerable expense to her own well-being (71, 223). Pitying Minta Doyle, who is about to be exposed to the "fangs" of Paul Rayley's passion, Lily is thankful that she has been spared what she perceives as the "degradation" and "dilution" inherent in heterosexual relations (154).

Unwilling to risk the loss of autonomy she senses in such relationships, Lily turns to Mrs. Ramsay, hoping to satisfy her longing for intimacy. In addition to her nurturing, emotionally fertile nature, Mrs. Ramsay appears to harbor within her some hidden truth that might put an end to Lily's quest for meaning:

> Sitting on the floor with her arms round Mrs. Ramsay's knees, close as she could get, smiling to think that Mrs. Ramsay would never know the reason of that pressure, she imagined how in the chambers of the mind and heart of the woman who was, physically, touching her, were stood, like the treasures in the tombs of kings, tablets bearing sacred inscriptions, which if one could spell them out, would teach one everything, but they would never be offered openly, never made public. What art was there, known to love or cunning, by which one pressed through into those secret chambers? (78–9)

Through her use of imagery, Woolf makes clear the direct relationship between Lily's search for truth and her longing for intimacy. The image of penetration in the last sentence is not simply phallic, but also suggests a longing for fusion with the mother. Lily continues to explore this relationship in the lines that follow:

> What device for becoming, like waters poured into one jar, inextricably
> the same, one with the object one adored? Could the body achieve, or the
> mind, subtly mingling in the intricate passages of the brain? or the heart?
> Could loving, as people called it, make her and Mrs. Ramsay one? for it
> was not knowledge but unity that she desired, not inscriptions on tablets,
> nothing that could be written in any language known to men, but inti-
> macy itself, which is knowledge, she had thought, leaning her head on
> Mrs. Ramsay's knee. (79)

Here Lily appears to recognize that her search for meaning and knowledge
is a psychological displacement of the longing for union with another.

Lily is not the only woman for whom the power of Mrs. Ramsay's maternal nature elicits such strong emotion. Despite their virginal resistance
to Mrs. Ramsay in her traditional role (14), her daughters cannot help pay-
ing homage to her beauty, which "called out the manliness in their girlish
hearts" (14). Mrs. Ramsay seems to show special affection for Prue, in
whom, perhaps, she narcissistically sees herself as an emerging young
woman. Prue responds to her mother with deep feelings of pride (298), and
assumes her mother's role among her siblings, trying to assure "that nothing
went wrong" (298).[10] Rose's infatuation with her mother has already been
noted; Mrs. Ramsay regrets that she cannot return her affection to the
same degree, and foresees a future of suffering for her (123).

Like Rose, Lily, too, is doomed to suffer, for Mrs. Ramsay is curiously
determined to reserve more of her nurturing and affection for the emotional
sustenance of men. In fact, Mrs. Ramsay exploits the unspoken feelings of
affection and identity between women to coerce them into aiding her in this
role, as when she silently urges Lily to engage Tansley in conversation during the dinner (138). Mrs. Ramsay occasionally reveals her irritation and
impatience with women who are reluctant to assume the traditional female
role and attend to men's needs. While wondering whether Paul and Minta
have become engaged during their beach walk, she decides to "speak seriously to Minta" (87) if the engagement has not taken place. As noted earlier, Mrs. Ramsay blames Augustus Carmichael's wife for the distrust he
appears to show for her (63). Placing a premium on the male admiration
she fails to receive from Carmichael, she expects other women to do the same
(13). Perhaps among the most deeply distressing aspects of Mrs. Ramsay's
attitude toward her own sex are her insistence that all women marry (77)—
and her patronizing view of Lily and her creative efforts:

> With her little Chinese eyes and her puckered-up face, she would never
> marry; one could not take her painting very seriously; she was an indepen-
> dent little creature, and Mrs. Ramsay liked her for it . . . . (29)

Mrs. Ramsay remains unavailable to Lily as well as other women for the
sustained, emotionally intimate relationship she craves. Yet she continues to
be the object of Lily's desire. This love, combined with the frequent irritation
and occasional anger that Lily feels toward Mrs. Ramsay, reflects the

fundamental ambivalence of the child toward its first and most revered love-object—its mother. Lily's anger also naturally extends to Ramsay, who, as the focus of Mrs. Ramsay's constant attention, has figuratively usurped Lily's daughter's place in Mrs. Ramsay's affections. The jealousy responsible for much of Lily's ambivalence toward Ramsay is aggravated by her anger at his egotism and domestic tyranny (72). Like Evelyn Murgatroyd in *The Voyage Out*, Lily seems to feel that women are "infinitely finer" than men (*VO* 247); Ramsay's unworthiness as his wife's spouse exacerbates Lily's dismay.

From a psychoanalytic perspective, the particular triangle of jealousy and longing depicted in Lily's relationship to the Ramsays suggests the pre-Oedipal fixation which girls demonstrate toward their mothers discussed by Juliet Mitchell in *Psychoanalysis and Feminism*. As Mitchell notes, in order to progress to heterosexual womanhood, girls must undergo "mother-*detachment*" (58), transferring their libidinal desire to the father during the Oedipal stage, and then to male partners in adulthood. To a large extent, Lily's psychological and artistic activity in the novel's final part focuses on the strong conflicting emotions which Lily experiences in thinking about Mrs. Ramsay, who must be demythologized—reduced to ordinary proportions—so that Lily may internalize her feminine qualities and undergo a rebirth into mature sexuality. Mrs. Ramsay's unavailability to women prevents the actual gratification of Lily's longing for intimacy, but aids her in the sense of forcing her to develop within herself those qualities she seeks in Mrs. Ramsay, enabling her to reach this new level of maturation.

The suggestion here of a kind of psychological fertilization taking place between women over a period of years does not appear in a context that would fail to support it. As noted earlier, Woolf alludes to the silent bonds of affection and understanding between women that harbor the potential for further intimacy between them. That this potential is usually not fully realized is due to the fact that in patriarchal cultures, female nurturing is usually harnessed and employed in service to men and children. In *To the Lighthouse*, there is even the hint of a wistful longing for a pre-patriarchal era when the original bonds between women remained inviolate and were not weakened or destroyed by the proprietary demands made by men upon women in marriage. The loss of Minta's brooch, a treasured heirloom from her grandmother, at approximately the same time as her engagement to Paul seems to suggest such a yearning:

> It was her grandmother's brooch; she would rather have lost anything but that, and yet Nancy felt, it might be true that she minded losing her brooch, but she wasn't crying only for that. She was crying for something else. We might all sit down and cry, she felt. But she did not know what for. (117)

The brooch is not merely symbolic of Minta's virginity, which is about to be sacrificed on the altar of marriage, but also of the legacy of the bonds of love and nurturing between women which have been eroded as a result of centuries of patriarchal domination.[11]

In the novel's final section, the torment of sorting out her feelings toward the Ramsays intimately influences Lily's attempt to recapture her aesthetic vision on canvas. By momentarily relinquishing her earlier reliance upon design principles in her painting, Lily enables herself to be influenced by Mrs. Ramsay's spiritual presence, allowing the material in her unconscious full expression in her art. Woolf's choice of imagery in the depiction of the creative process in this section strongly suggests the process of giving birth, not merely to one's aesthetic vision, but also to a new self. Mrs. Ramsay's influence in instigating these developments is affirmed. Both the process of painting and Lily's attendant personal growth enable her to relax her defensive efforts to protect her autonomy, and result in a broader, more receptive view which brings with it expansive feelings of acceptance and peace.

Lily's psychological growth in this final part involves several strands of activity. First, she must come to terms with her ambivalent feelings toward Mrs. Ramsay and accept her relationship with her husband. Like Bankes at the beginning of the dinner in the novel's first part, Lily feels somewhat guilty about her lack of emotion for Mrs. Ramsay, who has been dead for several years (217). It is only until she remembers how Mrs. Ramsay was able to conciliate her momentarily with Tansley that morning on the beach that Lily begins to recall Mrs. Ramsay's formidable skills as a peacemaker and unifier. However, she also recalls Mrs. Ramsay's manipulative behavior and her passion for matchmaking (261). Lily imagines the pleasure she would experience in telling Mrs. Ramsay of the failure of the Rayley marriage and of her continued satisfaction with her own single state, believing that she could now "stand up to" her (262). This brief intellectual triumph over Mrs. Ramsay and her "limited, old-fashioned ideas" (260) is almost immediately reversed by a sudden feeling of physical pain—"a hardness, a hollowness, a strain"—at the loss of the woman (266). As Lily recognizes, her longing for Mrs. Ramsay has finally revealed itself through her body (265).

Lily's acknowledgment of Mrs. Ramsay's emotional impact upon her proves to be cathartic, enabling her to view her from a new, more detached perspective. She begins to recall the ways in which others admired or criticized Mrs. Ramsay, and even tries to imagine how the woman herself viewed the world (294). Lily also takes a fresh look at the realities of the Ramsay marriage—"no monotony of bliss," full of the conflicts and reconciliations that other marriages contain (296). Lily's cathartic feeling of anguish, followed by a more detached appraisal of Mrs. Ramsay, enables her to drain her of her mythic force as a symbol of maternal power and so humanize her, making her a more manageable presence in Lily's psychic economy. This process reaches completion when Lily is able to recreate Mrs. Ramsay mentally as a part of everyday reality, recalling her sitting in the chair knitting the stocking for the lighthouse keeper's boy: "There she sat" (300).

Lily's dissociation of desire from the figure of Mrs. Ramsay coincides with a new development in her relationship to her husband. At the beginning of the final section, Woolf places Lily in a situation strangely akin to that of Mrs. Ramsay in the novel's opening section. Like Mrs. Ramsay at the beginning of the dinner, Lily, seated at the Ramsay breakfast table ten years later, feels oddly alienated from her surroundings. Everything appears to be "aimless" and "chaotic"; it seems "as if the link that usually bound things together had been cut" (219). Like Mrs. Ramsay earlier in that same day ten years ago, Lily is also seated at a window, and pretends to drink coffee in order to escape Ramsay's "imperious need" for sympathy as he passes by (219).

Later in the morning, Ramsay's efforts to elicit sympathy from Lily prevent her from resuming her painting. Unable to "imitate . . . the glow, the rhapsody, the self-surrender" (224) which Lily has observed in women offering solace and encouragement to men, she remains silent. It is only when Ramsay is rendered ordinary by the gesture of bending over to tie her shoe that Lily is suddenly "tormented with sympathy" for him; he becomes "a figure of infinite pathos" (230). Lily's recognition of Ramsay's vulnerability and humanity has correspondingly stimulated a human—and traditionally feminine—response within her. No longer the impersonal observer of others, she is now burdened with unexpressed sympathy for him which makes her attempt to paint even more difficult. Lily is unable to convey her sympathy for Ramsay until she has accepted the imperfections of the man and his relationship to his wife, and absolved him of his emotional excesses (308–9).

Lily's gift of forgiveness to Ramsay coincides with Carmichael's symbolic benediction upon the world as the two stand at the edge of the lawn looking out to sea:

> He stood there as if he were spreading his hands over all the weakness and suffering of mankind; she thought he was surveying, tolerantly and compassionately, their final destiny. (309)

At the same time, Lily recognizes a silent bond of understanding between herself and Carmichael. Both of the seemingly aloof, reserved characters have themselves undergone a kind of humanization that distantly approaches the sexually charged vitality of the Ramsay marriage.[12]

In the final section of *To the Lighthouse*, Lily's progress in painting closely accompanies her personal growth. The process of painting itself not only reveals Mrs. Ramsay's influence, but also symbolically reflects Lily's resolution of her conflict between the need for autonomy and the longing for intimacy. Lily consciously acknowledges the influence of Mrs. Ramsay as a fellow artist who has created enduring moments that remain in one's memory, "affecting one almost like a work of art" (240). Furthermore, Lily is aware that both she and Mrs. Ramsay share the same goal as artists, that of "making of the moment something permanent" (241). She even appears to credit Mrs. Ramsay for having enabled her to experience such moments both as an artist and as an individual:

> In the midst of chaos there was shape; this eternal passing and flowing . . . was struck into stability. Life stand still here, Mrs. Ramsay said. 'Mrs. Ramsay! Mrs. Ramsay!' she repeated. She owed it all to her. (241)

Mrs. Ramsay's subliminal influence upon Lily while painting is far more pervasive, however. In several instances, Lily's relationship to her art unconsciously imitates that of Mrs. Ramsay to life, her artistic medium. As noted earlier, Woolf has placed Lily in a situation that strikingly resembles Mrs. Ramsay's at the beginning of the dinner, which she eventually shapes into a work of art, an enduring moment. Lily's efforts to shed her consciousness of herself as an individual in preparing to paint approximate Mrs. Ramsay's deliberate shedding of her identity during quiet moments by becoming "a wedge-shaped core of darkness"(95). While painting, Lily displays Mrs. Ramsay's intuitive approach to creativity by momentarily setting aside formal concerns in order to allow unconscious impulses to direct the rhythmic strokes of her brush:

> With a curious physical sensation, as if she were urged forward and at the same time must hold herself back, she made her first quick decisive stroke. The brush descended. It flickered brown over the white canvas; it left a running mark. A second time she did it—a third time. And so pausing and so flickering, she attained a dancing rhythmical movement, as if the pauses were one part of the rhythm and the strokes another, and all were related . . . . (235–6)

Woolf depicts Lily's struggle to recapture her vision on canvas using the same martial imagery she employed in describing Mrs. Ramsay's struggle with life earlier in the novel: "this form. . . roused one to perpetual combat, challenged one to a fight" (236). During a moment of heightened awareness, Lily senses she is on the verge of a major insight: "A hand would be shoved up, a blade would be flashed" (266–7). Woolf's choice of imagery here evokes not only the Lady of the Lake of Arthurian legend, but also Mrs. Ramsay herself, who is portrayed earlier as "brandishing her sword at life" (92).

In the final part of the novel, Lily's continued manipulation of design elements in her painting also enables her to resolve the conflict posed by her longing for Mrs. Ramsay and her inability to accept her relationship with her husband. While painting, Lily delves into the past, recreating Mrs. Ramsay in her memories and noting the enduring moments of unity and peace Mrs. Ramsay has quietly bequeathed her. Under the influence of unconscious impulses, Lily's brush sculpts a large, empty space that appears to take on a life of its own, "looming out at her" (236). This space can be seen to have multiple symbolic associations. On the one hand, it appears to reflect Mrs. Ramsay's absence and Lily's accompanying feelings of loss and hollowness.

However, the language used to describe it evokes Ramsay's habit of approaching women from whom he seeks emotional support and threatening to inflict himself upon them. In this sense, it may represent the emotional barrenness that Mrs. Ramsay frequently senses in men (126).

Lily meets the challenge posed by the space by continuing to burrow into her memories, which are thrown up "like a fountain spurting over that glaring, hideously difficult white space" (238), and simultaneously modeling the space with greens and blues. Woolf's use of fountain imagery evokes that associated with Mrs. Ramsay earlier in the novel—"this delicious fecundity, this fountain and spray of life"—as she gives her husband the emotional support he craves (58). There appears to be a suggestion here of Lily's newly acquired emotional fertility, her ability to overcome sterility and emptiness with life-affirming energy. She has displayed this new ability in the overwhelming sympathy she suddenly feels for Ramsay earlier in the section. If the space is also viewed as representative of Mrs. Ramsay's absence and Lily's resulting feeling of hollowness, Lily's filling in the space can be seen as an effort both to imitate and to recreate Mrs. Ramsay psychically, in effect to nurture herself.

Like the empty space, the line which Lily paints in the middle of her picture after standing with Carmichael gazing in the direction of the lighthouse, which she intuitively senses the Ramsays have reached, appears to hold multiple associations. At the simplest level, the line may be seen to represent the male principle in Ramsay, who no longer poses a threat to Lily in her new psychological relationship to Mrs. Ramsay. Lily's placement of the line in the center of the modeled space, which can be associated with both Mrs. Ramsay and Lily in her new creative and emotional fertility, reveals her acceptance of Ramsay, both in relation to Mrs. Ramsay and to herself.[13]

Equally significantly, the inclusion of the line suggests Lily's confident assertion of her new sense of self. During the dinner in the novel's first section, Lily repeatedly turns to thoughts about her painting when threatened by fears of personal inadequacy (130), irritated by Mrs. Ramsay's solicitousness toward men (128), or sexually snubbed by Tansley or Paul Rayley (131, 154). In each of these instances, she defensively reaffirms her intention of moving the tree "to the middle" (130). Ten years must pass before Lily is capable of asserting her identity in this manner. The anguish of recalling the past and recapturing her vision has enabled her to give birth to a new self which triumphs over the sources of her former feelings of inadequacy. Mrs. Ramsay has been demythologized; Tansley, having married and moved to a London suburb, has lost his aura as one of Bankes's potential "great men" (292); Paul Rayley's marriage to Minta Doyle has failed (260). Lily's assertion of her identity now takes center stage, filling the space formerly defined by her feelings of emptiness and personal inadequacy, and by her unresolved longing for Mrs. Ramsay.

Woolf's use of the imagery of childbirth to describe the process of painting reinforces the central role that Lily's art plays in her personal development.[14]

Lily's position while painting evokes both a child who is about to be born and a mother who is giving birth. Earlier in the novel, Lily compares the anguish of attempting to capture her vision on canvas as follows:

> It was in that moment's flight between the picture and her canvas that the demons set on her who often brought her to the verge of tears and made this passage from conception to work as dreadful as any down a dark passage for a child. (32)

While identifying Lily with the child about to emerge, Woolf simultaneously identifies her with the mother/artist whose artistic conception culminates in the birth of the artwork, and whose desperate efforts to retain her aesthetic vision resemble the frenzied determination of a mother to retain possession of her infant:

> Such she often felt herself—struggling against terrific odds to maintain her courage; to say: 'But this is what I see; this is what I see,' and so to clasp some miserable remnant of her vision to her breast, which a thousand forces did their best to pluck from her. (32)

The rhythmic movement of Lily's brush strokes and her passive resistance to the force of her aesthetic vision, which "suddenly laid hands on her" (236), drawing her into a struggle for domination, all suggest the occasionally violent experience of the sexual act from the female perspective: "She was half unwilling, half reluctant. Why always be drawn out and haled away?" (236). The metaphor of the sexual act continues in Lily's response to the looming white space on her canvas:

> Then, as if some juice necessary for the lubrication of her faculties were spontaneously squirted, she began precariously dipping among the blues and umbers, moving her brush hither and thither . . . . (237)

As noted earlier, the "fountain" of memories in Lily's mind spurts over the glaring space, enabling her to model it with colors. Completing her painting, Lily experiences the "extreme fatigue" of a woman who has just given birth (310).

As depicted here, the creative process closely mirrors the sequence of events leading up to birth. The mind of the artist fertilizes itself, conceiving a vision that is made flesh with the birth of the work of art. Lily's artistic efforts, however, produce a new self as well as a completed painting. While making the transition from life's "fluidity" to the "concentration of painting," Lily again resembles the child about to be born,

> . . . an unborn soul, a soul reft of body, hesitating on some windy pinnacle and exposed without protection to all the blasts of doubt. (237)

Woolf's image of Lily as a swimmer about to dive into the ocean (235, 256, 269) suggests not only the feeling of isolation and fear experienced by the artist about to plunge into creative work, but also the similarity of this process to the ritual reenactment of death and rebirth in baptism. As Lily immerses herself further in her memories and her painting, she becomes suspended in fertile waters from which she occasionally surfaces to gaze at Augustus Carmichael or to follow the progress of the Ramsays' sailboat crossing the bay. Lily's placement of the line in the center of her canvas at the end of the novel reenacts the process of self-fertilization in which she has been involved; it also establishes the emergence of a new sexualized self, capable of its own nurturing.

Lily's psychological growth at the end of *To the Lighthouse* is brought about both by the influence of Mrs. Ramsay and her own efforts. In a sense, one can view Lily's completed painting as a collaboration between Mrs. Ramsay the social artist and Lily the painter.[15] Recalling her memories of the summer spent with the Ramsays, Lily draws upon her experience of the emotionally charged Ramsay marriage as well as Mrs. Ramsay's legacy of enduring moments—her social artistry—to regain her aesthetic vision and complete her painting. Through the agency of an unusually nurturing woman, a socially marginal artist-figure has experienced an immersion in life that provides the material for artistic creativity as well as an invaluable opportunity for her own sexual development. Although Lily has greatly expanded her empathic abilities and her capacity for self-nurturing, she nonetheless remains the celibate woman artist who rejects sexual relations in the interest of pursuing her art unhindered by the demands of others. In the later novels *Orlando* and *Between the Acts*, Woolf bridges the gap between artistic productivity and physical sexuality in women through the characters of Orlando and Miss La Trobe.

CHAPTER SEVEN

Orlando

Revising *Orlando: A Biography* in the early months of 1928, Woolf described the book in her March 18 diary entry as "all a joke; & yet gay & quick reading I think; a writers holiday" (*D3*: 177). The "joke" lies in Woolf's effort to write a fanciful biography based on the life of her friend and intimate Vita Sackville-West in which her subject first appears as a shy youth of sixteen during the English Renaissance and eventually matures into a capable, thirty-six-year-old modern woman. Spanning over three centuries and changing its subject's sex at some point during the Restoration, *Orlando* is nonetheless more than a *jeu d'esprit* that celebrates the personality, interests, and aristocratic heritage of Sackville-West. The book may also be viewed as an informal social history of England from the Renaissance to 1928 that portrays—and satirizes—the nation's changing values, mores, gender roles, and tastes over the centuries. In addition, it provides an irreverent history of the development of English literature and its modes of production during these years. As a self-conscious biography, *Orlando* can be considered an extended, albeit fanciful, meditation upon the problems facing biographers or historians in writing about a historical subject.[1] As psychobiography, the book explores the nature of sexual and personal identity, and the ways in which human beings experience time, especially the relationship between the past, memories of the past, and the present.[2]

By the time *Orlando* was published in October of 1928, Woolf's romantic involvement with Sackville-West had already peaked, but the two women remained affectionate friends. Descended from Renaissance poet Thomas Sackville, Earl of Dorset, Sackville-West was a dynamic aristocrat whose independent spirit and wide range of interests enabled her to lead what Woolf perceived to be a singularly exciting life. Sackville-West traveled widely and adventurously; engaged in lesbian relationships while simultaneously maintaining her marriage and family; spent a considerable amount of time managing Sissinghurst, the estate purchased by her husband (especially the gardens, for which she had a passion); proved herself a robust outdoorswoman and lover of animals; and wrote and published poetry and fiction as well as works on history, gardening, and travel.[3]

Perhaps more than any of Woolf's novels, *Orlando* may be viewed as a *Künstlerroman* as well as a *Bildungsroman* in that it covers over twenty formative years (though spread over more than three centuries) in the life of an aspiring young writer who ostensibly relinquishes his dream of literary fame after he becomes a woman and reaches maturity. Of course one must exercise much restraint in viewing the book as a significant example of either genre. As the life depicted is obviously fantastic and often comically rendered, the reader must question how seriously he or she should take the narrator's efforts to trace the subject's personal development, not to mention his/her artistic growth. Second, literature remains a beloved avocation for Orlando throughout his/her years of young adulthood; much of Orlando's life during this time is devoted to serving his queen or king at court or as an ambassador abroad and managing his/her large ancestral estate in the countryside. Furthermore, as a *Künstlerroman*, *Orlando* fails to examine in any depth the hero/heroine's evolution as a writer; the narrator provides only the most cursory information about Orlando's earliest literary efforts as well as "The Oak Tree," the single poem she completes during the course of the book and has published at the age of thirty-six.

Rather *Orlando* focuses upon the sequence of events in its subject's fantastic, centuries-spanning young life, his/her reactions to these events and the changing times, her experience of her sex change, her personal development, and the search for an authentic self at its end. As a *Künstlerroman*, however, *Orlando* does trace the hero/heroine's early fascination with literature, poetic language and writing, literary figures, and the literary scene, and makes somewhat of an effort to consider formally the relationship between literature and life.[4] The latter is of particular interest here, as Orlando the woman is Woolf's first female artist-figure to be artistically productive, socially integrated, and sexually active. In this fictional biography, as in her other fiction, Woolf continues to explore the relationship between the artist and social and sexual life. Orlando, like Lily Briscoe, emerges as an artist-figure who has achieved something of a balance between the desire to withdraw from the world to pursue one's art unhindered and the lure of a broader, more enriched life lived among others in the world at large.

In Orlando's case, though, the worlds of the Ivory Tower and the Sacred Fount appear to be more polarized, regressively evoking the two disparate spheres of existence perceived by Rachel Vinrace as she confronts gender-imposed limitations and her impending marriage in *The Voyage Out*. Furthermore, the vacillation between these extremes is more pronounced; Orlando, like Rachel, alternately becomes involved in social activity and then withdraws to his/her room—here, to continue working on "The Oak Tree." The relationship between involvement in social life, sexual relations, and artistic creativity ultimately remains ambiguous. Occasionally Orlando's experiences with others trigger thoughts approaching revelations and the concomitant urge to pursue and record them in verse. At other times, Orlando, like Rachel, retreats into a private world—one of reading and writing—when rebuffed by others. As the narrator provides so little information about Orlando's literary efforts, it is difficult to determine whether this work reflects his/her experience and observations of life or serves primarily as an imaginative escape for a sensitive, vulnerable personality.

Although Orlando easily surmounts Lily Briscoe's strong reservations concerning heterosexual involvement by marrying boldly and well, the marriage is an unusual one in that her seafaring adventurer-bridegroom departs immediately following the wedding, and Orlando remains solitary and independent for much of the time. Her maternity, perfunctorily announced at the end of a long, comical digression by the narrator on "natural desire" (294), hardly figures at all in her thoughts or her life beyond the moment of giving birth to her first son, whom the narrator then withdraws from the biography. The narrator's rather compromised accommodation of female heterosexuality, marriage, and motherhood in presenting Orlando's life suggests that Woolf continues to harbor fears about the dangers of heterosexual relations for aspiring female artists and writers.

At the beginning of the book, Orlando is introduced as a shy, very handsome, but rather clumsy Elizabethan boy of sixteen who spends his time swinging his sword at a shriveled head hanging from the attic rafters of his family estate, composing verse drama with titles such as "Aethelbert: A Tragedy in Five Acts" (16), and answering the call of nature by escaping from the house unseen and climbing a hill, where he stretches out under a favorite oak tree to commune with nature and daydream. The narration presents the oak tree as the geographic focus of Orlando's earliest and lifelong passion for the natural world and his country estate—a passion which first appears that of a lonely adolescent experiencing the first stirrings of desire:

> . . . he felt the need of something which he could attach his floating heart to; the heart that tugged at his side; the heart that seemed filled with spiced and amorous gales every evening about this time when he walked out. To the oak tree he tied it and as he lay there, gradually the flutter in and about him stilled itself . . . . (19)

Orlando returns to the oak tree after being jilted by the Russian princess Sasha, after reading a stinging assessment of his poetry, and upon returning to the family estate as a woman following a stint as ambassador of the Crown in Constantinople. The book concludes with Orlando as a woman standing by the oak tree in moonlight, welcoming her returning husband, Marmaduke Bonthrop Shelmerdine, which no doubt is meant to suggest a sense of completion and fulfillment in Orlando's life, as well as providing closure to the narrative.

Despite this final reunion with her husband and a life often lived intensely among others in service to the empire or in society, Orlando as both man and woman exhibits a strong preference for solitude—usually in nature or at his/her writing table. During the Renaissance and the Restoration, Orlando first serves his country as a courtier to Elizabeth I, who makes him her favorite and appoints him her treasurer and steward. During this time, he has a number of amorous involvements and falls in love with the princess Sasha, who eventually casts him off by returning to Russia without him. Under Charles II, he serves as "Ambassador Extraordinary" to Constantinople (118), where he cuts a dashing figure in the diplomatic community and orders a grand celebration upon receiving a dukedom from the king. He also spends time with gypsies in Turkey and purportedly marries one Rosina Pepita, a gypsy dancer.[5] As a woman during the Augustan age, Orlando frequently seeks the nocturnal company of a group of women prostitutes who regale her with stories of the seamy side of London life. She also attends Lady R.'s salon, where she meets Pope, who, together with Addison and Swift, become her friends and the recipients of her patronage. She is ardently pursued by the Archduke Harry, one of several unsuccessful suitors, and is rescued one day after having suffered a broken ankle alone on the moors by Shelmerdine—like Sasha, another romantic figure—whom she marries soon afterward.

With few exceptions, however—the relationship with Sasha being one—these experiences are rendered only superficially, with little attention given to Orlando's actual interactions with others as individuals. Rather, the narration emphasizes the breadth of adventures Orlando has experienced among others both in England and in Turkey. If anything, the narration continues to suggest that Orlando is one who prefers his/her own company best. As a youth, Orlando exhibits "a love of solitude" and solitary places, wanting "to feel himself for ever and ever and ever alone" (18). Exiled from the Court for having broken his engagement to Lady Margaret O'Brien O'Dare O'Reilly Tyrconnel, Orlando decides to go into seclusion on his country estate: "Solitude was his choice" (68). While there, he recalls his awkwardness and his "unfitness for the life of society" (83). The narrator comments on the figure of "romantic power" that Orlando cuts later in Constantinople, associating it with "a nature of extreme reserve. Orlando seems to have made no friends" (125). Adjusting to her new gender during the Restoration, Orlando decides to renounce the privileges she once enjoyed as a male because womanhood enables her to experience more fully "the most exalted raptures known to the human spirit, which are . . . contemplation, solitude, love" (160). At the age of thirty-six, Orlando considers how she feels about people generally, and reaches a rather unfavorable conclusion: "Chattering, spiteful, always telling lies" (311).

Coupled with Orlando's preference for solitude is his/her love of nature, symbolized by the oak tree. It is significant that the long poem that Orlando completes after several centuries' work is entitled "The Oak Tree," symbolically fusing Orlando's love of nature, solitude, and the family estate with the solitary activity of writing. As a young poet, Orlando is in the habit of describing nature at length (16). As a young woman, Orlando suffers from "the English disease, a love of Nature," which is "inborn in her" (143). Although comically rendered by the narrator, the Turkish landscape as well as her own estate elicits in her a passionate, mystical response:

> She climbed the mountains; roamed the valleys; sat on the banks of the streams. She likened the hills to ramparts, and the plains to the flanks of kine. She compared the flowers to enamel and the turf to Turkey rugs worn thin. Trees were withered hags and sheep were grey boulders. . . . She found the tarn on the mountain-top and almost threw herself in to seek the wisdom she thought lay hid there . . . . (143)

While experiencing these sights, Orlando is inspired to consider the nature of such abstractions as "Love, Friendship, Poetry" and Keats's pair, beauty and truth, and uses berries to make ink so that she can "describe the scenery" in a blank verse poem composed in the margins of "The Oak Tree" manuscript (145), which she keeps close to her breast. In a moment of homesickness, Orlando has a vision of her estate on a Turkish hillside and immediately decides to sail for England the following day. Orlando's status as "a passionate lover of animals" (32) reinforces her predilection for nature and its creatures. Betrayed during the Elizabethan era by the poet Nick Greene, whom Orlando supports with a quarterly pension, and who has ungratefully satirized his poetry, Orlando resolves to put his trust in "dogs and nature; an elkhound and a rose bush" (97). An era later, surfeited by his numerous social obligations as an ambassador in Constantinople, Orlando chooses "to take his dinner alone with his dogs" (123).[6]

It appears that the narration correlates the love of nature and solitude with writing, which in turn are opposed to the unusually active life Orlando leads at large. The relationship of writing to Orlando's life nonetheless remains ambiguous. Early in the novel, Orlando, rebuffed by the Court for having broken his engagement to Lady Margaret, retreats to the peace and solitude of his estate, embarking upon a program of intense reading and writing. At times, Orlando's writing habit simply appears to offer a refuge from a frequently frenetic life lived among others. Once he has refurbished the rooms of his estate, Orlando begins to offer "a series of very splendid entertainments to the nobility and gentry of the neighbourhood" (112). In the midst of the feasting, however, Orlando usually retires to his private quarters, where he resumes work on "The Oak Tree" manuscript. Sometimes Orlando appears to be impatient with specific relationships, and eagerly returns to his/her writing desk. Having rid herself of the Archduke and his flattering but ultimately undesired suit, Orlando remarks, "'Heaven be praised!'" (184), and turns once again to her poem. In this instance, however, she senses the loss of "life and a lover," and tries to employ the words in a line of poetry "which did not scan and made no sense with what went before—something about the proper way of dipping sheep to avoid the scab" (185).

Later in the book, having seen her new husband off to sea, Orlando immediately returns to the manuscript of her poem, doubting the validity of her new marriage since she would like nothing better than to be able to write:

> She was married, true; but if one's husband was always sailing round Cape Horn, was it marriage? If one liked him, was it marriage? If one liked other people, was it marriage? And finally, if one still wished, more than anything in the whole world, to write poetry, was it marriage? She had her doubts. (264)

Ostensibly Woolf is satirically challenging the conventional view of marriage and its importance in a woman's life, as well as questioning the prevailing notion of the Victorian era—first asserted in Byron's *Don Juan* years earlier—that love, not thinking and writing, is "woman's whole existence" (268). Orlando does achieve a compromise with "the spirit of the age," highly critical of women who place intellectual work of any kind above all else, that enables her to resume writing (266). A few pages later, the narrator perfunctorily announces the completion of "The Oak Tree:" "Orlando pushed away her chair, stretched her arms, dropped her pen, came to the window, and exclaimed, 'Done!'" (271). At the end of the poem's centuries-long gestation, the reader is still virtually ignorant of its subject and its evolution; all he or she knows with any certainty is that "The Oak Tree" includes lines describing techniques of animal husbandry. By the end of the book, the reader is left wondering whether the actual experiences of Orlando's unusually long and eventful life, including marriage and motherhood, have had any effect, for better or worse, upon the content or quality of her writing.

One must acknowledge here that as an aspiring writer whose life spans several centuries, Orlando is shown to become increasingly sophisticated in his/her choice of genres. His numerous early works—"plays, histories, romances, poems" (77)—tend to be about "some mythological personage at a crisis of his career" and bear such titles as "The Death of Ajax," "The Birth of Pyramus," and "The Return of Odysseus" (76). Nick Greene, the poet whom Orlando patronizes, mercilessly satirizes Orlando's tragedy "The Death of Hercules" in his own "Visit to a Nobleman in the Country," describing the work as "wordy and bombastic in the extreme" (95). In response to this devastating assessment, Orlando burns all his works, saving only the manuscript of "The Oak Tree."

Orlando's abandonment of turgid verse and prose concerning heroic subjects in favor of continuing work on "The Oak Tree," with minor excursions into "insipid verse" (238) during the Victorian era, is, of course, required as part of Woolf's effort to present a humorous informal history of the development of English literature within the biography. If one assumes that "The Oak Tree" is primarily a celebration of Orlando's country estate and the way of life it represents, then Orlando's decision to continue working on it may be seen as an indication of his/her coming of age as a writer who chooses to write about what he/she knows best. This choice is historically appropriate as well; Orlando finishes the long poem in the twentieth century, a period in which mythological subjects have virtually disappeared from the literary landscape and authors increasingly draw upon the experience of their own lives and times in creating literature.[7] Viewed this way, the completion of "The Oak Tree" seems to affirm the belief that literature should be based upon actual life and not upon myth, legend, or fantasy. In fact, Orlando's initial wish to bury a copy of the published poem under the oak tree for which it is named suggests her awareness of her debt to the tree and her estate, of which it is part, for having inspired the poem.

The narrator of *Orlando*, however, appears ambivalent about the relationship between literature and life. On the one hand, the Elizabethan period is presented as one in which life attempts to imitate art: "what the poets said in rhyme, the young translated into practice" (27). Later in the book, describing Orlando's love of literature as a common "disease" (like the love of nature), the narrator decries literature's tendency

> . . . to substitute a phantom for reality, so that Orlando, to whom fortune had given every gift—plate, linen, houses, men-servants, carpets, beds in profusion—had only to open a book for the whole vast accumulation to turn to mist. (74)

While Orlando thinks at her writing-table during the Victorian era, however, the narrator satirizes the view that thinking and writing do not constitute living:

> Life, it has been agreed by everyone whose opinion is worth consulting, is the only fit subject for novelist or biographer; life, the same authorities have decided, has nothing whatever to do with sitting still in a chair and thinking. (267)

Despite the ironic tone used here, the narrator does appear to believe that an author's work reflects his personality and his life experience. Earlier, he claims that "every secret of a writer's soul, every experience of his life, every quality of his mind is written large in his works" (209), and follows it with analyses of excerpts from Addison's and Swift's prose that demonstrate how they reveal the man (210–1). The hyperbole of the claim might suggest that Woolf's narrator is being ironic, but Woolf's own statements on authorship in her essays strongly suggest otherwise.[8]

Part of the ambiguity of the narrator's views concerning the relationship between life and literature originates in the more fundamental question of what life itself is—one that both the narrator and Orlando ask at different moments in the book. The narrator poses the question at the beginning of a comical digression in the manner of Sterne's *Tristram Shandy*, only to conclude, "Alas, we don't know" (271). While walking about Victorian

London some time later, Orlando asks the question herself, considering the matter further as she peruses literary reviews while seated in Hyde Park: "She looked at the paper and looked up; she looked at the sky and looked down. Life? Literature? One to be made into the other? But how monstrously difficult!" (285).

It may well be that the narrator's view of the relationship between literature and life is deliberately ambiguous, as this topic, much debated since the aesthetes, Dadaists, Surrealists and modernists challenged realism in literature, may have been one of the contemporary literary concerns that Woolf preferred to treat whimsically in the book, as is the case with other weighty questions such as defining the nature of life. If one had to choose which way the narration and Orlando's experience tend on this matter, one might conclude that the book espouses the view that literature and life are obviously interrelated, but that no more can be claimed with any assurance, at least in a mock biography of a fictional aristocrat with literary aspirations.

It would seem, though, that *Orlando* ultimately affirms the value of rich and varied life experience for the artist or writer. Orlando has managed a large estate, served the empire both at home and abroad, had numerous amorous involvements, exhibited a fondness for observing in disguise the urban street life of each era, changed sexes, married, given birth, and completed and published an award-winning poem that has gone into seven editions, ironically well after she has renounced her ambition to achieve fame as an author (312). As a worshipper of literature and its power to confer greatness upon individuals, Orlando has undergone considerable maturation, not only in relinquishing her quest for fame and vowing to write to please herself, but also in coming to value anonymous creation (106)[9] and realizing all too well the deficiencies and common humanity of such greats as Addison, Pope, and Swift (213). In the process, Orlando has made some valuable discoveries about the nature of literature itself: "What has praise and fame to do with poetry? . . . Was not writing poetry a secret transaction, a voice answering a voice?" (325).

As for Orlando's status as a woman, wife, and mother who has led an unusually exciting, centuries-long life and readily overcomes any initial difficulties posed to her writing by her sex change, one must remember that *Orlando* was written to celebrate the unusually independent, adventurous, bisexual life of Woolf's friend Vita Sackville-West, herself a prolific author. In this respect, the characterization of Orlando's relatively untroubled creative life is both an attempt to affirm Sackville-West's experience as an independent woman whose privileged circumstances enabled her to pursue the life of a writer, as well as an example of wish-fulfillment on Woolf's part as a woman writer aware of the difficulties posed by cultural expectations, marriage, and—through her sister Vanessa's experience—motherhood to female creativity.

One cannot help but notice Orlando's infrequent thoughts of her absent husband and the virtual disappearance of her children in the novel's final chapter. Apart from a vague intention to discuss fame with her sons (312), the only hint of maternal responsibility or concern provided by the narrator occurs during Orlando's disorienting experience of a London department store, where, among other things, she seeks a pair of boy's boots (300). If anything, it appears that "The Oak Tree," whose manuscript Orlando has habitually kept in her bosom, is far more valued as a "child" than her biological offspring. It is true that Sackville-West had an unusually liberating, unrestrictive marriage with her husband, also a bisexual and a diplomat frequently abroad on state business, and that her wealth would have accorded her much freedom from child-rearing. Nonetheless, Orlando's puzzling obliviousness to her children suggests that Woolf's portrait of the fictional Orlando as a successful woman writer, wife, and mother is a heavily mediated one, simultaneously disguising and reflecting Woolf's continuing reservations concerning the effects of heterosexual relationships and maternity upon female creativity.[10]

CHAPTER EIGHT

The Waves

Among Woolf's novels, *The Waves* (1931) stands out as her most experimental, earning it a reputation as a classic modernist text. The book's highly stylized rhythmic prose, unusually dense network of images, and lyrical interludes at the beginning of each chapter mark it as her most poetic novel as well.[1] The innovation of *The Waves* as fiction lies in both its structure and content. Lacking a narrator except in the interludes, the novel consists of a series of monologues spoken by six voices, each of which represents a character— Susan, Jinny, Rhoda, Neville, Louis, or Bernard. These voices trace the individual and collective psychological experience of six childhood friends from their earliest years through adolescence and young adulthood into middle age.[2] Unlike fiction in the realist tradition, *The Waves* contains no plot to advance any dramatic action, following instead a simple chronological sequence in presenting the thoughts and emotions of the characters as they experience life at different stages and in different settings.

Two dinner scenes are presented as milestones in the collective experience of the group. The first appears midway through the novel, during the characters' young adulthood, and is set in a London restaurant, where the group gathers to celebrate the imminent departure of Percival, its seventh member, for India. The second, a reunion at an inn near Hampton Court, occurs in the novel's penultimate chapter during the group's middle age, long after Percival has died in a riding accident in India. Concluding *The Waves* is a chapter-long monologue by Bernard, who attempts to sum up his and the group's experience by telling the story of his life to a chance acquaintance over dinner in a London restaurant.

To a degree not found in the other novels, *The Waves* is concerned with relating as closely as possible the nature of the individual's experience of others and the surrounding world at various stages in life. In presenting this subjective, phenomenological perspective, Woolf uses a uniform, stylized voice for all six characters that tests the capabilities of speech in its attempts to convey states of mind through such symbolic, non-rational means as figurative language. At the beginning of the novel, each of the voices associates its character with particular colors, images and motifs that recur throughout the novel; some of these eventually become associated with other characters as well.[3] These shared elements, in combination with the uniform cadence of the six voices, help to underscore the evolving collective identity shared by the six characters in the novel.[4]

Although the characters engage in creative activities of various kinds, none is a professional artist or writer in the traditional sense. Of the six, Neville comes closest to being a practicing artist or writer as a reclusive, discerning classicist who writes poetry as a youth and achieves considerable recognition for his scholarship as an adult. As a writer *manqué*, Bernard, whose voice and perspective are privileged in the novel, exhibits a number of traits commonly associated with writers—a formidable curiosity about others and daily life generally, finely honed skills as an observer, a sensitivity to the emotional states of others, an irrepressible need to formulate phrases descriptive of whom and what he observes and imagines, and a compulsion to make up stories about others as well as himself. In his ongoing search for the "true" story that accurately reflects the nature of living, Bernard is easily distracted and in the habit of leaving both his phrases and stories unfinished. As an adult, Bernard works at something other than writing that is not specified—perhaps in a government office—and never fulfills his promise as an aspiring writer. His concluding monologue, in which he tries to sum up his experience of life, can, however, be viewed as the "true" story he has sought to find and tell as a writer. One may even extend this story to encompass the many monologues preceding it, upon which it draws for details of Bernard's experience as well as that of the others.[5]

Although aesthetic creativity makes its appearance to a certain extent in Neville's and Bernard's lives, *The Waves* is primarily concerned with a much more fundamental, universal form of creativity—that of evolving individual and collective identities, an integral activity of every human being. Specifically, Woolf uses the novel to continue her exploration of a number of questions concerning the nature of identity: To what degree is it predetermined or conditioned? To what degree do we deliberately assume or construct an identity? Do we consist of multiple selves whom we choose to assume under different circumstances or in different company? How does the presence of others influence our sense of who we are? Where do the boundaries of self overlap or merge with those of others? Is there a collective identity that we share with close friends and family or simply as members of the same species? As in her earlier novels, Woolf is interested in representing those moments when the individual transcends the confines of his or her identity—the "damned egotistical self" (*D2*: 14)—to partake of a broader identity or to merge mystically with the universe.

As was the case with other modernist writers, questions of identity assumed greater urgency for Woolf in a postwar age in which civilization came to be viewed as tenuous and vulnerable, and human life subject to depersonalization and devaluation in an increasingly complex, mechanized culture. The reader becomes particularly aware of this world in the monologues of *The Waves*, especially those representing the characters' experience in the city. To a large degree, the novel concerns itself with the efforts of the characters to negotiate this difficult external world, to establish a sense of self within it, and to transcend these selves and the world on occasion through the collective identity they are momentarily able to forge as a group. First delineated in Woolf's earliest novels, the two realms of being—the social world and the private world of contemplation and imagination—reemerge in this novel as the characters variously assert themselves among others at large, withdraw into themselves and their imaginations, or evolve a rhythm of continuous movement between the two spheres, as is the case with Louis and Bernard. Although the establishment, challenging, evasion, or transcendence of identity, rather than aesthetic production, are presented as the main creative preoccupations of the characters in *The Waves*, the novel's focus upon the continuous interaction of the self with others in the external world makes it a valuable source for exploring Woolf's concerns regarding social and sexual involvement for unusually sensitive men and women. *The Waves* is also particularly revealing of the strategies that individuals adopt to sustain a sense of identity and self-worth in an increasingly indifferent, if not overtly hostile, world.

Of the six characters, three are women of widely differing temperaments who nonetheless confront the same limited range of life choices facing most of the female characters in Woolf's earlier novels. As a young child, Susan is dominated by the powerful emotions of love and hatred (185). Her love is most intense for her clergyman father, to whom she repeatedly refers, and the things of nature—the doves, squirrel, and setter that she keeps at her country home, for example. Enrolling in a girls' boarding school on the east coast with Jinny and Rhoda, Susan feels hatred for the institution and its regimented life, to which she must conform, and longs for the day when term ends and she can return to her family and nature (211). Susan's hatred also extends to urban life. Stopping in a London station on her way by train to the countryside, she vows that her children will never go to school in London, nor will she ever overnight there (217).

Earlier in the novel, a chance glimpse of Jinny kissing Louis behind a hedge sends Susan into a fit of jealousy that causes her to retreat from her playmates into the woods (183). As becomes increasingly evident, Susan's strong need to possess extends to people as well as animals. By returning to the countryside as a young woman, marrying a farmer, and giving birth several times, Susan literally creates for herself objects to possess and love in her children. Her maternity—"'the bestial and beautiful passion'" (267)—is particularly fierce, and pits her against the world at large: "'I shall push the fortunes of my children unscrupulously. . . . I shall lie basely to help them'" (267). Apparently willingly immured in her country home, Susan sets about creating a little world over which she as mistress has control: "'I possess all I see. . . . I am fenced in, planted here like one of my own trees'" (308). Susan is rooted in the earth, the element with which she is associated in the novel.

As she matures, however, Susan feels increasingly uncomfortable around her childhood friends. While at the dinner in honor of Percival in London, Susan notes that she will "'possess more'" than Jinny and Rhoda before she dies, but that, in contrast to them, she will "'be sullen, storm-tinted and all one purple'" (266). Jinny's cosmopolitan stylishness and sensuality particularly intimidate Susan, who is self-conscious about her plain dress and serviceable body (259). During the reunion at Hampton Court many years later, Susan realizes that her presence creates uneasiness among her friends as well; her "'hardness'" irritates their "'softness'" (325). There is something in Susan's determined directness, in her aggressive assertion of her simplicity that makes her appear defensive and fearful of the world beyond her farm in the countryside.

Reaching middle age, Susan consciously acknowledges dissatisfaction with the way of life she has chosen:

> 'Where can the shadow enter? What shock can loosen my laboriously gathered, relentlessly pressed-down life? Yet sometimes I am sick of natural happiness, and fruit growing, and children scattering the house with oars, guns, skulls, books . . . . I am sick of the body, I am sick of my own craft, industry and cunning, of the unscrupulous ways of the mother who protects, who collects under her jealous eyes at one long table her own children, always her own.' (308–9)

One senses here not only the common experience of middle-aged women who realize that some vital personal potential has been suppressed in embracing wifehood and motherhood so completely and exclusively, but also the perception by an intelligent woman of the considerable part played by her own insecurities in the choice of this traditional role, which she has assumed with such vehemence.

If Susan's temperament and insecurities lead her to retreat into maternity and nature, where she is able to create a smaller, more manageable world she can dominate, Jinny's take her in the direction of contemporary urban life, whose challenges she appears to face as a woman without fear. Jinny's own voice as well as those of the other characters associate her with the element of fire; her being vibrates with unspent physical energy and seeks its release as a child in ceaseless movement or in seeking out others upon which to expend itself: "'I dance. I ripple. I am thrown over you like a net of light'" (183). Reaching adolescence, Jinny becomes a narcissist, gazing at her image in mirrors and showing an inordinate concern for stylish clothing. Her imagination evolves a fantasy that eventually becomes a recurring reality in her adult life as an unmarried London socialite:

> 'I begin to feel the wish to be singled out; to be summoned, to be called away by one person who comes to find me, who is attracted towards me,

who cannot keep himself from me, but comes to where I sit on my gilt
chair, with my frock billowing round me like a flower. And withdrawing
into an alcove, sitting alone on a balcony we talk together.' (206)

As a narcissist and a sensualist, Jinny requires the constant attention and
adulation of men and uses her creativity to transform herself into a work
of art: "'My hair is swept in one curve. My lips are precisely red'" (245).
Jinny's creative life is centered in her physicality and its demands: "'My
imagination is the body's'" (329). Temperamentally unsuited for the
housebound role of wife and mother, she gravitates towards the glamour
and intrigue of urban social life, identifying it as her "'world'":

> 'Are we not lovely sitting together here, I in my satin; he in black and
> white? My peers may look at me now. I look straight back at you, men
> and women. I am one of you. This is my world.' (246)

Unlike Susan, Jinny appears to be able to accommodate herself to the
external world without difficulty, thriving as she does as an ornament at
the gathering places of London's rich and powerful. As she ages and
frankly acknowledges the waning of her beauty, Jinny seems to maintain
her gregariousness, her love of adventure and amorous intrigue, and her
sense of optimism about the future. But it is a pathetic, willed hopefulness
that results from her lack of rootedness and her compensating identification
with the ruling class and the empire that sustains it. Preparing to go out, she
thinks of "'the triumphant procession'" of British civilization in London's
streets, full of people superior to "'savages in loincloths'" (310–11):

> 'These broad thoroughfares . . . are sanded paths of victory driven through
> the jungle. I too, with my little patent-leather shoes, my handkerchief . . . my
> reddened lips and my finely pencilled eyebrows march to victory with the
> band.' (311)

Of the novel's three female characters, Rhoda is the most complex, the
most imaginative, and the most troubled. If Susan's element is earth and
Jinny's, fire, Rhoda is associated with water as "'the nymph of the fountain
always wet'" (356). Unlike the other five characters, Rhoda's attempts to
formulate an identity that will sustain her in the external world continually
fail. Like her element, she has no defining shape she can present to others,
and longs for her own dissolution, which she ultimately achieves through
suicide in middle age. Throughout *The Waves* Rhoda describes herself as
faceless (265), a nobody, and on one occasion compares herself to dissolving
foam spreading out on the beach (265).

From an early age, she exhibits an artist's temperament in her appreciation for color and her need for beauty as a means of ordering her turbulent
inner world. While reacting to the news of Percival's death, she considers
visiting Hampton Court, with its striking architecture and carefully
designed landscaping; there, she thinks, she may be able to "'recover
beauty, and impose order'" on her "'raked . . . dishevelled soul'" (287).

Perhaps the most telling indicator of an aesthetic temperament, Rhoda's unusually active imagination serves several purposes during the course of her life. As a young child, she floats petals in a basin and fantasizes a little world of ships launched on a sea in which she can assume an assertive, adventurous role (187). While at boarding school, Rhoda bolsters her flagging identity by imagining herself a powerful Russian empress confronting her disgruntled subjects: "'I am fearless. I conquer'" (213).

At other times, Rhoda exhibits the capacity to respond to positive experiences in the real world with satisfying visions. As a schoolgirl, she imagines herself in the world of the poems she reads; one "'about a hedge'" entices her to follow its length in her imagination, picking an array of pleasing country flowers (213). Years later, while attending a music hall performance as an adult, Rhoda ultimately derives a sense of stability and achievement from the experience by imaginatively reinterpreting the music-making of the musicians:

> 'The players take the square and place it upon the oblong. They place it very accurately; they make a perfect dwelling-place. Very little is left outside. The structure is now visible; what is inchoate is here stated; we are not so various or so mean; we have made oblongs and stood them upon squares. This is our triumph; this is our consolation.' (288)

Rhoda recalls this vision later during a troubled moment while riding a mule in the mountains of Spain and again while viewing Hampton Court with the other five, with whom she momentarily experiences a sense of wholeness and unity (335).

More often than not, though, Rhoda feels herself to be without a dwelling-place in the real world. As a fatherless child, she draws a closed loop she imagines as containing the world, but mentally situates herself "'outside of it'," while also hoping somehow to be saved from her eternal isolation (189). Unlike the other five, Rhoda's existential anxiety is so severe that she exhibits delusions of persecution, alienation from others and her own body, and self-destructiveness to a degree reminiscent of Septimus Warren Smith's condition in *Mrs. Dalloway*. Vehicles appear to pursue her; she feels "'alone in a hostile world. The human face is hideous. I want . . . to be dashed like a stone on the rocks'" (286).

Ultimately Rhoda uses her substantial imaginative powers to create a fantastic landscape into which she withdraws during particularly stressful moments. This landscape makes its first appearance in her mind while attending one of the same social functions so compellingly pleasurable to Jinny. Retreating to a window and gazing at the moon, Rhoda seeks "'draughts of oblivion':"

> 'The door opens; the tiger leaps. . . . terror rushes in . . . pursuing me. Let me visit furtively the treasures I have laid apart. Pools lie on the other side of the world reflecting marble columns. The swallow dips her wing in dark pools. But here the door opens and people come; they come towards me.' (247)

While summing up his life among his friends at the end of *The Waves*, Bernard, aware of Rhoda's habit of seeking escape in her imagination, refines her fantastic landscape further: "'Perhaps one pillar, sunlit, stood in her desert by a pool'" visited by wild animals (351). As Bernard later reveals, it is this imaginary landscape that ultimately claims Rhoda, who always seemed to be looking for "'some pillar in the desert, to find which she had gone'" by killing herself (371).[6] Unlike Septimus Warren Smith's, Rhoda's suicide is not so much an act of defiance as a means of escaping from an unbearable reality in which she feels she has no place.[7]

Like Rhoda, Louis, the son of a Brisbane banker, also feels himself to be an outsider; throughout his life he is extremely self-conscious about his colonial origins and his Australian accent (187). Unlike Rhoda, Louis combats this sense of otherness, of marginality by desperately trying to conform through imitation and denial: "'I will wait and copy Bernard. He is English'" (187). Even while lunching alone in a London restaurant, Louis is troubled by his difference, unable to order his meal "'with conviction'" and careful to imitate the behavior of the other diners (239).

Throughout *The Waves*, Louis also indulges in fantasies of greatness, imagining himself as one who has "'lived a thousand lives already':"

> 'What you see beside you, this man, this Louis, is only the cinders and refuse of something once splendid. I was an Arab prince; behold my free gestures. I was a great poet in the time of Elizabeth. I was a Duke at the court of Louis the Fourteenth. I am very vain, very confident; I have an immeasurable desire that women should sigh in sympathy.' (263)

As will be seen, these Prufrockian fantasies stem in part from Louis's sense of history and his desire to be part of the civilization he hopes to advance in his own time through his own efforts, but his habit of identifying with prominent historical figures must also be acknowledged as a form of compensation for his insecurity as a marginal figure in a foreign land.

As so many alienated colonials before him have done, Louis attempts to resolve the dilemma of otherness by vigorously identifying with the colonizer—in this case, the British empire—and doggedly carving out for himself what he considers to be an important and influential career within the empire's power structure as a shipping executive:

> 'My shoulder is to the wheel; I roll the dark before me, spreading commerce where there was chaos in the far parts of the world. If I press on, from chaos making order, I shall find myself where Chatham stood, and Pitt, Burke, and Sir Robert Peel. Thus I expunge certain stains, and erase old defilements; the woman who gave me a flag from the top of the Christmas tree; my accent; beatings and other tortures; the boasting boys; my father, a banker at Brisbane.' (292)

Attempting to shed his colonial heritage, Louis nonetheless continues to identify with his Australian banker father by embracing the paternal authority of the empire and entering its service in his father's field—commerce. Even as a boy, he seems destined for this path, repeatedly describing himself in his childhood as wearing "'grey flannels with a belt fastened by a brass snake'" (182).

Louis's success as a businessman also serves the function of fulfilling his need to impose order upon the world: "'We have laced the world together with our ships'" (315). This need first surfaces in his work as a serious young scholar and aspiring poet, who hopes to use words to structure a reality he dimly perceives. Lying on the grass listening to Bernard's stories, Louis perceives "'some other order, and better,'" which he hopes to put into words that evening (201). As a schoolboy, Louis naïvely assumes that he shall become a great poet, imagining his name among those of the "'unhappy poets'" inscribed one day on the walls of the school chapel (214). As an adult, he appears to abandon writing poetry for reading it, but retains a sensibility that continues to manifest itself in an almost mystical feeling for the past and his own experience of it, suspecting he has already "'lived many thousand years'" (220).[8]

As he reaches middle age, Louis evolves a dual existence, moving between an active life of practical affairs in the world, where he fosters the empire's growth, and a solitary life of reading and meditation in his attic at home, where he immerses himself in the past and ruefully contemplates what he considers to be his burdensome destiny as a force in the external world:

> 'My task, my burden, has always been greater than other people's. A pyra-
> mid has been set on my shoulders. I have tried to do a colossal
> labour. . . . As a boy I dreamt of the Nile, was reluctant to awake, yet
> brought down my fist on the grained oak door. It would have been hap-
> pier to have been born without a destiny . . . .' (315)

In middle age, Louis half-consciously appears to cling to a dream of a life other than that for which he rather grandiosely feels he has been marked. One cannot help but sense in this notion of destiny a defensive rationale for the successful but pedestrian life in commerce he has so eagerly embraced. The degree of Louis's self-delusion is evident in his pathetically reduced expectations for his future, hoping to "'inherit a chair and a rug; a place in Surrey'" with greenhouses and rare trees and fruits that others "'will envy'" (293).

At the end of *The Waves*, however, Louis's attainment of bourgeois respectability remains incomplete—perhaps, one suspects, deliberately so. In middle age, he has not married, has taken a mistress whose cockney accent conveniently enables him to feel socially superior, and has had an affair with Rhoda, a fellow dreamer and idealist, whom he views as his "'conspirator'" (274). Aware of their temperamental kinship, Bernard admiringly views Louis and Rhoda as "'authentics'" who do not define themselves through their personal relationships:

> 'To be myself (I note) I need the illumination of other people's eyes, and
> therefore cannot be entirely sure what is my self. The authentics, like

Louis, like Rhoda, exist most completely in solitude. They resent illumina-
tion, reduplication. They toss their pictures, once painted, face downward
on the field.' (255)

Unlike Bernard and Susan, Louis's and Rhoda's single states prevent them
from becoming socially integrated through marriage and parenthood; they,
with Neville, are Bernard's "'renegades'" who elicit the disapproval of the
herd by choosing to live apart from it (347).

If in Louis one can see the relinquishing of literary ambition in order to
devote himself to serving the empire and capitalism, Neville is able to sustain his aesthetic orientation as a solitary scholar, an option still possible in
an increasingly mechanized world. Like Rhoda, Neville is deeply susceptible to beauty. Like Louis, he hopes to become a famous poet. At Oxbridge
he writes poetry, which he shows to Bernard, and entertains thoughts of
greatness while watching Percival, whom he loves, lounging by the river:
"'Surely I am a great poet'" (231). As Bernard perceives, however, Neville's
rigorous scholarly temperament ultimately prevents him from attaining
this goal: "'You indulge in no mystifications'" (233).

Showing an early interest in the Latin authors, Neville becomes a metic-
ulous classicist, studying the "'exactitude'" of Latin and its "'well-laid sentences'" (196). Temperamentally Neville appears to be particularly well
suited for a solitary scholar's life. Unlike Bernard, whose curiosity causes
him to welcome contact with others beyond his own class, Neville in his
youthful arrogance exhibits a highly critical, elitist view of humanity generally. While on the train to London as a young man, he realizes that his
aversion to the everyday world in its banality may drive him reluctantly
into the relatively sheltered halls of academe:

> 'Let me at least be honest. Let me denounce this piffling, trifling, self-satisfied
> world; . . . I could shriek aloud at the smug self-satisfaction, at the medioc-
> rity of this world, which breeds horse-dealers with coral ornaments hang-
> ing from their watch-chains. . . . They will drive me in October to take
> refuge in one of the universities, where I shall become a don; . . . It would be
> better to breed horses and live in one of those red villas than to run in and
> out of the skulls of Sophocles and Euripides like a maggot, with a high-
> minded wife, one of those University women. That, however, will be my
> fate. I shall suffer.' (223)

It is never made clear whether Neville in middle age has in fact become a
university don. Unmarried and ostensibly homosexual, he remains in
London, having attained success as a classicist, and is most at his ease
working alone or sitting quietly with a friend or lover by the fire (300).

There is a vestige of the reclusive aesthete in Woolf's characterization of
Neville, whose sensitivity to beauty, preoccupation with Latin authors such as
Catullus and Virgil, and habit of reading French novels evoke the *fin-de-siècle*
traits of Augustus Carmichael in *To the Lighthouse*. As for the aesthetes,
life appears to imitate art for Neville. While walking along a London

street, he views those he passes as figures from Shakespeare and Dante whose roles are predetermined:

> 'Here's the fool, here's the villain, here in a car comes Cleopatra burning on her barge. Here are figures of the damned too, noseless men by the police-court wall, standing with their feet in the fire, howling. This is poetry if we do not write it. They act their parts infallibly, and almost before they open their lips I know what they are going to say, and wait the divine moment when they speak the word that must have been written.' (312)

Although Neville sheds some of his criticalness and exclusivity as he reaches middle age, he remains a recluse—one for whom the loss of Percival and other men he has loved is all the more painful. Realizing that "'Change is no longer possible. We are committed'" (324), Neville indulges in a rather grandiose view of the depth of his understanding of the universe as a way of consoling himself for a life that he senses has not been fully lived, devoted as it has been to scholarship and a series of hopeless loves:

> 'I am merely "Neville" to you, who see the narrow limits of my life and the line it cannot pass. But to myself I am immeasurable; a net whose fibres pass imperceptibly beneath the world. ... I detect, I perceive. Beneath my eyes opens—a book; I see to the bottom; the heart—I see to the depths.' (324)

It is significant that it is a book that opens beneath Neville's eyes; his knowledge of life appears to have arisen from his extensive exposure to literature rather than from direct experience of humanity in its diversity and frequent unseemliness. Like Rhoda and Louis, Neville, as one of Bernard's "'renegades',", remains an outsider, but for different reasons. Held captive in the shell of his self by his idealist's perfectionism, he studies the classics assiduously and nurses the wounds inflicted by unrequited love.

Of the six characters, Bernard has the greatest need for the company of others. As his voice confesses time after time, he is extremely uncomfortable when alone: "'I pine in solitude'" (327). In part, the presence of others satisfies his strong need for companionship and diversion, but more importantly, it provides him with an audience before which he may assume the persona of phrase-maker, teller of stories, commentator on and shaper of reality:

> '. . . I am a natural coiner of words, a blower of bubbles through one thing and another. . . . I conceive myself called upon to provide, some winter's night, a meaning for all my observations—a line that runs from one to another, a summing up that completes. But soliloquies in back streets soon pall. I need an audience.' (255)

Like Rhoda, Bernard's sense of self is fluid; unlike her, he actively seeks out others to help him define who he is. While at college, Bernard and Neville's continuing friendship provides them with the opportunity to shape each other as each seeks to develop an authentic self: "'Let me then create you. (You have done as much for me)'" (233). Bernard comes to believe that individuals are not separate and distinct—"'We are not single'" (221). Furthermore, he feels he has many personae that he assumes based on the circumstances or company in which he finds himself, not to mention the "'unborn selves'" (377) that will never emerge from within. This state of affairs is not entirely satisfactory, as Bernard notes while acknowledging his need for others. The discovery of a solid core that is distinctly Bernard continues to elude him (268).

Very early in life, Bernard assumes what perhaps becomes his most definitive persona—that of the phrasemaker and storyteller. As a schoolboy, he already has a reputation for spinning tales and ordering reality for his companions (200). Envisioning a writer's career for himself, Bernard keeps a notebook in which he methodically records his observations and phrases, and narcissistically imagines how his future biographer will describe him (227). At one point during his college years, Bernard very self-consciously (and humorously) attempts to construct an image of himself as a dashing Byronic figure, "'who, lightly throwing off his cloak, seizes his pen'" and scribbles a letter to the current object of his affection (228). Neville subtly discourages such posturing.

As self-conscious as Bernard appears to be about his story-telling persona, it nonetheless appears to be one that comfortably embodies his natural inclinations. Throughout the novel, Bernard is compelled by his curiosity to investigate life, mixing among others and imagining their private lives in the stories he tells. While at the London dinner for Percival, Bernard cannot help observing the other diners in the restaurant:

> 'There remains . . . the insoluble problem of the solitary man with the eyeglass; of the elderly lady drinking champagne alone. Who and what are these unknown people? I ask. I could make a dozen stories of what he said, of what she said—I can see a dozen pictures.' (275)

Perhaps more than any of Woolf's previous characters, Bernard exhibits a degree of receptivity to the world and to others most reminiscent of Pater's Marius.[9] Both share an irrepressible desire to observe the world around them and to be affected and stimulated by what they see and experience. As Bernard admits, he has "'a steady unquenchable thirst'" for taking in the things around him (221). Unlike Marius, however, there is a spontaneous, undisciplined element in Bernard that makes him liable to distraction and denies him the single-mindedness needed to complete his phrases and stories. Neville comments on his arrival at the restaurant for the dinner for Percival:

> '. . . unlike the rest of us, he comes in without pushing open a door, without knowing that he comes into a room full of strangers. He does not look in the glass. His hair is untidy, but he does not know it. He has no perception that we differ, or that this table is his goal. He hesitates on his way here. Who is that? he asks himself, for he half knows a woman in an opera cloak.' (259)

Bernard the storyteller is as much manipulated by life as he is a manipulator of it in attempting to give it structure and sequence through his stories. For Bernard, more so than for Louis or Neville in their efforts as poets, life is to be the primary subject of his fiction. In his plans as a young man for his novel, Bernard reveals himself to be an aspiring Balzac who hopes to produce his own version of *La comédie humaine*—a multiple-volume work that will encompass "'every known variety of man and woman'" (221). The lives of his friends and acquaintances as well as his own life and experiences are to become fodder for his fiction, as Neville is well aware (222–3). Bernard becomes obsessed with finding the perfect phrase to reflect the moment, the "'true story'" that will accurately delineate the nature of life, which unfortunately still eludes him as an adult (305–6). The rich diversity of life, its innumerable distractions, and his own domestic responsibilities as a husband and father continue to frustrate his effort, preventing him as a writer from achieving the fixity of purpose of the lady writing between the long windows at Elvedon, a scene he has observed with Susan in childhood that haunts him in middle age (343).

For Bernard, the image of the lady writing, like the notion of a "'true'" story explicating the nature of life, comes to be part of something "'beyond and outside our own predicament . . . symbolic, and thus perhaps permanent'" (349).[10] Life, he discovers, is intractable, refusing to allow itself to be encapsulated in any single "true" story. As he reaches middle age, Bernard wearily abandons his search for the perfect phrase, the true story, exhibiting "'distrust'" for "'neat designs of life . . . drawn upon half sheets of notepaper'" (341). Rather, he realizes that one can only experience a momentary sense of coherence in life that may well be illusory, as he feels he does when he decides to attempt a summation of his and his friends' shared lives at the end of *The Waves*: "' . . . something adheres for a moment, has roundness, weight, depth, is completed. This, for the moment, seems to be my life'" (341).

In telling the story of his life among his friends to a chance acquaintance over dinner in a London restaurant at the end of the novel, Bernard realizes that this is the "truest" story he knows, based as it is upon his own experience. And even in telling this story, Bernard is aware of the limits of his knowledge and understanding:

> 'Our friends—how distant, how mute, how seldom visited and little known. And I, too, am dim to my friends and unknown; a phantom, sometimes seen, often not. Life is a dream surely.' (367)[11]

In his maturity, Bernard comes to see that the best one can do as a writer is to look for "'something unbroken'" in "'phrases and fragments'" (361), to attempt to use language to structure one's experience of life in its unruliness and disorder.

No longer intent upon impressing potential readers or listeners with inventive figurative language, Bernard seeks a more serviceable "'little language'" such as that used by lovers and children that is closer to the texture of everyday life (381). As Bernard discovers, the creation of meaning is a human activity that every individual attempts daily: "'it is here, in this little room, that we make whatever day of the week it may be'" (353).[12]

At the end of *The Waves*, Bernard is momentarily tempted to have done with language altogether in the struggle to wrest order from the chaos that is life:

> 'When the storm crosses the marsh and sweeps over me where I lie in the ditch unregarded I need no words. . . . I have done with phrases.
>
> How much better is silence; the coffee-cup, the table. . . . Let me sit here for ever with bare things, this coffee-cup, this knife, this fork, things in themselves, myself being myself.' (382)

Bernard's moment of Mallarméan surrender to the ineffable nature of reality—his wish simply to be, and to experience the things of the world in their quiddity—does not last long, however. Roused by a sense that daybreak is approaching, Bernard feels the rhythmic, wave-like "'eternal renewal'" of daily life (383) calling him back to civilization and the distinctly human task of attempting to define and shape experience, to give form and meaning to our disordered, transient lives:

> 'And in me too the wave rises. . . . I am aware once more of a new desire, something rising beneath me like the proud horse whose rider first spurs and then pulls him back. What enemy do we now perceive advancing against us, you whom I ride now, as we stand pawing this stretch of pavement? It is death. Death is the enemy. It is death against whom I ride with my spear couched and my hair flying back like a young man's, like Percival's, when he galloped in India.' (383)

As an increasingly weary middle-aged married man and father who has long since found a relatively comfortable cranny for himself in the "'machine'" (285) that is twentieth-century life, Bernard is familiar with

> ' . . . satiety and doom; the sense of what is unescapable in our lot; death; the knowledge of limitations; how life is more obdurate than one had thought it.' (363)

Despite this knowledge, Bernard rallies and takes up his spear once again to resume the fight—here, the daily battle against chaos and dissolution.

The central creative activity of the six lives depicted in *The Waves* has been negotiating the relationship between the emerging self and the external world—attempting to evolve a serviceable, reasonably authentic identity while at the same time trying to forge a comfortable, secure framework for one's existence in an indifferent, mechanized world that has little tolerance for the nonconformity of figures such as artists, writers and thinkers. For most of the characters—Rhoda being the obvious exception—these efforts have resulted in a degree of personal compromise that leaves them unfulfilled in significant ways.

As collaborative creators, however, the six characters also manage to forge moments of unity that relieve them, if only fleetingly, of the burden of selfhood, imbuing them with a sense of wholeness. This occurs twice in the novel, once during the dinner for Percival in a London restaurant and many years later at Hampton Court, long after Percival's death:

> 'Now once more,' said Louis, 'as we are about to part, . . . the circle in our blood, broken so often, so sharply, for we are so different, closes in a ring. Something is made. Yes, as we rise . . . we pray, holding in our hands this common feeling, "Do not move, do not let the swing-door cut to pieces the thing that we have made, that globes itself here . . . . Do not move, do not go. Hold it forever."'
>
> 'Let us hold it for one moment,' said Jinny; 'love, hatred, by whatever name we call it, this globe whose walls are made of Percival, of youth and beauty, and something so deep sunk within us that we shall perhaps never make this moment out of one man again.' (275–6)

Although one understands that Woolf intended these moments to be viewed as transcendent ones in which egos and petty differences temporarily dissolve, there is something disturbing in the association of the moments with Percival's presence—either in actuality or in memory—which appears to act as a necessary catalyst to bring them about.

Throughout *The Waves*, relatively little is revealed about Percival—Neville is in love with him, the schoolboys view him as a natural leader, he is handsome, he has a reputation for brutal adherence to the truth, he is "'a great master of the art of living'" (284). Instead, he is frequently imagined by his childhood friends as a martial hero, an imperialist who, had he not died prematurely in a riding accident in India, would have served on the bench, become a military leader condemning "'some monstrous tyranny'," and eventually returned to them (281). Complementing this fantasy of Percival as a formidable colonial administrator and defender of the weak is the religious image of Percival (whose name evokes the knight of the Holy Grail) as a sacrificial Christ-figure with whom the six celebrate a Last Supper in London that they symbolically reenact at the "communion" dinner at Hampton Court several years later. Neville's reaction to the news of Percival's death evokes this image: "'He was thrown. . . . All is over. The lights of the world have gone out'" (280).[13]

For Neville, Percival serves the function of giving the group of six substance; in his absence, the friends are merely "'silhouettes, hollow phantoms'" (259).[14] Observing Percival seating himself next to Susan in the restaurant, Bernard notes how the six then take on "'the sober and confident air of soldiers in the presence of their captain';" they now "'love each other'" and have faith in their "'own endurance'" (260).

Although the placement of Percival in such an influential and inspirational position among his childhood friends is partly the result of Woolf's effort in *The Waves* to pay tribute to her deceased brother Thoby, after whom Percival is in part modeled, Woolf also appears to be suggesting something sinister about the nature of her era. If twentieth-century life—impersonal, mechanized, materialistic, competitive—is inhospitable to difference and thwarts the creative individual's attempts to find self-fulfillment in the expression of his or her creativity, it also breeds in human beings a fundamental insecurity that causes them to seek out forces beyond themselves with which they may identify in order to feel whole and empowered.

In Percival one may see the charismatic, distinctly masculine leader of men in service to the empire, who, like Europe's fascist leaders in the 1930s, has the ability to rally the unfulfilled, the disenchanted, the timid, and the downtrodden around him and enlist them in his cause.[15] As much as they have tried to develop serviceable identities as individuals struggling in an indifferent world, the six childhood friends of *The Waves* nonetheless feel themselves personally lacking in middle age, and so turn to the memory of Percival, the golden youth whose promise of human perfection and mastery is needed to affirm them, even if only momentarily.

CHAPTER NINE

The Years

In 1932, the year following the publication of *The Waves*, Woolf began working on her next novel, which she decided would be written in the realist mode of the earlier *Night and Day*: "I think the next lap ought to be objective, realistic, in the manner of Jane Austen: carrying the story on all the time" (*D*4: 168). In this "lap," however, Woolf wanted to create a new genre—the novel-essay, a form that would combine fiction with exposition. In her prototype, Woolf planned to alternate fictional chapters detailing the lives of an upper middle-class English family from 1800 to 2032 (*P* 9) with essays that would comment upon the issues and events represented in the fictional chapters:

> . . . there are to be millions of ideas but no preaching—history, politics, feminism, art, literature—in short a summing up of all I know, feel, laugh at, despise, like, admire hate & so on. (*D*4: 152)

By the end of 1932, Woolf had completed the first five chapters and six essays of her new work, which she initially entitled *The Pargiters* after the surname of the family whose members' lives she intended to trace.[1]

By early February of the following year, however, Woolf decided to excise the essays from her new novel: "I'm leaving out the interchapters—compacting them in the text" (*D*4: 146).[2] In his introduction to *The Pargiters*, first published in 1977, Mitchell Leaska surmises that Woolf would have found it difficult to sustain "a brand of rhetoric alien to her artistic temperament" (vii) in the essays. The five fictional chapters that remained would eventually be revised to become the 1880 chapter of the final work entitled *The Years* (1937).[3] Having eliminated the essays, Woolf set herself a new challenge, that of weaving the polemics of the essays into the fabric of fiction: "I mean intellectual argument in the form of art" (*D*4: 161). That Woolf believed that she had succeeded is evident in her own description of *The Pargiters*' fiction as "dangerously near propaganda" in her diary entry for April 13, 1935 (*D*4: 300).

For *The Years*, based upon *The Pargiters*, raises a number of issues that continued to concern Woolf in later life as well as during her earliest years as a novelist. Here, as in *The Voyage Out* and *The Waves*, Woolf continues her exploration of the nature of identity, this time within the context of the extended family—how it forms or eludes formation, how it occasionally merges with the identities of others, how it resists attempts to fix it, how it seeks its own dissolution. Like *To the Lighthouse*, *Orlando* and *The Waves*, the novel also concerns itself with time—Bergsonian *durée*, or mind time, as opposed to clock time, the experience of passing time, and the relationships between the past, memory and the present moment—here, in the minds of three generations of Pargiters over a period of fifty years.

As the excised essays reveal, however, *The Years* is especially concerned with social arrangements and institutions—in particular, the class system and the patriarchal Victorian family—and how they impinge upon the development of individual family members, particularly girls and women. Like *Jacob's Room* and *The Waves*, the novel seeks to reveal how social circumstances, mores and expectations affect individual lives, confining experience, suppressing or distorting desires, and curbing potentials. In this regard, the novel functions as a palimpsest containing observations and arguments made earlier in *A Room of One's Own* and, later, in *Three Guineas*, the latter of which, with *The Years*, Woolf felt to be "one book" (qtd. in Marcus, *Art & Anger* 113).

When read from this perspective, *The Years* reveals some of the more powerful social factors inhibiting aesthetic creativity in both sexes during the period treated by the novel. As in *Jacob's Room* and *The Waves*, the novel's cast of main characters does not include a practicing artist, novelist or poet— the dynamics of creativity are not a central concern of *The Years* — but several characters from the different Pargiter generations display inherent aesthetic talents or inclinations that might have flourished in a more nurturing climate. Not surprisingly, the older generation of Pargiters appears to suffer the restrictive effects of gender expectations more severely than the more recent ones.

As sons of Colonel Pargiter, the Victorian patriarch who served the empire in India for many years, Eleanor's brothers are subtly pressured to follow in his footsteps by pursuing careers in the army. Edward's early promise as a scholar has exempted him from this fate, and Colonel Pargiter takes pride in the aspiring classicist whose studies at Oxford he subsidizes. Eleanor must intervene on behalf of her older brother Morris, convincing her father to let him pursue the law, for which he has a "passion" (110). Martin, the youngest son, is not so fortunate, however. He is forced to join the army, where he serves in India and attains the rank of captain. Back in England after having completed his service, which he "'loathed,'" Martin acknowledges to his cousin Sara that he would much rather have become an architect (230).

That Martin's desire to be an architect was not just an idle fancy is made clear by his serious interest in the subject and his visceral response to the monumental buildings surrounding him in London. As he looks up at the dome of St. Paul's, he senses "something moving in his body in harmony with the building" (227). At home in his flat he is annoyed to discover that a friend has borrowed his biography of Sir Christopher Wren. Martin's aesthetic interests extend beyond architecture to include painting as well. While attending a dinner party at his cousin Kitty's in London, he notes the "famous Gainsborough" (252) in the dining room, and decides that the attractive Canaletto hanging in the stairwell is a copy. While strolling through Hyde Park with Sara on a fine spring day, he is taken by its "urbanity . . . the sweep and curve and composition of the scene" (240–1).

Although the novel does not reveal what Martin has been doing professionally, if anything, since having left the army, he appears to be quite comfortable financially, and seems to identify with his father in his concern for managing his financial affairs (224). As he ages, however, Martin also begins to exhibit the loneliness, the sense of being "out of it all" (5) that the retired Colonel experiences in the opening chapter of *The Years*. Soon a widower at loose ends, the Colonel wants to tell his daughter Eleanor about his long-time mistress Mira, who makes him feel wanted, but senses she would not welcome the news. In middle age, Martin still has not married, despite his fondness for women and children, indulging instead in a series of flirtations and affairs that he breaks off as soon as his lover becomes possessive or he becomes bored. One senses in him fear of becoming entrapped in an institution he knows all too well, one that affords its members very little freedom, privacy or honesty. Recalling his childhood among his family in Abercorn Terrace, Martin muses, "It was an abominable system . . . family life . . . . all those different people had lived, boxed up together, telling lies" (222–3).

To a lesser degree, his older brother Edward's life exhibits unfulfilled potential as well. Of the major characters in *The Years*, Edward's work as a critic and translator of Greek drama brings him closest to leading a writer's or artist's life. A fellow at Oxford, he is "at the top of his tree" (200) as a scholar by the time he has reached middle age. Personable and handsome, he has not only brought honor to his family by his scholarly success; he has also provided a spouse for his younger sister Millie in his old college friend Hugh Gibbs.

Already at this stage of his life, however, Edward senses opportunities lost, talents squandered. While reading his translation of *Antigone*, his cousin Sara recalls visiting him at Oxford, where he had expressed regret for his "'wasted youth'" (135). There is the suggestion that had his education and circumstances been otherwise, he might have become a poet. In *The Pargiters*, Edward as a third-year undergraduate attempts to write a poem to his cousin Kitty Malone, with whom he is in love, but his rigorous training as a classicist inhibits him:

> . . . the Greek language, the Greek metres were in his mind; & the first lines of his poem [*were, to*] would have seemed, to a critic, more like Greek than English. There was a tightness, a constraint about them. (*P* 69)[4]

In a fit of despair at his seeming lack of ability as a poet, he crumples the sheet and tosses it into the wastebasket.

Rejected in his youth by Kitty, who, being the daughter of an Oxford don, does not want to marry a future one, Edward never marries. As Lady Lasswade, Kitty observes him years later at the opera in London, "intellectual, handsome and a little remote" as he listens to the orchestra (183). By the time he appears at an advanced age at Delia's party, he strikes North as "established. Glazed over with the smooth glossy varnish" of the professional (407). More tellingly, however, he also looks like a desiccated insect that has been reduced to a hollow shell and wings (405). Later at the same party, Eleanor overhears Edward telling North that he would have liked to be something other than a classicist (427). Although successful as a scholar, Edward to a certain extent appears to be a victim of the cluster of peculiarly male values and ways of thinking inculcated at the universities. The rigor of his Oxford training in the classics has impeded his creativity; the inflexibility of the personality crystallized there has rendered him unable to recover from an early rejection and live a more fulfilled life in intimate relationship to another.[5]

The creativity and personal growth of Edward's sisters are also inhibited by gender-related factors. Of the four, Delia and Rose initially appear to hold the greatest promise for asserting their individual identities. Critical, restless, and frequently fantasizing a future role for herself as a kind of Maude Gonne sharing platforms with Parnell to champion the cause of Irish nationalism, Delia chafes against the restrictions imposed upon young women of her class. Many years later, having traded in her radical dreams for security and seeming contentment as the wife of a conservative Anglo-Irish country squire, she is still capable of declaring her girlhood at Abercorn Terrace as having been "'Hell'" (417).[6]

In her childhood fantasies, Rose, the youngest sister, named after her invalid mother, understandably identifies with the power of her father the colonel, imagining herself charging across the Indian plains on horseback: "'I am Pargiter of Pargiter's Horse . . . riding to the rescue!'" (27). As an adult, Rose becomes an ardent suffragette, leading a threadbare existence moving from one seedy lodging to another, speaking at rallies, throwing bricks through windows and being sent to prison. If anything, her experience of family life at Abercorn Terrace has kept her purposely rootless, seeking a broader, more empowering identity as a member of the nation's extended family of social reformers.

In *The Pargiters*, Woolf gives Delia and Millie artistic interests and ambitions. Delia, who plays the violin, wants to study music in Germany; Millie sketches and paints. As Woolf argues in the essay accompanying the first chapter, the education of brothers in the late 1800s always received priority over that of their sisters, most of whom had to forego formal education of any kind: "With three sons to educate, Captain Pargiter might reasonably have said, 'My dear, I would if I could—but just look as these

bills!'" (*P* 28). Millie's formal training as an artist would also have met a
second obstacle:

> ... though it would have been possible for her to go to the Slade (the
> Slade was opened to women in 18—), painting at the Slade meant paint-
> ing from the nude. ... because it was unthinkable that a girl <an English
> lady> should see a naked man, Captain Pargiter did not like the idea.
> (*P* 29–30)[7]

The most developed of the characters in *The Years*, Eleanor falls into the
role of the unmarried oldest sister who dutifully cares for her aging father
and maintains the family household.[8] At Delia's party, North wonders why
his aunt has never married: "Sacrificed to the family, he supposed—old
Grandpapa without any fingers" (372). A male bus rider mentally characterizes her as

> ... a well-known type; with a bag; philanthropic; well nourished; a spin-
> ster; a virgin; like all the women of her class, cold; her passions had never
> been touched . . . . (102)

To a certain extent, the characterization is apt, as Eleanor occupies her free
time visiting the sick, attending committee meetings, and eventually reno-
vating and renting out housing that she has marked with a terracotta sun-
flower plaque, which she had intended "to signify flowers, fields in the
heart of London," that has since "cracked" (101).

In the first chapter of *The Pargiters*, Eleanor's youthful plans for urban
rehabilitation are even more extensive, if naïve:

> '[*I think*] I should take a room, somewhere [*in quite*] <but in> a poor
> neighborhood: & [*& then*] I [*should get to know the people*]; & [*then*]
> I['d] pull down all these awful [*little*] slums &—well, start things fresh,
> [*in a better system.*]—if I had the money' (*P* 23)

As her experience maintaining the property on Peter Street teaches her,
such a project would be far from simple. But Eleanor's interest in social
work and urban renewal is genuine; what prevents her from doing more
are family obligations, her lack of money, and her lack of influence and
political power as a daughter of a retired army officer.

Such practical work appears to be Eleanor's natural bent, but she has
broader interests that she can only begin to explore once she is released
from domestic responsibilities by her father's death and the sale of the family
house. She reads the French historian and critic Ernest Renan and begins to
travel widely, first, on the continent; later, to India, with plans to visit
China as well. More and more Eleanor recognizes England's smallness
(199), becoming increasingly interested in other cultures and in a "New
World" first mentioned in Sara's ironic toast following a night raid on
London during the war. She longs for this world to materialize, hoping it
will provide greater liberty and the opportunity to "live adventurously,
wholly, not like cripples in a cave" (297). Eleanor reveals herself to be a

visionary of sorts, longing for a world free of the strife and limitations she has experienced in her own life.

As for the element of coldness in the stereotype of the philanthropic Victorian spinster, it appears that Eleanor's sexuality has indeed been repressed at an early age. In middle age, though, she recognizes the man she would have liked to marry in Renny, the French scientist who has married her younger cousin Maggie:

> She recognised a feeling which she had never felt. . . . For a moment she resented the passage of time and the accidents of life which had swept her away—from all that, she said to herself. (299)

Even as an old woman at Delia's party, she thinks aloud, "'If I'd known Renny when I was young . . .'" (386). The sexual impulse appears to have surfaced belatedly in Eleanor, but like so many women of her generation, she cannot fully acknowledge it for what it is, relegating it half-consciously to the realm of "'all that'."

Although Eleanor's life has been concerned primarily with the welfare of others rather than with aesthetic creativity, she shares with several of Woolf's major artist-figures—Lily Briscoe, Bernard, and Miss La Trobe, for example—a desire to escape the confines of individual identity and attain a deeper sense of wholeness and fulfillment by merging her identity with those of others. Her selflessness is evident early in the novel while attending a committee meeting, where her sense of her own individuality momentarily recedes as she focuses her attention on those seated around the table: "she was not anybody at all" (95). While considering her life many years later at Delia's party, Eleanor concludes that it has consisted of the lives of her family members and friends—"my father's; Morris's; my friends' lives; Nicholas's" (367). As do Rachel, Terence, and St. John at different moments in *The Voyage Out*, Eleanor senses a unifying pattern underlying reality and ordering experience. Listening to her friend Nicholas, she correctly anticipates his next sentence, and wonders,

> . . . Does everything then come over again a little differently? . . . If so, is there a pattern; a theme, recurring, like music; half remembered, half foreseen? . . . a gigantic pattern, momentarily perceptible? (369)

At the end of the novel, Eleanor experiences great joy simply in being a part of her circle of family and friends, and tries to encompass this momentary feeling of shared personal history and identity:

> She held her hands hollowed; she felt that she wanted to enclose the present moment; to make it stay; to fill it fuller and fuller, with the past, the present and the future, until it shone, whole, bright, deep with understanding. (428)

Woolf gives this sense of unity physical embodiment in the final scene of the novel, where Sara and Maggie observe the older generation of Pargiter brothers and sisters caught standing together for a moment before a window suffused with the light of approaching day:

> The group in the window, the men in their black-and-white evening dress, the women in their crimsons, golds and silvers, wore a statuesque look for a moment, as if they were carved in stone. Their dresses fell in stiff sculptured folds. Then they moved; they changed their attitudes; they began to talk. (432–3)

In this tableau-like rendering, the older Pargiters momentarily attain mythic proportions, partaking of eternity as monumental sculptures. Here, the creation of collectivity appears to assume the enduring quality of art. The brothers and sisters not only participate in this act of creation, but are themselves the work of art they have forged.[9]

The younger generation of Pargiters, however, has a far more difficult time creating this sense of unity among themselves. As young adults, their lives and minds are brutally altered by the experience of war—Sara and Maggie endure night raids in London while North enlists in the army. Maggie manages to escape the hopelessness and bitterness of her impoverished life in London through her marriage to Renny, an *émigré* French scientist and critic of the war who feels painfully compromised as a result of his munitions work on behalf of the British army. Rootless, physically deformed, highly imaginative, and cynical, Sara becomes a sardonic commentator upon her times. Preparing tea for North before he leaves for the front, she asks how much sugar "'a lieutenant in His Majesty's Royal Regiment of Rat-catchers'" wants (314).

In their late thirties at the time the novel ends, Peggy and North, sister and brother, comprise the youngest generation of Pargiters presented in the novel, and are portrayed as seriously alienated observers of the life around them. Peggy's work as a physician constantly confronts her with human suffering and degradation. Although she continually experiences feelings of despair, she believes that the professions are teaching her generation "not to live; not to feel; to make money, always money" (355). Describing herself as "hard, cold; in a groove already; merely a doctor" (354), Peggy negotiates her relationship to the external world by defensively assuming the role of scientific observer: "Take notes and the pain goes" (351). At times she has a vision of a realm of being which promises "real laughter, real happiness," and the world is made "whole, vast, and free" (390), but she cannot describe it successfully to others or sustain it for long. Rather, her bitterness and disillusionment resurface, causing her to disparage her own existence as well as that of her brother, whom she assumes will marry, start a family, and then "'Make money. Write little books to make money'" (390).

This pronouncement pains North particularly, as he has entertained hopes of becoming a writer. During his boyhood, he and Sara used to write "purple passages" (322) which they shared with each other. Having also written poetry in his younger years, North feels moved to write it again while ringing Sara's doorbell in her decaying neighborhood following his return from Africa (311). Having spent many solitary years on an African sheep ranch, North feels newly alienated in London, discovering himself "outside the doors of strange houses" and sensing he is "no one and nowhere in particular" (311). He also has not decided whether to remain in London or return to Africa. At Delia's party, which he, Sara and Peggy have all resisted attending, North repeatedly feels himself to be an "outsider" (403), much as does his uncle Martin after having completed his service to the empire in India.

Like his sister Peggy, North attempts to conquer his alienation by observing others, and, in his case, typing them, whether it is his wealthy aunt Kitty or the men whom he identifies at the party as having been educated in public schools and at Oxbridge (404). He writes off the party guests and his countrymen generally as being obsessed with "'money and politics'," a "stock" response that he has already given "twenty times" (400) to those who have asked how he finds England after his absence. Only Edward, who has "something behind that mask . . . . The past? Poetry?" seems to hold any promise of meaningful communication for him (408).[10]

North's difficulties appear to be those of any number of war veterans who have been traumatized by what they have seen and experienced on the battlefield—"he had been in the trenches; he had seen men killed" (404)—subsequently finding everyday society unbearable and retreating to the solitude of the wilderness, where they remain for years. North's return to London represents an attempt to determine whether he can live among his kind again. He understands the validity of his sister's wish to "live differently" (422), and himself longs for a "different life" that would allow him to retain his identity while simultaneously partaking of a broader one:

> To keep the emblems and tokens of North Pargiter . . . but at the same time spread out, make a new ripple in human consciousness, be the bubble and the stream, the stream and the bubble—myself and the world together . . . . Anonymously . . . . (410)[11]

Ultimately, however, North remains ambivalent about returning to the hectic, mechanized culture that is now twentieth-century England; he considers "silence and solitude . . . the only element in which the mind is free now" (424).

Of the three Pargiter women of the younger generations, Peggy, Maggie, and Sara, the latter is all too well acquainted with that state. Of the novel's major characters, Sara is perhaps the most marginalized as well as the most imaginative. Described as "sallow, angular and plain" (173) and deformed in early childhood by a fall, Sara does not have the physical desirability or the dowry to attract a husband. Instead, she moves from one boardinghouse to another in poor London neighborhoods, drawing upon her meager inheritance, and living "'in dreams . . . alone'" (370). As a young girl, Sara already exhibits an overactive imagination, weaving fantasies around sights, occurrences or the words of others and producing them aloud in language ranging from the lyrical to the baldly satiric. Watching a boy and girl at a garden party across the way from her bedroom window, she projects a hackneyed version of a romantic encounter in which a young swain confronts his beloved with a piece of his "'broken heart'" found on the ground (134).

As she grows older, Sara spends her days singing popular songs while accompanying herself on the piano, reciting poetry, reading widely in literature, observing the street life beneath her window, daydreaming in her chair and spinning fantasies aloud in the presence of others. In her imaginative exuberance, her echolalia and her utter disregard for propriety in pronouncing her thoughts, Sara appears to be dangerously near madness. The incisive, acerbic nature of her observations about others and life generally makes her appear a modern-day Cassandra, informing her companions that all is not well in their world. Having grown to love solitude, Sara agrees to accompany North to Delia's party only with the greatest reluctance. Her chief source of emotional sustenance is her intimacy with Nicholas, Renny's friend and a Polish *émigré* intellectual who is homosexual: "'I love him!'" she declares simply to North (324). Displaying a disarming mixture of childlike innocence and acute intelligence, Sara maintains her childish demeanor well into middle age; North describes her "'sitting on the edge of her chair . . . with a smudge on her face, swinging her foot up and down'" (324).

In Sara one may see a woman of great imaginativeness marginalized by her plainness, her deformity, her poverty, her lack of formal education, and her unusually high intelligence. There appears to be no place for a woman of Sara's temperament and gifts in her culture; had she been born in an earlier age, she would most likely have been labeled mad and put in an asylum. There is something of the Ivory Tower dreamer in her, but her unruly imagination and her lack of the discipline needed to sustain aesthetic creativity prevent her from becoming a poet, writer, or artist.

Like a number of Woolf's earlier novels, *The Years* also alludes to the tradition of the Ivory Tower aesthete. Woolf was working on the manuscript for the novel during the mid-1930s at a time when, as was noted earlier, Bloomsbury and Woolf in particular unjustly came under attack for supposedly being aesthetes who held themselves aloof from the pressing social and political concerns of the day.[12] The completed novel contains vestiges of the Ivory Tower aesthete in the generally unfavorable characterizations of two minor figures—Ashley, who is given no first name, and Tony Ashton, both of whom are Oxford friends of Edward.

As a rather supercilious undergraduate vying with Edward's other friends for his affection, Ashley makes his only appearance early in the novel as he interrupts Edward and Gibbs in Edward's rooms while the two are talking about country life:

> He was the very opposite of Gibbs. He was neither tall nor short, neither dark nor fair. But he was not negligible—far from it. It was partly the way

he moved, as if chair and table rayed out some influence which he could feel by means of some invisible antennae, or whiskers, like a cat. Now he sank down, cautiously, gingerly, and looked at the table and half read a line in a book. (52–3)

Edward characterizes Ashley as one who "could only talk about books" (53). Ashley is smitten by Edward's handsome features—"like a Greek boy" (54), but also perplexed by Edward's tolerance for Gibbs, "that clumsy brute . . . who always seemed to smell of beer and horses" (54). Correspondingly, Gibbs views Ashley as a "dirty little swine" who begins to "give himself airs" at his expense (54). The scene ends with Edward announcing his intention to go to bed, entering his bedroom and locking the door behind him. Gibbs leaves, but Ashley tries to get Edward to come out by calling him twice and rattling the door handle. Edward, listening behind the door, concludes that there will be a great "'row'" (56) with Ashley the next day as he hears him depart.

In the original version of this scene in *The Pargiters*, Ashley is named Jasper Jevons, and is described as "a smallish pale young man, whose physique obviously unfitted him for any game or any sport. Yet he moved beautifully" (*P* 71–2). Curiously, in the essay accompanying the chapter he is referred to as Tony Ashton, whose affection for Edward is rendered more problematic: "Tony not only loved him but objected to his loving anybody else. . . . Tony's love for him conflicted with the peculiar passion which he had for Kitty Malone" (*P* 82).

In *The Years*, Tony Ashton appears as another undergraduate, one who occasionally joins the students entertained by Kitty's father at home. Kitty dislikes him, noting that unlike those undergraduates, who are in the habit of falling in love with her, Ashton appears to be more interested in her cousin: "He always seemed to be cross-examining her about Edward" (62). In the original version in *The Pargiters*, Ashton is rendered a more sinister figure: "No, she did not like Tony Ashton. [*He was like a snake.*] There was something cold & clammy about him. <He was like a snake.>" (*P* 97). The essay accompanying the chapter is even more explicit in describing Kitty's aversion:

> . . . there was a coldness in his glance which led her to call him 'snaky'— meaning by that, that her body and his body had so little natural attraction for each other that they were singularly at ease. And yet, some stimulus was so lacking, that talking to Tony, in spite of her sympathy, left her cold. She would never be intimate with him, never wholly at her ease . . . . (*P* 116)

Later in *The Years*, Tony Ashton resurfaces at Kitty's London dinner party, where he is referred to as the man who has been lecturing on French poetry—specifically, Mallarmé—at Mortimer House in London (257, 261). Kitty recalls Edward and Ashton at Oxford, Ashton appearing a "snob on the surface; underneath a scholar" (261).

Although the portraits of Ashley and particularly Ashton are pared down in *The Years*, neither is particularly attractive, and Woolf appears to allude to their homosexuality in the novel with a curious indirection that one does not find in her portrayal of Neville, a sympathetically rendered homosexual scholar and one of the main characters in *The Waves*. One might speculate that in these curtailed portrayals, Woolf was raising and dismissing the homosexual aesthete in an effort to distance herself from the kinds of charges that had been leveled against her and Bloomsbury writers such as Strachey and Forster over the years.[13] With the writing of *Between the Acts*, the homosexual aesthete reemerges more fully rendered in the character of William Dodge, who is portrayed more favorably, although with some criticalness.

Despite the cameo appearances of aesthetes in *The Years*, the novel remains primarily concerned with the effects of social conditions and institutions such as the family upon individuals, their identities and their efforts to find meaning and fulfillment in life. As in Woolf's other later novels, the modern world in which they find themselves is not particularly hospitable to individuals and their needs. For that matter, neither is life generally. In the tradition of naturalist fiction, *The Years* provides numerous glimpses of urban poverty and depravity, ranging from the exhibitionist whom young Rose encounters one evening at the end of her supposedly respectable street to the drunkenness and abuse to be observed daily in Maggie and Sara's decaying neighborhood. The lives of servants such as Crosby are also rendered more fully, albeit condescendingly, in *The Years* than in any other of Woolf's novels.

As if to provide an overabundance of metaphors for the times, the novel is replete with images of deformity and disfiguration ranging from those incurred in service to the empire—Colonel Pargiter's missing fingers, lost in "the Mutiny" (13), and Uncle Horace's glass eye—to those reflecting sexual exploitation, such as the noselessness of an ostensibly syphilitic woman selling violets outside the Inns of Court. The physical degeneration of illness and aging is presented as yet another horror to be endured universally. To her children, the ailing elder Rose Pargiter is "soft, decayed but everlasting" (22).[14] Old Mrs. Chinnery sits in her wheelchair, her "hawk-like nose . . . curved in her shrivelled cheeks" below an infected eyelid (209).

The alienation of modern life is reflected in Crosby's mental preparations for doing daily "battle" in the shops along the High Street with already aching legs (304). In Sara's Cassandra-like utterances, one hears a condemnation of postindustrial urban life that echoes *The Waste Land*: "'Polluted city, unbelieving city, city of dead fish and worn-out frying-pans'" (340). In her mind, Peggy notes the rise of totalitarianism, one of the horrors characteristic of her times:

> On every placard at every street corner was Death; or worse—tyranny; brutality; torture; the fall of civilisation; the end of freedom. We here, she thought, are only sheltering under a leaf, which will be destroyed. (388)

As will be seen, this apocalyptic sense of the approaching end of time is shared by Isa Oliver, William Dodge, and their generation in *Between the Acts*, Woolf's last novel. In *The Years*, however, the ties of kinship and friendship, troubling and destructive though they frequently may be, are still capable of providing individuals like Eleanor Pargiter and her contemporaries with enduring moments of stability, wholeness, and hope in a troubled world, as the new day described in the novel's closing sentence suggests: "The sun had risen, and the sky above the houses wore an air of extraordinary beauty, simplicity and peace" (435).[15]

CHAPTER TEN

Between the Acts

Woolf's last novel, *Between the Acts*, published in 1941 without the final revision it would have received had she lived, is set in "a remote village in the very heart of England" (*BA* 16) on a June day in 1939. Throughout the novel are references to the particularly dry summer; the novel opens with a discussion in which the characters express their dismay that plans to bring a water line to the village have been held up. On more than one occasion, Isa Oliver, a relatively young woman in a troubled marriage, expresses her longing for water (66, 67, 104). In this novel, Woolf presents her version of Eliot's view of modern life as a parched wasteland, replete with alienated individuals, an atrophying collective identity, and an increasingly mechanistic culture which threatens to dissolve what tenuous bonds remain between the individuals who inhabit it.[1]

Among the main characters, Bart Oliver, the aging head of gentry he himself characterizes as "degenerate" (49), and his fragile widowed sister, Lucy Swithin, represent the survivors of an older order which is rapidly fading in England, even in its supposedly secluded countryside.[2] This last bastion of English indigenousness has been invaded by "a number of unattached floating residents" (75) brought to the area by the construction of a car factory and an airfield. Vacation bungalows and red brick villas, built by the urban *nouveaux riches*, have sprung up in age-old cornfields, much to the dismay of long-time residents whose families have lived on the land for centuries. The arrival of new (and distinctly twentieth-century) amusements such as dog tracks and movie theaters has further weakened the social ties between individuals, as has the advent of modern modes of transportation in the countryside. The recently expanded route of Mitchell's delivery boy, outfitted with a motorcycle, for example, no longer affords time for small talk with the kitchen staff (31).

The times have become increasingly secular. The Reverend Streatfield, curate of the local parish, complains about deepening absenteeism at church services, blaming "the motor bike, the motor bus, and the movies" (75). What was once a pre-Reformation chapel in the Olivers' house, Pointz Hall, has long since been a larder. The times have also become increasingly violent. Isa reads with horror a newspaper account of a gang rape in the Whitehall barracks (20), while Giles, her husband, is infuriated by news of the latest slaughter in the ugly civil war being won by the fascists in Spain (46).[3] The threat of an all-encompassing world war hangs like a pall over the thoughts of Isa's generation, which is fully aware that it may have no future. As William Dodge remarks, "'The doom of sudden death hanging over us . . . . There's no retreating and advancing . . . for us,'" nor for the older generation (114).[4]

The sense of stasis brought on by the threat of war is mirrored in widespread cultural degeneration. Bart Oliver is still able to quote from Byron's poetry, to which his mother introduced him (5), and sister Lucy continues to be an avid reader, beginning and ending her day with pages from Wells's *Outline of History.* Isa's generation, however, is "book-shy" (19); newspapers substitute for books in its world (20). The "shilling shockers" left behind by weekend visitors now clutter the shelves of the Oliver library, crowding out the classics (16). Guest Mrs. Ralph Manresa's populist posturings reflect the prevailing anti-intellectualism of the times (142). There is a growing suspiciousness of creative or artistic endeavor, which causes Dodge to deny twice that he is an artist and Isa to conceal her poetry from her husband by recording it in a bound volume that resembles an account ledger (15).[5]

Complementing the cultural decline are corresponding tendencies to utilize art as a form of escape or to compartmentalize it by distancing it from everyday life. Trapped in a troubled marriage, Isa is compared to "a captive balloon," locked "by a myriad of hair-thin ties into domesticity," a domesticity she "loathed" (19). She habitually constructs poetic phrases, which she utters under her breath, particularly in times of stress. A number of the phrases reflects a desire to escape into the empyrean in the manner of the Symbolist poets:

'Where we know not, where we go not, neither know nor care . . . . Flying, rushing through the ambient, incandescent, summer silent . . . [air].' (15)[6]

At other moments, her poetic utterances reflect a longing for the dissolution of death: "'That the waters should cover me . . . of the wishing well'" (103). It is significant that so much of her phrase-making arises from the pain of her imprisonment in a deeply frustrating role. One wonders whether her frustration has spurred her to produce poetry as an emotional release from the tensions of her life—whether her creativity would persist were her personal life more satisfactory. Isa's imaginative phrase-making provides her with a private world apart from that of her life with her husband and children. As the concealment of her recorded poetry demonstrates, Isa knows well that Giles would not approve of this activity, which most likely would exacerbate the tensions in their strained marriage.

William Dodge's alienation is of a different order than Isa's. His "twisted face" (37) reflects the defensive posture of one who anticipates scorn from those he meets. His homosexuality has also bred in him a poisonous self-contempt; in his mind, he characterizes himself as "'a half-man . . . a flickering, mind-divided little snake in the grass'" (73).[7] Manresa presents him as an artist, but he denies the vocation twice in the company of the Olivers. Dodge's refuge from the slings and arrows of social interaction is the realm of the beautiful. He shows a connoisseur's appreciation for old china, and finds himself drawn to the portrait of the unknown lady in the dining room during lunch with the Olivers and Manresa. Isa's "glass green eyes" and handsome figure make him wish to see her "against an arum lily or a vine" (105). Of the main characters, Dodge appears most moved by the beauty of the pageant in its natural setting:

> The children; the pilgrims; behind the pilgrims the trees, and behind them the fields—the beauty of the visible world took his breath away. (82)

As he asks himself in response to Mrs. Swithin, "Beauty—isn't that enough?" (82). Despite the seemingly *avant-garde* modernity of his casual dress, Dodge nonetheless represents the dwindling breed of aesthetes despised by the socially engaged young British writers of the 1930s who so troubled Woolf herself.

If aesthetic sensibility and the beautiful provide a refuge for individuals such as Dodge, they are suspect by others. Giles, Isa's stockbroker husband, is irritated by Dodge's homosexuality and his connoisseur's appreciativeness; for him, Dodge is "a teaser and twitcher; a fingerer of sensations" (60).[8] Giles is also a most reluctant spectator of the village's annual pageant, likening himself rather melodramatically to the enchained Prometheus, "manacled to a rock . . . forced passively to behold indescribable horror" (60). His rigid posture while seated in the audience (133) suggests his resistance to the pageant's attempts to move him as well as the frustration of enforced physical inactivity.

The quintessential modern man of affairs (in both senses of the word), Giles exhibits little patience for amateur theatrical productions, attending them only out of a sense of duty. The other attendees at the pageant are much more interested in the day's entertainment, but they, too, are wary of an art form that threatens to break out of its conventional boundaries and involve them in it. For them, art such as the drama is something to be appreciated, but from a discreet, intellectually informed vantage point. Members of the audience continually consult their programs to determine what will be represented in the next scene. The subject of the drama is often overshadowed by the delighted recognition of a seemingly unlikely villager cast in the character of a historical figure:

> From behind the bushes issued Queen Elizabeth—Eliza Clark, licensed to sell tobacco. Could she be Mrs. Clark of the village shop? She was splendidly made up. (83)

Such eager identifications serve to reinforce the artifice of the drama. Miss La Trobe's effort to engage the audience as participants at the end of the pageant involves violating the imaginary boundaries of the area designated as the stage by sending her actors romping into the audience armed with mirrors and other reflecting surfaces. Many among the audience are immediately affronted: "So that was her little game! To show us up, as we are, here and now" (186). Others, like Manresa, are not at all annoyed by the intrusion of art into their personal space; Manresa uses the reflecting surface directed at her as a mirror, and powders her nose. For Manresa, the artifice of theatricality and daily life itself are intricately intertwined; she sees no need to keep them separate, and irritates a number of friends and acquaintances by her consistently contrived behavior calculated for effect.

Although Bart Oliver is sensitive to La Trobe's intent in staging the final "act" of the pageant, he, like so many others, also turns away from the mirrors. For him, as for most of the gentry, art is something that must be objectified before it can be properly appreciated. Of the two portraits in his dining room, Bart views that of his robust ancestor with his horse as primarily a conversation piece. The portrait of the unknown lady, however, was "a picture:"

> In her yellow robe, leaning, with a pillar to support her, a silver arrow in her hand, and a feather in her hair, she led the eye up, down, from the curve to the straight, through glades of greenery and shades of silver, dun and rose into silence. (36)

The absence of a familiar subject in conjunction with the artist's cool, stylized treatment creates a strangeness that is ultimately mysterious. The content of the portrait becomes a matter of curved and straight lines and shades of muted colors that leave the viewer in an awed state of silent contemplation. For Bart, this is the true nature of art—unfamiliar, abstract, mysterious, and otherworldly, a view that one would not be surprised to find in a man of his time and background. The narrator's Keatsian description of an alabaster vase, placed in the house's "heart" and containing "the still, distilled essence of emptiness, silence" (37) echoes this view of the art object. Woolf sees the desire to keep art apart from life, or at least at arm's length from one's immediate experience, as a distinctly modern affliction—one that Miss La Trobe arduously seeks to overcome in the production of the pageant she has written. In the relationship of La Trobe to her art, the two tendencies noted earlier in Woolf's portrayals of artist-figures and their work reach their extremes.

Of all the practicing artists depicted in Woolf's fiction, La Trobe is undoubtedly the definitive outsider.[9] Members of the audience speculate about her mysterious origins:

> With that name she wasn't presumably pure English. From the Channel Islands perhaps? Only her eyes and something about her always made Mrs. Bingham suspect that she had Russian blood in her. (57–8)

Like her questionable origins, La Trobe's past is largely unknown and the subject of rumors: she had a tea shop, which failed; she had embarked on an acting career, which had also failed. Her sexual orientation is unclear and the subject of speculation; the villagers have heard that she had shared a cottage with an actress before they "quarrelled" (58). Her "abrupt manner and stocky figure" (63) reinforce her ambiguous sexual identity. Using martial imagery, the narrator likens her to "a commander pacing his deck" (62), issuing commands to his subordinates.

La Trobe also embodies Woolf's ideal of anonymity for artists and writers. Throughout the pageant, she conceals herself behind one of the trees, barking orders and prompting her actors. At the end of the pageant she refuses to disclose herself until most of the audience has departed. Bart discourages Lucy from thanking La Trobe, accurately sensing that she does not seek public acknowledgment of her artistry; rather, she prefers "darkness in the mud; a whisky and soda at the pub" (203). If La Trobe guards her anonymity closely, she also rejects any claims to superiority because of her status as an artist; the voice on the megaphone does not spare artists and intellectuals in its comments about the poverty of human nature:

> Don't hide among rags. Or let our cloth protect us. Or for the matter of that book learning; or skilful practice on pianos; or laying on of paint. (187)

Marginalized by her mysterious origins, her questionable background and her ambiguous sexual orientation, La Trobe is Woolf's best example of the anonymous outsider artist in her novels.

At the same time, though, La Trobe's art, the drama, requires a level of engagement in the common life of her culture and with actors and audience unparalleled by any other art form represented in Woolf's fiction.[10] Clearly an outsider, La Trobe has nonetheless lived a varied social and sexual life, and is quite knowledgeable about the history of English literature, upon which she draws in writing and producing the pageant.[11] She also has a shrewd understanding of human nature and uses it to manage her actors: "Vanity . . . made them all malleable" (64).

Unlike many practicing playwrights of the day, La Trobe is not simply satisfied with providing light entertainment to her audience to while away a summer's afternoon. Her dramatic goal is more ambitious: through the pageant, she hopes to engage her audience emotionally and imaginatively, enabling its members to acknowledge their common identity, both among themselves and with their ancestors.[12] In the minds of her audience, the pageant succeeds in raising fundamental questions about identity and human nature: "'D'you think people change?'"(120–1). Lucy later answers the question in her comment about the Victorians: "'I don't believe . . . that there ever were such people. Only you and me and William dressed differently'" (174–5). The figures of the villagers in sack cloth weaving in and out among the trees throughout the pageant convey a basic message of endurance and continuity in the face of change, a message one senses would be particularly reassuring to a society on the brink of war. La Trobe's pageant attempts to provide the "'centre. Something to bring us all together'" that a member of the audience says the community needs (198).

By employing villagers in the roles of various characters, both historically based and fictional, La Trobe's pageant has the added effect of providing examples of the unexpressed creativity present in most individuals. It is as if La Trobe's artistry supplies an answer to a question Lucy has raised well before the pageant has begun: "'People are gifted—very. The question is—how to bring it out?'" (59).[13] The audience relishes identifying fellow villagers in various roles, astonished by the transformation of some and delighted by the dramatic flair exhibited by others. This sense of untapped potential capable of being drawn out is also impressed upon members of the audience. During one of the intermissions, Lucy seeks out La Trobe to congratulate her, acknowledging the "'small part I've had to play! But you've made me feel I could have played . . . Cleopatra!'" (153).

Lucy's comment reflects one of the more ambitious of La Trobe's aims, that of making the audience see the importance of its role in the creation of art, ultimately by trying to draw it into the pageant itself at the end. This is a point that Bart, surprisingly prescient in his understanding of La Trobe and the intent of her work, makes before the pageant has even begun: "'Our part . . . is to be the audience. And a very important part too'" (58). The play's confrontational ending, in which the players rush into the audience with mirrors and other reflecting surfaces, attempts to point to the audience as a vital part of its action. The message is that the lives of the audience are an integral part of the historical procession represented by the pageant, and so constitute the raw material of art.

Actual lives are meant to become part of a drama that ultimately embraces all of reality, including that of the natural world, as La Trobe attempts to dissolve the boundaries between art and life. This is the "vision" that La Trobe wants her audience to experience, even though the text of the novel never articulates it as such. During particular moments in the play, the fusion of the two realms is complete, as, for example, when Albert, the village idiot, appears: "There was no need to dress him up. There he came, acting his part to perfection" (86).

But even from the beginning, the deliberate ambiguity of the pageant's staging contributes toward La Trobe's ultimate artistic goal. As the gramophone buzzes in the bushes, the audience wonders, "Was it, or was it not, the play?" (76). At several points during the pageant, the natural setting conspires with the art of the pageant to positive effect. Real swallows fly across a sheet that has been spread out on the ground to represent a lake (164). Pointz Hall serves as "'Home'" during the course of Budge the constable's monologue (172). Nature even bridges the lulls in the action that threaten to dissolve the emotion La Trobe has so painstakingly aroused. The collective bellowing of the cows in the field following the Restoration playlet "annihilated the gap; bridged the distance; filled the emptiness and continued the emotion" (140–1). Later, a brief shower sustains the momentum of the pageant: "'That's done it,' sighed Miss La Trobe . . . . Nature once more had taken her part" (180–1).

Just as the reality of the natural world is incorporated into the pageant, so at the end of the novel the pageant itself metaphorically assumes the properties of natural phenomena. In the evening, the Olivers have gathered together over dinner, at which point the pageant still remains fresh in the "sky" of their minds (212). If the play as art aims at permanence, it is ultimately transitory, as are the things of nature; very soon "it would be beneath the horizon, gone to join the other plays" (213) in the memories of those who have seen it. It is shortly after this moment that the novel's narrator metaphorically begins to transform the reality of the natural world into art as well. Isa contemplates the early evening sky, observing "the pageant fade," from inside the "shell" of the living room (216). As Bart and Lucy leave the room, the scene is gradually transformed, assuming mythic proportions as the windows and walls of the house drop away, and Isa and Giles are left alone to confront each other in a primordial context. Says the narrator, "Then the curtain rose. They spoke" (219).

With these lines, the real world of the novel actually becomes the beginning of a new play, a work of art. In fact, the scene with Isa and Giles bears a marked resemblance to the opening scene of the new play La Trobe has envisioned earlier as she leaves the grounds of Pointz Hall: "It would be midnight; there would be two figures, half concealed by a rock. The curtain would rise" (210). The narrator of the novel has effected a second fusion of art and reality first demonstrated by the pageant. There, elements of the real world were brought into the action of the pageant over time, ending with an attempt to incorporate the lives of the audience into the play. Here, the narrator of the novel transforms an evening confrontation between Giles and Isa into the beginning of a play, a new work of art.

More insistently than Woolf's earlier fiction, *Between the Acts* consciously presents the reader with specific examples in which daily reality intermingles with and gives rise to art. This is Woolf's mature vision of the relation between life and art. In its simplest form, the stuff of art is life, and vice versa. Moreover, in this final novel, Woolf refines her view of the artist-figure in relation to life and art, shedding any clinging vestiges of Beebe's Ivory Tower artist. La Trobe is Woolf's valued outsider, but she is not socially or sexually isolated. On the contrary, she has been involved in a number of particularly social ventures, from running a tea shop to acting to her current occupation of "getting things up" (58) as a playwright and stage director. Furthermore, she has known intimacy and deep feeling for at least one other:

> Since the row with the actress who had shared her bed and her purse the need of drink had grown on her. And the horror and the terror of being alone. (211)

Miss La Trobe is clearly a social creature, preferring in her moments of depression the company to be found at a local tavern to the isolation of her rooms.

Like other artist-figures in Woolf's earlier fiction La Trobe has her chosen medium—that of playwriting and directing her dramas. Unlike the Ivory Tower artist, however, La Trobe has little concern for her art as a refined, meticulously crafted product for others to admire. Her plays are scripted, of course, but have an impromptu, slap-dash quality that never aims at dramatic polish. In *To the Lighthouse*, Lily Briscoe shows a similar lack of concern for her artwork as product; she has attained her artistic vision in the process of completing her abstract portrait of Mrs. Ramsay after a ten-year hiatus, but knows full well that the canvas itself is destined for obscurity (309–10).

Like Lily, La Trobe practices her art with a vision in mind; her goal as an artist, however, is to convey that vision to her audience through the medium of the drama. The focus of La Trobe's efforts throughout the course of the pageant is her audience; she is very concerned with sustaining the emotion she has stirred in her scenes during those gaps in the action when her audience is in danger of being distracted. The music provided by the gramophone is a tool she uses repeatedly to continue the emotion and hold the audience's attention during such moments.

But how successful is she in conveying her vision to her audience?

> Hadn't she, for twenty-five minutes, made them see? A vision imparted was relief from agony . . . for one moment . . . one moment. Then the music petered out on the last word *we*. . . . She hadn't made them see. It was a failure, another damned failure! As usual. Her vision escaped her. (98)

As the pageant progresses, La Trobe agonizes over her ability to transmit her vision to her audience. At the end, she characterizes the play as a "gift" (209), ruefully acknowledging that even the momentary awareness that her play may have brought to her audience will, like the play, fade with time and be forgotten:

> But what had she given? A cloud that melted into the other clouds on the horizon. It was in the giving that the triumph was. And the triumph faded. (209)

Nonetheless, as an artist who is compelled to use her art as a medium for communicating with others, La Trobe has already begun to imagine her next play, the opening scene of which arises in her mind as she seeks comfort and forgetfulness in the village pub.

In *Between the Acts*, then, Woolf has chosen to foreground the importance of the relationship between audience and artist, de-emphasizing the significance of La Trobe's art as product.[14] In her role as the artist-figure in this novel, La Trobe is far more akin to Beebe's Sacred Fount artist, existing in the thick of life, although an outsider, and eager to communicate her vision to her audience through her art. In her desperation to convey her vision, La Trobe exhibits the characteristics of one who views herself as the servant of her audience, making herculean efforts in her attempt to transmit her message in dramatic form (150). In the margin of her script La Trobe has written, perhaps as a humbling reminder to herself, "'I am the slave of my audience'" (211).

With La Trobe, Woolf introduces a sacrificial element into her portrayal of the artist. As noted earlier, La Trobe stations herself behind one of the trees, where she conceals her presence from the audience, issues commands to her actors, and suffers when the moods she has evoked in various scenes threaten to dissipate. The tree becomes a crucifix of sorts, the site of her creative agony as an artist:

> Miss La Trobe leant against the tree, paralyzed. Her power had left her. Beads of perspiration broke on her forehead. Illusion had failed. 'This is death,' she murmured, 'death.' (140)

Later in the play, La Trobe experiences a similarly intense moment of suffering:

> Grating her fingers in the bark, she damned the audience. Panic seized her. Blood seemed to pour from her shoes. This is death, death, death, she noted in the margin of her mind; when illusion fails. (180)

After the pageant has ended, the crucifix-tree literally becomes a Tree of Life, affirming both her dramatic efforts and the real world of humanity and nature as it fills with chattering starlings "syllabling discordantly life, life, life, without measure" (209).[15]

But La Trobe knows that this moment of affirmation is fleeting. The audience that she has worked so hard to move and to unite through her pageant has already dispersed, its members carrying away fragments of the play in their memories that will gradually fade over time. Fully aware that her art is transitory, La Trobe, the suffering artist-slave of her audience, must be content to begin planning another play and await the next opportunity for producing it before an audience.

Although La Trobe represents Woolf's final image of the artist as Lemon's man or woman among others, socially aware and experienced, and passionately engaged in his or her art, the twentieth-century world in which Woolf positions this figure is no longer particularly hospitable to artistic creativity and its products. The pace of life has quickened, and civilization has assumed an increasingly mechanistic cast in its frantic attempts to improve the quality of daily life:

> Homes will be built. Each flat with its refrigerator, in the crannied wall. Each of us a free man; plates washed by machinery; not an aeroplane to vex us; all liberated; made whole. . . . (182–3)

The narrator's bitterly ironic tone is unmistakable. Even the end of La Trobe's pageant is immediately followed by a dreaded address by the Reverend

Streatfield, soliciting donations for the electrification of the parish church, an act that appears to put art in the service of advancing technology, here, in a space traditionally considered sacred.

Interrupting Streatfield's banal request, a dozen planes "in perfect formation like a flight of wild duck" (193) zoom overhead, reminding members of the audience of the war and its threat of imminent destruction.[16] A society facing possible annihilation appears to be able to give only limited attention to the arts at best.[17] The disturbing news of the war on the continent is everywhere; Giles angrily learns of massacres abroad, while Isa reads of the violence of a barracks gang rape at home. Dodge and Isa realize how tentative the war has made their lives. The pageant becomes one artist's effort to reassert a collective identity among her audience in the face of these uncertainties, but for Giles Oliver, attendance at the pageant becomes one more social obligation that he must patiently endure before returning to the real business of providing for a family in an uncertain world.

Surpassing the unfavorable climate for art created by an increasingly mechanistic world that is also threatened with destruction is an overriding sense of the transitoriness of all human endeavors, rooted as it is in a natural world fundamentally indifferent to it. If, as the existentialists would argue, it is up to the individual to give his or her existence meaning, Woolf would counter that such meaning is always merely a human construct, and therefore subject to dissolution over time. Of the main characters in *Between the Acts*, Lucy Swithin is overtly religious, but is also fascinated by the thought of England in prehistoric times,

> . . . populated, she understood, by elephant-bodied, seal-necked, heaving, surging, slowly writhing, and, she supposed, barking monsters; the iguanodon, the mammoth, and the mastodon; from whom presumably, she thought, jerking the window open, we descend. (8–9)

Despite the note of irony interjected by the qualifier and the action of opening the window, Lucy is unwittingly engaged in the Victorian activity of trying to reconcile her faith with the findings of science. Her attempts at "one-making," at integrating the natural and civilized worlds, however, are seen by the other characters for what they are—attempts at wish-fulfillment (175). If anything, *Between the Acts* ends by squarely subordinating its main characters to the roles assigned them by indifferent Nature as members of an animal species. As Giles and Isa are left alone in the living room, the scene assumes primordial proportions as the principals prepare to confront each other and then engage sexually:

> Before they slept, they must fight; after they had fought, they would embrace. From that embrace another life might be born. But first they must fight, as the dog fox fights with the vixen, in the heart of darkness, in the fields of night. (219)

Given this stark, Kurtzian reduction of the sphere of human activity to animalistic confrontation and copulation, where and how can the artist ply his or her art in such a world? If, as Isa has noted earlier, hatred and love are two of the three primal emotions (peace being the third), they are the two foregrounded here, and as such, are made to represent the primal elements of human interaction. Significantly, the second emotion leads to the most basic form of creativity—reproduction. As noted earlier, La Trobe has imagined just such a scene as the opening for her next play. Here, Giles and Isa become her protagonists as she appropriates this moment of confrontation for her art: "Then the curtain rose. They spoke" (219). The fundamental interactions of life—confrontation and reconciliation—become the raw material of art. Woolf's artist-figure, thoroughly grounded in the quotidian, uses her outsider's perspective to observe life closely in its elemental aspects, appropriating these in turn as the basis for her artistic vision.[18]

CHAPTER ELEVEN

Conclusion

As has been demonstrated, the question of the artist's relationship to others and the surrounding world is one that intrigued Woolf throughout her writing career; her consideration of the matter in her essays and fictional portrayals of artist-figures of varying kinds and degrees—practicing, amateur, and aspiring—attest to this lifelong preoccupation.[1] As these portrayals are also complex and highly individual, attempting to make generalizations based on them is fraught with difficulty and the danger of oversimplification.

If one examines the depiction of the major artist-figures spanning Woolf's fiction over the years, though, one can observe a steady movement away from the Ivory Tower toward the Sacred Fount—from living and working in isolation from one's fellows to plying one's art while living among them. As Woolf has suggested in "Life and the Novelist," the writer may craft his or her art at some remove from others, but only after having obtained the raw materials of that art from life, which he or she observes closely and experiences in all its richness as an ordinary human being living among his or her contemporaries. In *The Voyage Out*, Rachel Vinrace is made to appear wary of the external world, which threatens her emerging identity as an individual and a musician; conveniently, death resolves her dilemma, rescuing her from an increasingly compromised existence as an engaged young woman and restoring her to the natural world. In this first novel, there is no readily identifiable middle ground for fledgling artists— particularly women artists—to seek in making life choices as young people. One either practices one's art or scholarship in isolation, or one assumes the gender role expected of one in the world at large.

By the end of *To the Lighthouse*, though, Lily Briscoe has not only achieved a balance between the demands of her psyche and her art for distancing from others and her need for relationship and intimacy; she has also become capable of utilizing her own experience and memories of

Mrs. Ramsay and her family to stimulate her creativity as a painter. Furthermore, the process of recalling Mrs. Ramsay and resolving her conflicting feelings towards her and her husband while completing her portrait enables Lily to reach a new level of maturation as a woman and an artist. Here the artist not only draws upon life experience to create art; the process of recalling the subject in producing the artwork also has the reciprocal effect of nurturing the growth of the artist as a human being.

In *Between the Acts*, the artist-figure Miss La Trobe is rendered as a fully social and sexual being living among others daily and employing her art to communicate a vision to her fellows—in this case, actually a dual one which views the villagers as an integral part of England's history as well as the art of the pageant she so laboriously produces on their behalf. Here the artist as dramatist and producer breaks down the boundaries between art and life, utilizing life in the form of the villagers and the natural setting to create art, and using art in the form of the pageant to create a momentary sense of unity and kinship among her audience. Art's role in this novel expands beyond that of embodying a personal vision or fostering the artist's individual growth to that of engendering and attempting to sustain, if only momentarily, a collective identity among a community of individuals facing the fragmentation and dissolution of approaching war.

It is significant that in embracing life more fully, Woolf's major artist-figures also select artistic media that are increasingly social. Rachel's music-making, while capable of communicating the composer's vision or the performer's interpretation to an audience, nonetheless primarily serves a number of important psychological functions for her in helping her cope with a world she finds puzzling and alienating. As an art form, music is one of the most abstract and cerebral of the arts. Lily's art, painting, has a more direct relationship to the external world, which provides it with visual cues that give rise to the painter's vision. It is also itself visual, even though in its more abstract forms it may be nonrepresentational. La Trobe's art, drama, is one that involves perhaps the highest level of social interaction on the artist's part. Human beings are the tools of La Trobe's art, and the audience is an essential part of her pageant. From La Trobe's perspective, the communication of her vision to her audience is all, and determines whether her pageant is a success.[2]

In developing this view of the artist, Woolf increasingly distanced herself from the figure of the Ivory Tower artist, most frequently associated with aestheticism, a formidable legacy of her nineteenth-century literary and artistic heritage. In *The Voyage Out*, St. John Hirst, who, of the four main characters, exhibits the greatest potential for becoming an aesthete, chooses to forego his sequestered academic career in order to study for the bar in London. William Rodney, one of the main characters in *Night and Day* and a bachelor with antiquarian tastes who also writes antiquated verse drama, is portrayed as a finical, immature individual who objectifies Katharine as his fiancée and has difficulty developing a viable relationship to the world around him.

Rodney is the last aesthete portrayed as a major character in Woolf's novels. The figure reappears in a more limited form in such sympathetically rendered characters as Augustus Carmichael and William Dodge, but neither occupies a central position in *To the Lighthouse* or *Between the Acts*. Although Neville in *The Waves* and Edward Pargiter in *The Years* may be considered major characters, both are primarily practicing scholars and classicists rather than artist-figures, having relinquished their efforts to write poetry at an early age. More so than Edward, Neville exhibits the sensibility and temperament of the aesthete, but both men are presented as individuals whose creative potential has given place to the exercise of scholarly talents. Both also exhibit unfulfilled potential as human beings, having lost or been rejected by a beloved person at an early age. Among Woolf's minor characters are a number of aesthetes who are indifferently or unfavorably rendered. These include Everard Benson in *Jacob's Room*, "little Jim Hutton" (268) in *Mrs. Dalloway*, and Ashley and Tony Ashton in *The Pargiters* and *The Years*.

The demise of the Ivory Tower aesthete in Woolf's fiction reflects Woolf's growing impatience with those artists or writers who feel compelled to remove themselves from others and the world, either physically or psychologically. Her comments upon reading the memoirs of Bloomsbury friend G. Lowes Dickinson are characteristic: "Goldie depresses me unspeakably. Always alone on a mountain top asking himself how to live, theorising about life; never living" (D4: 360). In her essays, Woolf repeatedly makes the point that artists and writers must live among their kind in order to create meaningful art. Addressing her readers in "Mr. Bennett and Mrs. Brown," Woolf states, "Your part is to insist that writers shall come down off their plinths and pedestals, and describe beautifully if possible, truthfully at any rate, our Mrs. Brown. . . . for she is, of course, the spirit we live by, life itself" (CE1: 336). In "A Letter to a Young Poet," first published as a pamphlet in the Hogarth Letters series in 1932, Woolf admonishes the younger generation of British poets, of whom John Lehmann, the addressee, was one, about indulging in too much introspection and not exhibiting enough interest in the life around it:

> But how are you going to get out, into the world of other people? That is your problem now, if I may hazard a guess—to find the right relationship, now that you know yourself, between the self that you know and the world outside. (CE2: 191)

As was noted in the discussion of *The Years*, Woolf's critical cameos of the aesthete in her later novels may well indicate her discomfort at being associated with Bloomsbury's supposed aestheticism, especially during the highly politicized 1930s. One must also acknowledge, though, that the growing scarcity of aesthetes in Woolf's novels may simply reflect the waning of the figure as one of literary or even satiric interest in twentieth-century fiction. In real life, the poet or writer as aesthete seems to have disappeared from the Anglo-American literary scene with the maturation of such modernists as Pound, Eliot, and Faulkner.

If Woolf's interest in the Ivory Tower aesthete as an artist-figure diminished during her career as a novelist, she nonetheless retained significant elements in her work that reflect Pater's influence into her maturity as a writer. As was noted in the introduction, Pater tended to be associated—more wrongly than rightly—with the brand of aestheticism practiced by Wilde and the *fin-de-siècle* aesthetes and decadents satirized in the character of Bunthorne in Gilbert and Sullivan's *Patience* (1881). As the discussion of *The Voyage Out* has suggested, however, Woolf was particularly interested in Pater's portrayal in *Marius the Epicurean* of the eponymous hero as a sensitive young man and a close observer of life who made himself available and receptive to the experiences it placed in his way, allowing them to play upon his sensibilities and inform his view of the world. Woolf came to adopt this approach to the world as her own, and most of her aspiring or practicing artist-figures as well as a number of her other main characters exhibit this ability to varying degrees.[3]

The three young protagonists of *The Voyage Out*, Rachel Vinrace, Terence Hewet and St. John Hirst, are all active observers of the life around them. Of the three, Rachel is the most vulnerable to the impressions she receives, and appears adversely affected by them. Far more worldly, Terence demonstrates the aspiring writer's sensitivity in observing others and storing up impressions for later use in his work. Perhaps the least receptive to what he observes, St. John more often than not takes the stance of the merciless satirist in watching his fellows, lacking the maturity and charity to make allowances for them.

The social artist Clarissa Dalloway's skill in observing and reading the moods of others makes her a successful hostess. Both Clarissa and Peter Walsh demonstrate their finely honed awareness of their environment in their respective walks through London, which they continue to find fascinating, as did Woolf herself. Psychologically debilitated by his wartime experience, Septimus Warren Smith possesses the Paterian observer's receptivity to impressions to such a degree that they evoke extremes of emotion and agitation, threatening to render him even more mentally unstable. In fact, one could argue that Septimus's overdeveloped sensibility has made him so vulnerable to the shocks presented by his experience of the war that it has accelerated, if not instigated, his madness.

As an unusually intelligent and perceptive woman, Lily Briscoe in *To the Lighthouse* observes the life of the Ramsay family closely, but is unable to utilize the impressions it has made upon her creatively until ten years have passed. It is only then that she is able to draw upon the legacy of memories Mrs. Ramsay has bequeathed her in completing her painting and reconciling herself with the Ramsays as husband and wife. Like Lily, Augustus Carmichael exists at some remove from the lives of the Ramsays, but observes them actively when he is not lost in his opium-induced daydreams.

His successful wartime volume of poetry is the result of years of such close observation, and the suffering and disappointment in his difficult life. As another of Woolf's social artists, Mrs. Ramsay is highly attuned to those around her, constantly drawing upon her observations and intuition in shaping relations among her family and friends.

Orlando the aspiring poet makes a habit of disguising himself and prowling about Elizabethan London in order to observe and participate in its rich and varied nightlife. Later, as an eighteenth-century woman, she continues to feed her curiosity by befriending a group of prostitutes in order to experience the seamy side of London life vicariously. Even more than Orlando, Bernard in *The Waves* is a consummate observer of the urban scene, always curious about the lives of others and routinely seeking their company and confidences. As an observer, Rhoda, like Septimus, is extremely susceptible to the numerous shocks presented by daily life. Her method of coping with them falls just short of madness as she withdraws from others into a fantasy world of her own making.

Among the older generation of Pargiters in *The Years*, Eleanor Pargiter exhibits a growing hunger to observe and experience other cultures as she ages, expanding her awareness by traveling more frequently and widely. Like Clarissa Dalloway and Peter Walsh, Eleanor's brother Martin demonstrates a visceral awareness of London, its landmarks and its bustling life. As members of the troubled youngest generation of Pargiters, North and Peggy observe their fellows constantly. Their early experiences of war and human suffering as soldier and physician respectively have acquainted them all too well with the human condition, making them inwardly impatient with the frivolity and conventional behavior they observe in others. Like Septimus and Rhoda, Sara Pargiter's sensibility is so overdeveloped that she, too, must find some way of mediating her relationship to the world around her. Solitude, reading literature, spinning fantasies, and ironic commentary are her means of coping with the sordidness of everyday urban life.

Confined to her role as a wife and mother in a troubled marriage, Isa Oliver in *Between the Acts* finds daily reality almost too much to bear, escaping from it in her fantasies of Haines, "the gentleman farmer" (3), and in her poetic utterances. William Dodge's aesthete's sensibility makes him particularly responsive to beauty wherever he may find it—in the landscape surrounding Pointz Hall, in Isa's "glass green eyes and thick body" (105), or in a fragile, antique china cup, caught as it falls. Without illusions, Miss La Trobe has learned to read human nature closely, using her knowledge to extract the best performances from her amateur actors in practicing her art.

If, during the course of her fiction, Woolf's major artist-figures follow Henry James's Paterian dictum to observe perpetually, they are aided in this effort by their increasing identification as outsiders whose unique status as individuals working in the midst of life, but somehow marginalized by their class, gender, sexual orientation or marital status, gives them a more distanced, objective view of the world around them. A daughter of the mercantile class, Rachel Vinrace is not an outsider socially, but would become increasingly marginal were she to remain unmarried. As a woman who has already reached that state, Lily Briscoe psychologically as well as physically positions herself at the periphery of Ramsay family life, enjoying the advantage of observing her subjects objectively, her vision unclouded by any preformed allegiances to individual family members. If Lily is gradually drawn into the circle of life ten years later through her memories of time spent among the Ramsays, Miss La Trobe already finds herself at its center. As a woman who has loved and lost, and engaged in a number of failed business enterprises, each social in nature, she has a wealth of personal experience upon which to draw in practicing her art. As a woman with mysterious origins and an ambiguous sexual orientation, however, she stands apart from the largely homogenous, patriarchal culture in which she finds herself, which gives her greater artistic license in depicting it as she sees it in her pageant.

As Woolf eloquently argues in *Three Guineas*, a woman's gender is enough to make her an outsider in England: "Inevitably we [women] look upon society, so kind to you [men], so harsh to us, as an ill-fitting form that distorts the truth; deforms the mind; fetters the will" (105). If the female artist's status as an outsider simply by virtue of being a woman equips her with the perspective needed to identify and acknowledge the truths about society and human life, her gender nonetheless raises obstacles to the expression of those truths in her art. In her essay "Professions for Women," Woolf describes the insidious effects of "the Angel in the House"—an allusion to the self-sacrificing Victorian wife in Coventry Patmore's eponymous sequence of poems—which hovers over the shoulder of the woman writer as critic, discouraging her from expressing the truth as she sees it:

> . . . 'My dear, you are a young woman. You are writing about a book that has been written by a man. Be sympathetic; be tender; flatter; deceive; use all the arts and wiles of our sex. Never let anybody guess that you have a mind of your own. Above all, be pure.' (CE2: 285)[4]

If Woolf had reservations about women's ability to surmount the psychological barriers placed before them in expressing the truths about life in their art, she was also equally concerned about the physical and psychological difficulties posed by heterosexual relations to the aspiring woman artist. As has been seen, her earliest novels appear to overvalue the import of heterosexual relations for women. In *The Voyage Out*, Rachel senses a "terrible possibility" (176) imbedded in heterosexuality that threatens her autonomy as a woman and the free exercise of her art as a musician. Woolf's authorial decision to make illness and death carry Rachel off appears to reflect a view of heterosexual relations as so inimical to female aesthetic creativity that it must be avoided at all costs. In *Night and Day*, following Mary Datchet's loss of Ralph Denham to Katharine Hilbery, the narrator relegates Mary to the ranks of unfulfilled spinsterhood, in which even her work is depicted as a feeble effort to compensate herself for the loss of the love of her life. Conversely, Ralph and Katharine's impending union is presented as promising them greater independence and opportunities for personal growth.

Woolf's first significant example of women as social artists in her novels, Clarissa Dalloway is a wife and mother, but also exhibits reticence towards marital relations, choosing to sleep in a narrow bed in her attic. Her weak heart, which occasions her husband Richard's concern for her health, serves as a convenient justification for their nocturnal separation. With *To the Lighthouse*, Mrs. Ramsay the social artist, wife and mother of numerous children, is fully sexualized, but is shown to pay a price for her selfless devotion to her family's well-being: "boasting of her capacity to surround and protect, there was scarcely a shell of herself left for her to know herself by; all was so lavished and spent" (60). As a woman and artist, Lily Briscoe does not seem perturbed by her single state; if anything, she is relieved that she has managed to avoid marriage: "she need not undergo that degradation" (154). Although Lily attains a new degree of sexual maturation by the end of the novel, she remains the celibate female artist fearful of the compromises demanded by heterosexual relations and motherhood.

By the time of the writing of *Orlando*, Woolf appears somewhat more at ease with the image of the woman artist as a heterosexually active being. As a handsome young nobleman, Orlando is quite popular with Queen Elizabeth and the ladies of her court; as an eighteenth- and nineteenth-century noblewoman, Orlando has a number of suitors. When she marries, however, she chooses a spouse who conveniently spends most of his time as an adventurer at sea, allowing her much independence as a woman and poet. By the end of the novel, Orlando has given birth to at least one son, but puzzlingly her maternity and her children seem to occupy no space in her life or her thoughts, her children being literally invisible in the novel. Woolf may have intended to present Orlando as an example of the contemporary woman who can successfully be poet, wife and mother, but Orlando's seeming obliviousness to her children and her husband's frequent absence suggest Woolf's continuing reservations about the compatibility of wifehood and maternity with artistic creativity in women.

In *Between the Acts*, Woolf presents Miss La Trobe as an artist of the Sacred Fount, a social being who practices her art in the midst of life, using the villagers and a natural setting in her pageant. Although La Trobe is a sexualized artist figure, she is rumored to be lesbian and apparently has no children. One may see in Woolf's characterization of La Trobe another effort to protect her women artists from the seemingly inimical effects of wifehood and motherhood. Even at the end of her writing career, Woolf remained deeply skeptical about the ability of women artists to negotiate the demands of heterosexual relationships and motherhood successfully.

Although during the course of Woolf's career, her artist-figures become increasingly involved in the life around them, her women artist-figures who are not social artists refrain from embracing wifehood and maternity fully, if at all. If Woolf understood the serious disadvantages these could pose to women's aesthetic creativity through her observations of Vita's and her sister Vanessa's lives as well as those of other women, she also acknowledged the limitations imposed by marriage and family responsibilities upon men as would-be artists and writers.

His father dead, Ralph Denham in *Night and Day* reluctantly becomes the head of his large, middle-class family as its oldest son. He fantasizes a life for himself as a writer in the countryside, but his sense of duty to his family keeps him practicing law in London. In *To the Lighthouse*, Mrs. Ramsay and Charles Tansley as well as Ramsay himself suspect that the burdens of domesticity have prevented him from writing the important philosophical work many assumed he would produce. An inveterate storyteller and an aspiring writer, Bernard in *The Waves* has married, fathered children, and reached middle age. His family responsibilities have caused him to take a job in London, and his writing career never materializes. Instead, he resigns himself to telling the story of his and his friends' lives to a chance acquaintance in a city restaurant one evening.

If heterosexual coupling and parenthood appear to hamper would-be artists and writers of both sexes in Woolf's world, aspiring male artists and writers face additional gender-specific obstacles as well. Perhaps the greatest of these is the externally or internally imposed need to serve the empire. His friends assuming that he would become a writer, Peter Walsh is expelled from Oxford for his socialist views and rejected by Clarissa. In despair, he follows family tradition and expectations by enlisting in the colonial service in India, where he spends the formative years of his young manhood as a government official and writes letters that Clarissa considers "dry sticks" (9) to his friends back home. Lacking the scholarly promise of his older brother Edward, Martin Pargiter is obliged to follow in his father the colonel's footsteps by serving in the army in India, an experience he later admits he detested. Eleanor, like Martin himself, feels he should have become an architect.

Coming of age shortly before the Great War, Jacob Flanders, Septimus Warren Smith, and North Pargiter, all of whom have aspired to be authors or poets, succumb to patriotic fervor and the expectations of their families and friends by enlisting in the infantry to fight the Hun in the trenches of France and Belgium. Jacob is killed and Septimus later descends into madness, which ultimately results in his suicide; North, badly shaken by his experience of the war, retreats to an isolated sheep ranch in Africa for a number of years. His return to society and London, where he feels himself to be an outsider, is only tentative at best.

Louis's early scholarly promise and poetic ambitions in *The Waves* fall victim to his needs as an insecure middle-class colonial whose Australian banker father denies him the university education given Bernard and Neville. Identifying himself with the mother country's power structure as a form of compensation, Louis works his way into it by following his father into business and becoming a shipping executive, extending the empire's influence abroad. His evenings spent reading and daydreaming in his attic represent what remains of his youthful hopes and intellectual ambitions.

One must note that Woolf's novels also reveal another world of "shadow people" (*ND* 265), particularly women—individuals prevented by a combination of their class, gender, lack of education or personal circumstances from ever achieving their full potential as human beings. Among these are such characters as Evelyn Murgatroyd in *The Voyage Out*, whose only hope of avoiding marginality lies in finding a respectable husband who will rescue her from her status as an illegitimate child and orphaned young woman. There are also the impoverished, unmarried women scholars—Miss Allan, Miss Kilman, and Lucy Craddock—who, no matter how intelligent and diligent they may be, face a life of isolation and obscurity. Also among the group are daughters fallen from the comfort of a relatively secure childhood such as Sara Pargiter, whose unmarriage-ability and inadequate inheritance doom her to a marginal existence. One must also mention the *demimondaines* of Jacob's acquaintance who include the fickle Florinda and the young prostitute Laurette, women whom class and circumstance have reduced to a life of sexual exploitation in return for a meager, uncertain subsistence.

In the world of early twentieth-century British urban life as Woolf comes to view it, men and women are more valued for what they can do on behalf of the empire—furthering industry and trade, fighting in wars, administering colonies, serving in Parliament, giving birth to more males to perpetuate these activities—than for what they are capable of achieving as disinterested artists and writers. One may see in the evolution of Woolf's novels the gradual emergence of this world, which becomes increasingly inhospitable to aesthetic creativity, unless, of course, it can be made to serve the interests of the empire. It is this sense of a world that has turned its back on the arts, especially in times of approaching war, that gives Miss La Trobe's dramatic efforts in *Between the Acts* their particular poignancy. But it is a world whose "scraps, orts and fragments" (*BA* 189) she, as an artist of the Sacred Fount, feels obliged to acknowledge, experience, and embody in her art.

Notes

1 Beebe's statement evokes Leopold Bloom, the other of Joyce's two major self-reflexive characters.

2 In her essay on Defoe published in *The Common Reader* (1925), Woolf identifies him as belonging to "the school of the great plain writers, whose work is founded upon a knowledge of what is most persistent, though not most seductive, in human nature" ("Defoe," *CE1:* 68). For Woolf, Defoe has the gift of emphasizing "the very facts that most reassure us of stability in real life ... until we seem wedged among solid objects in a solid universe" ("Phases of Fiction," *CE2:* 58). In her diary entry for August 5, 1920, Woolf expresses admiration for Cervantes's "deep, atmospheric, living people casting shadows solid, tinted as in life" (*D2:* 56). Chekhov's appeal lies in his interest in the functioning of the mind: "he is a most subtle and delicate analyst of human relations" ("The Russian Point of View," *CE1:* 241).

3 Woolf actually had an opportunity to see Holman Hunt when she attended a party one evening with her half-brother George Duckworth at the Hunts' home on Melbury Road:

> There we found old Holman Hunt himself dressed in a long Jaeger dressing gown, holding forth to a large gathering about the ideas which had inspired him in painting "The Light of the World", a copy of which stood upon an easel. (MB 154)

4 The character of Ridley Ambrose, Rachel Vinrace's finical, cantankerous scholar-uncle who is editing Pindar's *Odes* in *The Voyage Out*, also appears to have been modeled to a certain extent upon Woolf's father. Ambrose's wife Helen expends considerable energy setting up a study for him, first on board the *Euphrosyne*, and later in their South American villa, from which he rarely emerges during the rest of the novel.

5 In *Bloomsbury: A House of Lions*, Leon Edel relates how Leslie Stephen gave Woolf a ring on her twenty-first birthday: "It was as if there were a marriage

and also a laying on of hands, a literary succession" (92). Edel also notes that a short time after Stephen's death in 1904, Woolf took to smoking a pipe, as did her father: "Few Victorian daughters dared to take such liberties" (92).

6   For example, Woolf anticipates that *The Pargiters* "will be the longest of my little brood" (*D4*: 176), and compares the protracted writing and revising of *The Years* to "a long childbirth" (*D5*: 31).

7   In *World within World*, Stephen Spender writes, "She inquired of everyone endlessly about his or her life: of writers how and why they wrote, of a newly married young woman how it felt to be a bride, of a bus conductor where he lived and when he went home, of a charwoman how it felt to scrub floors" (141).

8   That Woolf had read Mallarmé at least in middle age, if not earlier, appears evident in her letter of August 13, 1920 from Rodmell to Roger Fry, who was translating his poems. In it she expresses pleasure in reading Fry's translations and regrets leaving her copy of Mallarmé in London (*L2*: 439). Woolf was most likely first introduced to the Symbolist poets by Fry, Clive Bell, and Lytton Strachey, all of whom read French literature (Strachey's *Landmarks in French Literature* was published in 1912). Christopher Reed states that around 1917, Fry "became interested in the aesthetics of poetry and began what would become a lifelong project translating Mallarmé" (16). As Hermione Lee notes in her biography of Woolf, Fry continued to translate Mallarmé's poetry during the final years of his life (645). The translations, with a commentary by Charles Mauron, were posthumously published in 1936 (*L6*: 84n1). In Woolf's *The Years*, one Tony Ashton is referred to as the man who has been giving lectures on Mallarmé at Mortimer House in London (261). For a discussion of Woolf and the French Symbolists' stylistic affinities, see Marilyn Zucker's "Virginia Woolf and the French Connection: A Devotion to Language" in *Virginia Woolf & Communities: Selected Papers from the Eighth Annual Conference on Virginia Woolf*, ed. Jeanette McVicker and Laura Davis (New York: Pace UP, 1999) 29–35.

9   Woolf's analysis of highbrows, middlebrows, and lowbrows in her humorous essay "Middlebrow" (*CE2*: 196–203) which she had intended to send as a letter to *The New Statesman*, calls to mind the third chapter of Arnold's *Culture and Anarchy* (1869), "Barbarians, Philistines, Populace." As much as Woolf admired Ruskin, she thought that the isolation of his privileged, sheltered life had hampered his development:

We remember how for years after most men are forced to match themselves with the real world "he was living in a world of his own", to quote Professor Norton again, and losing the chance of gaining that experience with practical life, that self-control, and that development of reason which he more than most men required. ("Ruskin," *CE1*: 206)

10   S. P. Rosenbaum speculates as to why Woolf found *Marius the Epicurean* so appealing: "here was a historical novel quite unlike those of Scott she had been brought up on—a novel that concerned itself, as its subtitle declares, with 'sensations and ideas' instead of the passionate events of historical romance" (*Victorian Bloomsbury* 144).

11 Woolf began taking lessons in Greek as well from Clara Pater in October 1900 (Gordon 84). Clara and her brother would serve as models for Miss Craye and her dead brother in Woolf's short story "Moments of Being: 'Slater's Pins Have No Points'" (Meisel 23). Clara Pater also serves as the source of the character Lucy Craddock, Kitty's tutor in Oxford in *The Years* and its original essay-portion in manuscript, since published posthumously as *The Pargiters* (1977) (Meisel 27). Meisel speculates that Woolf "probably managed to extract, at least in atmosphere, a blend of aestheticism and women's educational rights from her tutor, both of which provided effective antidotes to life with father and the Duckworths" (20–1).

12 Forster's portrayal of Cecil Vyse in *A Room with a View* appears to evoke not only the popular image of the finical aesthete but also Pater himself. One may detect allusions to Pater's asceticism and his fondness for religious art and church ritual in Forster's physical description of Vyse:

> He was mediaeval. Like a Gothic statue. Tall and refined, with shoulders that seemed braced square by an effort of the will, and a head that was tilted a little higher than the usual level of vision, he resembled those fastidious saints who guard the portals of a French cathedral. Well educated, well endowed, and not deficient physically, he remained in the grip of a certain devil whom the modern world knows as self-consciousness, and whom the mediaeval, with dimmer vision, worshipped as asceticism. A Gothic statue implies celibacy, just as a Greek statue implies fruition, and perhaps this was what Mr. Beebe meant. (100–1)

13 It may well be that Woolf was bowing to the prevailing view of aestheticism when she made the following statement in her essay "The Narrow Bridge of Art," first published in *The New York Herald Tribune* on August 14, 1927:

> Modern literature, which had grown a little sultry and scented with Oscar Wilde and Walter Pater, revived instantly from her nineteenth-century languor when Samuel Butler and Bernard Shaw began to burn their feathers and apply their salts to her nose. She awoke; she sat up; she sneezed. (*CE2*: 223)

14 In her letter of August 29, 1908 to her sister Vanessa Bell, Woolf writes:

> I finished Moore last night; he has a fine flare of arrogance at the end— and no wonder. I am not so dumb foundered as I was; but the more I understand, the more I admire. He is so humane in spite of his desire to know the truth; and I believe I can disagree with him, over one matter. (*L1*: 364)

> Many years later, writing to her niece Judith Stephen on May 29, 1940, Woolf refers to *Principia Ethica* as "the book that made us all so wise and good" (*L6*: 400).

15 There are a number of ironies associated with these individuals as critics of Bloomsbury. As David Gadd notes in *The Loving Friends: A Portrait of Bloomsbury*, Bloomsbury rallied behind Lawrence when *The Rainbow* (1915)

was banned by attempting to get the ban lifted: "Lytton tried hard, without success, to get the *New Statesman* to take up the case, and Clive tackled the rest of the press. Whether Lawrence was grateful or not, there was no resumption of contact between them" (63). Quentin Bell rightly points out that Eliot, "the great opponent in literature of Bloomsbury and of all that Bloomsbury stood for, found in Leonard and Virginia Woolf publishers and friends" (*Bloomsbury* 85).

16   In her diary entry for July 19, 1919, Woolf expresses serious misgivings about social reformers as a group:

It seems to me more & more clear that the only honest people are the artists, & that these social reformers & philanthropists get so out of hand, & harbour so many discreditable desires under the disguise of loving their kind, that in the end there's more to find fault with in them than in us. But if I were one of them? (D1: 293)

To a limited degree, Woolf did become "one of them" by joining her husband at Labor Party meetings. Following one such meeting on October 1, 1935, in Brighton, Woolf reports her feeling of alienation in her diary entry the next day:

The immersion in all that energy & all that striving for something that is quite oblivious of me; making me feel that I am oblivious of it. (D4: 345)

Although in his autobiography, Leonard Woolf described his wife as "the least political animal that has lived since Aristotle invented the definition," he noted that Woolf was "highly sensitive to the atmosphere which surrounded her, whether it was personal, social, or historical" (27).

17   Evidence of this theme can also be found in the poetry of the Symbolists, in Wilde's *Salomé* (1896), in Richard Strauss's operatic version of the play (1905), and in the work of painters such as Moreau, Klimt, and Munch. The motif of woman as vampire-seductress was particularly prevalent in *fin-de-siècle* European art and culture. See also Nina Auerbach's *Woman and the Demon: The Life of a Victorian Myth* (Cambridge: Harvard UP, 1982), Virginia M. Allen's *The Femme Fatale: Erotic Icon* (Troy, NY: Whitston, 1983), and Bram Dijkstra's *Idols of Perversity: Fantasies of Feminine Evil in Fin-de-siècle Culture* (New York: Oxford UP, 1986).

18   In "Phases of Fiction," Woolf praises Austen for her ability to withhold her individuality from the writing of her fiction:

It may be the very idiosyncrasy of a writer that tires us of him. Jane Austen, who has so little that is peculiar, does not tire us, nor does she breed in us a desire for those writers whose method and style differ altogether from hers. (CE2: 76)

Of Turgenev, Woolf writes, "He is the most economical of writers. One of his economies is at once obvious. He takes up no room with his own person. He makes no comments upon his characters. He places them before the reader and leaves them to their fate" ("A Giant with Very Small Thumbs," *BP* 110). In "Henry James," Woolf quotes James himself on the "impersonality" of his writing:

In this impersonality the maker himself desired to share—"to take it", as he said, "wholly, exclusively with the pen (the style, the genius) and absolutely not at all with the person", to be "the mask without the face", the alien in our midst, the worker who when his work is done turns even from that and reserves his confidence for the solitary hour. . . . (*CE1*: 285)

One must note here that unlike Austen and Turgenev, James was a living presence in Woolf's life. As a friend of Leslie Stephen and a frequent visitor to 22 Hyde Park Gate, James knew Woolf from her girlhood. As a young woman, Woolf read James's fiction with irritation as well as admiration. James died in 1916; from 1917 to 1922 Woolf published six reviews of James and his critics in the *Times Literary Supplement*. In *Covert Relations: James Joyce, Virginia Woolf, and Henry James* (Charlottesville: UP of Virginia, 1990), Daniel Fogel explores at length the impact of James's literary legacy upon Joyce and Woolf.

19 For an analysis of this trend in Woolf's mature fiction, see Maria DiBattista's *Virginia Woolf's Major Novels: The Fables of Anon* (New Haven: Yale UP, 1980).

CHAPTER TWO

1 A number of critics have commented on the influence of Austen and the novel of manners in the writing of Woolf's earliest novels. Katharine Dalsimer, for example, notes that *Persuasion* in particular is featured in the conversation of the characters in *The Voyage Out*, and that Clarissa Dalloway gives Rachel a copy of the book before disembarking (132). Lisa Williams considers *The Voyage Out* to be the novel that "most resembles Austen's novels," but that "rewrites Austen" by ending in Rachel's death instead of her marriage (29). John Lehmann states that the novel "appears to set out as a social comedy, in the manner of E. M. Forster perhaps, but as it goes on it acquires, intermittently, a new dimension, a visionary and poetic quality that foreshadows the novels of Virginia Woolf's maturity" (44).

2 According to Lyndall Gordon, Woolf as a young woman debated such topics as the Greeks versus the moderns, Racine versus Shakespeare, and romance versus realism with her brother Thoby (77). *The Voyage Out* also airs a number of concerns that occupied the Bloomsbury group in its early years. Among these are the advocacy of frank, wide-ranging discussion between the sexes (*VO* 162), the difficulty of knowing others and communicating successfully with them, as evidenced by Rachel's conversations with Dalloway (*VO* 66), Evelyn Murgatroyd (*VO* 251), and Miss Allan (*VO* 255), and the importance of emotions, which Hirst and Hewet discuss one evening in Hirst's hotel room (*VO* 106). In her introductory essay in *Melymbrosia: An Early Version of The Voyage Out*, Louise

DeSalvo notes that this earlier version of the novel, which she edited for publication in 1982, "bristles with social commentary and impresses one with Woolf's engagement with the most significant problems of Edwardian and Georgian England" and then supplies a long list of topics discussed in the work (xxxvi-ii). For more on this early version of *The Voyage Out*, see DeSalvo's *Virginia Woolf's First Voyage: A Novel in the Making* (Totowa, NJ: Rowman & Littlefield, 1980).

3   Many critics have commented on the multiple meanings of the novel's title. These include the literal reference to Rachel's journey to South America as well as the metaphorical meanings—Rachel's movement out into the world of men and women, her journey of self-discovery, and her final but premature voyage out of life. Woolf's narrator lyrically describes the *Euphrosyne*, the ship owned by Rachel's father that bears her to her tragic destiny, as

... a bride going forth to her husband, a virgin unknown of men; in her vigour and purity she might be likened to all beautiful things, worshipped and felt as a symbol. (32)

The ship comes to symbolize Rachel and her fate; unfortunately death will become her bridegroom in this Woolfian variation on the age-old theme of Death and the maiden.

4   In her discussion of Fanny Burney's fictional heroines in *The Female Imagination*, Patricia Meyer Spacks notes Burney's recognition of "the incompatibility between the yearning for self-discovery and self-development and society's pressure toward comformity" experienced by young women (133). The female *Bildungsroman* underscores this dilemma: "women have not created important fictional heroines who find gratification through doing something in the world" (318). "Where," Spacks asks, "is the female equivalent of *Portrait of the Artist as a Young Man?*" (157).

As if to account for Spacks's observation, Christine Froula argues that genres like the *Künstlerroman* "marked with the features of fathers and sons refashion the natural law of sexual difference into social and culture laws of gender that foster male culture even as they repress female culturemaking" ("Gender" 157). Contrasting Joyce's *Portrait* and Woolf's *The Voyage Out*, Froula notes that while Stephen Dedalus "is nurtured, first and last, by fathers, Rachel has no culturally empowering mothers, natural or symbolic" (159). As *Künstlerromane*, both novels

... figure cultural inheritance governed by the law of the father: the son inherits a male-gendered cultural wealth, from which his own symbol-making takes its features, while the daughter inherits not a patrimony but matrimony, a role outside symbolic culture which does not empower symbolic acts. She receives no maternal inheritance from which to trace her own name and voice but instead suffers, sometimes fatally, images of her own repression in the father's texts. (162)

5   In her essay "Mr. Kipling's Notebook," Woolf herself notes that this habit is characteristic of young writers: "Between the ages of sixteen and twenty-one,

speaking roughly, every writer keeps a large notebook devoted entirely to landscape" (*BP* 63).

6 Peter Stansky echoes Naremore: "In many ways it is a traditional first novel, recounting the education of its central character, who can be taken to stand for the author herself" (67). More specifically, in this novel Katharine Dalsimer sees Woolf "contemplating the possibilities life offers a young woman. Marriage held terrors for her, and her first novel is at once an exploration and an enactment of those terrors" (133). Woolf had been working on the novel for several years before marrying in 1912.

According to George Spater and Ian Parsons, Woolf modeled the novel's principal characters to varying degrees on friends and relatives. To a certain extent, her parents served as models for the Ambroses, Helen Ambrose being a composite of her mother and her sister Vanessa Bell. Lytton Strachey was Woolf's model for St. John Hirst (84). Leon Edel argues that Hewet "is Virginia when he talks of his ambition to write novels and his desire to find words that will render human silences. He is also a version of Clive Bell (Heward was a Bell family name)" (155). J. K. Johnstone suggests that Rachel and Hewet "express the two different sides of their creator's character—her dreamy, sensitive, intuitive femininity; and her active, companionable, intellectual masculinity" (321–2). Spater and Parsons state that Woolf drew upon her own voyage to Lisbon and her experience of illness in describing Rachel's sea voyage and her "delirium" at the end of the novel (84). Further, they state that Helen Ambrose's chair-side companion is a copy of Moore's *Principia Ethica*, and note that the *Euphrosyne*, the name of the ship that carries Rachel to South America, was taken from the title of an anthology of verse published in 1905 that included contributions by Lytton Strachey, Clive Bell, Saxon Sydney-Turner, and Leonard Woolf, among others (84).

7 In *Virginia Woolf: Public and Private Negotiations*, Anna Snaith examines Woolf's thinking on the subject of public and private life, a topic that recurs throughout her work and in her letters and diaries, giving particular attention to *A Room of One's Own* and *Three Guineas*. That an intelligent young woman from the upper middle class would be particularly absorbed by this matter is not surprising, given the dramatic increase in the involvement of women in the public sphere in the late nineteenth century (see Snaith's summary, 20–4). As Snaith observes,

Historically, Woolf's use of the terms [public and private] was influenced, and played through, the ideology of separate spheres. For a woman living at the turn of the century, the division of public and private would have had immense significance even as it began to be challenged. (11)

8 Perhaps the poems that most clearly delineate the two spheres as Arnold viewed them are "Stanzas from the Grand Chartreuse" (1855), whose speaker bemoans the passing of a more intellectual and spiritual age that, like the monks of the Grand Chartreuse, valued study and contemplation, and "Stanzas

in Memory of the Author of 'Obermann'" (1852), in which the speaker reluctantly bids farewell to the writer Étienne Pivert de Senancour (1770–1846), sequestered in the Alps, and prepares to return to the contemporary world, which he views as fallen and disordered. This poem in particular succinctly summarizes the artist's or writer's dilemma:

> Ah! two desires toss about
> The poet's feverish blood.
> One drives him to the world without,
> And one to solitude. (93–6)

Among the essays that comprise Arnold's *Culture and Anarchy* (1869), "Sweetness and Light" presents a version of the two realms in the form of culture, which also includes the scientific passion for knowledge and the moral and social passion for doing good in the service of attaining "perfection," and contemporary British society, which Arnold criticizes for its "belief in machinery" (104) and its fundamental materialism: "He who works for sweetness and light, works to make reason and the will of God prevail. He who works for machinery, he who works for hatred, works only for confusion" (112). Not surprisingly, Arnold argues that the Oxford tradition promotes the "beauty and sweetness" that are "essential characters of a complete human perfection" (106).

9   Maurice Beebe notes that among the Symbolist poets, Baudelaire was a "visionary" who "attempts to see beyond the surface to a deeper reality that will cause him to forget the physical degradation of existence, the chaos of appearances, the tyranny of time" (132). Edward Engelberg finds in Mallarmé's "Les fenêtres"

> ... the dilemma facing the Symbolist poet: he seems forever alienated from an ideal world and also forever acutely conscious not only of this separation but also of the sordid reality from whose perspective he is obliged to seek the azure of the ideal world. (32)

Des Esseintes, the protagonist of Huysmans's novel *À rebours* (1884), deliberately retires from social life in order to cultivate his senses and exercise his imagination in seclusion.

10   As Howard Harper notes, one of the traits that reflect the modernity of *The Voyage Out* is the novel's concern with "the nature of the process of perception itself" (13). In *Between Language and Silence: The Novels of Virginia Woolf*, Harper examines the narrative consciousness in each of Woolf's novels and the implications of the choice of perspectives it makes in presenting the action of the novel. According to Harper, each novel

> ... represents a psychological voyage out of a familiar but oppressive reality toward a realm that is unknown and exciting, and which seems to promise wholeness. The narrative consciousness struggles to transcend the limited roles ordained by the family and society. Although the struggle involves sexual

conflict, the final transcendence can be achieved only in a detached, distanced, almost asexual identity which can comprehend experience without drowning in it. This personality can emerge only after all passion is spent. In *The Voyage Out* it is essentially an observer, but in the later works it becomes more and more closely identified with the role of the creative artist—painter, writer, dramatist. (56)

11   Woolf's characterization of Clarissa Dalloway in *The Voyage Out* is quite different from, and far less sympathetic than, that of Mrs. Dalloway in the eponymous novel published ten years later. Like Mrs. Manresa, also a wealthy man's wife, in *Between the Acts*, Clarissa as she appears in *The Voyage Out* frequently assumes the role of the flirtatious woman-child, disguising her manipulative nature under a veneer of artless enthusiasm. One senses in her the frustration of a strong intelligence that has few meaningful arenas in which to exert itself.

12   Rachel foresees an unsympathetic and unattractive matron in the engaged young woman: "She appeared insincere and cruel; she saw her grown stout and prolific, the kind blue eyes now shallow and watery, the bloom of the cheeks congealed to a network of dry red canals" (261).

13   Music appears to serve a similar function for Lucy Honeychurch, the young heroine of Forster's *A Room with a View*, which Woolf had read and reviewed in 1908, the year of its publication:

It so happened that Lucy, who found daily life rather chaotic, entered a more solid world when she opened the piano. She was then no longer either deferential or patronizing; no longer either a rebel or a slave. The kingdom of music is not the kingdom of this world; it will accept those whom breeding and intellect and culture have alike rejected. (33)

14   Throughout *The Voyage Out*, Rachel expresses dissatisfaction with external reality: "'it's the world that tells the lies and I tell the truth'" (293). On several occasions, the unreality of the everyday world strikes her as dreamlike. After a particularly trying Sunday spent among the guests at the hotel, Rachel's exasperation with "the imposition of ponderous stupidity" begins to dissipate as she tells herself, "'It's a dream. . . . We're asleep and dreaming'" (258). Apart from their Shakespearean echoes, Rachel's words suggest the disaffection of a Platonist for the visible world. In *Marius the Epicurean*, Pater describes Marius's constitutional idealism, "his innate and habitual longing for a world altogether fairer than that he saw" (36). While seated resting in an olive garden during a journey, Marius has a revelation in which he perceives the "*Great Ideal*" (257) operating in the universe, and concludes, "Must not all that remained of life be but a search for the equivalent of that Ideal, among so-called actual things—a gathering together of every trace or token of it, which his actual experience might present?" (258).

15   There are numerous instances of the perception of a "pattern" by the novel's characters. During a conversation with Rachel, Hewet detects "an order, a

pattern which made life reasonable" (299). While seated with Hewet in the hotel's hall, observing the guests passing through, Rachel, recently engaged, speculates that they, like herself, now knew "where they were going; and things formed themselves into a pattern not only for her, but for them, and in that pattern lay satisfaction and meaning" (314). In *Marius the Epicurean*, Marius, drawn to Christianity, visits the house of the young Christian widow Cecilia, and discerns in her gracious maternity "the sanction of some divine pattern thereof" (351). Pater describes what Marius had longed for most during his life of vigilant observation:

> Throughout that elaborate and lifelong education of his receptive powers, he had ever kept in view the purpose of preparing himself towards possible further revelation some day—towards some ampler vision, which should take up into itself and explain this world's delightful shows, as the scattered fragments of a poetry, till then but half-understood, might be taken up into the text of a lost epic, recovered at last. (379–80)

16 Hewet's comment recalls Dr. Johnson's derogatory remark concerning women who preach: "'Sir, a woman's preaching is like a dog's walking on his hinder legs. It is not done well; but you are surprized to find it done at all'" (Boswell 327).

17 The sea serves a number of functions for Rachel. She frequently turns to it to escape from disturbing occurrences or annoying companionship. The sea also provides an imaginative retreat where she can give her fantasy full sway. Startled by the sight of the Ambroses embracing on shipboard, Rachel turns away to peer into the ocean:

> One could scarcely see the black ribs of wrecked ships, or the spiral towers made by the burrowings of great eels, or the smooth green-sided monsters who came by flickering this way and that. (27–8)

The sight of seabirds rising and falling on the waves calms her after having broken away from Dalloway's embrace in her cabin (76). Irritated by Hewet's questions while seated atop a cliff, Rachel turns her gaze toward the sea (215). Woolf underscores Rachel's otherworldly dimension in Hewet's description of her as having at first looked "like a creature who'd lived all its life among pearls and old bones" (293). On the afternoon in which Rachel's fatal illness manifests itself, Hewet has been reading to her the passage from Milton's *Comus* invoking the water sprite Sabrina, a preserver of imperiled virginity, whose description curiously suggests the paintings of such Pre-Raphaelite artists as Burne-Jones and *fin-de-siècle* artists as Toorop, Klimt, Rackham, and Beardsley in its linearity:

> Sabrina fair,
>   Listen where thou art sitting
> Under the glassy, cool, translucent wave,
>   In twisted braids of lilies knitting
> The loose train of thy amber dropping hair,

> Listen for dear honour's sake,
>   Goddess of the silver lake,
>   Listen and save! (*VO* 327)

As Rachel succumbs to delirium, she finds herself a modern-day Sabrina submerged in a watery world much like the sea of her earlier imaginings:

> . . . she fell into a deep pool of sticky water, which eventually closed over her head. She saw nothing and heard nothing but a faint booming sound, which was the sound of the sea rolling over her head. While all her tormentors thought that she was dead, she was not dead, but curled up at the bottom of the sea. There she lay, sometimes seeing darkness, sometimes light, while every now and then some one turned her over at the bottom of the sea. (341)

Rachel's dissolution in illness becomes a metaphoric return to the sea-womb, a merging with the broad, impersonal forces of the universe.

18 There is considerable irony in Pepper's comment, as he has joined the voyage to South America in order to "get things out of the sea" (19). In *The Voyage Out*, the collecting mania appears to be a distinctly male one and is tainted with colonial exploitation as Woolf depicts it. Mrs. Flushing's husband is in the business of buying native ornaments and clothing for very little—"'they don't know what they're worth, so we get 'em cheap'" (235)—and selling them to fashionable Englishwomen.

19 Woolf's later novels actually include instances of, or references to, sexual violation in urban settings. In *The Years*, the child Rose Pargiter is subjected to the lewd gestures of an exhibitionist on the sidewalk near her London home (29). Isa Oliver reads of the gang rape of a naive young woman in the Whitehall barracks in *Between the Acts* (20).

20 Confiding in Helen, Hirst remarks, "'There never will be more than five people in the world worth talking to'" (161). On more than one occasion, Hirst exhibits considerable contempt for the hotel guests, declaring them "'all types'" who can be counted upon never to stray from their predictable roles (107).

Woolf may have had Pater's Sebastian van Storck of *Imaginary Portraits* (1887) in mind when she has Hirst describe his beloved friend Bennett, a reclusive scholar

> . . . who lived in an old windmill six miles out of Cambridge. He lived the perfect life . . . very lonely, very simple, caring only for the truth of things, always ready to talk, and extraordinarily modest, though his mind was of the greatest. (205)

21 A good example of the view of Rachel as having at some level chosen death in an effort to escape the potential threat to her autonomy posed by her engagement may be found in Phyllis Rose's biography of Woolf:

> Rachel's illness inevitably seems connected with her engagement to Terence—she withdraws into herself as she always does when threatened, but now in a final and ghastly fashion; her purity and integrity are preserved through death. (72–3)

Lisa Williams considers Rachel's death "to be part of her unwillingness to move from a more female centered world to one of marriage, even if it is to an almost 'maternal' male" (42). Christine Froula views Rachel's "identification with drowned things" as representing "an alternative to human culture as structured by the marriage plot" ("Out of the Chrysalis" 144). Summarizing the significance of Rachel's death for Woolf as a writer, she suggests that if it "records the failure of Woolf's imaginative project" in this novel, "it is also a symbolic, initiatory death that precedes the rebirth of Woolf's authority in the more powerful representations of female creativity in her later female *Künstlerromane*" (136).

22   Although his intent is somewhat different, Hewet's plans to write a novel about silence, "the things people don't say" (216), call to mind Mallarmé's concern for the inadequacy of words as a means of communication and of evoking the ineffable in human sensation and experience. As his career progressed, Mallarmé's poetic productivity steadily diminished and the poems themselves became increasingly cryptic.

During Rachel's illness, Hewet experiences a glimpse of an underlying reality that brings him peace:

Surely the world of strife and fret and anxiety was not the real world, but this was the real world, the world that lay beneath the superficial world, so that, whatever happened, one was secure. (343)

CHAPTER THREE

1   In his Rede Lecture on Woolf, Forster states of *Night and Day*:

This is an exercise in classical realism, and contains all that has characterised English fiction, for good and evil, during the last two hundred years: faith in personal relations, recourse to humorous side-shows, geographical exactitude, insistence on petty social differences: indeed most of the devices she so gaily derides in *Mr. Bennett and Mrs. Brown*. The style has been normalised and dulled. (*Virginia Woolf* 13)

2   Woolf may well have had Wordsworth in mind in creating Richard Alardyce. The narrator's description of Alardyce's portrait in the Hilbery home bears a strong resemblance to the famous tinted pencil portrait of Wordsworth as a young man drawn by Henry Edridge in 1806:

The sensual lips were slightly parted, and gave the face an expression of beholding something lovely or miraculous vanishing or just rising upon the rim of the distance. (319–20)

Tennyson may also have been a model; Alardyce's period of dissipation recalls Tennyson's years of depression and alcoholism prior to gaining literary recognition in the 1840s.

3   One must note that from the novel's conception, Woolf drew upon her sister Vanessa Bell as the model for Katharine Hilbery. In a letter to Bell dated July 30,

1916, Woolf writes, "I am very much interested in your life, which I think of writing another novel about" (*L2*: 109). In another letter to her dated April 22, 1918, Woolf notes, "I've been writing about you all morning, and have made you wear a blue dress; you've got to be immensely mysterious and romantic, which of course you are" (*L2*: 232). *Night and Day* is also dedicated to Vanessa.

But Katharine exhibits much of Woolf as well, as both Woolf and her sister were involved in the same enterprise of trying to craft identities as creative individuals apart from that of their father. Vanessa's medium proved to be painting rather than writing and editing, those of Leslie Stephen. Lyndall Gordon notes some of the traits Katharine shares with Vanessa in particular: "her dependence on reason, her silent stoicism, her secret commitment to mathematics, an equivalent to Vanessa's painting and, like that, in conflict with a Victorian sense of responsibility as the daughter at home" (166).

As in *The Voyage Out*, a number of the characters in *Night and Day* are based on Woolf's friends, relations, and acquaintances. Leonard Woolf serves as the model for Ralph Denham. Woolf's aunt Anne Thackeray Ritchie is portrayed in Mrs. Hilbery (Bell, *VW1*: 11; Gilbert and Gubar 3: 16), and William Rodney is based upon Walter Headlam, a fellow of King's and an old friend of the Stephen family (*L2*: 414; Bell, *VW1*: 118).

4   Rodney's "pearl in the center of his tie" (*ND* 52) evokes the "necktie rich and modest, but asserted by a simple pin" (43) worn by Eliot's Prufrock, who is equally obsessed with appearances. Woolf would most likely have been familiar with the poem; the Egoist Press in London had published Eliot's *Prufrock and Other Observations*, a collection of early poems, in 1917. Two years later, in 1919, the same year as the publication of *Night and Day*, the Woolfs' Hogarth Press published a collection of seven new poems by Eliot (Lehmann 42).

Denham's incredulous reaction to the news of Katharine's engagement to Rodney—"'That little pink-cheeked dancing-master to marry Katharine?'" (303)—recalls Dr. Johnson's dismay upon learning that Mrs. Thrale had wed Gabriel Piozzi, an Italian musician and her dancing teacher.

5   Upon arriving at Stogdon House in Lincolnshire, Rodney is irritated by the temporary loss of a box containing clothes he had selected for Katherine to wear (196). During a critical conversation with her while seated under an oak tree in the countryside, Rodney notices "with distress" a wayward strand of hair upon her shoulder and some leaves clinging to her dress (246). He wishes she would attend to these matters, "of more immediate importance to him than anything else" (246).

6   As Howard Harper notes, in the culture Katharine inhabits, a "woman can transform or escape from her given world through her choice of a marriage partner. In the view of the narrative consciousness here . . . this is almost the only meaningful choice that she can make" (68).

7   It is noteworthy that Woolf gives Cassandra the same surname as the Restoration dramatist Thomas Otway, whose *Venice Preserv'd*, first produced in London in

1682, became a stock tragedy in the London theater repertory during the following century. Rodney is obviously interested in Restoration drama; his book collection includes the Baskerville edition of Congreve (73). Rodney gives the manuscript of his own verse play to Cassandra to read (280). Woolf's assignment of Otway's surname to Cassandra appears to reinforce the sense of a natural affinity between her and Rodney. Woolf may also have been playfully borrowing some of her characters' names from Forster. A Sir Harry Otway, a comical minor character who, like Cassandra's father Sir Francis Otway, lives in the countryside, appears in Forster's *A Room with a View* (1908).

8   As Quentin Bell notes, "When in *Night and Day* Ralph Denham brings Katharine Hilbery to visit his family in Highgate, Virginia is surely remembering that first visit to the Woolf family" in Putney, another London suburb (*VW2*: 3). Denham's family lives on Mount Ararat Road, a street name which evokes the image of Noah's ark coming to rest following the Flood. The Denham family, like Leonard Woolf's family, appears to be a socially isolated one attempting to survive in a challenging new world following the death of the father.

9   The novel's narrator also suggests an element of danger here by comparing Denham to "one of those lost birds fascinated by the lighthouse and held to the glass by the splendor of the blaze" (395). In Jungian terms, the mysterious, idealized image of Katharine that Denham worships constitutes a projection of his anima.

10   Leonard Woolf idealized his future wife in a similar manner, referring to her as "Aspasia" in his diary and equating her in his imagination with distant snowy hills unexplored by humankind (Gordon 150).

11   Although meant to illustrate the couple's emotional state, this rather Wagnerian transfiguration strikes one as overblown; the language indicates the extent to which Woolf at this stage in her writing career was still influenced by the rhetoric and diction of an older literary style. The explorer image serves Woolf's purpose of gentle satire eight years later in *To the Lighthouse*, when Mr. Ramsay earnestly reconsiders his strenuous attempts to reach "R" (54–7).

12   Woolf's image of the flame here evokes that of Pater in the controversial conclusion to the first edition of *Studies in the History of the Renaissance* (1873) in which he urges his readers to experience the visible world as intensely as they can:

Not the fruit of experience, but experience itself, is the end. A counted number of pulses only is given to us of a variegated, dramatic life. How may we see in them all that is to be seen in them by the finest senses? How shall we pass most swiftly from point to point, and be present always at the focus where the greatest number of vital forces unite in their purest energy?

To burn always with this hard, gemlike flame, to maintain this ecstasy, is success in life. (249–50)

13   Chelsea's Cheyne Walk, where Woolf situates the house of the literary Hilberys, has numerous literary associations. As Jean Moorcroft Wilson notes in *Virginia Woolf, Life and London: A Biography of Place*, George Eliot died

at Number 4 in 1880 (210). From 1862 to 1882, the year of Woolf's birth, Rossetti lived at Number 16 (210). Carlyle Mansions, at the end of Cheyne Walk, had two famous literary occupants, Henry James and T. S. Eliot (211). Carlyle himself had lived nearby at 24 Cheyne Row (211). Wilson submits that in Woolf's novels, though,

> . . . Chelsea quite unequivocally stands for social privilege as opposed to intellect. The symbolism of *Night and Day* centres round the contrast between Katharine Hilbery's socially privileged but intellectually arid home in Cheyne Walk, Chelsea, and Ralph Denham's socially inferior but intellectually lively house in the suburbs at Highgate. Katharine's decision to marry Ralph involves leaving her Chelsea home. In doing so she frees herself to pursue her own intellectual interests, which are not understood by her family. (155)

One might add in support of Wilson's argument that the street's name suggests hobbling, reinforcing the view of Katharine as a capable young woman intellectually hampered by her family and her social class.

14   In *Archetypal Patterns in Women's Fiction*, Annis Pratt discovers in Katharine's fantasized "magnanimous hero" the "green-world-lover archetype"(22). Pratt argues that as the heroines of women's novels approach the age of marriage, "comprehended as submission to the patriarchy," their memory of the natural world, which represents freedom and the state of innocence, "erupts with the power of a struggle for personal authenticity" (22). When this happens, the young heroine often "turns away from 'appropriate' males toward fantasies of a figure, projected from within her own personality, more suitable to her needs" (22). Examples of the green world lover archetype from novels written by women include Heathcliff in *Wuthering Heights* and Alexandra's Great Corn God, a dream figure who carries her off in Cather's *O Pioneers!* (22). In Jungian terms, one may view such fantasy figures as projections of the woman's animus. Denham comes to be equated with the "magnanimous hero" in Katharine's psyche relatively early in their courtship. While chiding Denham for idealizing her, she says, "'You're going to go on dreaming and imagining and making up stories about me as you walk along the street, and *pretending that we're riding in a forest*'" (382–3; italics mine).

15   Katharine's habit of hiding her sheets of figures and equations between the pages of a dictionary (45) anticipates Isa Oliver's effort to conceal her poems from her husband by recording them in a book that resembles an account ledger in *Between the Acts* (15).

16   Early in the novel the narrator states quite bluntly that Katharine chooses mathematics as her subject for study because "in her mind mathematics were directly opposed to literature" (46). As Perry Meisel notes, part of Katharine's aversion to literature lies in the fact that it is "a primary systematic presence" (187) in the novel that "structures life" (186) in the Hilbery home. Mornings and evenings are spent writing or reviewing the writings of others; Mr. Hilbery edits a review while Mrs. Hilbery and Katharine attempt to produce a biography

of Alardyce, the presiding literary genius of the household (187). In *The Singing of the Real World: The Philosophy of Virginia Woolf's Fiction*, Mark Hussey argues that Woolf's treatment of the elder Hilberys' literary activities in *Night and Day* represents a questioning of the kind of literary "dogmatism" that she viewed as "deadening and restrictive" (69): "This generation has made a religion of literature: their responses are dogma, the editor of an 'esteemed review' is a 'minister of literature' . . . they have a certain idea of what literature is and what it should not be" (69). Further: "Literature is shown as the opiate of an intellectual élite who consider it their birthright, to guard and interpret" (68).

It becomes clear why Katharine's secret passion must become something other than literature in the psychological economy of the novel. However, the choice of mathematics strikes readers as arbitrary. As Howard Harper remarks, the novel's

> . . . narrative consciousness hasn't the faintest idea of what 'mathematics' might be about: it is an unknown realm, an arcane language which, in this naïve view, has none of the ambiguities or uncertainties of literary language. Although Katharine is alleged to know "mathematics," to her it means nothing more than the negation of literature. (63)

17 Unlike the Hilberys, the Denham family appears to be far more advanced in its views regarding women, education, and the professions. Ralph's younger sister Hester tells Katharine that she is reading for an examination and eagerly hopes to be able to enter Newnham (376).

18 The *Oxford Companion to English Literature* (5th ed., 1985) reports that Sarah Grand, writing in *The North American Review* in 1894, is believed to have coined the phrase "to describe a new generation of women, influenced by J. S. Mill and other campaigners for women's rights, who believed in Women's Suffrage, abolition of the double standard in sexual matters, Rational Dress, educational opportunities for women, etc." (697). For discussions of the emergence of this figure in late Victorian fiction, see Lloyd Fernando's *"New Women" in the Late Victorian Novel* (University Park: Pennsylvania State UP, 1977) and Gail Cunningham's *The New Woman and the Victorian Novel* (New York: Barnes & Noble, 1978). Jane Marcus believes that Woolf's New Woman, Mary Datchet, is modeled partly on the suffragette Margaret Llewelyn Davies (*Art & Anger*, 210).

19 In *Bloomsbury and Modernism*, Ulysses D'Aquila comments upon Woolf's work addressing envelopes for the Adult Suffrage Movement in 1910: "Undoubtedly, she found her labor uninspiring and her co-workers an unimaginative lot, and several years later, writing *Night and Day*, she to a degree satirised [sic] the feminist movement and the women to whom it was a religion" (193).

20 Woolf's narrator again resorts to Pater's image of the flame, this time to describe how Mary views the "essential thing" (259) that she feels she lacks: "In the eyes of every single person she detected a flame; as if a spark in the brain ignited spontaneously at contact with the things they met and drove them on" (259). In *The Voyage Out*, Terence Hewet tries to explain to Evelyn Murgatroyd his

appreciation for individuals in their essentiality: "'It's just them that we care for,'—he struck a match—'just that,' he said, pointing to the flames" (193).

21 As Howard Harper notes, "Although Mary's work is alleged to be important, it has very little reality in the narrative consciousness, which remains preoccupied with other things" (68).

22 Woolf's overvaluation of the import of heterosexual relationships for women in these early novels is quite understandable given her upper middle-class family background and the Victorian social world of her formative years spent at 22 Hyde Park Gate. See the Introduction, above, and the biographies by Bell, Rose, Gordon, and Lee.

CHAPTER FOUR

1 J. K. Johnstone characterizes Woolf's first short story collection *Monday or Tuesday* (1921) as "a prelude to *Jacob's Room*," which drew upon the "highly individualistic techniques" used in the short stories (320). Having finished writing *Jacob's Room*, Woolf records being "on the whole pleased" with her effort in her diary entry for July 26, 1922:

> There's no doubt in my mind that I have found out how to begin (at 40) to say something in my own voice . . . . (*D2*: 186)

2 As in Woolf's first two novels, the protagonist of *Jacob's Room* appears to be partly based on an actual person in her life—her brother Thoby Stephen, who died of typhoid fever in London in November 1906 following a journey with Vanessa, Virginia, and Adrian Stephen to Greece. Lyndall Gordon interprets Jacob as Woolf's effort "to recast Thoby in the figure of the lost generation of the first world war" (168). Phyllis Rose notes some of the similarities between the two:

> The bare bones of Jacob's life are those of Thoby's: childhood at the seashore, Cambridge, London, a trip to Greece, early death. Thoby Stephen appealed to people as Jacob does, not for anything you could put your finger on, except his beauty, but for some indefinable quality of distinction emanating from him. (106)

Howard Harper notes an even closer factual correspondence between Jacob's life and that of Rupert Brooke, whom Woolf knew. Like Brooke, Jacob attends Rugby and King's College, Cambridge, where he matriculates in October 1906, as did Brooke, who died of blood poisoning in Greece in 1915 (105n5).

3 Judy Little argues that Woolf's use of the *Bildungsroman* genre in *Jacob's Room* is parodic. In the novel, according to Little, "the traditional male growth-pattern, full of great expectation, falls like a tattered mantle around the shoulders of the indecisive hero, heir of the ages. The musing and amused narrator mocks the structure of her story; she mocks the conventions of the

hero's progress; and, by implication, she mocks the values behind those conventions" (105).

4   Among Woolf's novels, *Jacob's Room* contains an unusually high number of characters. As David Dowling notes, over 160 distinct characters have been counted in this relatively short novel (129).

5   In ascribing this research topic to Miss Marchmont, Woolf appears to be alluding to synesthesia—the mixing of sensory effects, of which the Symbolists were quite fond. Among the well-known Symbolist works employing this technique are Baudelaire's sonnet "Correspondances" (1857), Rimbaud's sonnet "Voyelles" (1871), and Huysmans's novel *À rebours* (1884).

6   The reader is not told exactly what kind of job Jacob has. Based on the brief description of a typical work day provided by the narrator at the beginning of the eighth chapter, Jacob's position appears to be a leisurely one in an office of a private law firm or one of the Inns of Court, as it is located near, if not in, Gray's Inn, involves signing letters, and leaves "some muscle of the brain new stretched" (90) at the end of the day. According to the narrator, Mrs. Flanders addresses her letter to her son as "Jacob Alan Flanders, Esq., as mothers do" (90), which might suggest that he is clerking or has even become a lawyer, but is not necessarily the case.

7   As was noted earlier, Woolf read and admired Chekhov, as her comments in "The Russian Point of View," an essay published in *The Common Reader* (1925), make clear, but not chiefly for the naturalist elements in his work:

> Tchekov . . . is aware of the evils and injustices of the social state; the condition of the peasants appals him, but the reformer's zeal is not his—that is not the signal for us to stop. The mind interests him enormously; he is a most subtle and delicate analyst of human relations. But again, no; the end is not there. Is it that he is primarily interested not in the soul's relation with other souls, but with the soul's relation to health—with the soul's relation to goodness? These stories are always showing us some affectation, pose, insincerity. Some woman has got into a false relation; some man has been perverted by the inhumanity of his circumstances. The soul is ill; the soul is cured; the soul is not cured. Those are the emphatic points in his stories. (*CE1*: 241)

Woolf gently satirizes the Chekhovian character in Mrs. Sandra Wentworth Williams, who feels tender concern for the suffering of others, especially the poor. See the following note.

8   As the narrator describes her, Mrs. Wentworth Williams could easily have stepped out of a Chekhov play:

> . . . she stood, veiled, in white, in the window of the hotel at Olympia. How beautiful the evening was! and her beauty was its beauty. The tragedy of Greece was the tragedy of all high souls. The inevitable compromise. She seemed to have grasped something. She would write it down. (141–2)

As a cue to her readers, Woolf equips Mrs. Wentworth Williams with "a little book convenient for traveling—stories by Tchekov" (141).

9 In his marital unhappiness and seeming obliviousness to his surroundings, Mr. Clutterbuck appears to be a prototype for Augustus Carmichael in *To the Lighthouse.*

10 Woolf's narrator satirizes Oxbridge and the men it produces in short sketches of three Cambridge dons—Sopwith, who invariably serves chocolate cake to undergraduates and former students in his rooms; Erasmus Cowan, the classics professor who intones Virgil and Catullus between sips of port; and old Professor Huxtable, whose mind in reading reflects the methodical march of soldiers:

Now, as his eye goes down the print, what a procession tramps through the corridors of his brain, orderly, quick-stepping, and reinforced, as the march goes on, by fresh runnels, till the whole hall, dome, whatever one calls it, is populous with ideas. Such a muster takes place in no other brain. (40)

Woolf continues her critique of the predominantly masculine values promoted by the British educational system in *A Room of One's Own* and *Three Guineas*, the latter of which treats more explicitly the expression of these values in government and the military.

11 Elsewhere in the novel, the narrator reflects upon a stark, ugly reality lying concealed beneath the visible world: "who, save the nerve-worn and sleepless, or thinkers standing with hands to the eyes on some crag above the multitude, see things thus in skeleton outline, bare of flesh?" (162). At other times, chaos is seen to lurk beneath the quotidian, and the activities of civilized life, down to the most insignificant daily rituals, serve to maintain the illusion of order and keep chaos at bay:

Sunlight strikes in upon shaving-glasses; and gleaming brass cans; upon all the jolly trappings of the day; the bright, inquisitive, armoured, resplendent, summer's day, which has long since vanquished chaos; which has dried the melancholy mediaeval mists; drained the swamp and stood glass and stone upon it; and equipped our brains and bodies with such an armoury of weapons that merely to see the flash and thrust of limbs engaged in the conduct of daily life is better than the old pageant of armies drawn out in battle array upon the plain. (163)

This last image evokes the famous one of a chaotic world at the end of Arnold's "Dover Beach:"

And we are here as on a darkling plain
Swept with confused alarms of struggle and flight,
Where ignorant armies clash by night. (35–7)

The war, of course, represents the eruption of unfettered chaos, which claims Jacob's relatively orderly life. For more on Woolf's response to the wars of her era and their impact upon her work, see *Virginia Woolf and War: Fiction,*

Reality, and Myth (Syracuse: Syracuse UP, 1991), a collection of essays edited by Mark Hussey, and Karen L. Levenback's *Virginia Woolf and the Great War* (Syracuse: Syracuse UP, 1999).

12 Among the other natural objects that foreshadow Jacob's death is the jawbone of a sheep that the child Jacob has picked up during his afternoon at the beach and kicks away from him in bed at night (14). The galloping riderless horse which startles Clara Durrant in Hyde Park at the end of the novel (167) adumbrates not only Jacob's demise, but also the chaos of war generally.

13 In writing these short sentences, Woolf most likely had in mind the well-known lines from Wordsworth's "Ode: Intimations of Immortality from Recollections of Early Childhood:"

> But trailing clouds of glory do we come
> From God, who is our home:
> Heaven lies about us in our infancy!
> Shades of the prison-house begin to close
> Upon the growing Boy,
> But He beholds the light, and whence it flows,
> He sees it in his joy;
> The Youth, who daily farther from the East
> Must travel, still is Nature's Priest,
> And by the vision splendid
> Is on his way attended;
> At length the Man perceives it die away,
> And fade into the light of common day. (64–76)

CHAPTER FIVE

1 Interestingly, Septimus's name contains within it the Latin roots for "septic," or "infected," as well as the number seven, associated with the Deadly Sins of Christianity and evoking Septimus's unbearable feeling of guilt. There is also an irony in Woolf's choice; Septimus's famous namesake, the Roman emperor Septimus Severus (AD 146–211), was a highly skilled military commander who conducted several successful campaigns in the provinces during the closing years of the second century and fathered Caracalla, one of Rome's most ruthless emperors.

2 Alex Zwerdling gives a more critical assessment of the Dalloways' social selectivity; they

> . . . shut out not only the Septimus Smiths and the Doris Kilmans but the artists as well. The novel makes it clear that their world is consistently and uneasily philistine. Though a token poet makes an appearance at Clarissa's party, her set has a deep distrust of writers, precisely because they might disturb its complacency. (127)

3 There is a certain irony in Clarissa's characterization of Lady Bradshaw, as she herself undoubtedly appears to others to be such a wife. The two women are

quite different, however. As Patricia Meyer Spacks notes, "Mrs. Dalloway *uses* the forms that Lady Bradshaw merely submits to; but they are the same forms, the women inhabit the same society" (268).

4   A model for this character may well have been Marianne North, an unmarried Victorian painter of flowers who traveled around the world to capture her subjects on canvas. She gave her collection of paintings, for which she funded the construction of a gallery in 1882, to the Royal Botanic Gardens at Kew, one of the Woolfs' leisure destinations and the setting of Woolf's short story "Kew Gardens." North's paintings can still be seen in the gallery, which remains open to the public.

5   Clarissa Dalloway is the first of Woolf's fictional social artists, women skilled at bringing people together and creating moments of meaning and community. Mrs. Ramsay in *To the Lighthouse*, of course, is another. Phyllis Rose suggests that Woolf may have been attempting "to bridge the gap between her own activities and the more usual activities of women of her class by trying to present the efforts of hostesses as versions of artistic creation" (151). Geneviève Sanchis Morgan makes the case that the frequent appearance of the hostess in Woolf's works "functions as a metaphor for the female artist" (90), and that Woolf's use of hostess and seamstress figures "argue[s] for a poetics of domesticity" (91). Further: "By creating 'modernist' works that not only depict the domestic realm, but are also products of this same realm, Woolf strategically rejects the public, male-identified sphere as the cradle of aesthetic vision" (93). Marianne DeKoven views *Mrs. Dalloway* as "the clearest instance of Woolfian fiction as reinvention of feminine privacy," an effort that "permeates her work from its inception through the mid-thirties" (238). These observations can be seen to reflect a refinement of the broader modernist project to reclaim the interiority of the artist-figure generally, a trend that one can observe in the writings of authors as diverse as Joyce, Richardson, Lawrence, Thomas Wolfe, and Faulkner, as well as Woolf herself. As such, it can be viewed as a reaction to the realism of so much Victorian and Edwardian fiction, more concerned with depicting social life than exploring the private, individual consciousness and its sources of aesthetic inspiration, both internal and external.

As Morgan notes (and the biographies reveal), Woolf had ample exposure to the world of London society hostesses, having attended parties held by Emerald Cunard, Sybil Colefax, and Nancy Corrigan, who were quite prominent during the 1920s (91). It should also be noted, though, that Woolf was ambivalent about the hostess role, as the narrator's characterization of the hostess in *Orlando* suggests:

The hostess is our modern Sibyl. She is a witch who lays her guests under a spell. In this house they think themselves happy; in that witty; in a third profound. It is all an illusion (which is nothing against it, for illusions are the most valuable and necessary of all things, and she who can create one is among the world's greatest benefactors), but as it is notorious that illusions are shattered by conflict with reality, so no real happiness, no real wit, no real profundity are tolerated where the illusion prevails. (199–200)

Clarissa shares this ambivalence somewhat, feeling she is, as will be noted again later, "something not herself" (259) when giving a party, but to a far lesser degree than Woolf. For more on Clarissa's artistry as a hostess, see Jacob Littleton's "*Mrs. Dalloway*: Portrait of the Artist as a Middle-Aged Woman," *Twentieth Century Literature* 41.1 (1995): 35–53.

6   As J. K. Johnstone notes, in Woolf's introduction to the 1928 Modern Library edition of *Mrs. Dalloway*, she states that Clarissa and Septimus are "'one and the same person'" (qtd. in Johnstone 341), Septimus succumbing to the despair and madness that Clarissa successfully resists. As Littleton remarks, "Septimus replicates Clarissa's threatened position. They are threatened more than other characters because, more than any others, their private selves diverge from public expectations of them" (48). Spater and Parsons, among others, note that Clarissa is modeled after Kitty Maxse, a society woman and girlhood friend "who died in 1922 after a fall which Virginia believed was suicide" (114). Shirley Panken, a psychoanalyst, sees in Woolf's portrayal of Septimus "the objective depiction of her early breakdown" (12).

     Woolf uses shared imagery—especially that of trees, birds, and webs or nets—to connect Septimus to Clarissa, and the consciousnesses of both at different times in the novel register the same line from *Cymbeline*, "Fear no more the heat o' the sun." Panken delineates what she perceives to be a number of similarities between the two characters and Woolf herself:

     Septimus, Clarissa, and Woolf are enormously self-devaluating. Clarissa and Woolf caricature their bodies, feel unfeminine, aged, or asexual; Septimus loathes and distorts his body functions, which seem true for Woolf during her emotional crisis in 1913. All three are sexually ambivalent, feel isolated, and are spectators to life. Woolf shares Septimus' [sic] and Clarissa's confusion regarding sexual identification. (137)

     Woolf employs bird imagery to link Clarissa and Septimus to Peter as well; both Clarissa and Septimus have "beaked" noses (14, 20), Septimus reminds his wife of "a young hawk" (222), and Peter's eyes are "still a little hawklike" (249) as he heads toward the Dalloways' house in the evening.

7   Only once does the novel mention Clarissa's witnessing the accidental death of her talented young sister. Peter recalls Clarissa's comment that the sight "was enough to turn one bitter" (118). As Howard Harper points out, Clarissa, like a number of Woolf's female characters, also lost her mother in girlhood (115); the narrative only alludes to the pain of this loss once, during the party, when Mrs. Hilbery (also of *Night and Day*) remarks to Clarissa how much she reminds her of her mother as she appeared one day in a garden: "And really Clarissa's eyes filled with tears" (267). In *Virginia Woolf and the Fictions of Psychoanalysis*, Elizabeth Abel sees in the deaths of the mother and the sister, coupled with the loss of Clarissa's girlhood intimacy with Sally Seton and her marriage to Dalloway, the loss of a pre-Oedipal

"pastoral female world" centered in Bourton, her childhood home, which has since been replaced by "the heterosexual and androcentric social world" of Dalloway and London (31).

One can only speculate as to how deeply these losses have been felt by Clarissa and how they have shaped her relationship to her father, her husband and daughter, her life, and her own mortality. The novel also highlights the fact of death's real and constant presence during the war, even in the lives of Clarissa's privileged friends and acquaintances. While running her morning errand, Clarissa recalls the death of Mrs. Foxcroft's son and the stoicism of Lady Bexborough, directing a bazaar, "with the telegram in her hand, John, her favourite, killed" (5). As Clarissa observes, the times "had bred in them all, all men and women, a well of tears" (13).

8   According to Phyllis Rose, "One of Woolf's concerns in this novel is the strategic value of frigidity, its use in preserving a woman's sense of autonomy and selfhood" (144).

9   That this is an important matter for Clarissa is evidenced by her silent assessment of Sir William Bradshaw in connection with Septimus's suicide during the party in the evening (281).

10 According to Alex Zwerdling, "In Sally, Peter, and Clarissa, Woolf traces the process of socialization from the extended moment in which each was intensely alive—young, brash, open, taking emotional risks—to the stage of conventionality" (137).

11 Zwerdling views Peter's "whole personality in middle age" as "a flimsy construct designed to reassure himself that the passion and radicalism of his youth are not dead" (135).

12 Howard Harper suggests that Peter psychologically "embodies a consuming male desire which has been disarmed and transformed into a lifelong devotion" (123).

13 In introducing Miss Isabel Pole and her lectures on Shakespeare in Waterloo Road, Woolf may well be remembering, and gently satirizing, her own experience as an evening lecturer at a London college for workers while a young woman (Bell VW1: 105–6; Lee 218–20). See also Lindsay Martin's "Virginia Woolf at Morley College," *The Charleston Magazine* 4 (1991/2): 21–5. Interestingly, in *Night and Day*, a man named Septimus is one of the young people expected at Mary Datchet's apartment to hear William Rodney read his paper on the Elizabethan use of metaphor (50).

14 The narrator characterizes the relationship between Septimus and Evans, whom Rezia saw as "a sturdy, red-haired man, undemonstrative in the company of women" (130), as follows:

It was a case of two dogs playing on a hearth-rug; one worrying a paper screw, snarling, snapping, giving a pinch, now and then, at the old dog's ear; the other lying somnolent, blinking at the fire, raising a paw, turning and growling good-temperedly. They had to be together, share with each other, fight with each other, quarrel with each other. (130)

Some critics view Septimus and Evans, as well as Clarissa and Sally Seton, whose kiss on her lips Clarissa recalls as "the most exquisite moment" (52) of her life, as repressed homosexuals victimized by a patriarchal culture. For example, Jane Marcus values the novel for

> . . . its objective relating of the psychiatric establishment to the political establishment, its indictment of the class system, patriarchy, and imperialism, and its uncanny ability to condemn capitalism for destroying the lives of two unlikely figures [Clarissa and Septimus] at opposite ends of the scale, consumed by guilt at their repressed homosexuality. (*Art & Anger* 176)

Gay Wachman views the novel "as a survey of suppressed lesbianism (or homosexuality in the case of Septimus) whose motive force was Woolf's growing interest in Vita Sackville-West" (349).

It is certainly possible to acknowledge a lightly disguised homosexual subtext in the depiction of each of these same-sex relationships. There seems to be a lack of evidence, though, that Clarissa's life has been "destroyed" by the repression of her lesbianism. I would also add that female sexual reticence in heterosexual relationships is not necessarily linked to a particular sexual orientation, especially for women of Clarissa's generation, who were subjected to numerous Victorian taboos concerning the expression of female sexuality generally, and may have been subjected to childhood sexual abuse as well, as Woolf herself apparently was (see DeSalvo's book on the subject).

As for Septimus's guilt, the text makes the case that it stems from his not having been able to feel (137), to mourn the loss of Evans—which can be interpreted as a vital defensive reaction on the part of an extremely sensitive psyche to the horrors of war surrounding it at the time. In *Psychoanalysis, Psychiatry and Modernist Literature*, Kylie Valentine offers a different view of Septimus's inability to feel; his "experience of war is of induction into a masculinity that allows no acknowledgement of grief or fear; and it is this foreclosing of emotional honesty, not grief or fear alone, that brings about madness" (128).

15   Panken views *Mrs. Dalloway* as

> . . . a courageous foray into little-understood channels of mental illness: the recourse to messianism and sublimity; emergence of delusional mechanisms and body distortions; the sense of extreme isolation, and occasionally, of depersonalization. (139)

Septimus hears voices, talks to himself and to the deceased Evans, has manic moments, and exhibits paranoia and megalomania—behaviors that might suggest differing diagnoses. Valentine, however, views Septimus as well as Woolf herself as "resisting subjects of clinical scrutiny;" their symptoms "do not conform to ready clinical categories" (132).

16   In enjoying the hot sun here and earlier in the novel (140), Septimus appears to have reached the desired state recommended in the line from *Cymbeline*—

"Fear no more the heat o' the sun"—which enters the consciousnesses of both Clarissa and Septimus during the course of the day, linking them. There appears to be something sane and wise in Septimus at such moments.

17 One is reminded here of Hawthorne's valorization of the sanctity of the human heart in his fiction. That Woolf would have been familiar with Hawthorne is clear; Hermione Lee notes that Leslie Stephen read aloud from his works as well as those of other authors to his family during Woolf's girlhood (111). As Quentin Bell reports, "Before she was thirteen, Virginia was trying to imitate the novels or at all events the style of Hawthorne" (*VW1*: 51).

18 This sentence appears in the first American edition of the novel, published by Harcourt, Brace & World in 1925, and in subsequent Harcourt editions.

CHAPTER SIX

1 Of all her novels, *To the Lighthouse* is Woolf's most autobiographical. Her original conception of the book made her father the pivotal character:

> This is going to be fairly short: to have father's character done complete in it; & mothers; & St. Ives; & childhood; & all the usual things I try to put in—life, death &c. But the centre is father's character, sitting in a boat, reciting We perished, each alone, while he crushes a dying mackerel . . . . (*D3*: 18–9)

As the novel evolved, however, Mrs. Ramsay and Lily Briscoe would emerge as its central characters. As Alex Zwerdling notes, Woolf did not intend the Ramsays to replicate her parents exactly, and was annoyed by assumptions that they did (181). Some critics, including Zwerdling (185), suggest that in Ramsay and his wife, Woolf presents exaggerated versions of traditional Victorian gender roles for the sake of contrasting them and emphasizing the tyranny of their restrictiveness. In *Free Women: Ethics and Aesthetics in Twentieth-Century Women's Fiction*, Kate Fullbrook states that the Ramsays

> . . . are both deformed—overdeveloped in certain areas, underdeveloped in others, and these ethical/gender deformities are read by them as points of pride, to be passed on to the next generation as ideals despite their own hidden dissatisfaction with the roles they so warmly embrace. (101)

In her diary, Woolf comments upon the therapeutic effect of having embodied her parents in fictional form:

> I used to think of him & mother daily; but writing The Lighthouse, laid them in my mind. . . . (I believe this to be true—that I was obsessed by them both, unhealthily; & writing of them was a necessary act.) (*D3*: 208)

As Sybil Oldfield notes, in the holograph manuscript of the novel, the artist-figure who became Lily was initially envisioned as a much less substantial character named Miss Sophie Briscoe, a somewhat scatterbrained woman of fifty-five who is an amateur sketcher of cottages and hedgerows (94). Diane Gillespie notes that neither Roger Fry nor Vanessa Bell detected Vanessa in Woolf's portrayal of Lily (196), but that Woolf's "observations of her sister's work foreshadow Lily Briscoe's creative process" (107).

Aspects of Woolf herself seem to appear in both Lily and Cam, whose position as the youngest Ramsay daughter mirrors that of Woolf in the Stephen family. As Jane Marcus notes, in *The Wise Virgins* (1914), Leonard Woolf's *roman à clef*, the heroine, based on Woolf, is named Camilla (*Art & Anger* 177). Gayatri Spivak sees Cam as linked to James, himself a composite of Woolf's brothers Adrian and Thoby; both characters resolve Oedipal issues with their parents in the final part of the novel (319).

Woolf was able to tap much material for the novel's setting and the characters' activities from recollections of her childhood summers spent at St. Ives in Cornwall, which she describes quite vividly in "A Sketch of the Past," a private memoir first published in *Moments of Being: Unpublished Autobiographical Writings* (1976), a collection edited by Jeanne Schulkind that was reissued in a revised edition in 1985. However, both Lyndall Gordon and Susan Gubar independently note that Woolf may have been influenced by Katherine Mansfield's stories, specifically, "Prelude" and "At the Bay," in writing *To the Lighthouse* (Gordon 185–6). As Gubar observes,

> Mrs. Ramsay's passion for putting people in pairs, as well as her grandmother's recipe for Boeuf en Daube, are strongly reminiscent of Mrs. Fairfield's kitchen and Alice's duck dinner [in 'At the Bay'], just as Minta Doyle's loss of a brooch on the beach recalls the lost and found gems at the bay. (45)

"Prelude" was first published by the Hogarth Press in 1918.

2   As Phyllis Rose suggests, in making Mrs. Ramsay and Lily Briscoe the novel's central characters, Woolf "dramatizes the working out of a way in which she can see herself as her mother's heir while still rejecting the model of womanhood she presents. She does this by conceptualizing Mrs. Ramsay as an artist" (169). Shirley Panken notes that Mrs. Ramsay is nonetheless an idealization of Julia Stephen: "in *To the Lighthouse*, Woolf managed to have the mother's activities center on husband and children, much more than was the case in the Stephen household" (164).

Mark Hussey suggests that Woolf chooses painting as Lily's medium in order

> . . . to see *her* specific problems as a novelist in a fresh way. She knows well where the line comes between the two modes, and uses painting to distance herself from literature so that she will not be too close to her own difficulties to see them clearly. (*Singing,* 72)

3   The frequent association of yellow with Carmichael evokes the Gilded Age and *The Yellow Book* (1894–7), a highly controversial magazine based in London that published the poetry and prose of the aesthetes and decadents, among

others. Its more prominent contributors included James, Yeats, Bennett, Gosse, and Dowson. At the beginning of the second part of *To the Light-house*, Carmichael keeps late-night company with Virgil, who, like other Latin poets of Peacock's Silver Age, was favorite reading among the aesthetes. It is no surprise that Carmichael might prefer Virgil on the eve of the war; as Carolyn Heilbrun notes, Virgil was Dante's guide through the *inferno* (*Toward* 161).

Critics have also noted similarities between the portrayal of Carmichael and the life and character of De Quincey, who significantly influenced the work of Poe and Baudelaire. See, for example, John Ferguson's "A Sea Change: Thomas De Quincey and Mr. Carmichael in *To the Lighthouse*," *Journal of Modern Literature* 14.1 (1987): 45–63. Woolf was fond of De Quincey and published "Impassioned Prose," a review of his work, in the *Times Literary Supplement* in 1926, the year before the publication of *To the Lighthouse*.

4   While acknowledging Ramsay's moodiness, Bankes mentions Carlyle to Lily as another man who, like Ramsey, "could not behave a little more like other people" (71). According to Bankes, Carlyle was a "crusty old grumbler" who could become angered by a meal getting cold (71). For Carlyle's views on great men, see his *On Heroes, Hero-Worship & the Heroic in History*, a popular series of lectures first published in 1841.

5   The model for Mrs. Ramsay was more successful in pursuing similar interests. As Lyndall Gordon notes, during her young widowhood prior to marrying Leslie Stephen, her second husband, Woolf's mother became seriously involved in nursing the sick. Continuing this work following her marriage to Stephen, Julia eventually published *Notes from Sick Rooms* in 1883, a book that Gordon characterizes as "the work of a professional" (20). The book was reprinted by the Hogarth Press years later.

6   As a close observer of the life around her, Lily is one of a number of heirs of Pater's Marius in modernist fiction. One might attempt to characterize the difference between them as observers as follows: Marius consciously exposes himself to the varied stimuli surrounding him, wanting to be affected by them emotionally and spiritually, as well as intellectually. Because of her need to master her emotions, Lily does not show such conscious receptivity; rather, she usually attempts to assess what she observes critically. It is only in the third part of the novel that Lily enables herself to confront and acknowledge her previously unconscious responses to all that she has observed and experienced during her earlier stay with the Ramsays.

7   Outwardly, Woolf's characterization of Lily as a celibate woman artist appears to conform to a tendency in female *Künstlerromane* that Jean Wyatt deems lamentable:

Stories of artists' lives—at least those told by middle-class white women—tend to polarize a woman's possibilities: a woman can carve out for herself the autonomous space necessary for creating works of art; or she can relax into a sensual and emotional intimacy—not both. (103)

Further:

> The concept of autonomy as absolute self-containment and absolute self-reliance that governs most female artist novels is a product of the oedipal stage, a period when girls feel the pressures of gender training in a male-dominant society. Faced with the demand that they accept the subordinate female role embodied by their mothers, girls can either accept that role and continue to identify with the mother who has nurtured them through preoedipal times; or they can strike out towards autonomy and the power to define the self differently. But then they risk the loss of the mother's love. That either-or split, engraved in the unconscious of women writers, results in the dichotomy that rules most female artist fantasies: a woman has to choose between a nurturing and sensual love and the autonomy requisite for art. (104)

Drawing upon the theories of D. W. Winnicott and Otto Kernberg, Wyatt challenges this assumption, suggesting that intimacy with another allows one to "relax into an ambiguous space where the distinction between self and other loses its clarity" (103). In such a space, "one can more easily recognize and accept creative impulses from the unconscious" (103). Such circumstances "can trigger a parallel collapse of the mental dividers that keep categories discrete, releasing their contents into a potentially fruitful jumble" (124). One might argue that something very close to this process occurs in the final part of *To the Lighthouse*, where Lily's powerful memories of Mrs. Ramsay blur the distinction between the deceased woman and herself, releasing impulses in Lily that enable her to recapture her vision and complete her painting.

8   As Lily explains to William Bankes, whose taste in art is quite traditional, she is not aiming at representational realism in portraying Mrs. Ramsay and James. As a Post-Impressionist who rejects the fashionably pale Impressionist palette of Mr. Paunceforte, who has set the trend for painters visiting the village lately (23), Lily is more concerned with abstract shapes and *chiaroscuro*: "Mother and child then—objects of universal veneration . . . might be reduced . . . to a purple shadow without irreverence" (81). As Diane Gillespie notes, observations that Lily's and Woolf's aesthetics are quite similar to those of Post-Impressionism's Bloomsbury champion, Roger Fry, are "critical commonplaces" (108).

9   Noting Vanessa Bell's "apologetic attitude" in expressing enthusiasm for her art, Gillespie suggests that Lily, like Vanessa, "hesitates to draw attention to her work or to expose herself to possible negative criticism by revealing too much commitment to her art" (201). It is sad that Lily minimizes the importance of her painting even with Bankes, who takes an interest in it and would never make such rankling statements as Tansley's "Women can't write, women can't paint" (130), which Lily recalls with bitterness several times in the novel.

10 Not surprisingly, Prue becomes the victim of this traditional gender role, dying of an illness related to her first childbirth less than a year after her marriage. Woolf's half-sister Stella Duckworth Hills was pregnant with her first child

when she died in 1897, just three months after her wedding. Woolf was fifteen years old at the time.

11 The female characters in *To the Lighthouse* also share an ability to transform everyday reality through the use of imaginative powers. As mentioned earlier, Mrs. Ramsay transmutes the ugly reality of a skull nailed upon the nursery wall into a delightful landscape for Cam by wrapping it in her shawl, enabling her youngest daughter to fall asleep (172). Ten years later, Cam, like her mother, uses her imagination to transform a potentially threatening reality into a pleasurable fantasy. The sea, which her father and Macalister have characterized as cruel and deadly—a number of sailors had lost their lives during a recent winter storm (244)—becomes a magical realm where "pearls stuck in clusters to white sprays" (272). Mrs. Ramsay uses the artistry of her grandmother's recipe for *boeuf en daube* to work her magic at dinner, where she is also delighted by Rose's skillful arrangement of fruit, which appeals to her as a hiker's world of hills and valleys in miniature (146).

Like Mrs. Ramsay, Nancy and Cam experience intimations of a world beyond everyday reality that they share as individuals. Woolf's use of linking imagery seems to suggest a mystical transmission of this awareness from woman to woman. When Mrs. Ramsay sheds her identity to become a "wedge of darkness," she discovers a realm that offers limitless possibilities, thinking of exotic lands like India, which she has not visited, and imagining herself entering a Roman church (96). Under the influence of Minta Doyle, Nancy experiences a glimpse of a similar world:

. . . when Minta took her hand and held it, Nancy, reluctantly, saw the whole world spread out beneath her, as if it were Constantinople seen through a mist, and then, however heavy-eyed one might be, one must needs ask, 'Is that Santa Sofia?' 'Is that the Golden Horn?' So Nancy asked, when Minta took her hand. (112)

Ten years later, seated in the boat crossing the bay, Cam suddenly experiences a transcendent moment of joy which briefly illuminates for her a mysterious, concealed world:

. . . the drops falling from this sudden and unthinking fountain of joy fell here and there on the dark, the slumbrous shapes in her mind; shapes of a world not realised but turning in their darkness, catching here and there, a spark of light; Greece, Rome, Constantinople. (281)

Woolf's inclusion of Rome and Constantinople in this passage connects Cam's vision with those of Mrs. Ramsay and Nancy. In addition, the image of the "fountain of joy" calls to mind the fountain imagery associated with Mrs. Ramsay and her nurturing ability (58, 264). Woolf's use of this image in relation to Cam also suggests the belated influence of Mrs. Ramsay upon her daughter's development. Relinquishing her anger for her father during the crossing, Cam suddenly feels affection for him, seeing him as something other than the "tyrant" her brother sees (282). Woolf seems to suggest that this surge of feminine sympathy constitutes an initiation into womanhood, an indication of Cam's coming of age as a woman.

12   The positioning of Lily and Carmichael as archetypal figures on the lawn overlooking the bay at the end of *To the Lighthouse* foreshadows the "two scarcely perceptible figures" on "the high ground" in La Trobe's final vision in *Between the Acts* (212). At the end of that novel, Isa and Giles Oliver embody the figures, imbuing them with the fertile potential of their own highly charged relationship.

13   From the perspective of Mitchell's discussion of the daughter's pre-Oedipal fixation on the mother, the placement of the line in the center of the space reflecting Mrs. Ramsay's absence seems to suggest the process of mother-detachment and the successful transference of desire to the father. Immediately after mentally recreating Mrs. Ramsay sitting in her usual spot, Lily turns away from her painting and gazes out over the bay, searching for Ramsay's boat: "She wanted him" (300).

The process of Lily's painting, including the significance of the glaring space and the final stroke in her second attempt to capture Mrs. Ramsay on canvas at the end of the novel, has been the subject of numerous interpretations. Patricia Caughie sees in Lily's "wave-like rhythm" while painting "the oscillating relations between the thing and the process that produces the thing," a movement that embodies both "continuity and change" ("'I must not settle'" 378). Caughie characterizes the view of artistic production presented by Woolf here as one that wishes "to maintain a multiple perspective and to participate in an ongoing activity," rather than needing to create a "lasting product" (378). Elizabeth Abel sees a shift from masculine, formalist concerns in Lily's first attempt to paint Mrs. Ramsay to an effort to address boundary issues with the mother-figure in her second, mentally placing herself in the position occupied by Mrs. Ramsay's son James in the first painting (*Virginia Woolf* 77–8). Brandy Brown Walker utilizes Kristeva's theory of the *sujet en process* (subject in process) to examine the psychological significance of Lily's last stroke. According to Walker, in her second painting, Lily tries "to reconcile on the one hand, her yearning for a reunion with the maternal figure that would take her out of speech and expression in the symbolic, and on the other hand, her need to take up a position with respect to paternal law" represented by Ramsay (34–5). Walker argues that Lily ultimately rejects these competing options with her final brushstroke, which "breaks the hold of the limiting binary" (36). In his article "Fluidity versus Muscularity: Lily's Dilemma in Woolf's *To the Lighthouse*," André Viola provides an in-depth psychoanalytic interpretation of Lily in relation to Mrs. Ramsay by drawing upon the theories of Klein, Kristeva, Irigaray, Lacan, and Chodorow, among others, as well as classical mythology to explore the tension between Lily's need to maintain her distance from a suffocating, devouring mother-figure and her pre-Oedipal desire to merge with her. He views Lily's final brushstroke as reflecting "the daughter's hard-won victory over paralyzing inhibitions" (286).

14 As was noted earlier, Woolf employed metaphors of sexuality and childbirth to describe her own literary production. Her comment in her diary upon completing *To the Lighthouse* is representative:

> The blessed thing is coming to an [end] I say to myself with a groan. It's like some prolonged rather painful & yet exciting process of nature, which one desires inexpressibly to have over. (*D*3: 109)

15 Jean Wyatt sees a fusion of the two women in the production of the painting:

> It can be argued that the painting itself furnishes the transitional ground where identities meet and merge: the painting is filled with Mrs. Ramsay's presence, but it is Lily who recreates her. The art work itself recaptures the diffuse blending of self and mother. (117)

Grace Stewart views Lily's painting as

> ... her *womanly* offering to the patriarchal world; it is a discharge of bodily emotions welling from the mother/daughter cathexis, a fountain of feeling which includes pain, sorrow, and compassion for separation from the source of sustenance, a sorrow which she feels and a compassion which she can offer in turn to males like Mr. Ramsay. (73–4)

Lyndall Gordon makes the important point that unlike the male modernist *Künstlerromane* whose artist-figures such as Stephen Dedalus and Paul Morel eventually break "from family ties and conventional ambitions," *To the Lighthouse* presents Lily the artist as "an heir, evolving naturally, almost biologically, from the previous generation" (200). Some critics go further, viewing Lily as heralding a new breed of women in Woolf's novels and in twentieth-century fiction generally. As Sandra Gilbert suggests, "Woolf here embodies the mystery of the future, with all the questions about new forms that it implies, in an icon of the new analogous to Elizabeth Dalloway but far more closely examined: Lily Briscoe" (3: 28).

CHAPTER SEVEN

1 That Woolf showed a particular interest in biography as a genre is not surprising, as she grew up in a household in which her father was editing and writing entries for the mammoth *Dictionary of National Biography*. In fact, the narrator of *Orlando* slyly refers to the work during a digression on how human beings experience time in the book's final chapter: "The true length of a person's life, whatever the *Dictionary of National Biography* may say, is always a matter of dispute" (305–6). As Lyndall Gordon notes, as a young woman, Woolf was evolving her own theory of biography in the biographical reviews she wrote from 1908 to 1910; she "examined the hidden moments and obscure formative experiences in a life, rather than its more public actions" (94). As S. P. Rosenbaum remarks, most of the reviews written by Woolf for the *Times Literary Supplement* toward the end of this period were of lives of authors

(*Edwardian Bloomsbury* 346). As Andrew McNeillie reminds us, biography was a favored genre among Bloomsbury writers: "The practice of the 'new' biography, of the biographical essay, and of the autobiographical memoir—life-writing as Woolf called it—were to one degree or another common across Bloomsbury" (4). Among its chief practitioners was Lytton Strachey, whose irreverent *Eminent Victorians* (1918) and *Queen Victoria* (1921) would become successful as well as controversial works.

Of *Orlando*, James Naremore writes that the book pointedly satirizes the traditional biography in its "use of comic paraphernalia like the mock preface and index, the occasional pretended distrust of imagination, and the abortive attempts at pedantry" (216). As a number of critics, including Naremore, has noted, Woolf believed that the successful biographer could not rely on facts alone in arriving at the truth of a person and his or her life; *Orlando* "is meant to show us the futility of biographical fact and the necessity for art in the depiction of personality" (Naremore 217). In her own essay "The Art of Biography," first published posthumously in *The Death of the Moth and Other Essays* (1942), Woolf applauds the biographer who can supply "much more than another fact" about his subject: "He can give us the creative fact; the fertile fact; the fact that suggests and engenders" (CE4: 228). In an extended discussion in her essay "Fictionality, Historicity, and Textual Authority: Pater, Woolf, Hildesheimer," Judith Ryan argues that in its mixing of fact and fiction, biographical reporting and fictional narration, *Orlando* follows an important precedent set by Pater's *Marius the Epicurean*. Toward the end of "The Art of Biography," Woolf expresses her view of biography as a relatively new genre that will undergo much change in the years to come: "Biography . . . is only at the beginning of its career; it has a long and active life before it, we may be sure—a life full of difficulty, danger, and hard work" (CE4: 227). Woolf herself would try her hand at a serious full-length biography when writing a life of Roger Fry in the late 1930s.

For more on Woolf's interest in and views on biography, see Hermione Lee's biography, 8–15. See Naremore's chapter on *Orlando* and the "new" biography (190–218) as well as Thomas S. W. Lewis's "Combining 'The Advantages of Fact and Fiction': Virginia Woolf's Biographies of Vita Sackville-West, Flush, and Roger Fry" in *Virginia Woolf: Centennial Essays*, ed. Elaine K. Ginsberg and Laura Moss Gottlieb (Troy, NY: Whitston, 1983) 295–324 for an analysis of Woolf's efforts to employ her theory of biography in her own work. See also Elizabeth Cooley's "Revolutionizing Biography: *Orlando, Roger Fry*, and the Tradition," *South Atlantic Review* 55.2 (1990): 71–83.

2   Sandra Gilbert views Woolf's exploration of the nature of sexual identity as a project she shared with other modernist women writers, utilizing "the 'female female impersonator,' whose masquerade of 'femininity' ironically comments on the fictionality of the 'feminine' even while implicitly fetishizing a vanished 'womanhood'" (3: xvi).

Orlando contains two digressions on time that appear to reflect the theories of French philosopher Henri Bergson (1859–1941), who differentiated between measured time and time as it is intuitively experienced by human beings (*durée*). Woolf's narrator's first digression on the subject elaborates on this key distinction:

An hour, once it lodges in the queer element of the human spirit, may be stretched to fifty or a hundred times its clock length; on the other hand, an hour may be accurately represented on the timepiece of the mind by one second. This extraordinary discrepancy between time on the clock and time in the mind is less known than it should be and deserves fuller investigation. (98)

In the second digression, the narrator whimsically argues that

. . . the most successful practitioners of the art of life, often unknown people by the way, somehow contrive to synchronise the sixty or seventy different times which beat simultaneously in every normal human system so that when eleven strikes, all the rest chime in unison, and the present is neither a violent disruption nor completely forgotten in the past. (305)

Bergson's lectures at the Sorbonne influenced a number of writers of Woolf's time, including Proust and Eliot. Ulysses D'Aquila attempts to account for the appeal that Bergson's theories had for Woolf's contemporaries:

. . . he was able to put intuition on a par with the intellect, and indeed to show that the new Einsteinian physics was a scientific expression of a profoundly intuitive, not to say spiritual, world-view in which matter was ultimately equated with pulsating atomic energy. (220–1)

3   Sackville-West's most well-known novels are *The Edwardians* (1930) and *All Passion Spent* (1931), both first published by the Hogarth Press. Her poem *The Land*, published in 1926, won the Hawthornden Prize in 1927 (Naremore 203). Woolf actually quotes from it in *Orlando*, where it is renamed "The Oak Tree." Woolf drew heavily upon *Knole and the Sackvilles* (1922), Sackville-West's history of her extensive Kentish ancestral estate, in describing Orlando's country estate. Although *Orlando* pays considerable attention to its subject's writing habit and alludes to specific works by Sackville-West, Spater and Parsons state that Sackville-West's status as a fellow writer did not figure largely in Woolf's attraction to her:

Virginia's interest was not because of Vita's writing, which Virginia thought was produced with a 'pen of brass,' but rather because of Vita's love of high adventure, her noble connections and her virile beauty, the essential elements of the traditional fairy tale. (135)

For a biography of Sackville-West, see Victoria Glendinning's *Vita: The Life of V. Sackville-West* (New York: Knopf, 1983). Nigel Nicolson, one of the sons of Sackville-West and Sir Harold Nicolson, has published a book about his parents entitled *Portrait of a Marriage* (New York: Atheneum, 1973). He has also edited and published their letters, *Vita and Harold: The Letters of Vita Sackville-West and Harold Nicolson* (New York: Putnam's, 1992). For more on Woolf's relationship with Sackville-West, see Joanne Trautmann's *The Jessamy Brides: The Friendship of Virginia Woolf and V. Sackville-West* (University Park: Pennsylvania State UP, 1973) and Hermione Lee's biography, 478–504. See also *The Letters of Vita Sackville-West to Virginia Woolf* (New York: Morrow, 1985), edited by Louise DeSalvo and Mitchell Leaska. For an extended discussion of Woolf's choice of Orlando as the name for Sackville-West's fictional persona and parallels between *Orlando* and Ariosto's *Orlando Furioso* (1532), see Howard Harper's chapter on the book (163–203) and note 3 (340–1) of Madeleine Moore's notes and commentary in "Virginia Woolf's *Orlando*: An Edition of the Manuscript," *Twentieth Century Literature* 25.3/4 (1979): 303–55. Harper's chapter also treats in depth Woolf's use of material from Sackville-West's *Knole and the Sackvilles* and the significance of Sackville-West's ancestral estate for herself and her fictional persona. Frank Baldanza's "*Orlando* and the Sackvilles," *PMLA* LXX (1955): 274–9 details a number of correspondences between *Orlando* and *Knole and the Sackvilles*.

4   One should note that these subjects also provide the narrator with a wealth of opportunities to satirize literature as an ongoing cultural product—its practitioners, pretensions, trends, patrons, critics, and purveyors. The narrative itself mocks a number of literary styles and conventions. Prime examples include the narrator's blazon enumerating Orlando's physical beauties (15) and the catalog of objects in the manner of Swift used to describe the monument reflecting Victorian materialism erected in St. James's Park (232). The narrator encases Orlando's sex change within a masque replete with allegorical figures—here, Purity, Chastity and Modesty (134–8), indulges in Shandy-like digressions on various subjects, imitates the Augustans' epigrammatic style (203) and the high Romantic drama of *Wuthering Heights* (262), and ascribes Dickensian names to family servants and retainers (several of these, such as Mrs. Grimsditch the housekeeper and Mr. Dupper the chaplain, bear the names of actual individuals listed in a catalog of the Knole household staff under Richard Sackville, third earl of Dorset, from 1613 to 1624. See Baldanza 277).

5   This allusion to Sackville-West's Spanish grandmother is a good example of the private jokes based on Sackville-West's ancestry and life embedded in *Orlando*. *Pepita*, Sackville-West's biography of her grandmother and mother, Victoria Sackville, was published by the Hogarth Press in 1937.

6   In his essay "Orlando's 'Caricature Value': Virginia Woolf's Portrait of the Artist as a Romantic Poet," John Moses makes the case that Woolf's portrayal of Orlando is that of a fundamentally Romantic artist-figure in his/her love for nature and preference for solitude: "In this reclusiveness s/he joins the ranks of the solitary figures so very prominent in Romantic literature—the Ancient Mariner, Childe Harold, the poet of *Alastor*, Endymion" (50). Moses also offers as evidence his characterization of Orlando's "developing aesthetic" (42) as a thinker and writer as essentially Romantic.

7   One might argue that mythological subjects continued to live in the poetry of modernists such as H.D. and Pound. More characteristic of the modernists,

though, is their appropriation of myth and legend in depicting contemporary subjects in their works, as *The Waste Land* and *Ulysses* illustrate. Modernist mythmaking—the elevation of the present-day to the realm of myth—can also be seen at work in Williams's *Patterson* and Hart Crane's *The Bridge*. For instances of classical mythology still used as the subject of Western art in the early twentieth century, see, for example, Richard Strauss's opera *Elektra* (1909), the choreography of Martha Graham, and the line drawings and etchings of Picasso.

The "topographical" poem, which includes the country house poem, of which "The Oak Tree" seems to be an example, appears in English literature as early as the Renaissance with Jonson's "To Penshurst" in *The Forest* (1616). Marvell's "Upon Appleton House," Denham's *Cooper's Hill* (1642), and Pope's *Windsor Forest* (1713) continue the tradition in later years.

8   As discussed earlier, Woolf shared with Pater as well as her father the belief that good writing reflects its author's personality. Edmund Wilson summarizes the Symbolists' concern with this principle:

Each poet has his unique personality; each of his moments has its special tone, its special combination of elements. And it is the poet's task to find, to invent, the special language which will alone be capable of expressing his personality and feelings. (21)

Time after time in her essays, Woolf praises writers for works that reflect their unique personalities. For her, Sir Thomas Browne is "one of the first of our writers to be definitely himself" ("Reading," *CE2*: 28). Woolf notes with approval that Hazlitt's essays are "emphatically himself" ("William Hazlitt," *CE1*: 155). In discussing George Moore's fiction, Woolf considers,

But are not all novels about the writer's self, we might ask? It is only as he sees people that we can see them; his fortunes colour and his oddities shape his vision until what we see is not the thing itself, but the thing seen and the seer inextricably mixed. ("George Moore," *CE1*: 338)

Woolf was also aware of the danger to writing of too much self-consciousness, especially when one has grievances to air, as does Charlotte Brontë in *Jane Eyre*:

The desire to plead some personal cause or to make a character the mouthpiece of some personal discontent or grievance always has a distressing effect, as if the spot at which the reader's attention is directed were suddenly twofold instead of single. ("Women and Fiction," *CE2*: 144)

In "The Modern Essay," Woolf summarizes the challenge posed by the matter of personality in writing:

. . . it is only by knowing how to write that you can make use in literature of your self; that self which, while it is essential to literature, is also its most dangerous antagonist. Never to be yourself and yet always—that is the problem. (*CE2*: 46)

Like the Symbolists, Woolf was concerned with finding forms of literary expression that would best reflect her own mind. In Shakespeare's plays, she senses "the perfectly elastic envelope of his thought" ("The Narrow Bridge of Art," CE2: 221). Woolf's diaries document her search for such forms. In her entry for October 4, 1922, she announces, "At last, I like reading my own writing. It seems to me to fit me closer than it did before" (D2: 205). While assessing the progress of her work as a whole in her entry for November 16, 1931, Woolf states, "I think I am about to embody, at last, the exact shapes my brain holds" (D4: 53).

9   Although Lily Briscoe is the first of Woolf's artist-figures to approach anonymous creation by acknowledging the strong likelihood that her artwork will be ignored by future generations, Orlando is the first to conclude that anonymous creation is preferable to personal fame. Surveying his large, centuries-old estate and imagining the generations of the dead who once inhabited it, Orlando thinks,

Not one of these Richards, Johns, Annes, Elizabeths has left a token of himself behind him, yet all, working together with their spades and their needles, their love-making and their child-bearing, have left this. (106)

These thoughts cause Orlando to decide to refurbish the house as his own modest contribution to the ongoing maintenance of the estate by countless generations:

Why, then, had he wished to raise himself above them? For it seemed vain and arrogant in the extreme to try to better that anonymous work of creation; the labours of those vanished hands. Better was it to go unknown and leave behind you an arch, a potting shed, a wall where peaches ripen, than to burn like a meteor and leave no dust. (106–7)

John Moses argues that Orlando's view of anonymity implies "a dismissal of stereotypical male traits; obscurity and self-abnegation are preferenced over a public life, the will to power, self-aggrandizement, and ego-gratification" (52).

As was noted in the introduction, Woolf's artist-figures increasingly exhibit a growing desire for anonymity. This trend culminates in Miss La Trobe, who, although plying her decidedly social art with others in public, does not seek fame, and deliberately conceals herself from the audience at the end of the pageant, waiting until most have departed before emerging from the bushes.

10 Grace Stewart argues that in deciding to write Sackville-West's biography as a fantasy involving a sex change, Woolf gives Orlando the writer the advantages of being a man of "experiences" as well as a modest, sensitive woman: "the hero-ine [sic] can both *do* and *be*" (30). Further, "By choosing to escape reality in this literary form, Woolf indicates the tensions a female writer normally faces and sidesteps a direct confrontation with them" (30).

From another perspective, one may see in this fanciful biography Woolf's effort to develop what Carolyn Heilbrun describes as "new ways of writing the lives of women" (*Writing* 18). Like Phyllis Rose, Heilbrun notes that in recent years, students of biography have come to acknowledge that "biographies are fictions, constructions by the biographer of the story she or he had to tell" (28). This activity is not limited to biographers alone: "We tell ourselves stories of our past, make fictions or stories of it, and these narrations *become* the past, the only part of our lives that is not submerged" (51). Heilbrun argues that women "have been deprived of the narratives, or the texts, plots, or examples, by which they might assume power over—take control of—their own lives" (17).

In this sense, Orlando's fictional triumph over a Victorian legacy that discourages women from writing, the limitations of marriage as an institution, and the constraints of childbearing and rearing may be viewed as Woolf's attempt to provide Sackville-West with just such an empowering narrative. As Howard Harper argues, the narrative of *Orlando* consistently privileges feminine values and endows Orlando at thirty-six with an unusual degree of wholeness and strength:

> The change of sex in the center of the story represents the crucial transformation of the relatively juvenile masculine values of Orlando's youth into the more feminine values of maturity. The masculine values are not denied or destroyed, but subsumed into a larger value system in which the more feminine traits are dominant. The successive eras of *Orlando* show this feminization as an evolutionary process leading toward higher, more fully and subtly developed, forms of awareness. The boy slicing at the head of the Moor at the beginning of the book is thus revealed as a primitive stage in the evolution of the androgynous woman who is in full command of her own personality and heritage at the end. (202)

Chapter Eight

1 Ulysses D'Aquila characterizes *The Waves* as Woolf's "most extreme move away from materialism" in fiction (224). As David Gadd suggests,

> Perhaps in *The Waves* she had gone as far as she could towards her objective as a novelist—to produce a book from which all that was external, adventitious, 'phenomenal,' factual, had been distilled and what remained was the essence of life itself, free of all impurities and irrelevancies. (162)

Mark Hussey argues that the novel's "reputation as a classic text of modernism owes much to its abstruseness; its hostility to 'common reading' seems to qualify it for a special prominence among notoriously 'difficult' works of modern art" (*Singing* 82). As "antireading," he continues, *The Waves* "does not allow for the participation of the reader, but continually dictates through a highly self-conscious structure" (86). Viewing the novel as a critique of "the ideology of white British colonialism and the Romantic literature that sustains it," Jane Marcus argues that in

> ... its loving misquotation and textual appropriation of Romantic poetry, *The Waves* may participate more fully in postmodernism as Linda Hutcheon

defines it [in *A Poetics of Postmodernism: History, Theory, Fiction* (New York: Routledge, 1988)] than it does in that modernism where its tenuous canonical place is earned by praise for technical difficulty and apparent anti-realism as a representation of consciousness. ("Britannia" 145)

2   Like many of the characters in Woolf's fiction, those in *The Waves* are thought to have been partly or substantially modeled after her friends, her relatives, or herself. Percival is supposed to reflect traits of Thoby Stephen and J. K. Stephen (Marcus, "Britannia" 149); Bernard, Roger Fry (Harper 235; Johnstone 362) and Desmond MacCarthy (Marcus, "Britannia" 139; Spater and Parsons 119); Louis, Leonard Woolf (Harper 228; Panken 196; Spater and Parsons 119), Maynard Keynes (Johnstone 362), and T. S. Eliot (Dowling 176; Marcus, "Britannia" 155); Neville, Lytton Strachey (D'Aquila 228; Johnstone 362; Spater and Parsons 119); Susan, Vanessa Bell (D'Aquila 228; Panken 194); Jinny, Kitty Maxse "or perhaps Mary Hutchinson" (Spater and Parsons 119); and Rhoda, Woolf herself (Panken 196). Shirley Panken also notes resemblances between Neville, Bernard and Woolf as creative individuals (196, 198), and suggests that writing the novel enabled Woolf to gather "friends and family ('us four') around her, resurrecting her brother Thoby in guise of Percival, a shadowy, athletic hero who dies young, and who assumes an integrative function in the novel, bringing the friends together" (194). As was noted earlier, Woolf met many of her male Bloomsbury friends, including her future husband, through her brother Thoby.

3   For a discussion of the significance of colors, images and motifs associated with the six characters, see Howard Harper's chapter on *The Waves*, 204–51.

4   As James Naremore notes, "All the language in the book has the same remarkable sensitivity to rhythm and metaphor, the same characteristics of repetition and alliteration, even sometimes the same use of rhyme, euphony, and assonance" (158). "The speeches," he observes, "often seem like one pervasive voice with six personalities" (152). In *The Lyrical Novel: Studies in Hermann Hesse, André Gide, and Virginia Woolf*, Ralph Freedman argues that as a result of Woolf's artful use of linking imagery and motifs, the six characters appear "not as a social group but as a single organism—one symbol of a common humanity" (252). David Dowling elaborates on this collective identity:

Just as the six personae are waves in the eternal sea, so their experiences, with the individual variations of temperament and experience, draw on a common pool of deep emotions and symbolic referents. . . . together they seem to emanate from a Jungian collective unconscious. (185)

5   According to Howard Harper,

The speeches of the first chapter show the emergence of consciousness in the nursery and early childhood. Each successive chapter continues the lives which the voices represent. But the final chapter subsumes the whole story into the consciousness of Bernard, the writer. (231–2)

6 The image of the pillar in Rhoda's imaginary desert suggests that found in Tennyson's dramatic monologue "St. Simeon Stylites" (1842), a satiric treatment of the famous ascetic who in the poem hankers after sainthood, takes pride in his self-mortification, and reveals his madness in his obsession with numerical precision and his use of overextended metaphors while seated upon a pillar in the desert. Woolf would no doubt have been familiar with the poem, but it is perhaps more likely that the image of the pillar hermit is used here to suggest a sense of ontological guilt and the concomitant need for expiation that may also contribute to Rhoda's suicide.

7 In *Free Women: Ethics and Aesthetics in Twentieth-Century Women's Fiction*, Kate Fullbrook sees in Rhoda

> . . . the female outsider who feels the close pressure of nothingness and the radical danger in life from the time she is a child. There is no place for this woman who won't be just a body, no social niche in the ranks of power that can accommodate her intellectual force or her metaphysical bent. (108)

8 Ulysses D'Aquila views Louis's seemingly mystical sense of the past as further evidence of Jung's race-consciousness at work among the six voices of *The Waves*:

> This hints, it would seem, if not at some idea of reincarnation, at least at a belief that the psychic background of every individual is not bounded by his personal culture, but rather encompasses the entire cultural history of the human race. (226)

9 In the closing paragraphs of Bernard's final monologue, Harold Bloom perceives a "restrained exultation, profoundly representative of Woolf's feminization of the Paterian aesthetic stance" (5).

10 John Lehmann argues that Woolf "intends the 'lady writing' as an image of the artist at her task beyond time and contingency" (85).

11 The difficulty of knowing others is a recurring theme in Woolf's fiction, particularly in the early novels. In *The Voyage Out*, Richard Dalloway remarks to Rachel, "'How little, after all, one can tell anybody about one's life!'" (68). Momentarily feeling defeated by life, Ralph Denham complains to Mary Datchet in *Night and Day*, "'I doubt that one human being ever understands another'" (254). In that novel, Katharine Hilbery's reserved, mysterious nature initially causes Denham to create and worship an idealistic image of her that bears little resemblance to the woman. In *Jacob's Room*, the narrator's attempts to probe the enigmatic Jacob Flanders repeatedly result in frustration: "It is no use trying to sum people up" (154). As the novel's title suggests, the narrator must resort to an examination of the contents of Jacob's room in an attempt to define him.

12 These lines evoke the scene of the dinner in *To the Lighthouse*, where the Ramsays and their guests create an oasis of light and order around the dinner table, temporarily holding the forces of darkness and dissolution at bay (146–7).

13 As was noted earlier, Woolf had an opportunity to view a copy of Pre-Raphaelite painter Holman Hunt's *The Light of the World* (1853–6) at the painter's home

one evening while attending a party there with her half-brother George Duckworth (*MB* 154); the original hangs in a side-chapel of Keble College Chapel at Oxford. The painting depicts a regally crowned and robed Christ knocking on a wooden door in the darkness with a burning lantern hanging from his left hand.

14   These lines evoke the eponymous speakers in Eliot's *The Hollow Men* (1925), who exhibit "Shape without form, shade without colour" (11).

15   Jane Marcus offers the following interpretation of Percival's significance for the six, as well as for their generation:

> . . . *The Waves* reveals that the primal narrative of British culture is the (imperialist) quest. Bernard and his friends idolize Percival, the violent last of the British imperialists, as his (imagined) life and death in India become the story of their generation. Percival embodies their history, and Bernard, the man of letters, ensures by his elegies to Percival that this tale, the romance of the dead brother/lover in India, is inscribed as *the story* of modern Britain. ("Britannia" 144)

CHAPTER NINE

1   In his introduction to his edition of *The Pargiters* published in 1977, Mitchell Leaska explores the possible etymology and significance of the family surname: "With curiosity aroused, one turns to the *Oxford English Dictionary* and . . . finds no 'pargiter'—but 'pargeter' which means 'a plasterer; a whitewasher'; and by figurative extension refers to 'one who glosses and smoothes over'" (*P* xiv). Leaska argues that the fictional sections and essays that make up *The Pargiters* show the extent to which *The Years* would "succeed in conveying the lives of the Pargiters—a family who because of the sexual premises of the age and their accompanying economic circumstances were themselves pargeters, and taught their children to be" (*P* xix).

2   Jane Marcus states that Woolf's husband was instrumental in this decision:

> *The Years* was planned as a new form of her opera for the oppressed, alternating chapters of fact and fiction. The documentary chapters have been reprinted in *The Pargiters*. It is too bad that Leonard talked her out of it. He was fearful of mixing fact and fiction. Her fearlessness went into the writing of both books. But she was justifiably terrified of what the male critics would say. (*Art & Anger* 196)

3   As Leaska notes in his introduction to *The Pargiters*, the novel underwent eight title changes before being published as *The Years*: *The Pargiters, Here and Now, Music, Dawn, Sons and Daughters, Daughters and Sons, Ordinary People, The Caravan, The Years* (*P* xv n4).

4   Leaska provides the following explanation of his editing practices: "[word] = a reading editorially supplied. [*word*] = a deletion editorially restored. <word> = an insertion made by Virginia Woolf. <[*word*]> = an insertion deleted but editorially restored" (*P* xxiii).

In the fourth essay of *The Pargiters*, Woolf elaborates further on Edward's difficulty in writing the poem entitled "To Persephone" to his cousin Kitty:

It was not only that nature and education both made it difficult for him to express his genuine emotion in a genuine way; it was also that he was writing a poem to a girl whom he scarcely knew. . . . It contains elements of falsity. For when the writer idealises his subject he almost always sentimentalises himself. Without being like Mrs. Pugh and piecing together the scraps of poetry on a sheet of newspaper, one may be sure that Edward's poem to Persephone was largely a poem to himself. In his ignorance of her, self-love and self-pity were sure to enter into it, however much the contortions of the metre might disguise them . . . . (*P* 83)

5   As an outsider, Woolf alludes to the pervasive influence of public school and university education upon the men of her social class in the fourth essay of *The Pargiters* without attempting to describe exactly what that influence might be. The ironic tone suggests its unfavorable nature:

To understand what Dr. Bealby meant when he preached the words that came to Edward's mind—indeed had become part of his creed, and were to influence him all his life—about belonging to a great and famous fellowship, about 'being moved, as it were, all together, in something like a rhythmic harmony,' about receiving and handing on an influence which derived from Jew, Greek, and Roman, an influence which made for 'the sterner and more robust virtues—fortitude, self-reliance, intrepidity, devotion to the common weal; readiness for united action and self-sacrifice'—to understand what effect such teaching had had upon . . . Edward Pargiter and thousands upon thousands of other young men, so that as they sat in their rooms at Oxford and Cambridge, they felt themselves, as Edward felt himself, dedicated to carry on the tradition, with whatever expansions and modifications the University might suggest, to give the full effect of all this, and of infinitely more than all this, upon the whole mind and nature of an intelligent and vigorous young man, would be entirely impossible for anyone who had not spent ten years first at Rexby and then at Benedict's. (*P* 77–8)

In *Three Guineas*, Woolf would critically examine such patriarchal institutions as England's military, its state church, and its political system, nurtured and run by men equipped with such an education.

6   In the second and third essays of *The Pargiters*, Woolf examines in detail the restrictions imposed upon young women like Delia, Millie, and Eleanor, who are largely confined to their homes and prevented from receiving either a formal education or the education in life that greater access to the city and its streets provides their brothers:

That three healthy girls should be sitting round a tea table with nothing better to do than to change the sheets at Whiteleys and peep behind the blinds at young men who happen to be calling next door may seem incredible. And yet the facts drawn from life seem to support that picture. (*P* 33)

7   The end of the second essay of *The Pargiters* in particular includes a discussion
    of the limiting effect of "street love," or common sexual behavior as observed
    outside the home, on the freedom of movement of the Pargiter daughters:

    . . . the influence of this street or common love was felt at every turn—it
    affected their liberty; it affected their purses; and since their mother was
    an invalid, it greatly diminished their chances of meeting friends, since it
    was impossible to go to a party without a chaperon. (*P* 38)

    In discussing young Rose's encounter with the exhibitionist on the sidewalk
    near her home and her instinctive concealment of it from her family in the
    third essay, Woolf reveals how young women of the time were discouraged
    from acknowledging their own burgeoning sexual interest and experienced
    guilt as a result of such encounters. For young Rose,

    . . . what she could not say to her sister, even, was that she had seen a sight
    that puzzled . . . her, and shocked her, and suggested that there were things
    brooding round her, unspoken of, which roused curiosity and physical
    fear. (*P* 50)

8   In portraying Eleanor in this role, Woolf most likely had in mind the experi-
    ence of her half-sister Stella Duckworth and her sister Vanessa, who per-
    formed such functions for Leslie Stephen following their mother's death. See
    Woolf's vivid account of Stephen's treatment of Vanessa as she unwillingly
    assumed this role in "A Sketch of the Past" (*MB* 124–5).

9   In ascribing mythic proportions to the elder Pargiters as they stand before the
    window, this scene adumbrates the concluding scene of *Between the Acts*, in
    which Isa and Giles Oliver assume similar proportions as the two figures La
    Trobe has imagined for the opening scene of her next play:

    Isa let her sewing drop. The great hooded chairs had become enor-
    mous. And Giles too. And Isa too against the window. The window was
    all sky without colour. The house had lost its shelter. It was night before
    roads were made, or houses. It was the night that dwellers in caves had
    watched from some high place among rocks.
    Then the curtain rose. They spoke. (219)

    As has been seen, the creation of such moments of collective identity and
    unity as the Pargiters experience here occurs in Woolf's earlier fiction as well.
    In *To the Lighthouse*, Mrs. Ramsay crafts such a moment during her dinner
    with her family and guests as the candles are being lit and the party around the
    table forms an oasis of light, holding darkness and dissolution at bay. In *The
    Waves*, the group of six characters creates two such moments—first, with Per-
    cival at the farewell dinner for him in a London restaurant, and many years
    later, during their reunion dinner at Hampton Court.

10 Howard Harper suggests that for the unattached of Peggy and North's genera-
    tion, books and art serve an unusually compelling function in their troubled
    lives: "they can objectify our existential anguish, can transform it from the

merely personal to the universal, make it more fully meaningful" (270). Feeling "marooned" standing by a bookcase during Delia's party, Peggy pulls out a volume that she opens at random, expecting to find words in it that reflect her thoughts exactly, which they obligingly do:

> '*La médiocrité de l'univers m'étonne et me révolte,*' she read. That was it. Precisely. She read on. '... *la petitesse de toutes choses m'emplit de dégoût*...' She lifted her eyes. They [the dancing guests] were treading on her toes. '... *la pauvreté des êtres humains m'anéantit.*' She shut the book and put it back on the shelf.
>
> Precisely, she said. (383)

One can readily imagine Sara reading literature for this purpose as well.

11   In its hope of expanding human awareness anonymously, this desire appears close to Woolf's own goals as a mature writer, seeking some way of representing collective experience in her experimental fiction without drawing attention to herself as author or narrator. Of her fictional artist-figures, Miss La Trobe in *Between the Acts* comes closest to achieving this ideal, directing a pageant representing the collective historical experience of her countrymen while concealing herself behind a tree.

12   As Andrew McNeillie notes, the Bloomsbury group "began to seem redundant" in the 1930s: "Urgent political events in Europe, the march of fascism ... all conspired to make the Moorean contemplation of 'beautiful objects', and so on, a luxury no one could justify" (19). Regina Marler summarizes the common objections to Bloomsbury that contributed to this view:

> The homosexuality of many Bloomsberries, their pacifism during World War I, their feminism, their private incomes, their championship of French art and literature—all were black marks. By the early 1930s, 'Bloomsbury' had become a term of abuse, suggesting everything from giggling effeminacy to political indifference. (11)

13   Further evidence that Woolf may have been trying to distance herself indirectly from aestheticism at this time may be found in the fifth essay of *The Pargiters*, in which she portrays Walter Pater as an opponent of women's higher education by referring to an unflattering episode from his life recounted by Thomas Wright in *The Life of Walter Pater* (1907):

> ... there was that incident when one of the new women's colleges aped the men's colleges and gave a 'gaudy.' 'It was a brilliant affair, and almost every Oxfordian of note,' whatever he may have felt secretly about women's colleges, 'was present. Walter Pater, whose views upon women were too well-known, one would have thought, to accept an invitation from such a source, was present. And in the course of the evening, the lady Head of the house dropped her white kid glove in front of Pater; and

Pater, at least, thought that she did it on purpose. Therefore, he 'instead of gallantly picking it up, walked on and trod on it.'

Did [n't you see *that*? whispered a friend who stood near.

'Didn't you see how I rewarded the action?' followed Pater. 'If I had not remembered how, in spite of the honours heaped upon him by Queen Elizabeth, Sir Walter Raleigh was in the end led out to execution, perhaps I, too, might have made a fool of myself. Believe me, my dear sir, it was an insinuation of the devil that caused this woman to drop her glove.'] (*P* 125–6)

The material in brackets has been supplied by Leaska from the 1969 Haskell facsimile edition of Wright's 1907 biography of Pater.

Woolf's letter dated April 7, 1937 to Stephen Spender, one of the young writers of the 1930s who were so critical of Bloomsbury at the time, offers additional evidence that she felt the need to repudiate aestheticism and defend herself as a socially engaged writer. In *The Years*, she states, she wanted to supply a "picture of society as a whole; give characters from every side; turn them towards society, not private life; exhibit the effect of ceremonies; Keep one toe on the ground by means of dates, facts" (*L6*: 116).

14 In portraying the elder Rose Pargiter's lingering illness in *The Years* and Delia's ambivalent reaction to her death, Woolf appears to be recalling her own experience at age thirteen of her mother's death at 22 Hyde Park Gate:

I remember very clearly how even as I was taken to the bedside I noticed that one nurse was sobbing, and a desire to laugh came over me, and I said to myself as I have often done at moments of crisis since, 'I feel nothing whatever.' (*MB* 92)

Julia Stephen's death struck her as unreal, and she, like Delia, felt that her father, brothers, and sisters were all acting a role that was expected of them as a bereaved family:

. . . the atmosphere of those three or four days before the funeral was so melodramatic, histrionic and unreal that any hallucination was possible. We lived through them in hush, in artificial light. Rooms were shut. People were creeping in and out. People were coming to the door all the time. We were all sitting in the drawing room round father's chair sobbing. (*MB* 92)

15 The Pargiters of Eleanor's generation, unlike North and Peggy, are still able to attain such moments, drawing strength and solace from their shared history as siblings and cousins who have suffered the tyranny of late Victorian family life together. As Janis Paul suggests, *The Years* "demonstrates the need to transcend the limitations of past social forms in the present-day world, while at the same time it points out the loss of communion that occurs without those social forms" (185–6). Alex Zwerdling states that in the novel,

. . . the force of family life that had once seemed merely oppressive gradually grows to something of great constancy. For despite all the domestic conflict and frustration and misery the novel records, Woolf also makes it clear that these are the ties that bind. (174).

CHAPTER TEN

1   Among those noting the resemblance between elements in *Between the Acts* and *The Waste Land* are Spater and Parsons: "Much of the aridity of *Between the Acts* is reminiscent of T. S. Eliot's *The Waste Land* and, not surprisingly, Eliot thought it her best novel" (122–3). That Woolf knew the poem well is clear; as Leon Edel notes, she set the type for the 1923 Hogarth Press edition of the poem herself (247). For more on Woolf's view of and relationship with Eliot, see Hermione Lee's biography, 432–47.

2   Alex Zwerdling states that *Between the Acts* "is rooted in an acute longing for an earlier, more civilized phase of English culture as well as in her observation of the barbaric present" (308).

3   As Shirley Panken notes, "Preoccupation with violence, death and suicide is striking throughout the novel" (253). A number of commentators detects in *Between the Acts* an unstated correlation between domestic violence and the violence of war and totalitarian regimes that is rendered more explicit in *Three Guineas*. As Alex Zwerdling remarks,

> The pervasive feeling of contained violence in the personal relationships of the novel—the conflict between Isa and Giles, Giles's instinctive hatred of William Dodge, the perpetual disturbance generated by Mrs. Manresa, etc.—are not directly caused by contemporary public events but are meant to embody similar forces in a microcosmic setting. (304)

Whereas Zwerdling sees Isa and Giles's marital discord as "a paradigm for war itself" (220), Jane Marcus goes a step further, arguing that Woolf's novel "shows us how fully she saw the source of the violence of war in the violence of human sexuality" (*Art & Anger* 151). In a related observation, Annette Oxindine posits a relationship between violence against women in particular and the atrocities of war that might also be seen as causal. In her essay "Outing the Outsiders: Woolf's Exploration of Homophobia in *Between the Acts*," she notes that the rape in the barracks that Isa reads about was an actual one that the *Times* reported in 1938, and "vividly connects the violence of war with violence against women" (119).

4   See Woolf's diary entry for January 26, 1941: "Yes, I was thinking: we live without a future. Thats whats queer, with our noses pressed to a closed door" (*D5*: 355). As Sandra Gilbert notes, the Battle of Britain was at its peak while Woolf finished working on her drafts of the novel (3: 4). Bombs were being dropped on London by enemy planes that flew over southern England on the way to their targets. As noted earlier, the collection of essays entitled *Virginia Woolf and War: Fiction, Reality, and Myth* (Syracuse: Syracuse UP, 1991), edited by Mark Hussey, and Karen Levenback's *Virginia Woolf and the Great War* (Syracuse: Syracuse UP, 1999) examine Woolf's reaction to the wars of her era and their impact upon her work.

5   Some commentators give a highly critical assessment of the quality of Isa's poetry. Among them, Alex Zwerdling states that Isa does not show her work to others

"because it could scarcely survive a daylight scrutiny. The lines she writes are a kind of geriatric pastoral, full of echoes from an older poetic dispensation and quite incapable of conveying the reality of her own experience" (314). Elizabeth Abel characterizes Isa's efforts as "a poetry of evasion and cliché" (*Virginia Woolf* 129).

6   Zwerdling comments that Isa's poetry "must be seen simply as an escape from the tensions and abrasions of the real world in which she finds herself. Its aim is ascent, imaginative departure" (315).

7   Woolf may well have intended a connection between Dodge's characterization of himself and the scene in which Gerald crushes a snake unsuccessfully trying to swallow a toad: "It was birth the wrong way round—a monstrous inversion" (99). Historically psychiatry has used the word *inversion* to describe homosexuality.

8   Annette Oxindine states that "Dodge's otherness helps to maintain the value of 'normalcy'," which supports the view that homosexuals, like other marginalized individuals, "serve an important function in the community; they provide their oppressors with an outlet for anger that might otherwise be self-directed or lead to self-reflection about one's own potential otherness" (121).

9   By the end of her career, Woolf had come to think of herself in such terms: "I'm fundamentally, I think, an outsider. I do my best work & feel most braced with my back to the wall" (*D5*: 189). That Woolf drew upon her own experience in creating the character and work of La Trobe is likely, as in 1940 the Rodmell Women's Institute asked her to write and produce a play for the village (*L6*: 391). Although there is some disagreement as to whether Woolf actually did (Panken 252; Putzel 254), she did attend rehearsals of the Institute's plays, but complained about the boredom and disillusionment she experienced in watching them (*D5*: 288). Shirley Panken views her involvement as "a reaching out, an extending of herself; she wished to be part of the collective or community feelings uniting England at this point in history" (252).

Phyllis Rose suggests a further correlation between Woolf and La Trobe the playwright, viewing *Between the Acts* "as Woolf's *Tempest*, a *Tempest* written in time of war, her assessment of her own art and her farewell to it" (231–2). Other commentators such as Sybil Oldfield have remarked upon the resemblance of La Trobe to British composer Ethel Smyth, Woolf's friend and ardent admirer (99).

10   It is interesting to speculate why Woolf chose drama as the medium of the central artist-figure in *Between the Acts*. As noted above, Woolf herself was involved in the theatrical efforts of the Rodmell Women's Institute at the time. She had also been reading Dickens during the previous year; her comments in her diary entry for April 13, 1939 suggest that she may have begun to view the drama as the *Ur*-form of all literature:

... I read about 100 pages of Dickens yesterday, & see something vague about the drama & fiction: how the emphasis, the caricature of these innumerable scenes, forever forming character, descend from the stage. Literature—that is the shading, suggesting, as of Henry James, hardly used.

All bold & coloured. Rather monotonous, yet so abundant, so creative: yes: but not *highly* creative: not suggestive. Everything laid on the table. Nothing to engender in solitude. Thats why its so rapid & attractive: nothing to make one put the book down & think. (*D5*: 214–5)

That Woolf had a deep and abiding respect for the genre is evident in her essays on Greek tragedy and Renaissance drama (see "On Not Knowing Greek," "Notes on an Elizabethan Play," and "The Narrow Bridge of Art"). As was noted earlier, Woolf herself wrote *Freshwater: A Comedy*, a satirical play about her great aunt and pioneering Victorian photographer Julia Margaret Cameron and her circle of artists and writers on the Isle of Wight. The play was performed privately in Vanessa Bell's studio in 1935 (Bell, *VW2*: 189). Lucio Ruotolo edited the play, published in the U.S. by Harcourt in 1976.

In her essay "Incomplete Stories: Womanhood and Artistic Ambition in *Daniel Deronda* and *Between the Acts*," Allison Booth examines the function of theater in George Eliot's and Woolf's respective novels: "For the authors themselves and for their created societies, theater challenges genre and convention by dissolving the marriage plot of the novel of manners and enacting a communal ritual apparently coextensive with the history of a people" (121).

11   Lyndall Gordon argues that during the last ten years of her life, Woolf wanted to become, like the character Bernard in *The Waves*, a "preserver of national achievement" (283). La Trobe's pageant, which constitutes an often comical, if not satiric, history in brief of English literature, can nonetheless be seen as an attempt to affirm the nation's impressive literary achievement even as it raises fundamental questions about the relationship between art and life. That the pageant's intent is to demonstrate the close interrelation of the two is evident in Woolf's earliest plans for the novel:

. . . why not Poyntzet Hall: a centre: all lit. discussed in connection with real little incongruous living humour; & anything that comes into my head; but 'I' rejected: 'We' substituted . . . . we all life, all art, all waifs & strays—a rambling capricious but somehow unified whole . . . . (*D5*: 135)

12   Alex Zwerdling argues that contrary to the prevailing view among critics, the pageant does not seek to promote a common identity among its audience and participants; he views it as "providing us not so much with a comprehensive vision of the past as with a prehistory of the present. It follows English culture through its historical stages to emphasize the gradual but persistent decay of the sense of community" (317). As for the pageant's final, confrontational sketch,

This vision of contemporary life as essentially discontinuous, a collection of 'scraps, orts, and fragments,' has been prepared for by every previous section of the pageant, as Miss La Trobe traces the gradual triumph of individualism over communal identity. (319–20)

Elizabeth Abel takes a similar position, arguing that La Trobe

... wants to generate a shared aesthetic illusion, but she also wants to dispel the illusions of community (elicited by music and language, then disrupted by rapid shifts of tone) and art (called into question by the minimalism of her stage effects, which allow real people and places to show through). She insistently presents the discontinuity of experience, salutary in contrast to demands for uniformity. (*Virginia Woolf* 127–8)

13   The novel provides numerous examples of Woolf's belief in the creative potential of ordinary people, ranging from the lively imaginations of Mrs. Sands's kitchen girls, who insist that a lady once drowned in the pond and that her ghost lingers there, to the inexplicable flair of Candish the butler for flower arrangement:

Yellow, white, carnation red—he placed them. He loved flowers, and arranging them and placing the green sword or heart-shaped leaf that came, fitly, between them. Queerly, he loved them, considering his gambling and drinking. The yellow rose went there. (35)

See also Woolf's diary entry for May 31, 1940, with its (albeit wry) observation, "Shows what a surplus of unused imagination we possess" (*D5*: 290–1).

14   Pamela Caughie views this shift in emphasis as evidence of what she considers to be Woolf's postmodernism. Woolf's novels about artist-figures, she argues, are concerned with creating an audience for her art, and "teaching us how to create the literature of the future, which will be a collaborative act. This last novel in particular raises questions about who will occupy the position of reader/listener/audience" (*Virginia Woolf* 56). Caughie states that "Woolf's concern is not the relation of art to life but the relation of art to audience. It is in the use of art by its audience that we must locate its meaning and value, not in some correspondence between art and life, whether subjective or objective" (50).

It is true that Woolf becomes increasingly preoccupied with the significance of audience in her later years. Her wartime diary entries vividly attest to this concern as Woolf the writer bemoans the lack of an "echo" from a reading public that now seems otherwise engaged (*D5*: 293, 299). Certainly Woolf's choice of drama as La Trobe's medium highlights the role of the audience in the production and reception of art to a degree not given it in relation to other media such as literature and painting in her fiction. Note, though, that during a moment of frustration, La Trobe longs to be free of the demands of an audience: "Audiences were the devil. O to write a play without an audience—*the* play" (180). Woolf's ongoing exploration of the relationship between art and life, begun in her earliest fiction, continues unabated in *Between the Acts*.

15   Note that La Trobe not only metaphorically shares the travails of the sacrificial deity, but also imitates the Creator as a sorcerer/dramatist:

... she was not merely a twitcher of individual strings; she was one who seethes wandering bodies and floating voices in a cauldron, and makes rise up from its amorphous mass a re-created world. (153)

16 This was a sight which Woolf herself had seen and recorded in her diary entry for July 26, 1940 (*D5*: 306).

17 Woolf the writer bemoans this point frequently in her wartime diary entries:

> . . . the war—our waiting while the knives sharpen for the operation— has taken away the outer wall of security. No echo comes back. I have no surroundings. I have so little sense of a public that I forget about Roger [her biography of Fry] coming or not coming out. (*D5*: 299)

18 In one of her last diary entries Woolf noted,

> No: I intend no introspection. I mark Henry James's sentence: Observe perpetually. Observe the oncome of age. Observe greed. Observe my own despondency. By that means it becomes serviceable. Or so I hope. (*D5*: 357-8)

CHAPTER ELEVEN

1 Woolf's essays on individual authors frequently applaud a poet or novelist for his or her active engagement in life. In "The Pastons and Chaucer," Woolf notes that Chaucer "never flinched from the life that was being lived at the moment before his eyes" (*CE3*: 11). She admires Dr. Johnson for his "love of pleasure, his detestation of the mere bookworm, his passion for life and society" ("Dr. Burney's Evening Party," *CE3*: 141-2). Of Henry James in his later years at Lamb House, Woolf writes that he was "no meagre solitary but a tough and even stoical man of the world, English in his humour, Johnsonian in his sanity, who lived every second with insatiable gusto" ("Henry James," *CE1*: 285). In her essay on Rupert Brooke, whom she knew personally, Woolf expresses admiration for "his inquisitive eagerness about life, his response to every side of it, and his complex power . . . of testing and enjoying, of suffering and taking with the utmost sharpness the impression of everything that came his way" ("Rupert Brooke," *BP* 89).

  In writing about women authors in particular, Woolf often notes the damage wrought by their enforced isolation and limited exposure to life. In "*Aurora Leigh*," she comments on the adverse effects of Elizabeth Barrett's sheltered life before eloping with Robert Browning:

> . . . it cannot be doubted that the long years of seclusion had done her irreparable damage as an artist. She had lived shut off, guessing at what was outside, and inevitably magnifying what was within. (*CE1*: 214)

As Woolf notes, George Eliot's social isolation as a result of her liaison with G. H. Lewes, in combination with her growing fame as a writer, caused her to lose "the power to move on equal terms unnoted among her kind; and the loss for a novelist was serious" ("George Eliot," *CE1*: 199).

  In a number of essays, Woolf makes general observations about the relationship between the artist or writer and life that reveal how critical she believed it to be. In "The Leaning Tower," she aphoristically—and humorously—argues that

Life and books must be shaken and taken in the right proportions. A boy brought up alone in a library turns into a bookworm; brought up alone in the fields he turns into an earthworm. (*CE2*: 169)

In the same essay, while comparing the writer's task to that of the painter or sculptor, she states, "Two words alone cover all that a writer looks at—they are, human life" (*CE2*: 162). In "The Artist and Politics," Woolf argues,

. . . it is a fact that the practice of art, far from making the artist out of touch with his kind, rather increases his sensibility. It breeds in him a feeling for the passions and needs of mankind in the mass which the citizen whose duty it is to work for a particular country or for a particular party has no time and perhaps no need to cultivate. (*CE2*: 231–2)

Woolf considers the matter of the search for truth in "On Not Knowing Greek":

Truth, it seems, is various; Truth is to be pursued with all our faculties. . . . It is not to the cloistered disciplinarian mortifying himself in solitude that we are to turn, but to the well-sunned nature, the man who practises the art of living to the best advantage . . . . (*CE1*: 9)

2   The importance of communication between the writer and his or her audience is a major theme of the essays collected in *The Common Reader* (1925). In "Montaigne," Woolf applauds the French moralist and essayist's views on the subject:

Communication is health; communication is truth; communication is happiness. To share is our duty; to go down boldly and bring to light those hidden thoughts which are the most diseased; to conceal nothing; to pretend nothing; if we are ignorant to say so; if we love our friends to let them know it. (*CE3*: 23–4)

Woolf approvingly notes the ability of John Evelyn's diaries to transmit "a perceptible tingle of communication" to her own contemporaries across the centuries ("Rambling Round Evelyn," *CE3*: 49). In "Addison," she pays tribute to the man's ground-breaking work as a prose writer: "undoubtedly it is due to Addison that prose is now prosaic—the medium which makes it possible for people of ordinary intelligence to communicate their ideas to the world" (*CE1*: 93). In "The Patron and the Crocus," Woolf notes that "writing is a method of communication; and the crocus is an imperfect crocus until it has been shared" (*CE2*: 149–50).

3   Woolf's essays contain numerous descriptions of experiencing her immediate environment intensely. She concludes "Impressions at Bayreuth" with a Paterian analysis of her experience of the evening following an opera performance that includes suggestions of synesthesia, a technique used by the Symbolist poets and writers:

. . . we wander with *Parsifal* in our heads through empty streets at night, where the gardens of the Hermitage glow with flowers like those other magic blossoms, and sound melts into colour, and colour calls out for words, where, in short, we are lifted out of the ordinary world and allowed merely to breathe and see—it is here that we realize how thin are the walls between one emotion and another; and how fused our impressions are with the elements which we may not attempt to separate. (*BP* 22)

In "Street Haunting: A London Adventure," Woolf describes her loss of identity in the intensity of observing and experiencing urban life:

The shell-like covering which our souls have excreted to house themselves, to make for themselves a shape distinct from others, is broken, and there is left of all these wrinkles and roughnesses a central oyster of perceptiveness, an enormous eye. (*CE4*: 156)

In her essays on individual authors, Woolf notes with approval their skill and receptivity to experience as observers. Commenting on William Cowper's close observation of nature, she states, "It is this intensity of vision that gives his poetry, with all its moralising and didacticism, its unforgettable qualities" ("Four Figures," *CE3*: 185). She values Dorothy Wordsworth's notebook for providing exact, succinct renderings of what she sees: "the plain statement proves to be aimed so directly at the object that if we look exactly along the line that it points we shall see precisely what she saw" ("Four Figures," *CE3*: 202). Reading Christina Rossetti's poetry, Woolf is impressed by her "keen sense of the visual beauty of the world . . . your eye, indeed, observed with a sensual Pre-Raphaelite intensity that must have surprised Christina the Anglo-Catholic" ("'I am Christina Rossetti'," *CE4*: 58–9). In "Phases of Fiction," Woolf notes approvingly, "The mind of Proust lies open with the sympathy of a poet and the detachment of a scientist to everything that it has the power to feel" (*CE2*: 84).

4   As Woolf would readily admit, Victorian mores forbidding the expression or description of sexuality in art plagued men and women alike as artists and writers. In the third essay of *The Pargiters*, she discusses the taboo against describing a character's sexual feelings in fiction:

This instinct to turn away and hide the true nature of the experience, either because it is too complex to explain or because of the sense of guilt that seems to adhere to it and to make concealment necessary, has, of course, prevented both the novelist from dealing with it in fiction—it would be impossible to find any mention of such feelings in the novels that were being written by Trollope, Mrs Gaskell, Mrs Oliphant, George Meredith, during the eighties . . . . In addition, there is, as the three dots used after the sentence, 'He unbuttoned his clothes . . .' testify, a convention, supported by law, which forbids, whether rightly or wrongly, any plain description of the sight that Rose, in common with many other little girls, saw under the lamp post by the pillar box in the dusk of that March evening. (51)

Bibliography

Abel, Elizabeth. "'Cam the Wicked': Woolf's Portrait of the Artist as her Father's Daughter." *Virginia Woolf and Bloomsbury: A Centenary Celebration.* Ed. Jane Marcus. London: Macmillan, 1987. 170–94.
———. *Virginia Woolf and the Fictions of Psychoanalysis.* Chicago: U of Chicago P, 1989.
Allen, Virginia M. *The Femme Fatale: Erotic Icon.* Troy, NY: Whitston, 1983.
Annan, Noel. "Bloomsbury and the Leavises." *Virginia Woolf and Bloomsbury: A Centenary Celebration.* Ed. Jane Marcus. London: Macmillan, 1987. 23–38.
Arnold, Matthew. *Culture and Anarchy, with Friendship's Garland and Some Literary Essays.* Ed. R. H. Super. Ann Arbor: U of Michigan P, 1965.
———. *Poetical Works.* Ed. C. B. Tinker and H. F. Lowry. London: Oxford UP, 1969.
Auerbach, Nina. *Woman and the Demon: The Life of a Victorian Myth.* Cambridge: Harvard UP, 1982.
Balakian, Anna. *The Symbolist Movement: A Critical Appraisal.* New York: Random House, 1967.
Baldanza, Frank. "*Orlando* and the Sackvilles." *PMLA* 70 (1955): 274–9.
Beebe, Maurice. *Ivory Towers and Sacred Founts: The Artist as Hero in Fiction from Goethe to Joyce.* New York: New York UP, 1964.
Bell, Quentin. *Bloomsbury.* 1968. New York: Basic, 1969.
———. *Virginia Woolf: A Biography.* 2 vols. New York: Harvest-Harcourt, 1972.
Bloom, Harold, ed. *Modern Critical Views of Virginia Woolf.* New York: Chelsea House, 1986.
Booth, Allison. "Incomplete Stories: Womanhood and Artistic Ambition in *Daniel Deronda* and *Between the Acts.*" *Writing the Woman Artist:*

Essays on Poetics, Politics, and Portraiture. Ed. Suzanne W. Jones. Philadelphia: U of Pennsylvania P, 1991. 113–30.

Boswell, James. *Life of Johnson.* London: Oxford UP, 1966.

Carlyle, Thomas. *On Heroes, Hero Worship & the Heroic in History: Six Lectures; Reported, with Emendations and Additions.* London: James Fraser, 1841.

Caughie, Pamela L. "'I must not settle into a figure': The Woman Artist in Virginia Woolf's Writings." *Writing the Woman Artist: Essays on Poetics, Politics, and Portraiture.* Ed. Suzanne W. Jones. Philadelphia: U of Pennsylvania P, 1991. 371–97.

———. *Virginia Woolf & Postmodernism: Literature in Quest & Question of Itself.* Urbana: U of Illinois P, 1991.

Caws, Mary Ann. *Women of Bloomsbury: Virginia, Vanessa and Carrington.* New York: Routledge, 1990.

Cooley, Elizabeth. "Revolutionizing Biography: *Orlando, Roger Fry,* and the Tradition." *South Atlantic Review* 55.2 (1990): 71–83.

Cunningham, Gail. *The New Woman and the Victorian Novel.* New York: Barnes & Noble, 1978.

Dalsimer, Katharine. *Virginia Woolf: Becoming a Writer.* New Haven: Yale UP, 2001.

D'Aquila, Ulysses. *Bloomsbury and Modernism.* New York: Peter Lang, 1989.

DeKoven, Marianne. "Constructing Feminine Aesthetic Spaces." *Virginia Woolf & Communities: Selected Papers from the Eighth Annual Conference on Virginia Woolf.* Ed. Jeanette McVicker and Laura Davis. New York: Pace UP, 1999. 234–49.

DeSalvo, Louise A. "'A View of One's Own': Virginia Woolf and the Making of *Melymbrosia.*" *Melymbrosia: An Early Version of The Voyage Out.* Ed. Louise A. DeSalvo. New York: The New York Public Library, Astor, Lenox and Tilden Foundations, 1982. xxiii-xl.

———. *Virginia Woolf: The Impact of Childhood Sexual Abuse on Her Life and Work.* Boston: Beacon, 1989.

———. *Virginia Woolf's First Voyage: A Novel in the Making.* Totowa, NJ: Rowman & Littlefield, 1980.

DiBattista, Maria. *Virginia Woolf's Major Novels: The Fables of Anon.* New Haven: Yale UP, 1980.

Dijkstra, Bram. *Idols of Perversity: Fantasies of Feminine Evil in Fin-de-siècle Culture.* New York: Oxford UP, 1986.

Dowling, David. *Bloomsbury Aesthetics and the Novels of Forster and Woolf.* New York: St. Martin's, 1985.

Edel, Leon. *Bloomsbury: A House of Lions.* Philadelphia: Lippincott, 1979.

Eliot, T. S. *The Complete Poems and Plays.* New York: Harcourt, 1971.

Engelberg, Edward. *The Symbolist Poem: The Development of the English Tradition.* New York: Dutton, 1967.

Ferguson, John. "A Sea Change: Thomas De Quincey and Mr. Carmichael in *To the Lighthouse*." *Journal of Modern Literature* 14.1 (1987): 45–63.

Fernando, Lloyd. *"New Women" in the Late Victorian Novel*. University Park: Pennsylvania State UP, 1977.

Fogel, Daniel Mark. *Covert Relations: James Joyce, Virginia Woolf, and Henry James*. Charlottesville: UP of Virginia, 1990.

Forster, E. M. *A Room with a View*. New York: Vintage International-Random House, 1989.

———. *Virginia Woolf*. New York: Harcourt, 1942.

Freedman, Ralph. *The Lyrical Novel: Studies in Hermann Hesse, André Gide, and Virginia Woolf*. Princeton: Princeton UP, 1963.

Froula, Christine. "Gender and the Law of Genre: Joyce, Woolf, and the Autobiographical Artist-Novel." *New Alliances in Joyce Studies*. Ed. Bonnie Kime Scott. Newark: U of Delaware P, 1988. 155–64.

———. "Out of the Chrysalis: Female Initiation and Female Authority in Virginia Woolf's *The Voyage Out*." *Virginia Woolf: A Collection of Critical Essays*. Ed. Margaret Homans. Englewood Cliffs, NJ: Prentice-Hall, 1993. 136–61.

Fullbrook, Kate. *Free Women: Ethics and Aesthetics in Twentieth-Century Women's Fiction*. Philadelphia: Temple UP, 1990.

Gadd, David. *The Loving Friends: A Portrait of Bloomsbury*. 1974. New York: Harcourt, 1975.

Gilbert, Sandra M., and Susan Gubar. *No Man's Land: The Place of the Woman Writer in the Twentieth Century*. 3 vols. New Haven: Yale UP, 1988–94.

Gillespie, Diane Filby. *The Sisters' Arts: The Writing and Painting of Virginia Woolf and Vanessa Bell*. Syracuse: Syracuse UP, 1988.

Glendinning, Victoria. *Vita: The Life of V. Sackville-West*. New York: Knopf, 1983.

Gordon, Lyndall. *Virginia Woolf: A Writer's Life*. 1984. New York: Norton, 1986.

Gubar, Susan. "The Birth of the Artist as Heroine: (Re)production, the *Künstlerroman* Tradition, and the Fiction of Katherine Mansfield." *The Representation of Women in Fiction*. Ed. Carolyn G. Heilbrun and Margaret R. Higonnet. Baltimore: Johns Hopkins UP, 1983. 19–59.

Hafley, James. "Walter Pater's 'Marius' and the Technique of Modern Fiction." *MFS* 3.2 (1957): 99–109.

Harper, Howard. *Between Language and Silence: The Novels of Virginia Woolf*. Baton Rouge: Louisiana State UP, 1982.

Heilbrun, Carolyn G. *Toward a Recognition of Androgyny*. 1973. New York: Harper Colophon, 1974.

———. *Writing a Woman's Life*. 1988. New York: Ballantine, 1989.

Henke, Suzette. "Virginia Woolf's *To the Lighthouse*: In Defense of the Woman Artist." *Virginia Woolf Quarterly* 2 (1975): 39–47.

Hill, Katherine C. "Virginia Woolf and Leslie Stephen: History and Literary Revolution." *PMLA* 96 (1981): 351–62.

Hussey, Mark. *The Singing of the Real World: The Philosophy of Virginia Woolf's Fiction.* Columbus: Ohio State UP, 1986.

——, ed. *Virginia Woolf and War: Fiction, Reality, and Myth.* Syracuse: Syracuse UP, 1991.

Johnstone, J. K. *The Bloomsbury Group: A Study of E. M. Forster, Lytton Strachey, Virginia Woolf, and Their Circle.* 1954. New York: Octagon, 1978.

Leavis, F. R. *The Common Pursuit.* London: Chatto & Windus, 1952.

Lee, Hermione. *Virginia Woolf.* 1996. New York: Knopf, 1997.

Lehmann, John. *Virginia Woolf and her World.* 1975. New York: Harvest-Harcourt, 1977.

Lemon, Lee T. *Portraits of the Artist in Contemporary Fiction.* Lincoln: U of Nebraska P, 1985.

Levenback, Karen L. *Virginia Woolf and the Great War.* Syracuse: Syracuse UP, 1999.

Lewis, Thomas S. W. "Combining 'The Advantages of Fact and Fiction': Virginia Woolf's Biographies of Vita Sackville-West, Flush, and Roger Fry." *Virginia Woolf: Centennial Essays.* Ed. Elaine K. Ginsberg and Laura Moss Gottlieb. Troy, NY: Whitston, 1983. 295–324.

Little, Judy. "*Jacob's Room* as Comedy: Woolf's Parodic *Bildungsroman.*" *New Feminist Essays on Virginia Woolf.* Ed. Jane Marcus. Lincoln: U of Nebraska P, 1981. 105–24.

Littleton, Jacob. "Mrs. Dalloway: Portrait of the Artist as a Middle-Aged Woman." *Twentieth Century Literature* 41.1 (1995): 35–53.

Marcus, Jane. *Art & Anger: Reading Like A Woman.* Columbus: Ohio State UP, 1988.

——. "Britannia Rules *The Waves.*" *Decolonizing Tradition: New Views of Twentieth-Century "British" Literary Canons.* Ed. Karen R. Lawrence. Urbana: U of Illinois P, 1992. 136–62.

Marler, Regina. *Bloomsbury Pie: The Making of the Bloomsbury Boom.* New York: Henry Holt, 1997.

Martin, Lindsay. "Virginia Woolf at Morley College." *The Charleston Magazine* 4 (1991/2): 21–5.

McNeillie, Andrew. "Bloomsbury." *The Cambridge Companion to Virginia Woolf.* Ed. Sue Roe and Susan Sellers. Cambridge: Cambridge UP, 2000. 1–28.

Meisel, Perry. *The Absent Father: Virginia Woolf and Walter Pater.* New Haven: Yale UP, 1980.

Miller, C. Ruth. *Virginia Woolf: The Frames of Art and Life.* London: Macmillan, 1988.

Mitchell, Juliet. *Psychoanalysis and Feminism.* 1974. New York: Vintage-Random House, 1975.

Moore, George Edward. *Principia Ethica.* Cambridge: Cambridge UP, 1962.

Moore, Madeline, ed. "Virginia Woolf's *Orlando*: An Edition of the Manuscript." *Twentieth Century Literature* 25.3/4 (1979): 302–55.

Morgan, Geneviève Sanchis. "The Hostess and the Seamstress: Virginia Woolf's Creation of a Domestic Modernism." *Unmanning Modernism: Gendered Re-Readings.* Ed. Elizabeth Jane Harrison and Shirley Peterson. Knoxville: U of Tennessee P, 1997.

Moses, John W. "*Orlando*'s 'Caricature Value': Virginia Woolf's Portrait of the Artist as a Romantic Poet." *English Romanticism and Modern Fiction: A Collection of Critical Essays.* Ed. Allan Chavkin. New York: AMS, 1993. 39–81.

Naremore, James. *The World Without A Self: Virginia Woolf and the Novel.* New Haven: Yale UP, 1973.

"New Woman." *Oxford Companion to English Literature.* 5th ed. 1985.

Nicolson, Nigel. "Bloomsbury: The Myth and the Reality." *Virginia Woolf and Bloomsbury: A Centenary Celebration.* Ed. Jane Marcus. London: Macmillan, 1987. 7–22.

———. *Portrait of a Marriage.* New York: Atheneum, 1973.

Oldfield, Sybil. "From Rachel's Aunts to Miss La Trobe: Spinsters in the Fiction of Virginia Woolf." *Old Maids to Radical Spinsters: Unmarried Women in the Twentieth-Century Novel.* Ed. Laura L. Doan. Urbana: U of Illinois P, 1991. 85–103.

Oxindine, Annette. "Outing the Outsiders: Woolf's Exploration of Homophobia in *Between the Acts*." *Woolf Studies Annual* 5 (1999): 115–31.

Panken, Shirley. *Virginia Woolf and the "Lust of Creation": A Psychoanalytic Exploration.* Albany: State U of New York P, 1987.

Pater, Walter. *Marius the Epicurean: His Sensations and Ideas.* New York: Modern Library, 1950.

———. *The Renaissance.* 1935. New York: Chelsea House, 1983.

Paul, Janis M. *The Victorian Heritage of Virginia Woolf: The External World in her Novels.* Norman, OK: Pilgrim, 1987.

Pratt, Annis. *Archetypal Patterns in Women's Fiction.* Bloomington: Indiana UP, 1981.

Putzel, Steven D. "Frame, Focus and Reflection: Virginia Woolf's Legacy to Women Playwrights." *Virginia Woolf and the Arts: Selected Papers from the Sixth Annual Conference on Virginia Woolf.* Ed. Diane F. Gillespie and Leslie K. Hankins. New York: Pace UP, 1997. 252–9.

Reed, Christopher. "Through Formalism: Feminism and Virginia Woolf's Relation to Bloomsbury Aesthetics." *The Multiple Muses of Virginia Woolf.* Ed. Diane F. Gillespie. Columbia: U of Missouri P, 1993. 11–35.

Rose, Phyllis. *Woman of Letters: A Life of Virginia Woolf.* 1978. New York: Oxford UP, 1979.

Rosenbaum, S. P. *Edwardian Bloomsbury: The Early Literary History of the Bloomsbury Group.* Vol. 2. London: Macmillan, 1994.

————. *Victorian Bloomsbury: The Early Literary History of the Blooms-bury Group*. Vol. 1. New York: St. Martin's, 1987.

————, ed. *The Bloomsbury Group: A Collection of Memoirs, Commentary and Criticism*. Toronto: U of Toronto P, 1975.

Ryan, Judith. "Fictionality, Historicity, and Textual Authority: Pater, Woolf, Hildesheimer." *Neverending Stories: Toward A Critical Narratology*. Ed. Ann Fehn, Ingeborg Hoesterey and Maria Tatar. Princeton: Princeton UP, 1992. 45–61.

Sackville-West, Vita. *The Letters of Vita Sackville-West to Virginia Woolf*. Ed. Louise DeSalvo and Mitchell A. Leaska. 1984. New York: Morrow, 1985.

Sackville-West, Vita, and Harold Nicolson. *Vita and Harold: The Letters of Vita Sackville-West and Harold Nicolson*. Ed. Nigel Nicolson. New York: Putnam's, 1992.

Silver, Brenda R., ed. "'Anon' and 'The Reader': Virginia Woolf's Last Essays." *Twentieth Century Literature* 25.3/4 (1979): 356–441.

Snaith, Anna. *Virginia Woolf: Public and Private Negotiations*. New York: Palgrave, 2000.

Spacks, Patricia Meyer. *The Female Imagination*. New York: Knopf, 1975.

Spater, George, and Ian Parsons. *A Marriage of True Minds: An Intimate Portrait of Leonard and Virginia Woolf*. 1977. New York: Harvest-Harcourt, 1979.

Spender, Stephen. *World within World*. New York: Harcourt, 1951.

Spivak, Gayatri C. "Unmaking and Making in *To the Lighthouse*." *Women and Language in Literature and Society*. Ed. Sally McConnell-Ginet, Ruth Borker and Nelly Furman. New York: Praeger, 1980. 310–27.

Stansky, Peter. *On or About December 1910: Early Bloomsbury and Its Intimate World*. Cambridge: Harvard UP, 1996.

Stewart, Grace. *A New Mythos: The Novel of the Artist as Heroine 1877–1977*. St. Albans, VT: Eden, 1979.

Symons, Arthur. *The Symbolist Movement in Literature*. New York: Dutton, 1919.

Thoreau, Henry D. *Walden*. Ed. J. Lyndon Shanley. Princeton: Princeton UP, 1971.

Trautmann, Joanne. *The Jessamy Brides: The Friendship of Virginia Woolf and V. Sackville-West*. University Park: Pennsylvania State UP, 1973.

Valentine, Kylie. *Psychoanalysis, Psychiatry and Modernist Literature*. New York: Palgrave Macmillan, 2003.

Viola, André. "Fluidity versus Muscularity: Lily's Dilemma in Woolf's *To the Lighthouse*." *Journal of Modern Literature* 24.2 (2000/2001): 271–89.

Wachman, Gay. "Pink Icing and a Narrow Bed: *Mrs. Dalloway* and Lesbian History." *Virginia Woolf and the Arts: Selected Papers from the Sixth Annual Conference on Virginia Woolf*. Ed. Diane F. Gillespie and Leslie K. Hankins. New York: Pace UP, 1997. 344–50.

Walker, Brandy Brown. "Lily's Last Stroke: Painting in Process in Virginia Woolf's *To the Lighthouse.*" *Virginia Woolf and the Arts: Selected Papers from the Sixth Annual Conference on Virginia Woolf.* Ed. Diane F. Gillespie and Leslie K. Hankins. New York: Pace UP, 1997. 32–8.

Williams, Lisa. *The Artist as Outsider in the Novels of Toni Morrison and Virginia Woolf.* Westport, CT: Greenwood, 2000.

Wilson, Edmund. *Axel's Castle: A Study in the Imaginative Literature of 1870–1930.* New York: Scribner's Sons, 1969.

Wilson, Jean Moorcroft. *Virginia Woolf, Life and London: A Biography of Place.* 1987. New York: Norton, 1988.

Woolf, Leonard. *Downhill All the Way: An Autobiography of the Years 1919 to 1939.* New York: Harvest-Harcourt, 1967.

Woolf, Virginia. *Between the Acts.* New York: Harvest-Harcourt, 1969.

———. *Books and Portraits: Some Further Selections from the Literary and Biographical Writings of Virginia Woolf.* Ed. Mary Lyon. 1977. New York: Harcourt, 1978.

———. *Collected Essays of Virginia Woolf.* 4 vols. New York: Harcourt, 1967.

———. *The Common Reader, First Series.* New York: Harvest-Harcourt, 1953.

———. *The Diary of Virginia Woolf.* Ed. Anne Olivier Bell with Andrew McNeillie. 5 vols. New York: Harcourt, 1977–84.

———. *Freshwater: A Comedy.* Ed. Lucio P. Ruotolo. New York: Harcourt, 1976.

———. *Jacob's Room & The Waves.* New York: Harvest-Harcourt, 1950, 1959.

———. *The Letters of Virginia Woolf.* Ed. Nigel Nicolson and Joanne Trautmann. 6 vols. 1975–80. New York: Harvest-Harcourt, 1977–82.

———. *Moments of Being: Unpublished Autobiographical Writings.* Ed. Jeanne Schulkind. New York: Harcourt, 1976.

———. *Mrs. Dalloway.* New York: Harvest-Harcourt, 1953.

———. *Night and Day.* New York: Harvest-Harcourt, 1948.

———. *Orlando.* New York: Harvest-Harcourt, 1956.

———. *The Pargiters: The Novel-Essay Portion of The Years.* Ed. Mitchell A. Leaska. New York: Harvest-Harcourt, 1977.

———. *Roger Fry: A Biography.* New York: Harvest-Harcourt, 1976.

———. *A Room of One's Own.* New York: Harbinger-Harcourt, 1957.

———. *Three Guineas.* New York: Harbinger-Harcourt, 1966.

———. *To the Lighthouse.* New York: Harvest-Harcourt, 1955.

———. *The Voyage Out.* New York: Harvest-Harcourt, 1948.

———. *The Years.* New York: Harvest-Harcourt, 1965.

Wordsworth, William. *Poems, in Two Volumes, and Other Poems, 1800–1807.* Ed. Jared Curtis. Ithaca: Cornell UP, 1983.

Wright, Thomas. *The Life of Walter Pater*. 2 vols. London: Everett, 1907.

Wyatt, Jean. *Reconstructing Desire: The Role of the Unconscious in Women's Reading and Writing*. Chapel Hill: U of North Carolina P, 1990.

Zucker, Marilyn. "Virginia Woolf and the French Connection: A Devotion to Language." *Virginia Woolf & Communities: Selected Papers from the Eighth Annual Conference on Virginia Woolf*. Ed. Jeanette McVicker and Laura Davis. New York: Pace UP, 1999. 29–35.

Zwerdling, Alex. *Virginia Woolf and the Real World*. Berkeley: U of California P, 1986.

Index